RIO BRAVO AND BUGLES ON THE PRAIRIE

Two Full Length Western Novels

GORDON D. SHIRREFFS

WOLFPACK
PUBLISHING
— EST 2013 —

Rio Bravo and Bugles on the Prairie
Paperback Edition
Copyright © 2022 (As Revised) Gordon D. Shirreffs

Wolfpack Publishing
5130 S. Fort Apache Rd. 215-380
Las Vegas, NV 89148

wolfpackpublishing.com

Paperback ISBN 978-1-63977-290-2

RIO BRAVO AND BUGLES ON THE PRAIRIE

RIO BRAVO

CHAPTER ONE

The sun was dying in a welter of rose and gold beyond the Escabros as Lieutenant Niles Ord rode Dandy into the shallow rushing waters of the Rio Bravo. The bay splashed across, throwing aside sheets of water tinted the color of blood by the sun. Niles looked up the steep side of the low mesa before him as Dandy clattered out on the pebbly bank. Fort Bellew sprawled amidst a waste of mesquite, prickly pear, and high-stalked *pitahaya*. The eroded adobes and sagging jacales of the lonely post were dwarfed by the somber, brooding Escabros.

Niles turned, resting his right hand on the cantle, to watch his twenty-man patrol take the ford. Thirty days of patrol had honed them thin. The rasping voice of Sergeant Jared Ershick rose above the clatter and the splashing. Ershick hated field duty, and had taken his spite out on the men. Niles scanned the taut fourteen-dollar-a-month dogfaces as the troopers crossed the river. Days of cautious riding through the country of Asesino, grim war chief of the Chiricahuas, eating lousy food, harried by the torrid heat of Arizona, always thirsty, had taken the starch out of the men of B Company.

Niles spat into the clear water. He had overlooked

some minor infractions of the tough patrol, but Ershick never missed a chance to crucify any trooper who broke the least regulation.

The troopers clattered past. In the last file was the Apache girl, Little Deer, riding her calico pony. She seemed as fresh as the day they had captured her, three weeks before. She bent her head and looked away as she felt Niles looking at her.

Niles touched the bay with his spurs and rode up the incline after the patrol. He glanced back at the rough country through which they had come almost as though looking for the beefy figure of Francis Xavier Feeley, one of the best yellowlegs who had ever forked a McClellan. But Feeley would never answer Boots and Saddles again, at least not on earth. A chewed slug, driven by a Chiricahua rifle, had smashed his spine the first week of the patrol. "Feeley, F.X., Sergeant, from Duty to Killed in Action," said Niles aloud. The cold regulation words could never tell what kind of noncom Feeley had been. But the patrol knew it, and Jared Ershick knew it. With the smallness of his kind he had wrought revenge on the men below him. If Niles could help it, Sergeant Ershick would never again ride on any patrol of his.

Niles passed the patrol and swung down from Dandy. A trooper cantered out to take the bay. Niles eased his legs and walked toward the headquarters building. He wondered if Elias Boysen was sober. Never in the two years Niles had served at Fort Bellew had he known a time when Captain Boysen was cold sober.

"Mr. Ord, sir!"

Niles turned at the sound of Sergeant Ershick's voice. The noncom jerked his head toward the Apache girl, who still sat her calico. "What about *her,* sir?"

Niles shoved back his hat. Little Deer regarded him without expression. She had been the only captive they had taken in the brawl at Verde Canyon. She couldn't be more than seventeen, but her figure was already full. Niles had been forced to watch her closely in bivouac, for troopers on patrol are always hungry for liquor and women; any kind of women. It hadn't taken her long to realize Niles was her protector.

Niles walked to the side of the calico pony. He spoke in soft, slurring Apache. "There is a good woman here, Little Deer. It is the daughter of the Sergeant Ershick. Go with him. Be quiet and no harm will come to you. Do you understand?"

Her sober, liquid eyes studied him. She nodded. "I will do as you say, Nantan," she said softly. The mingled odors of sweat, grease, and smoke clung to her filthy deerskins.

"Take her to Marion, Ershick," said Niles

"I don't know whether Marion will want a stinking squaw in her care, Mr. Ord," said Ershick.

"Is that your thought or your daughter's?"

"There's no regulation covering this, sir!"

For a moment Niles eyed the gaunt face. There was almost the look of a fanatic about Jared Ershick. A damned dangerous fanatic. Niles raised a hand. "Put her in *my* quarters then, damn it!" he said. Niles spun on a heel and strode toward headquarters, he glanced back as he reached the shelter of the *ramada*. A slim woman was standing beside the Apache girl, holding out her hands. It was Marion Ershick. Niles grinned. Marion would take over. Jared Ershick was afraid of the calm girl he had somehow sired. Little Deer would be safe enough with Marion.

Niles entered the small headquarters office. A strange officer sat at Boysen's desk under the light of a harp lamp. There was a touch of gray in the dark curling hair. Dark eyes studied Niles. A major's leaves were on the shoulders of the beautifully tailored shell jacket. Niles saluted. "Lieutenant Niles Ord, sir."

The field officer returned the salute and held out a slim hand. "Major Roland Dane, Mr. Ord. I've taken over command of Fort Bellew." Dane glanced at a chair. "You look tired. Sit down. How was the patrol?"

Niles sat down. "We contacted some of Asesino's band of Chiricahuas at Verde Canyon, sir. Sergeant Feeley was killed in the fight. We killed three warriors. The rest escaped. We captured a young Apache woman."

Dane clasped his hands together. His dark handsomeness and immaculate uniform made Niles all the more conscious of the trail filth he had accumulated in thirty days, and of the three days' reddish stubble on his face. He shifted in his chair. The odor of sweat-soaked wool rose about him.

Dane smiled. "Why is it a handful of naked savages can make fools of you officers?"

Niles flushed. "The Chiricahuas are not exactly naked savages, sir."

Dane waved a hand. "I've heard that story before. Slackness, perhaps, or a desire to stay close to the comforts of a post, may have something to do with the deplorable record of you officers here in the Southwest."

Niles felt his temper rise. Roland Dane. The name was familiar. He riffled through the files of his memory.

The Major got up and walked to a window facing the darkening parade ground. "I saw your patrol come in, Mr. Ord. I can't say that I was pleased with their appearance." Dane turned. "The Apache woman. Why did you bring her back?"

"It is the policy of this department to bring in as many captives as we can."

"One squaw is rather a poor showing for the work of an officer and twenty troopers, isn't it?" asked Dane with a trace of ironic amusement in his cultured voice.

Niles gripped his temper. "Under ordinary circumstances I would agree, sir, but Little Deer is one of the wives of Asesino."

"So?"

"It might lead him into a trap."

"A thin thread, Mr. Ord."

Someone walked across the boardwalk beneath the *ramada* in front of the building. The door swung open.

Niles' breath caught short in his throat. A woman stood there eying him. Blonde hair was coiled at the back of a shapely head. A pert forage cap with the crossed sabers of the Cavalry on it was pinned to the golden tresses. A blue riding costume, straight from New York, clothed the full body. Niles stood up. The last time he had seen Sylvia Henry she had been wearing a quite similar costume. She came forward, stripping off a riding glove.

Dane glanced at Niles. "You knew Sylvia before, I believe, Ord."

The touch of her smooth hand brought all the old memories back, as though someone had opened a box of forgotten love letters. She had lost none of her beauty; in fact, she was more attractive than ever. The lure that had brought them together five years before smashed at him like a carbine butt. It was the way Sylvia Henry affected a man. It had almost cost Niles his commission then, but she had been after bigger game. Yet in the few months he had known her she had never held anything back from him.

"Doesn't it seem strange that we should meet again, Niles?" she asked. She pressed his hand for a fraction of a second and then withdrew hers. "I had no idea you were here at Fort Bellew until we arrived last week."

"I've been here two years, Sylvia." He wanted to tell her that she had driven him out there.

"I knew you were out West somewhere. California, I thought, or perhaps in the Dakotas."

Niles wondered if Roland Dane could read his eyes. He knew damned well Sylvia could. The long dead memories boiled up to the surface. The nights together. The perfume of her body and the warmth of her. He knew now the thought of her had never really died.

Dane eyed Niles closely. "My wife knew you in Washington five years ago," he said.

Niles nodded. "Yes." His voice seemed to come from a long way off. He wanted to grip her harshly; to feel her respond as she had always done.

Sylvia laughed. "It's nice to have old friends here in the wilderness. Did you know Captain Boysen was in Roland's class at the Academy?"

Niles turned to the Major. "Is Captain Boysen still here?"

Dane nodded. "My orders were to take command here, not to relieve Boysen from duty. The Captain will remain under my command until further orders."

Sylvia lifted the long skirt of her riding habit. "I must get ready for dinner, Niles," she said. "You're dining with us, of course?"

"If you like."

She tilted her beautiful head to one side. "Roland and I need a new face at our table." She left the room.

Dane watched her cross the dark parade ground. "She's lonely," he said, almost as though to himself. He turned. "Has she changed?"

Niles smiled. "She's more lovely than ever, Major Dane."

For a fraction of a second the mask Dane seemed to wear slipped, and Niles looked into the eyes of a totally different man. "Yes," Dane said quietly, "she is lovely." He waved a hand. "Well, go and clean up. Dinner is at seven."

Niles crossed the parade ground to his quarters and glanced back toward headquarters. Dane was still standing at the window, outlined against the yellow light. How much did he know? The whole aspect of life at Fort Bellew had changed for Niles. It had been a niche of refuge for him; a niche whose price was hardship and danger. But it had helped erase some of Sylvia. Now she had come back through the mists, the wife of his commanding officer. Niles was trapped. The implacable administration machinery of the War Department did not take into consideration old love affairs in the assignments of its officers. An inadequately numbered military force faced thousands of hostiles from the Canadian border down to Mexico. The War Department had problems of its own.

Niles entered his quarters. Lieutenant Baird Dobie looked up from his desk as Niles scaled his campaign hat at a peg. His lean, saturnine face broke into a grin. "Back from the wars," he said. "You want to talk about it?"

Niles pulled his soggy shirt over his head and swabbed his armpits with it. "Feeley is dead. We tangled with Asesino again. They got away into the hills, as usual. I brought in one of his squaws. Little Deer."

"Feeley gone?" Dobie stood up and shook his head. "He took me in hand when I came out here four years ago and kept me alive." Dobie watched Niles pull at his boots and gave him a hand. "How did the estimable Sergeant Ershick pan out?"

Niles reached for the bottle on Dobie's desk. "I mean to break him, Baird. He's a damned martinet, and yellow to boot. I can't stand the sight of him."

Baird nodded. "If it hadn't been for Marion, I'd have recommended his demotion months ago. He's pulled every trick out of the hat to keep from going on field duty."

Niles filled two glasses and handed one to Dobie. He dropped on his bunk and watched the dust rise from the blankets and drift slowly toward an open window. "So Boysen finally got relieved?"

"Yes, and about time, too, although they left the sot here to sweat under the man who relieved him. I don't like Boysen, but they should have sent him somewhere else. He's been drinking steadily ever since Dane took over."

"Our new commanding officer wasn't exactly pleased with the appearance of my patrol."

"He hasn't been pleased with anything."

Niles sipped at his drink. "His name is familiar."

Baird laughed harshly. "You never heard of Roland Dane? The *beau sabreur!* Fought all through the war with Custer and never forgot it. Congressional Medal of

Honor man. Light of Washington society the last five years. Wealthy—enough money to buy a dozen like you and me. Did you meet his wife?"

"Yes."

Baird looked closely at Niles. "You knew her before?"

Niles drained his glass and looked squarely at Baird. "Yes. I knew her before."

Baird reached for the bottle. "Sylvia!" he said. "She can't be the *same* Sylvia!"

"She is."

"For the love of God!"

Niles looked down at the floor. "I thought I had forgotten her."

"How could you forget a woman like her?"

"I thought I'd never see her again."

Baird refilled the glasses. "Does *he* know?"

Niles shrugged. "If he didn't when he married her, he does now. She wanted wealth and prestige, something a shavetail named Niles Ord couldn't give her."

"She's a magnificent animal, Niles."

Niles looked up at his friend. "You might as well say the rest of it, Baird."

"Say what?"

"The thought in your mind: that she's a high-class prostitute."

"Oh, shut up!"

Niles shook his head. "I never realized it myself at the time. She was always so damned clever about such things. In her own way, she might have loved me. I've always cursed the day I met her."

Baird dropped on his bunk and elevated his feet to the edge of his desk. He ran a hand through his thin sandy hair. "We've been drunk together. Fought Apaches together. Kept each other from going loco in this heat-sodden, lonely, stinking outpost of hell. It was your friendship that kept me going when nothing else mattered. Believe me, Niles, I'd hate to see you leave here, but I'd rather face this misery alone if I could know you were safe away from Dane and his wife."

Niles leaned back against the wall and closed his eyes. "What puzzles me is why a man with his standing was sent out here to Hell's Half Acre."

Baird lit a cigar. "My cousin is in the War Department, Niles. I received a letter from him right after you left on patrol. Dane went too far for the gentle tastes of Washington. Marrying Sylvia Henry and bringing her into the social circle he moved in was more than the brass could stand. She was cut short, tried to get him to resign, and failed. In all his useless, spendthrift life, he had only a few glorious moments. Swinging a saber in a hell-for-leather charge behind George Armstrong Custer. Appomattox stopped that. Later he was with Custer's Seventh at the Battle of the Washita, on temporary duty, as an aide. That was in '68. In '69 he did a little fighting against the Kiowas and then hurried back to Washington to be with the lovely Sylvia."

Niles spat into the littered beehive fireplace. "He'll get no saber-swinging charges out here. He'll be lucky if he sees the Apaches whom he's fighting against. His sentries will have their throats cut fifty feet from his campfires. This isn't a war of glory against a half-starved rebel cavalry, or a camp of sleeping Cheyennes. It's war of attrition, and I hope to God he learns it."

Baird inspected the end of his cigar. "You couldn't tell *him* that. Watch your step, son. I don't like the smell of this situation. Now you'd better get cleaned up. I can smell you clean over the stink of this cigar. We're due to dine in regal splendor with the Danes this evening. God help us, one and all." Baird got up and placed his forage cap on his head, tilting it at the right angle. "I'm going to get another bottle. See you."

Niles gathered his toilet articles. He looked about the room he and Baird had shared for so long. Baird's assigned room was across the hall, filled with their extra gear. They had bunked together for almost two years.

Hanging above the fireplace was the half armor of a Spanish soldier that Baird had found deep in a forgotten canyon with the skeleton still in it. An Apache lance stood in a corner, the blade formed from a French cavalry saber, although God alone knew how an Apache had found it. On a table was a set of chessmen carved from bone by the skilled hands of First Sergeant Joe Bond, the black figures in the likeness of Apaches, the white in the likeness of Cavalry troopers. Their bookcase was between the two beds, lined with technical manuals, classics, magazines, and the lurid French novels that Baird read in the original. The place had been home for Niles for two years; it seemed now more like a prison cell.

Niles thrust his Colt beneath his waistband. No one walked the confines of Fort Bellew at night unarmed. In the last six months three men had been found with slashed throats within a hundred yards of the post. No trace of Apaches had been found. Nothing but the sprawled bodies staring at the sun with eyes that did not see.

Niles left the rear door of the quarters and crossed the flinty earth to the wash house. A faint trace of light still showed to the west, just above the brooding Escabros. Somewhere up there Asesino sat in council with his warriors, planning more deviltry as he swilled his tiswin. The thin string of forts, undermanned and isolated, did little but annoy him. The hills were dotted with the burned shells of ranch houses. Mines were abandoned and weeds grew in the middle of once busy roads and trails. No white man in his right mind would willingly enter the Escabros. Asesino ruled them like a medieval robber baron.

Niles looked across the parade ground as he opened the wash-house door. Two men were talking in front of the brightly lit commanding officer's quarters. There was no mistaking Roland Dane and the gaunt figure of Sergeant Jared Ershick. Niles somehow knew they were talking about him.

CHAPTER TWO

Captain Elias Boysen sat at the Danes' table holding his empty wineglass in a hand that trembled spasmodically. The yellow candlelight accentuated the dark circles beneath his eyes and the sickly pallor of his puffy face. He had been well fortified when he had arrived at the dinner, and had emptied his wineglass three times since he had sat down, barely picking at his food. His lifeless hair curled untidily at the back of his thick neck, greasing the collar of his blouse.

Baird Dobie glanced at Niles as Major Dane talked steadily with one slim hand grasping the neck of the wine decanter. Now and then he swirled the ruby contents, seemingly studying the rich color of the wine. Boysen's bloodshot eyes flicked constantly from the wine decanter to the handsome face of Roland Dane. Niles could not look at the craving face of the besotted officer.

Sylvia Dane sat across the table from Niles. She wore a low-cut gown of white, exposing the deep cleft between her full breasts. The soft light brought out the creaminess of her smooth skin. The hunger that had been buried deep in Niles clawed its way to the surface, aided by the rich wine. For he still wanted her as he had known her long ago. It seemed incredible that this beautiful woman had once been his. Her clear blue eyes held his now and then, and somehow he knew she still would not refuse him anything. He looked away.

"Elias and I were in the same class at the Academy, Baird," said Roland Dane in his well-modulated voice. "Elias was the high-point man, while I, alas, stood almost at the bottom. Isn't that right, Elias?"

"A good class, '58," mumbled Boysen.

"I never thought Elias would serve under me," continued Dane. He swirled the wine. "Yet fourteen years have made changes. Wine, gentlemen?"

Dane carefully filled the glasses of Baird Dobie, Niles, stolid Jim Ashley, the post quartermaster, Surgeon Orville Blanchard, and young Thorpe Martin, the junior officer of B Company. Elias Boysen extended his glass and then bit his lip as Dane spoke again. "Elias had quite a record in the war. You were with Sherman, were you not, Elias?"

"Yes."

"On the march to Savannah?"

"Yes. Yes."

Niles gripped his glass in desperation. Why in God's name didn't Dane fill the thirsty man's glass?

Dane at last reached across the snowy tablecloth and carefully filled Boysen's glass until the red liquid almost bulged over the top. Boysen drew back his shaking hand, obviously afraid he'd spill the wine on the exquisite cloth. Sylvia Dane shot a look of anger at her husband, lifted the glass, and sipped a little from it. She placed the glass close to Boysen's hand. Boysen drained half the wine.

Roland Dane's face was expressionless. "We must begin a reorganization here, gentlemen. I have asked for two more companies and possibly a Gatling gun or two. Mr. Ord will assume command of B Company. Mr. Dobie will act as executive officer, with Mr. Martin as junior officer."

Sylvia smiled and placed a hand on her husband's arm. "Roland, *must* you talk business?"

He bowed slightly. "Of course I realize it *is* out of

place, but I mean to waste no time in getting this post on an efficient basis."

Jim Ashley flushed. "We've been left out of the picture pretty much out here, sir. No replacements for months. A few remounts now and then. No new equipment to speak of."

Dane waved a hand. "No excuses are necessary. The frontier seems to breed a studied carelessness in junior officers. I have dedicated myself to changing that. At Fort Bellew, in any case."

Baird Dobie emptied his glass and looked at Niles, then at Sylvia. Almost as though he spoke aloud, the thought came to Niles: The egotistical ass. He knows why he was shipped to the Southwest. The reason was sitting at the table. Sylvia Dane.

Dane leaned forward. "Had you never thought of sending out smaller patrols, Elias? You would have been able to cover more territory in less time than the present patrols take."

Boysen shook his head. "Our patrols are small enough as it is."

"Perhaps... for men lacking combat spirit. Surely one U.S. cavalryman can handle a dozen Apaches?"

Niles couldn't help himself. "The Apaches say that no trooper carrying a cookstove can catch them in their own country. They ride their own horses to death and then use them for food. They always camp high, miles from water, if necessary, to avoid being surprised. They bring raw gold in and trade it to unscrupulous merchants for repeating rifles. They go on the reservations to get food and blankets and then disappear to raid again. It isn't like fighting white men, sir."

Dane smiled. He passed a hand caressingly along the side of his dark gray-streaked hair. "How long have you been out here, Mr. Ord?"

"Almost four years. The last two here at Bellew."

"Perhaps that is too long?"

"He knows the Apaches as few officers do," interrupted Dobie.

Dane's amused glance took in Baird Dobie. "So I understand. Speaks the language like a Chiricahua. Is it a difficult tongue to learn, Ord?"

"I didn't find it so."

"Perhaps to be able to talk with women like Little Deer?" Dane laughed.

Niles flushed despite himself. "Just what do you mean, sir?"

Sylvia stood up. "We'll have our coffee in the living room."

Roland Dane filled his glass and drained it. He eyed Boysen and then shoved the decanter in front of the Captain. He stood up. "I have some fine cigars upon which I'd like your judgment, gentlemen."

As they stood up, the Mexican woman who had been employed as maid entered the dining room from the kitchen. It was Teresa, daughter of Porfirio Armendez, who ran a woodcutting camp in a *cienaga* farther up the Rio Bravo.

As Sylvia led the way from the dining room, followed by her husband, Baird Dobie stopped beside Niles. "Watch yourself," he said in a low voice. "Ershick has been shooting off his big mouth. For God's sake, let Dane have his way! You've too damned good a record to let him ruin it. Look what he's already doing to Boysen."

Elias Boysen sat back in his chair. His lower lip was slack. He clumsily wiped a thread of spittle from his mouth and reached unsteadily for the decanter. As Teresa passed by him he made a quick movement with his free hand for her flowing skirts. She drew back and shot a look of hate at him.

"Dane is a sadist," whispered Baird to Niles. "He hates you and Boysen; Boysen for being the man he was, and you for being the man you are."

Sylvia was standing in the dark hallway, letting the officers pass. Niles was last. She placed a hand on his arm and looked up at him. Her soft lips were parted. Her perfume came strongly to Niles. It was the same kind she had always used. "He hates me," she said. "I'm afraid of him, Niles."

"You? Afraid of a man? You got what you wanted."

"I was wrong. I've bitterly regretted my marriage."

"Let sleeping dogs lie, Sylvia. Don't try to wreck my life again. I mean to transfer as quickly as I can."

She gripped the aiguillette that festooned his dress blouse. "No! You can help me. Niles, you *must* help me."

He gently disengaged her fingers. "You don't know a small post like this, Sylvia. There is no privacy here." He walked into the lamplit living room. Roland Dane looked up from his armchair. He knows, thought Niles.

Tattoo echoed softly from the sleeping hills as Niles and Baird left the Danes' quarters. Niles inhaled the cool fresh air. He stepped aside as Boysen lurched from the porch and bumped against him. Boysen eyed them for a moment and then muttered unintelligibly. He swayed off across the parade ground which was silvered by the moonlight. Baird watched him go. "Let's get to bed," he said. "I've stood enough for tonight. Did you ever see a man crucified the

way Boysen was tonight? Dane never lost a chance to sink his spurs into him."

"The swine! Can't he satisfy himself some other way?"

"He can't control Sylvia. He has to take it out on someone who's helpless to resist him. He means to get you, too."

"I'm getting out of here, Baird."

"He'll never recommend your transfer. Believe me."

Hoofs hammered on the hard ground. Baird nodded. "There goes Boysen. Every time he gets full lately, he rides upriver to the camp of Porfirio."

Niles watched the officer descend the mesa to the river trail. There was plenty of liquor up there. Fort Bellew had no hog ranch just outside its limits such as a larger post would have. The so-called hog ranch was the direct descendant of the old sutler's store. Some of the larger posts had as many as two or three just beyond post limits, where rotten liquor and greasy food were dispensed.

"What's the attraction up there besides liquor?" asked Niles as he and Baird crossed the parade ground.

Baird relit his cigar. "Ana. Porfirio's cook. She's part Mex, part Apache, and all bad."

Niles listened to the fading hoofbeats. "Does Dane know about it?"

"He must. Everyone else on the post does."

Marion Ershick was standing on the porch in front of her father's quarters on Soapsuds Row. Niles touched Baird's arm. Baird nodded and went into their quarters. Niles walked over to Marion and took off his dress helmet.

"I wanted to tell you that Little Deer is all right, Niles," she said.

The moonlight silvered the white shawl she wore over her slim shoulders. Her soft brown hair was braided and piled atop her head. Her oval face had a maturity that belied her twenty years. Niles had never been able to understand how a man like Jared Ershick, with the juices long drained from his system, had ever fathered Marion.

"I knew you'd take care of her," he said. "Are you afraid of her, Marion?"

She laughed. "Heavens, no! She's like a child. Yet so mature in some ways for her age that it *is* rather frightening. But I trust her. She's asleep in the lean-to room behind mine."

"She'll do anything I ask. I told her about you."

She glanced back at the quarters. "Father hates her. He made me take her food to her rather than have her in the house. He told me tonight the only good Apache was a dead one."

"There are some Apaches whose friendship I prefer and value above that of many white men."

"Sergeant Bond brought some of Mary's clothing for

her. I didn't want to accept it. It's been just two months since his wife died. Joe said she would have liked the thought."

"Joe Bond has a heart of gold, if you can get beneath the tough crust he's grown over it."

"Dad hates him. I never knew why. I suppose it's because Joe got the first sergeantcy three months ago. Father was sure he'd get it."

Niles glanced back at Dane's quarters. "He might get it yet."

"You seem troubled, Niles."

"I'm all right, Marion."

Marion Ershick looked across the parade ground. "She *is* beautiful, isn't she?"

"Yes."

"You never really forgot her, did you?"

"How did you know I knew her before?"

She looked away. "I helped her unpack when she came here. She asked me many questions about you."

Niles bit his lip. "You'd better go in now. Your father wouldn't like seeing us together."

She tilted her head to one side. "An enlisted man's daughter and an officer. It just isn't right, is it?"

Niles smiled at her. "It is ... to *us*, Marion. You know that. Good night."

He watched her as she went into her quarters. Marion Ershick was loved by everyone at Fort Bellew. She had been engaged to smiling Corporal Tom Colter, but Colter had died at Padre Pass with an Apache lance in his gut a week before he was to be promoted to sergeant. They were to have been married when he got his third stripe. When gentle Mary Bond had died, Marion had been left one of three women on the post: Ellen O'Boyd, genial Irish wife of Mick O'Boyd, the farrier sergeant; Teresa, who occasionally worked for the commanding officer; and Marion. Niles had always liked Marion, but now, when he contrasted her warm loveliness with Sylvia's glacial beauty, he suddenly realized he thought a great deal of Marion Ershick, despite her father.

Niles scratched a lucifer against a thumbnail and lit a cigar. He walked slowly to Officers' Row. A shadow moved in front of the commanding officer's quarters. It was Sylvia Dane, enveloped in a dark cloak. There was no mistaking her. She stopped at the end of the *ramada* and looked across at Soapsuds Row. Niles shrugged and went into his room. The sight of a man being interested in another woman had always aroused Sylvia. She hadn't changed.

Baird was already in his bunk when Niles came in. His eyes were closed. Niles took off his dress uniform and put it away. He dropped on his bunk and lay for a long time puffing his cigar. Taps came and went. A cool desert wind scrabbled gently about the adobe quarters.

"Niles," said Baird.

"Yes?"

"I'm taking out the next patrol in three days. You interested in taking it instead?"

"For thirty more days of hell? No, thanks!"

Baird was silent for a few minutes. "I was thinking of you, Niles. Think it over. The offer is always good."

CHAPTER THREE

T
he second day after Niles's return from patrol his attention was drawn to the bulletin board. A slip of paper fluttered in the wind. Niles read it aloud: "'Sergeant to First Sergeant: Ershick, J. vice Bond, J., reduced to Sergeant.'" For a moment seething rage boiled up in him, only to be replaced by a cold hate that had always made Niles dangerous.

Baird Dobie gripped Niles by the arm. "Take it easy, Niles. It's only the poison beginning to work."

Across the post he could see Sylvia Dane mounting her mare near the corrals. She adjusted her riding skirt over the sidesaddle, as an orderly went to get his horse. She had started the dangerous habit of riding for a time each morning, sometimes in the afternoon, in a country that was ruled by the Army as far as its carbines could range. In the short-handed post, one trooper was with Sylvia about two hours a day, forcing other troopers to double up on the duty roster.

"I'm going to see Major Dane," said Niles.

"You won't lose your temper? We can't afford to lose you, Niles. *Now,* of all times."

"I'll take it easy," said Niles. He strode off, his booted

heels slamming against the hard *caliche* of the parade ground as though he'd like to smash it to powder.

Dane was in his quarters. Niles rapped briskly against the thick door, sheeted with iron against bullets and fire arrows. "Come in!" called Dane. He was sprawled in an easy chair by the fireplace, slim hands steepled on his chest. "I've been expecting you, Ord," he said quietly.

"Sir, it's customary to consult a company commander on promotions and demotions."

"Customary, but not necessary." The dark eyes studied Niles. "Ershick is a good man, more of an administrative soldier than a field soldier."

"On the frontier, sir, a good first sergeant must be both."

Dane waved a hand. "I've started a campaign to snap this post into some sort of efficiency. I have a definite purpose in promoting Ershick. At this time it doesn't serve my purpose to inform you of my plans."

"Perhaps the Major would prefer me to submit a request for transfer?"

Dane shook his head. "No. You know your business; as a *field* soldier, that is. Boysen is a drunken sot. Dobie is lackadaisical. Ashley is too busy marshaling his beans and bacon to bother about much else. Martin is a young idiot."

Niles bit his lip.

Dane sat up straight. "You can say what is on your mind."

"It didn't take the Major long to form opinions on his officer personnel."

"I've been a soldier for a number of years. What else is bothering you?"

"I don't like the practice that Mrs. Dane has started here of riding out each day. In the first place, it's too dangerous; in the second place, she requires an orderly. It plays hell with the duty roster in a post where we've been short-handed for months."

Roland Dane rubbed his jaw. "My wife has a mind of

her own. A strong mind, I might add. However, I'll stop her from riding beyond the post limits. Any other complaints?'

"I'd like to replace Mr. Dobie on tomorrow's patrol."

Dane shoved a box of cigars toward Niles and shrugged when Niles shook his head. He took a cigar and clipped it. As he lit up, he studied Niles over the flare of the match. "I thought you might want to stay with your company, now that you're the commanding officer. Patrol work is not exactly pleasant out here. Why do you want to go again so soon?"

"Asesino will never forget that we have one of his wives as captive. He'll be up to some deviltry. I'd rather be out in the field facing him than waiting here to see what he'll do."

"Is that the only reason, Mr. Ord?"

"Yes," lied Niles.

Dane leaned against the stone mantel of the big fireplace. "You were friendly with Sylvia in Washington, were you not?"

"Yes."

"Isn't that the real reason you want to avoid post duty?"

Niles flushed. "If the Major is through, I'd like permission to leave, sir."

Dane nodded. He reached up to touch the fine Castellani saber that hung above the fireplace. As Niles reached the door the Major's voice rapped out. "Ord!"

Niles turned.

Dane had unsheathed the exquisite weapon. "How well *did* you know Sylvia?"

If he starts for me with that damned saber, I'll kill with my bare hands, thought Niles.

"Well?"

Niles spoke quietly. "I have duties to perform, sir."

Dane looked down at the gleaming blade. "Go on, then. I had no right to ask you, or any other man, that question."

Niles closed the door and breathed deeply of the crisp morning air. There was a touch of heat in the atmosphere. Carbines thumped hollowly from the small post range where the recruits were firing for record. A trooper whistled as he crossed the parade ground. Niles went to the stables. Sergeant Bond, a stubby unlit pipe in his mouth, was supervising morning stables. There was a dark, un-faded arc below his three stripes, where the bottom of his first sergeant's insignia had been cut away.

Niles leaned against a post. "It was done without my knowledge, Joe," he said.

Bond turned. There was no expression on his broad face. The gray eyes, so often like granite when Bond was berating a trooper, had a humorous light in them. "I knew that," he said. "I bucked for first sergeant because of Mary. It doesn't matter now. I'd like some field soldiering for a change."

"I'm taking out the patrol tomorrow. You can replace Forgan, if you like. He's got a devilish felon on his left hand."

"Too much rotgut whiskey for Tim Forgan. I'd like to go with you, sir. It'll be like old times. You mind the stories we'd tell about the campfires?"

Niles grinned. "Yours were all lies compared to mine, Joe. But they were more interesting."

Bond raised a broad hand. "Ah..." His face broke into a wide grin. "What about Asesino, sir?"

Niles spread out his hands. "He's like a drop of mercury on a platter. Here one day, gone the next. And the very devil to pick up."

"Nato came in at dawn. Damned-fool Johnny Raw recruit nearly shot him before the corporal of the guard passed the man in."

"*Bueno!* Take the company for pistol practice after morning stables."

Bond removed the pipe from his mouth. "First Sergeant Ershick has posted a new drill schedule, sir. There will be saber drill this morning."

Their eyes met. "For God's sake," said Niles, "we don't even take the damned thing with us on patrol!"

"Aye."

Niles shrugged. "The Major approved the new schedule, no doubt?"

"Yes, sir."

"Then it *will* be saber drill. Don't forget the right and left moulinets, Joe."

"I won't, Mr. Ord."

Niles left the stables and made a short cursory inspection. The flag snapped in the dry desert wind, the warped pole quivering steadily with the vibration. From the blacksmith shop came the steady ring of metal on metal. A white-aproned K.P. was scouring a brass pan behind the troop mess, the sun sending shafts of reflected light from it. There was a rattle of carbine fire from the range and smoke drifted toward the hills. Niles walked toward headquarters building. The one incongruous note on the whole post was the squatting figure of Nato in the dubious shade of headquarters.

Nato was broad-chested, like all of his race, but was half a head taller than most of the others. A battered campaign hat was pulled low and square on his glossy mane of jet-black hair. He wore a faded calico shirt above a buckskin kilt, and his leather bag of *hoddentin,* the sacred pollen of the tule, hung from his cartridge belt. His *n'deh b'keh,* the button-toed, thigh-length moccasins, were worn thin. His long-barreled Sharps rifle leaned against the wall.

Nato looked up as Niles approached. *"Sikisn.* Brother," he said in soft Apache. *"Nantan-*Na-txe-ce."

It was the name given to Niles by the Apaches. Chief Never Still. Niles proffered his hand and the Pinal Coyotero shook it awkwardly, leaving a trace of grease on Niles's palm.

Nato gravely accepted a cigar, which he tore apart and stuffed into a filthy pipe. Niles touched a lucifer to the tobacco. The scout inhaled deeply and then nodded.

"You have traveled far, my brother?" asked Niles in the scout's language.

"Very far."

"You are hunting?"

Nato's eyes glistened. "A great panther, a chief of all panthers, leaped at me as I rode my *thlee*. Nato shot once." The scout touched the Sharps. "He died."

"Nato is the greatest of hunters. You killed some other game?"

"No."

The Coyotero puffed at his pipe. He gazed off at the distant heights of the Escabros. There was no use rushing him. Yet he had not traveled far and fast to tell of killing a panther.

Roland Dane came out of headquarters and glanced quickly at the squatting scout. "Who is this?" he asked Niles sharply.

Niles stood up. "Nato, a government scout, sir."

"An Apache?"

Nato did not even look up at Dane.

"The word Apache is not known in their language, sir. They call themselves Tinneh, or a variation of the same word, simply meaning 'The People.' They also call themselves Shis-inday—'men of the woods.'"

Dane waved an impatient hand. "Thanks for the scholarly dissertation. They'll be known as Apaches while I'm in command here."

Niles shook his head. "It is a name given to them by their enemies. In Navajo or Zuni it simply means 'The Enemy.' Nato is a Pinal Coyotero, a loyal scout, who hates Chiricahuas, and particularly Asesino."

"He could do with a bath."

Niles flushed. "He understands English much better than he lets on, sir. He's a good man. Once he killed a Tonto who tried to kill me. He saved me from drowning in the Rio Bravo. He's my good friend, sir."

Dane glanced at Niles with a trace of amusement. "What does he want?"

"He was just about to tell me, sir."

"Tell him to get on with it."

Nato looked up at Dane. *"Nantantco?* Great chief?"

"Yes."

"Hackeguti?"

"No. He is not angry."

"Can't he speak English, Ord?" snapped Dane.

"Yes. We usually speak in his language so that I may learn better."

Nato touched Niles's leg. "Talk now," he said in English. He pointed to the north. "Many signal fires. One long smoke. Asesino." Here Nato spat. "Gathering Tinneh."

"The Chatterers?"

"Chiricahuas. Yes. *Te-dagudnti.* Joined-Together-Friendly Groups. On-Top-of-Mountains People. Many-Go-to-War People. Spotted-on-Top People."

"What is this gibberish?" demanded Dane.

"Asesino is gathering his allies. White Mountain Apaches."

Nato grunted. "Tontos. The Fools. Arivaipas. The Girls. Many. *Many.*"

"How many?"

Nato held out both hands. *"Go-nay-nan-ay.* Ten, many times."

"Why is he doing this?"

"Squaw gone. Little Deer. Asesino runs about. The *heshke* is on him. The killing craze. He has cut himself and spat blood. He curses the white-eyes."

Niles looked at Dane. "Asesino has cursed us for taking his favorite squaw. He is gathering tribal divisions of the Tinneh for war purposes. He generally fights only with his own people, the Chiricahuas. But if he convinces the others that they should go to war, there will be hell to pay from the Mogollon Rim clear down to the Sonora border."

"So?"

Niles shrugged. "I'd like to try to mess up his game."

"You're going on a routine patrol!"

"Routine? With signal smokes throughout the Escabros? We'll have to travel like ghosts, sir. The canyons will be filled with Tinneh coming to Asesino's council fire."

"All because of a dirty squaw?"

Niles shook his head. "There's more to it than that, sir. A woman means less to Asesino than a horse does. And if you've ever seen an Apache handle a horse, you'll know what I mean. The point is that he's found a means to bring his force up to great strength. Heretofore, most of the allied tribal divisions have left him to fight his own battles. Now he has a crusade. A crusade to get back his squaw.

Believe me, Major, he'll build it up to a fare-thee-well. I'd suggest that this information be sent at once to department headquarters. I'll try to get messages back from my patrol. This is damned serious, sir."

Dane was not listening to him. He was watching his wife as she posted past the gatehouse. The wind caught her blonde hair, and she held it with one gloved hand as she rode toward the corrals. Young Second Lieutenant Thorpe Martin, whose father owned several banks and a railroad or two, ran out to meet her. He helped her down, laughing as she said something to him. The orderly led the mare to the stables. Sylvia strolled toward her quarters, talking vivaciously to the goggle-eyed kid.

Nato relit his pipe. "It is the young *nantan's* squaw?" he asked Niles.

"No. It is the squaw of the *nantanco.*"

Nato digested this, sucking on his pipe. "Perhaps that is why he is so angry. He wishes to fight with knives with the *nantan eclatten.*"

Niles grinned at Nato's reference to Martin. Raw virgin lieutenant. "The white-eyes do not fight each other with knives because a man talks with another man's squaw," he said in Apache.

"So? Someday these two men *will* fight. The *nantanco*

smells of hate. He drags his moccasins on the ground. *Hacke-da-nats-itsi!"*

The Coyotero said the last phrase with such vehemence that Dane looked down at him. *Hacke-da-nats-itsi.* Angry, a sound moves back and forth overhead. Niles felt a cold foreboding. Nato's mother was a *diyi,* a medicine doctor. Pretty Mouth was her name, although she had but half a face left after escaping from an attacking mountain lion. She was noted for her powers of prophecy, and for her ability to locate lost or stolen property. Niles felt sure some of her occult powers had been inherited by her son.

"I will go on patrol tomorrow with Tzit-jizinde?" asked the Coyotero.

"The Man Who Likes Everybody will not go," said Niles. "Lieutenant Dobie will stay here while I lead the soldiers."

"Enju! That is good." Nato stood up. He picked up his rifle and trotted toward the quartermaster warehouse.

Roland Dane was still watching his wife and Martin.

"If you'll excuse me, sir," said Niles, "I have much to do getting ready for the patrol."

Dane waved a hand. His eyes never left the two strolling toward him.

Niles went to his quarters. Baird Dobie was in the room, filling his tobacco pouch. "What did Nato have to say?" he asked.

"Asesino is gathering Arivaipas, Tontos, and White Mountain Apaches for a big council. It looks bad, Baird."

Baird filled his pipe, watching Sylvia Dane and Thorpe Martin through the window. "Thorpe is making a fool of himself. He hangs on every word she says."

Niles looked past his friend's shoulder. Sylvia was laughing and had touched Martin's face with her hand. He was mooning like a sick calf. Roland Dane was gone. A pang of jealously swept through Niles. Sylvia always touched your face when she was trying to convince you of her sincerity.

Baird leaned against the wall. "Well?"

"She's playing with fire again."

Baird shrugged. "Thorpe can buy or sell any of us. He has a hell of a lot more *dinero* than Dane, and his society position outranks Dane's by quite a few files."

Niles reached for the bottle. "I'm glad I'm getting out of here."

"Ask for Thorpe to go along with you. He needs field experience. All he's done since he's been here is take stables, inspect the sanitary sinks, do close-order drill, and pester Mess Sergeant Antonelli with what he doesn't know about running a post mess."

"He'll be in the way, Baird."

Baird walked to the door. "It's up to you. Forget her, Niles. Don't open the old wound. Forget her and help Thorpe Martin to escape her net. If you don't, he'll fly right into it, and get stuck by Roland Dane's Castellani saber. She's egged Dane far enough now. Fort Bellew isn't exactly the place to line up a new affair and try to fire up an old one all at the same time."

Niles nodded. "What about you?" he asked.

Baird slanted his forage cap rakishly. "I've got my eyes on Little Deer, Niles. You can teach me enough Apache to get by." He slammed the door behind him as one of Niles's dress boots hit the wall.

Niles heard Sylvia's laughter carry to him on the wind. He gripped his glass so hard some of the liquor slopped on the floor. He emptied the glass and dropped on his bunk. He tried to think of anything else, the liquid eyes of Little Deer, the wholesomeness of Marion Ershick, but always standing between them was the laughing face of Sylvia Dane.

CHAPTER FOUR

A cold morning wind swept dryly across the parade ground as the patrol formed outside of the barracks. Hoofs rapped against the hard earth. Sergeant Bond was bellowing as he lined up the sleepy men. "Suck in your guts! Wipe the sleep outa them pretty blue eyes, Mulligan! Yuh got a loose spur, Vassily! Wipe the egg off'n that chin, Jacony!"

Niles grinned as he swung his gun belt about his slim waist with practiced ease and buckled it. He settled the heavy holstered .44 Colt, balanced by the sheath knife at his left hip. He took his sweat-stained campaign hat and looked at Baird Dobie. "Sounds good to have Joe Bond out there with a healthy dislike for a sloppy outfit, Baird."

Baird nodded. "Odd how one noncom can scrape them raw saying the same things."

"You mean Ershick?"

"Yes. There isn't a man out there who wouldn't go to hell and back for Joe Bond."

Niles picked up his Henry rifle and the pair of desert moccasins Nato had given him. "This will be a short patrol, Baird. I have a feeling we'll run into some of Asesino's bunch not too far from here."

"God forbid! All the same, I envy you."

Niles waved a hand. "I'm off before you change your mind." He left the quarters and walked to his horse. He eyed the small command. The bays were laden with ninety pound packs.

Joe Bond was calling the roll. "Sergeant Gorse!"

"Here!"

"Corporal Cassidy!"

"Yo!"

"Corporal Pierce!"

"Yo!"

"Corporal Schimmelpfennig!"

"Yo!"

So on down the line. Niles eyed the fourteen-dollar-a-month faces, dark with desert tan beneath the floppy-brimmed campaign hats. Argyll, Boyle, D'Angelo, Finnegan, Gottschalk, Highboy, Jacony, Mulligan, O'Brien, O'Hallihan, O'Toole, Reelfoot, Vassily, and Walzik. Some of them were old in the service, carrying the memories of Yellow Tavern and Brandy Station. Some of them had fought against Kiowas, Comanches, Cheyennes, Sioux, and Apaches. Others had never fired a shot in anger. D'Angelo carried his trumpet on its worsted yellow sling. Behind the line of troopers was Nato, sucking on his pipe, holding the reins of a sad-looking bayo coyote that had more bottom in it than the smart-looking, well-groomed bays of B Company.

Mulligan, Niles's orderly, took the Henry rifle and slid it into its sheath and made the desert moccasins fast to the straps of Niles's cantle pack. A breath of sour liquor came to Niles. He glanced at the orderly. "You were up the river last night, Mulligan?"

Mulligan nodded. The white worms were moiling in his gut. "Aye, sorr."

"You knew we had patrol today. You'll sweat blood when the sun comes up."

Mulligan nodded. "Aye, sorr." He glanced toward

Captain Boysen's quarters. "And I won't be the only wan, Mr. Ord. Captain Boysen, he—"

"Shut up!" said Niles.

Mulligan shrugged and went to his horse. Niles passed down the line, followed by Sergeant Bond. The horses were in fine condition. Major Dane appeared at the end of the line and eyed Niles. Niles hurried to him and saluted.

Dane glanced at Niles's bay. "I see you don't carry the issue carbine, Mr. Ord?"

"That's my own repeater, sir. I prefer it."

"It's not regulation, Mr. Ord."

Niles turned "Private Mulligan!"

The black Irishman trotted up.

"Take my Henry rifle into my quarters. You'll find an issue carbine in there. Place it in my sheath."

"Yes, sorr!"

Dane held up a hand. "Take those moccasins back to Mr. Ord's quarters too, Mulligan."

"Yes, sorr!" The Irishman did as he was told.

Dane pulled down his shell jacket. "No offense, Ord. This is a regular Army patrol. I'd like it to look like one!"

Niles looked past his commanding officer. Baird Dobie stood at the door to their quarters. As Mulligan trotted past carrying the issue carbine, Baird raised an arm and pointed across the river. His meaning was clear. He'd get the Henry rifle and moccasins to Niles.

Sergeant Bond reported. "All present, sir!"

"Move them out, Sergeant Bond!"

Dane raised a hand. "Just a minute. I have a few words to say." He paced to the front of the small command. "You men are going out on patrol. I'd like each of you to bring back credit for at least one Apache. The sooner we begin wiping them out, the quicker we'll be able to take credit for being United States cavalrymen! If any man brings back Asesino, dead or alive, he can count himself a sergeant from that date. Good luck, men!"

Bond glanced at Niles. Niles nodded. Bond rattled

out his commands. The patrol mounted and rode toward the gate. Nato followed them. Niles looked at the Major. Dane passed a hand along the side of his sleek head. "Good luck, Ord."

"Thanks, sir. I may need it."

The dark eyes held Niles' for a second. "We may have reinforcements by the time you get back, along with orders to take the field against these filthy Apaches. I hope to ride with you the next time."

Niles swung up on Dandy and saluted. He kneed the bay away from his commanding officer. Marion Ershick was standing in front of her quarters. Little Deer was beside her, looking out of place in one of Mary Bond's calico dresses. Niles drew rein in front of them. "Goodby, Marion," he said.

"I had hoped you'd let Baird Dobie take this patrol, Niles."

"Why?"

"We don't see much of you any more."

Niles doffed his campaign hat. "Maybe I'll send Baird anyway." He looked at Little Deer. "My sister, are you well?"

"Yes, Never Still. The white-eyed *nahlin* is good to Little Deer. Will you be gone long?"

"A short time."

"Enju! Yadalanh, Never Still."

"Yadalanh, Little Deer."

Niles touched the bay with his spurs and rode toward the gatehouse. Dust drifted up from the passage of the patrol as they followed the road to the ford. The sun glinted from metal. Niles turned in his saddle. Sylvia Dane was nowhere in sight. He turned and acknowledged the "Present arms!" of the sentry at the gate and then rode down toward the river.

Nato was sitting his bayo coyote at the edge of the rushing water. He pointed with his pipe. High atop a pinnacled peak, a puff of smoke detached itself and sped upward, to be followed by two more. "Asesino," said Nato. "He knows we have left the fort."

They were an hour on the trail when a trooper came up behind them, riding hard. He drew rein beside Niles and handed him his Henry rifle and the desert moccasins. "Compliments of Mr. Dobie, sir," he said.

"Thanks, Tankersly. Tell him to post a double guard on the corrals. He might need it before we get back." Niles tied the moccasins on the cantle pack and placed the Henry rifle across his thighs. He waved the patrol on.

———

IT WAS late afternoon when Niles halted the patrol in a deep canyon north of the fort. He slid from the saddle, pulled off his boots, and replaced them with the desert moccasins. He slung his field glasses about his neck and took his repeater. He jerked his head to Nato and started up the steep, brushy slope. It was hard going, and by the time they reached the top of the canyon wall Niles felt his wind harsh in his throat. Far below them the troopers and their mounts looked like chessmen. Nato squatted on a rock as Niles studied the jumbled terrain to the north of them. Scrub trees and brush stippled the brown and yellow slopes like cloves in a ham. There was no sign of life other than an eagle drifting high overhead.

For a long time Niles watched the lifeless slopes. Nato suddenly shifted. He touched the glasses and took them from Niles's hands. He looked through them and then handed them to Niles. He pointed at a knife-edged ridge two miles away. Niles focused the glasses. The brush swam into view. Then Niles picked up a lone horseman.

His brown body blended into the coloration of the rocks. His dun shaft of a lance showed above his shoulder. He dipped out of sight. A few minutes later a file of braves rode the high trail. Fifteen of them. Two more braves followed them when they had passed from sight.

Niles recased the glasses and shoved back his hat. The collected sweat ran down his face. He gave Nato a cigar and lit one for himself. Nato shifted and pointed northwest. A steady thread of smoke rose high in the hot, windless air. "Gathering," he said.

They camped that night high on a brushy mesa. The horses were watered at a *tinaja*. The rock pan was inches deep in brown water, thick with wrigglers, but there was no other supply within a day's ride. The horses were picketed in a draw and the men bedded down in a circle of rocks. There were to be no fires.

Niles and Sergeant Bond, smoked a bedtime pipe. "Gorse is not taking this patrol well," said Bond softly. He glanced at the form of the Sergeant, who was already wrapped in his blanket.

"Why?"

"You know his trouble, sir."

Niles nodded. Millard Gorse had been a sergeant major during the war. He had been a first sergeant at Fort Craig in New Mexico, and had joined the company six months before as a sergeant. His face was drawn and lean, marked deeply by the heavy drinking he indulged in. For months Niles had been thinking of reducing the man to the grade of corporal. He had a deep thirst in him, yet was never seen to drink with the others.

"He'll sweat it out of him this trip," said Niles.

"I doubt it. What he has deep in his soul will not be sweated out of his body by the sun. The scar is on his soul, sir."

"A woman?"

"Yes. Pretty as a picture. He showed me a daguerreotype of her one time."

"So?"

Bond tamped the tobacco in his pipe. "Crazy about her. Married her during the war. Didn't know her very well then. Gorse was a hero. She was a young girl. After the war she couldn't stand frontier duty. Lost a kid from cholera at some post in Kansas. She left him."

"So?"

"He saw her in Tucson last month."

"She's coming back?"

Bond shook his head. "Not her."

"Why?"

Bond looked at Niles. "Gorse and some of the boys went into a hurdy-gurdy house down there. He waited while the boys went in to see Jersey Kitty, the most popular of the girls."

"So?"

Bond shook his head. "Four of the boys went in first. Then Gorse went in. You won't believe who Jersey Kitty was, sir."

Niles took his pipe from his mouth. "God, no!" he said.

"Aye. Gorse went loco. The boys had a hell of a time with him. I wanted to leave him behind, but he insisted on coming."

Niles looked at the emaciated form beneath the issue blanket. "Keep an eye on him, then. I'll arrange a transfer. for him when we get back."

"Will that solve it, sir?"

Niles shook his head.

Bond sucked at his pipe. "Belike Asesino will. Well, good night, sir." The noncom stood up. "Mr. Ord."

"Yes?"

"It's good to be with you again." The Sergeant went to his blankets.

A shadowy form materialized. Niles caught the odor of greasy buckskin as Nato squatted beside him. The Coyotero had scouted north when the patrol had halted for the day. "Trail used much today," he said. "The drop-pings of many *thlees.*"

"How many?"

"Four hands or more."

Niles relit his pipe and looked at the impassive face of the Coyotero. Forty braves riding to join Asesino. The *bronco* Chiricahua usually had between forty and fifty warriors of his own tribe. Not counting the other tribes that might send men to his inflammatory council fire, that gave him close to one hundred warriors. The entire post personnel of Fort Bellew numbered less than a hundred. Roland Dane might need his reinforcements and his Gatling gun before long.

Niles finished his pipe. "We ride north tomorrow, Nato," he said.

"Enju!" The Coyotero went to his bed. Niles heard him say his prayers, *"Gun-ju-le, chil-jilt, si-chi-zi, gun-ju-le, inzayu-ijanale."*

Niles translated the prayer and said it softly aloud: "Be good, O Night; Twilight, be good. Do not let me die!"

Niles emptied his pipe and walked toward his bed, passing the form of Sergeant Gorse. The noncom's eyes were wide open, but he gave no sign of seeing Niles. Niles shivered a little at the set look on the man's face. He was like a laid-out corpse.

Niles rolled into his blankets and placed his head against his saddle. The odor of sweat-soaked wool, the nitrogen odor of horses, the rich odor of tanned leather clung about him. It was good to be away from Fort Bellew and its load of trouble. A coyote howled far across the dark mesa as he closed his eyes.

CHAPTER FIVE

Niles moved the patrol out an hour before dawn. Nato led the way on foot, leading his bayo coyote. Niles had damned good eyes and prided himself on his ability to see at night, but even with the first faint traces of the dawn in the eastern sky it was like moving about at the bottom of an inkwell. There was no talking among the men of the patrol, but Niles could almost feel the mental cursing with which each man lightened the burden. The hoofs clattered on rock now and then. Boots accidentally dislodged stones. The patrol descended the mesa two miles from the camp and Niles called a halt. He had done what he had planned to do; he had moved away from the skyline before daylight broke.

Niles called Bond aside. "Make fires of dry wood just at daybreak. Shield the glow if you can. When you've made coffee, put out the fires and cover the ashes carefully with sand."

"Where are you, going, sir?"

"Nato and I will scout ahead up the canyon. D'Angelo will come as courier."

Nato swung up on his boyo coyote. Niles followed him. D'Angelo brought up the rear. The Italian was the dandy of B Company. He had fought with Garibaldi's Redshirts in Sicily and Italy, was a veteran of the battles of Calatafimi, Palermo, and Milazzo in Sicily, and later had seen action at the Volturno in Italy. Upon Garibaldi's capture at Aspromonte, D'Angelo had fled from the Royalists and arrived in New York to enlist in the Union Army in the fall of 1862. He had fought with Judson Kilpatrick's hard-riding Federal Horse, and later had served on the Mexican border. There was no better soldier in the company, in drinking, making love, and fighting. His trumpeting was inspired.

The sun tipped the eastern ranges when Nato led the way into a side canyon and dropped the reins of his horse. Niles took his Henry rifle and handed the reins of his bay to the trumpeter. "Stay here, D'Angelo. Nato will bring you any message I have for Sergeant Bond."

The Italian smiled. "Ees Indians ahead?"

"Yes."

The trumpeter blew a kiss. "Ees better than the Forta Bellew. Ees excitement!"

Nato followed an almost indistinguishable trail up the side of the canyon. It was damned hard going and the sun warmed Niles's back when at last the Coyotero hit the dirt and motioned Niles down. Niles fell flat and crawled up to the scout. Nato pointed west.

On the near side of a conical butte they could see the movement of men. Two Apaches trotted up a trail, seemingly nothing but a faint line on the rugged side of the butte. "Up," said Nato.

Niles followed the trail with his eyes and uncased his field glasses. An Apache stood on a flat rock at the top of the trail, watching the two warriors coming toward him. Beyond the guard was a faint trace of smoke against the gray sky. "Asesino?" Niles asked over his shoulder.

"I think so, Brother."

"There is not much room up there for horses."

Nato pointed down at the base of the butte. There

was movement down there in the thick shadows, as yet not dispelled by the rising sun. "Many *thlees*," said Nato.

"Ummm..." said Niles. He looked up at the butte. There was no way of getting up there for a look-see. The country at the foot of the butte was badly cut up, too risky for an ambush. But the horses... That was a thought.

Niles lay flat on the ground. "Can you lead us west of that butte, Nato?"

"Muy malo," the scout said in Spanish. *"Malpais."*

"But *is* there a way?"

"Yes. *Dan juda.* All bad. Take long time. Hard on *thlees.*"

Niles watched the two warriors vanish atop the butte. "Asesino has big medicine," he said softly. "Big talk. Maybe we can let some of the hot air out of his bag." He turned to Nato. 'Tell the trumpeter to go back to Sergeant Bond. Bring the men up to the canyon at the foot of this ridge. Tell him to tell Sergeant Bond to come up here when the men are down below."

The Coyotero nodded and vanished like a slithering snake. Niles studied the horse herd. There were a hundred to a hundred and fifty in the herd, probably watched by boys and untried braves still using the head-scratching stick and drinking cane. If Niles could get up the canyon from them and stampede that herd through the rough country, they would be scattered from hell to breakfast. Then let Asesino talk all the war he wanted to.

When Bond squirmed over the lip of the ridge his face was purpling. "For God's sake, Lieutenant!" he gasped, "If you're trying to get to heaven the hard way, don't bring me in on it. I can figure an easier way."

Niles grinned, "Hell, Joe," he said, "maybe you should have sent up a *younger* man. Like Corporal Schimmelpfennig."

"Schim? Oh, my God. He drinks so damned much beer, all he needs is hoops around that gut of his to make him look like a barrel."

Niles handed the glasses to the noncom and spoke of his plan. Bond shifted his chew and spat reflectively. "I like it," he said slowly. "Except if we *don't* drive that herd, we'll be bottled up behind them and every damned Apache on that butte will be dumping rocks and bullets down on us."

Niles rubbed his bristling jaw. "It'll take us a hell of a long time to get west of the butte, because we've got to travel under cover every damned foot of the way. That means a fireless, and maybe a waterless, camp tonight. I mean to hit them at dawn tomorrow. If they're still there then."

Bond nodded. "They'll be there. When Asesino gets wound up, he'll talk most of the day. Then the rest of them have to talk. Then the *tiswin* gets passed around. I think we can bet on it that they'll still be up there."

Niles slapped the big noncom on the back. *"Enju!* Let's go. You need any help going down?"

Bond drew back his head. "Lieutenant, sometimes you try my patience. Just look out I don't fall on you."

They worked their way down the slope. Niles sent Nato ahead with D'Angelo and Jacony as connecting files. Then came Niles with the main body and Sergeant Bond. Corporal Cassidy brought up the rear with Argyle and O'Hallihan.

Niles glanced at Millard Gorse as they led their horses to the north. The Sergeant's face was impassive. Behind him was beefy Corporal Schimmelpfennig. The big German stayed close to Gorse. It came to Niles that Joe Bond had arranged for that seeming friendship. The German was big enough to take care of Gorse if anything should happen.

Corporal Kermit Pierce rode a few files behind Gorse. The laconic, tobacco-chewing Tennesseean was the finest shot in the troop. Niles wondered if that was another one of Bond's examples of foresightedness. One way or another, Gorse would be stopped if he tried anything reckless or foolish to stamp out the memory of his wife.

Muy malo, the Coyotero had said, and he had not exaggerated in the least. The canyon they traversed was a hell of shattered rock, shintangle brush, and tangled scrub trees. The sun beat down into the huge trough of rock, filling it with a soaking heat like a great woolen blanket. They halted ten minutes out of the hour. It was only then that Niles allowed the thirsty troopers a mouthful of water from their canteens. By midafternoon Niles called a halt and the soggy troopers dropped where they stood. Niles rode ahead to contact Nato. D'Angelo pointed upward as he slid from his lathered horse. "Esa looking, Meester Ord. Esa *always* looking, that one."

Niles worked his way up a talus slope, pulling himself along by the brush. His shirt was black with sweat and his lungs were full of fire when at last he found the Coyotero squatting in the dubious shade of a pinnacle of rock. The tall butte was now to the south of them. Niles studied it with his glasses, the scout shading the lens with his filthy hat. There was no way of seeing the herd in the canyon far below the butte. Niles looked at Nato. "Are they still there?"

"Asesino there."

"How do you know?"

Nato felt inside his filthy shirt and drew out a piece of denticulated spar crystal. *"Chalchihuitl* know."

There was a positive tone to the Coyotero's voice.

"How much longer before we reach the canyon where the *thlees* are?"

"Go-nan-nay."

Ten hours. It was after three o'clock. Allow an hour's rest for the men. March until midnight. Rest until three hours before dawn. That would give them an hour's leeway before they hit the herd. Niles nodded. He returned down the canyon wall and led the weary bay back to the resting place. Bond was stoking his pipe. The men were scattered about on the hard earth.

"Christ," said Schimmelpfennig, "in my bloodt iss fire yedt."

"It's just the beer working around, Schimmy," said Walzik.

"Yah? Beer yedt! I should punch in your headt yedt for mentioning beer in a furnace like diss."

"There ain't even water in here, much less beer," growled Reelfoot.

Gorse lay with his arm over his eyes. "There's death in this place. I know," he said.

"Shut up," said Pierce.

The men looked at each other out of the corners of their eyes. O'Toole looked up. "Holy Mother," he said in an awed voice. "Look!"

Heads snapped up. Niles reached for his rifle.

A ragged buzzard floated on the updraft of hot air from the canyon, not a hundred feet above them. His greedy eyes seemed to be inspecting them. A horse whinnied and the bird of prey drifted off as silently as it had come. O'Toole crossed himself.

Bond lit his pipe. "The boys are getting tense," he said.

"They'll be a hell of a lot more tense by dawn tomorrow, Joe."

"Aye. But it's a soldier's life. The drudgery of training, post duty, lousy pay, and then the fight, short but wild, which burns the dross from a man's system."

Niles eyed the stolid noncom. "The Army for you, eh, Bond?"

"Aye. I know no other life." The wise gray eyes studied Niles. "Nor will you."

Niles rested his head on his canteen. "I wonder why."

Bond shrugged. "With me it was a home before I met Mary. Maybe it was because I needed someone to tell me what to do when I was a younker. Mary seemed to understand. I offered to leave after the war, but she wouldn't have it. Even after she lost two babies from the heat and hard living. Aye! She knew me well enough. I couldn't have gone home and worked as a clerk or a watchman. It was the flag, and wearing the blue; the rut the Army sets you in. After a time any other life doesn't appeal to you. If I *had* gone home, the sight of a soldier or the music of a band would have set me neighing like a fire horse put out to pasture."

Niles half closed his eyes. "Rather like pouring the hot fluid metal of youth into a mold. As it cools the impurities rise to the surface and form a scum, leaving the pure metal of a soldier."

Bond tamped the tobacco down into his pipe. He glanced at Sergeant Gorse. "Aye," he said quietly. "But in some of us the impurities remain, to show up at times of stress."

Niles shifted a little. "In some of us?" he asked. "Why not in all of us?"

The men rested as well as they could in the heat. It was four o'clock by Niles's repeater watch when they started on again. There was no conversation from the weary men as they slogged over the broken ground or crashed through thickets of catclaw and mesquite. Darkness came and still Niles went on. A faint moon rose and gave them some light. His shirt was stinking with sweat, and his feet, socks, and boots were all molded into one. A blister was forming on his left heel.

Once the moon rose, they had light to help them pick their way along, but the going was no easier. A cool wind finally felt its way into the canyon. At midnight they stopped again and picketed the horses. Sentries were placed and the command ate embalmed beef and hard-tack washed down by the little water they had remaining.

Niles was aroused by Sergeant Bond. The moon was low by now. Niles felt his shirt clinging clammily to his body. The men stumbled to their horses. Niles gathered his small command together. "We've got a two-hour march ahead of us. At the end of that time we'll be close in on the Apache herd." Niles looked at the dim faces beneath the wide hat brims. "You may be cursing me now, but when we scatter Asesino's herd, he'll be afoot for some time and not so damned cocky. This night's work may, in time, save your life or the life of one of your bunkies. Another thing: I'll trade one large blister for a shirt that stinks worse than mine."

Corporal Schimmelpfennig laughed. "Nodt for mine, Mr. Ord! Only I can standt it."

They went on through a narrow part of the canyon and debouched into a wider area where the going was easier. Niles plodded on mechanically. Only the ghostly appearance of Nato, squatting beside the rough trail, brought him back to reality. The Coyotero spoke quickly in loose Apache, using his hands to express some of his thoughts. "We are close, Never Still. Short time until dawn."

Niles stopped his command. He called Bond. "I'm going ahead with Nato," he said. "I'll leave my watch with you. In half an hour bring the men up. Wrap any loose metal in strips of cloth. Remove spurs. Clamp onto those windpipes if the horses get wind of the herd. The wind is to the south, blowing across the canyon, so they shouldn't smell us, though God knows how they'd miss whiffing these shirts."

"Yes, sir."

Niles handed him Dandy's reins. "See you," he said.

"Good luck, sir."

Niles took his Henry rifle and followed the silent scout through the dimness. Nato led the way around a long curve in the canyon and then up a brushy slope. He squatted in the brush and pointed up. Niles saw the conical butte thrusting itself into the velvety darkness. It beat him to figure how Nato had led them so precisely to the spot.

For a time it seemed to be darker, and then there was a subtle change in the east. The false dawn. Below him Niles heard the occasional thud of a hoof as Bond brought up the patrol.

The sky grew lighter. Niles looked down into the

canyon that wound past the base of the conical butte. He could distinguish darker patches now, obviously the Apache herd. In a few minutes it was light enough for him to use his glasses. The ridge sloped down, fairly free of brush. The herd was scattered from one wall of the canyon to the other. Niles tightened his belt and drew his Colt, twirling the cylinder and slipping the pistol back into its sheath. His gut became queasy and then settled. There was a dryness in the back of his throat, not entirely from thirst. Sergeant Bond materialized. Niles pointed down the slope. "We'll ride with pistols at the ready. Pair the men off to watch each other. I want no man left behind if unhorsed!"

Bond nodded and went down the slope. There came the faint sound of rumps slamming against damp leather as the patrol mounted. Nato shifted. "Dawn, long time let me live," he said in Coyotero as he cast a pinch of *hoddentin* toward the east. He called attention to his prayer with a sharp exclamation. *"Ek!"*

D'Angelo brought up Niles' horse and that of the Coyotero. The sky was clear enough now for fair visibility. Niles swung up on his bay and drew his Colt. Bond was in the rear with Sergeant Gorse. On the right was lean Corporal Pierce. On the left was Corporal Cassidy. Corporal Schimmelpfennig was spaced down the line. D'Angelo, the trumpeter, was behind Niles. Niles looked at the Italian. 'Trumpeter! When we hit the bottom of the slope, blow the Charge, and put some spit into it! Keep blowing until we're past the herd or have driven it up the canyon."

Niles settled his hat and touched Dandy with his spurs. He raised an arm, waving the men on, and rode hard down the slope. The drumming of the hoofs was the only sound for a short time. The nearest Apache horses were a good two hundred yards away when D'Angelo lipped into the Charge. The thrilling notes seemed to bounce like rubber balls from wall to wall of the canyon. A startled warrior jumped up from behind a bush, throwing aside his blanket. He leveled and fired his rifle. The cottony smoke drifted off. A young warrior rose from behind a rock. His heavy rifle banged.

Nato whooped tremulously. Niles yelled. The high-pitched, terrifying Rebel yell broke from leather-lunged Corporal Pierce, and then they hit the first horses. Dandy shouldered aside a bayo coyote mare. Niles turned in the saddle. His men were sweeping the canyon like a dirty blue-and-bay broom. Apache horses milled in terror, whinnying and neighing as the first troopers closed in on them, shrieking and cursing. Guns rattled from the brush. Trooper O'Brien shouted as his bay went down, pitching him over its head. The Irishman hit the ground running, cast a wild look over his shoulder, and then screamed at the top of his lung, *"Mulligan!* Damn your Irish soul, pick me up!"

Mulligan kneed his bay close to O'Brien and kicked his right foot out of the stirrup. O'Brien gripped it and swung up behind his mate. He drew and fired his Colt full into the face of a screaming Apache boy. The face exploded into red jam and then the dust covered him.

It was a hell of crashing rifles, thudding hoofs, yelling men, and neighing horses. Niles bent low as an Apache sighted on him. Nato swung over, gripped his Sharps by the barrel, and smashed the rifleman into the dust.

Corporal Cassidy drove his horse at another herder. The bay reared. The forehoofs smashed into the herder's chest and the bay was past. Niles fired twice at two herders hiding behind a thicket. One of them went down and the other rolled into cover.

The herd was streaming to the east, smashing through thickets and over rocky slopes. Half a dozen of them were down with broken legs, their eyes wide with terror as the patrol crashed over and past them.

Niles caught a flash of the frenzied face of Sergeant Millard Gorse close beside him. "Through the valley of the shadow of death, eh, Mr. Ord? Is *that* the way you want it?" he screamed, and then he was gone in the swirling dust.

Rifles popped futilely from the high trail and the top of the butte, and then it was over. The patrol rode hard through the swirling dust. D'Angelo stopped his steady trumpeting. Niles dropped back among the hard-riding men. "Bond!" he yelled. "Close up! Take the rear! Anyone missing?"

"I don't think so, sir."

A mile from the butte Niles slowed the men to a walk. He ordered four men to dismount and take positions beside the trail with ready carbines. Bond shoved back his hat and wiped the sweat from his face. He grinned as he pointed at the pillar of dust rising ahead of them. "Damned bangtails will run all the way to the New Mexico border," he said.

Niles looked about, mentally calling the roll. Nato. Sergeant Bond. Corporal Pierce. Corporals Cassidy and Schimmelpfennig. Suddenly he looked at Bond. "Who's missing?"

Bond turned in his saddle and looked long and hard down the dusty canyon. "Sergeant Gorse," he said quietly.

"We'll go back!"

Bond shook his head. He looked Niles full in the eyes. "He rode *back* toward the ridge, sir. I couldn't stop him at all."

Niles looked to the west. "Through the valley of the shadow of death," he said quietly.

Bond looked at Niles with a queer expression on his dust-caked face. "Sir?"

"Nothing, Sergeant Bond. Nothing at all. Take the rear with four men. We're riding for the Rio Bravo!"

Niles led the way with Nato. He unsheathed his carbine, firing and dropping a dun mare that stood by the side of the trail. "Get every one you can, men!" he called out. "Let's see how far and fast Asesino can *walk* on the warpath!"

The crackle of carbine fire echoed through the canyon as the troopers fired at the strays. It was filthy work for cavalrymen. Yet they were damned if they did and damned if they didn't. As Niles fired, he seemed to see the tragic face of Millard Gorse in front of him.

CHAPTER SIX

The patrol worked westward as far as Squaw Tanks, south as far as Keg Butte, and then north again to circle the brooding Escabros for the long haul back to Fort Bellew. Day after monotonous day, week after week, fulfilling the thirty days in hell. Now and then, there was an ominous thread of smoke against the hazy sky, and always there was the feeling of being watched by hostile eyes, but never in all that time, after the stampeding of Asesino's herd of horses, did they see an Apache other than patient Nato, the Coyotero. It was a time of utter loneliness, when the time-tried jokes and stories of the brown-faced troopers finally died away into the silence of strict endurance.

On the last day before Fort Bellew, Niles looked back at the thin line of men. Dust shrouded the patrol. The lean jaws worked away at chewing tobacco. Everything about them was a neutral dust color. The mingled odors of horse nitrogen, leather, and stinking wool clung about them, broken now and then by the clean sweep of the dry sweet wind. White crescents of sweat showed beneath the armpits of the faded blue shirts. The soft whisper of leather, the thud of hoofs, the dull clicking of equipment blended into a monotonous rhythm. Oddly enough, as

Niles looked at his tiny command, he seemed to see the long gray line of cadets sweeping across the parade ground at West Point in the teeth of a cold wind from across the Hudson.

The dust-hoarse voice of Sergeant Bond brought Niles back to reality. "I don't like it," he said.

Niles stood up in his stirrups to ease his weary body. "What?" he asked.

Bond shifted his wad of sweet chewing. "The whole damned thing," he said. "It isn't like that side-winder Ase-sino to let us get away with such a quiet patrol."

Niles looked at the hazy hills. "No. He'd have rounded up his horses by now. Maybe he's sitting up there watching us now. It'd be like him to hit us close to the fort just to prove he wasn't scared of us."

"Aye."

A thin streamer of dust rose ahead and Nato appeared riding hard. He drew up beside Niles. "There is no sign of them ahead," he said, gravely accepting a cigar from Niles.

"Nothing?"

"Here and there a little dung of *thlees*. A few tracks."

Niles eased back his hat and let the collected sweat run down his face. The sun was like a saber cut across the back of his neck. He swabbed his face with his filthy yellow scarf, wincing as the cloth rubbed across the sunburn. "Go on ahead, then," he said, "on the fort trail. Report back if you see anything."

The Coyotero drummed his heels against the sides of his horse and rode away from the patrol.

Niles glanced at Joe Bond. "Nothing," he said. "Nothing at all? I wonder if Asesino is home."

Bond spat a thin brown stream. "His home is in hell and his father and mother are devils."

Niles eyed the somber hills. "I wonder if Millard Gorse is in hell with him."

Bond shrugged. "The man lived his hell on earth, Mr. Ord."

"Where did he go, I wonder?" Niles filled his pipe. "Across the border? Back to Tucson?"

Bond shook his head. "He's dead."

The long day dragged to a close. They forded the rushing Rio Bravo, rode up onto the mesa, and entered the drab fort. The men swung down, muscle-stiff and wooden-legged. Niles returned Bond's salute. "Dismiss the men," he said. He watched them lead the horses to the corral, knowing the time that must be spent taking care of the horses before they took care of themselves, bone-weary as they were.

Niles wiped some of the dust from his face and slapped his uniform with his hat. He handed the reins of his horse to Mulligan and walked to headquarters. Roland Dane was at his desk, reading a thick book that Niles recognized as Army regulations. The Major returned Niles's salute. "Well?" he asked. There were dark circles beneath his eyes.

Niles told of his patrol.

"You lost Sergeant Gorse?"

"The man was deranged, sir."

"You didn't go *back* for him?" The officer's tone was sharp.

"The Apaches were alert. I had the patrol to think about."

Dane slammed the book shut. "You should have gone back, damn it all! God knows what has happened to that man. In my experiences against the Cheyennes and Kiowas we never rode deliberately away from a man, leaving him in the hands of the hostiles. That wasn't Custer's way!"

Niles shifted a little. The acid tones cut into Niles like a whip of nettles. He couldn't help himself, not after thirty days in hell. "I seem to remember something about Major Elliott, Sergeant Major Kennedy, and eighteen troopers being left behind at the Washita," he said quietly. "Seven hundred men leaving a battlefield with the loss of one man killed and twenty missing. *Custer's* way!"

Dane threw back his head and eyed Niles. Thin lines etched themselves at the corners of his mouth and for a moment Niles almost thought the man would strike him. Dane gripped the edge of his desk. "I should throw the lie in your teeth, Ord," he said, "but this is not the time or the place." He stood up. "Go to your quarters and clean up. Get some food. Present yourself here in an hour and a half with sidearms. I want you to accompany me to make an arrest."

Niles stared at his commanding officer. "I've just put in thirty days on patrol, sir. Surely a junior officer or a non-com can make an arrest."

Dane's unfathomable eyes held steady on Niles. "This is an unusual case," he said softly.

There was something coldly evil in the man's tone. A trooper passed by headquarters whistling "The Captain's Name Was Murphy." A mule bawled from the corral. Dane looked down at the thick book of regulations on his desk. "Captain Boysen absented himself from the post last night without permission," he said. "He is at the camp of Porfirio the woodcutter. We are going to arrest him for being absent without leave!"

Niles felt a revulsion against the man seated before him.

There was no doubt in his mind that Roland Dane had driven the drunken officer from the post.

"You may leave now," said Dane.

Niles saluted and left the room. He strode across to his quarters. A woman called to him from Dane's quarters. It was Sylvia Dane. He kept on. The whole damned post reeked of evil. He almost wished he were still out in the hills scouting against Asesino.

Baird Dobie was seated on his bunk, in his drawers, staring moodily at a half-empty bottle on his desk. He glanced up at Niles. "I don't know whether to empty it and get stinking, or go over the hill, Niles. Welcome home," he added as an afterthought.

Niles peeled off his stinking uniform and swabbed his body with a towel. "What's the grisly story, Baird?"

Baird filled two glasses. "We've practiced saber drill. The charge. Pistol drill. Foot drill. Every damned kind of drill in the rotten book. With Roland Dane striding around the post like an avenging angel and Elias Boysen lying in his bunk sloppy drunk. We've had dinner at the Danes' every third night, with Sylvia Dane dressed like Queen Elizabeth and just as immoral. With Roland Dane filling Boysen's glass before it was even empty. With Thorpe Martin goggling at her like a boy looking at a fresh-baked pie cooling on a window ledge. Jesus Christ, Niles! I could throw up all over the place every time I look at Roland Dane and his bed-loving spouse!"

Niles sat down on his bunk and downed his drink, holding the glass out for a refill. "What happened to Boysen?"

"After dinner last night he was so damned drunk he fell over his own feet in the middle of the Danes' parlor. Dane ordered him to stay in his quarters. Boysen went down to Porfirio's camp. He hasn't been back. By God, Niles, Dane *forced* the man into it! I have no use for the drunken sot, but that polished sadist sitting over there like a damned spider in his web is responsible for Boysen's situation. Dane and no other!"

"I'm to go with Dane to the woodcutter's camp to arrest him."

"Why? There are other officers here."

Niles shrugged. "Who can figure out Dane's twisted reasoning? I'll have to go."

"How was the patrol?"

Niles rapidly sketched in the details.

Baird lay back on his bunk. "We'll never see Millard Gorse again. Maybe it's just as well."

Niles bathed and dressed. He had no appetite. He shrugged into his shell jacket and hung his Solingen saber at his side. He slid his Colt into its holster and placed his forage cap on his head. "God help us all," he said. "How is Little Deer?"

Baird Dobie looked up at Niles. "Well enough. Boysen got drunk one night and roughed her up a bit before I stopped him. That bastard Ershick thought it was real funny."

A cold feeling came over Niles. "Sometimes I have a feeling we're on a one-way ride to hell with the slide greased," he said.

"Amen, sonny. Amen!"

Niles touched the peak of his cap and left the quarters. Mulligan brought up a horse for him. "Is the Lieutenant going out on a evenin' av pleasure, sorr?" the Irishman asked.

Niles glanced at the impassive face of the trooper. He knew. Niles looked up at the dusk-shrouded hills. "Yes," he said. "Pleasure for someone."

"Kape away from the ladies down there, sorr. They have a nasty habit of lavin' a man with something he will not like, Mr. Ord."

"Damn you, Mulligan! Keep a checkrein on that loose lip of yours or I'll have you bucked and gagged!"

Mulligan held up a hand in protest. "Just a bit av a joke, sorr!"

"Keep your jokes for the barrack room, then!"

Niles led the bay across the parade ground. Roland Dane was waiting beside his horse. Without a word he mounted and they rode toward the gate. Here and there about the post men stood under the *ramadas* eying them. It was a damned disgrace and Niles felt unclean as he passed the gatehouse and rode down toward the river.

The moon was rising to tint the eastern ranges as they followed the river trail beside the rushing Rio Bravo. Ice-chip stars sprinkled the deep-blue blanket of the sky. The wind soughed through the scrub trees. Roland Dane glanced at Niles. "You don't like it, do you?" he asked.

"No, sir."

"You're wondering why I picked you?"

"Yes."

Dane guided his bay past a fallen tree. "I picked you because I can rely on you. There may be trouble."

"I expect it. Porfirio is a good man in his rough way. He won't like this mess."

Dane laughed. "I had him up at the post a week ago and told him not to serve his rotgut to the men or I'd drive him from the country. He didn't like it."

"He's done a lot for us, sir. Sent valuable information to us about the movement of the hostiles."

"The greasy swine fattens on the money these men take down there for his rotgut and loose women."

Niles shrugged. "There's little enough amusement for the men here, sir. It's a place to let off steam."

"It weakens them."

Niles eyed the Major. "They don't have their own women with them, sir, or choice wines and brandies. You can't pen up men like animals. Studs have hot blood."

Dane placed a hand on the cantle of his saddle and looked back at the distant yellow lights of Fort Bellew. "I'll agree to that," he said quietly. "Officers and men both."

The camp of Porfirio was sprawled in a *cienaga* near the river. Jacales formed a crude square. A fire blazed in the center of the camp. Cords of wood stood ready to be transported to the market. Wagons stood in a row behind the jacales, and mules milled about in a peeled-pole corral. A woman laughed as the two officers came up the rise. A sentry, wearing a black steeple hat, his thin body shrouded in a garish *serape,* came out of the shadows bearing a long-barreled rifle. He nodded as he saw the two officers and watched them with curious eyes as they dismounted near the big jacal of Porfirio. Niles rapped on the door, glancing back over his shoulder. Half a dozen Mexicans squatted near the fire, smoking thin twisted cigars, watching the two officers.

The door opened, emitting a gush of warm air redolent of the odors of greasy food, pungent liquor and unwashed bodies. Porfirio eyed Niles. "Welcome, *Teniente,*" he said quietly. "Please to come in."

They followed the thick-bodied Mexican into the one big room of the jacal. A covered pot sat in the coals of the beehive fireplace. Beds had been rolled up and placed against the walls for seats. A candle flickered in front of an image of the Virgin of Guadalupe set in a niche in the mud-plastered wall. Porfirio indicated seats for them. The Mexican's pock-marked face was impassive. His liquid eyes showed no surprise at the visit. He took a bottle of *aguardiente* from a shelf and filled three glasses, placing them on a box in the center of the room.

Roland Dane leaned forward. "Is Captain Boysen here?" he asked coldly.

"*Sí*"

"Where?"

Porfirio wiped his thick black mustache both ways. "With the woman Ana."

"Take us to him!"

"All in good time."

Dane threw back his head. "Now!"

Porfirio looked at Niles. "This man is not my *patrón*" he said in swift Spanish to Niles. "Why does he come here and give orders?"

Niles held up a hand. "The Captain Boysen is absent without leave," he said.

"So?" Porfirio shrugged. "He comes here often."

"He must return with us."

"There is no one keeping him here." The Mexican smiled slyly. "With the exception of Ana."

Niles stood up. "Take us to him," he said. "There will be trouble if you do not, *amigo.*"

"Trouble?" asked Porfirio softly. "No! I have twenty men here, well armed, to do my bidding."

"We are friends, Porfirio!"

"*Sí! We* are friends. But this cockerel with the fine

sword and shiny pistol, with hate in his eyes, *he* is not a friend."

"Show us to him, Porfirio."

Porfirio downed his drink and stood up. "Follow me," he said. "It is not a pretty sight."

They followed the woodcutter across the firelit area between the rows of buildings. Liquid eyes studied the two Americans. Porfirio stopped at a jacal near the river and thrust open the door. There was a startled exclamation from a woman. A guttering candle lantern hung in a corner. Ana drew a *serape* over her thin, sweaty *camiseta* and stood back against the dirty wall. Her dark eyes looked from one to the other. The room was overheated, and heavy with the odors of cheap perfume, rotten liquor, and sweat. Dane eyed the full-bodied woman up and down. "Where is the Captain?" he asked.

She looked at the sagging bed in the darkest corner. A man lay there with his head hanging back over a dirty pillow. It was Elias Boysen. His dark hair was plastered with grease and sweat, hanging down over his pallid face like thread stretched across yellow linen. One arm hung down to hold a bottle, sitting on the packed earth floor. His eyes were open, but unseeing. "Who is it, Ana?" he asked.

She shifted and glanced at the door. "Officers. From the fort, Elias."

Boysen rolled his head to one side. "Tell 'em I'll be back in the morning."

Dane's lips drew back in a sneer of disgust. "Get up, Boysen," he said.

Boysen eyed Dane. "Roland," he said. "The *beau sabreur.* Have a drink. Good Bacanora mezcal! Better than that sugary swill you pour out of your fancy crystal decanters."

"Damn you!" said Dane thinly. "Get up! That's an order!"

Porfirio jerked his head at the woman. She passed close to Niles and smiled, and then vanished into the shadows. The woodcutter placed a hand on Niles's arm. "No trouble," he said. "Get him out of here." He left the room.

Boysen lifted the bottle. Dane crossed the room in quick plunging steps. He kicked the bottle from the slack fingers. It smashed against the wall, flooding the room with the pungent odor of mezcal. "Get up, you drunken sot!" he barked. "You poor excuse for an officer! Get up, you filthy bastard!"

Boysen grinned. "Now, Roland. Don't call the kettle black."

Dane reached down and twisted his fingers in the front of Boysen's sweaty undershirt. He dragged the bigger man to his feet with surprising strength. "Damn you! Damn you! *Damn you!* Lying here like a hog, with a diseased doxie! You stink of her cheap perfume and reeking sweat! You're a damned disgrace to us all!"

Boysen looked vacantly at Niles. "Ord! What the hell is this? Get this ass out of here."

Dane freed his right hand. It caught Boysen hard across a flabby cheek. He slapped hard on both sides of the dirty face. Boysen's head rocked back and forth. Spittle flew from his loose mouth. Dane shoved him back against the wall so hard that dried mud fell in a hard patter about them. He smashed a fist against the helpless man's mouth. He panted like an angry woman.

Niles, sickened at the sight, gripped Dane by the shoulder and whirled him about, ripping his hand open on the Major's oak leaf. "Enough!" he said. "For God's sake, man! He's helpless."

Niles looked into the staring eyes of Roland Dane. The Major raised a hand as though to strike and then let it drop. He broke away from Niles, gripped Boysen by the shoulder, and whirled him about. He planted a foot against the drunken officer's rump and kicked him toward the door. Boysen crashed through it, followed by the enraged Dane. Dane kicked him again, sending him sprawling in the dust. The Mexicans watched the disgusting scene.

Niles gripped Dane by the shoulder. "Damn you!" he said. "It's bad enough as it is. Let him alone, or by heaven, I'll buffalo you with my Colt!"

Dane eyed Niles for a moment. "Get him on his horse," he said. "The disgusting swine." He strode toward his bay.

Niles pulled Boysen to his feet. A woodcutter handed Boysen his greasy blouse and the officer shrugged into it. He wiped the blood from his mouth. Niles took him by an arm. He guided him to the horse that was brought over by Porfirio. Niles gave him a boost up into the saddle.

Ana came out of the shadows. "The money!" she cried. "He has not paid!"

"Shut up!" said Niles. "I'll pay tomorrow."

"Now!"

Dane spurred forward. "Get out of sight," he said, "you whore!"

Ana planted her hands on her broad hips. "Whore? You talk of a *whore?* You with that painted bitch up there on the mesa making sheep's eyes at anything in trousers. Paaah!"

Dane spoke out of the corner of his mouth. "Get him started on the trail. I'll cover you."

Niles took the reins of Boysen's horse. The firelight flickered on the liquid eyes of the Mexicans who had gathered behind the raging woman. Here and there the light glinted dully on drawn knives and pistols. Porfirio leaned against a jacal, watching the Major. Niles led Boysen's horse toward the trail.

"Pay!" screamed Ana. She thrust out her two hands, letting her *serape* fall. A full breast hung over the edge of her dirty *camiseta*. She ran forward and gripped the bridle of Dane's bay. Dane circled the bay on the forehand, dragging the shrieking woman on her knees across the rough earth. A Mexican raised a knife. Roland Dane drew out his Colt and cocked it. "Stand back!" he cried furiously.

Ana dragged at the bridle. The bay was nervous. It shied and blew and then reared. A knife flashed through the air and skidded across Dane's pistol wrist. The heavy Colt fell and hit the ground butt first. The handgun bellowed. For a scant moment the scene was almost like a tableau. The encircling woodcutters. The impassive Porfirio. The woman, with her mouth agape. Then she fell forward as the echo of the pistol shot slammed back and forth between the walls of the canyon. Blood stained the thin material of the *camiseta*. Roland Dane sank steel into his excited horse and followed Niles. "Get out of here!" he yelled.

The hoofs drummed on the hard-packed earth. Niles looked back across his shoulder. The woman was ringed by the woodcutters. She was screaming like a stricken mare. She had been hit hard, but not hard enough to kill her, or she wouldn't be screaming like that.

Niles jerked at the reins of Boysen's bay. A wave of revulsion flowed through him as they cleared the camp area and followed the river trail. He had met many men in his life whom he had disliked, but none as much as the two that rode with him beside the rushing Rio Bravo.

CHAPTER SEVEN

A cool searching wind sprang up in the darkness just before dawn. Niles awoke and lay with his hands cupped at the base of his neck, staring at the darkness. A door banged somewhere along the line of quarters. It was no use trying to sleep. He sat up and pulled on his trousers and boots, shrugging into his shirt. From across the room he heard the steady breathing of Baird Dobie. Niles buckled on his pistol belt and picked up his hat. He went outside and stood in the darkness of the *ramada*. The lights from the guardhouse shone through the night. A tumble-weed scraped against the side of the building and then rolled across the parade ground. Niles lit a cigarette and walked toward the guardhouse. Thorpe Martin was officer of the guard, and more than once Niles had suspected that he let his noncoms make the rounds.

Trooper Raskob was on duty at the gate. "How is it, Raskob?" asked Niles.

"Quiet, sir. Almost too damned quiet, if you know what I mean, begging the Lieutenant's pardon."

Niles nodded. He looked toward the dim bulk of the hills, gradually taking shape in the faint gray light of the false dawn. He went into the guardhouse. Thorpe Martin was asleep in the little cuddy near the door. Offut, the corporal of the guard, jumped to his feet when he saw Niles. "You're up early, sir," he said.

Niles glanced about the dimly lit room. The men off guard were sleeping quietly. Yet there was a foreboding in the windy darkness outside, something he could not explain: He sat down on a chair and tilted it back against the wall. He closed his eyes.

He could still clearly see the scenes of the night before when he and Roland Dane had brought Captain Boysen back to the post and tumbled him into his bed. Dane had invited him in for a drink before he went to bed. Sylvia had been there, searching their faces for knowledge of what had happened at the woodcutter's camp, but neither of them had spoken of it. The look in her eyes as Niles had left the quarters was more vivid than the disgusting scenes at Porfirio's camp and the bright crimson stain on the dirty *camiseta* of the breed woman Ana at the camp. Niles opened his eyes. Was it possible that he still loved her, knowing her at last for what she really was? He shook his head. Corporal Offut looked up curiously from the tattered magazine he was reading. Niles closed his eyes again and this time dropped off into an uneasy sleep.

"Lieutenant Ord, sir! Wake up, sir!"

Niles opened his eyes. The guardroom was flooded with cold gray light. Corporal Offut was standing before him. "There's something going on down by the river, sir. Will you take a look?"

Niles hit the floor with both feet and followed the non-com out into the windy open. Half a dozen men of the guard were standing with ready carbines, staring down toward the thick brush that lined the bank of the river on each side of the ford. Thorpe Martin stood on a rock near the gate.

"What is it, Thorpe?" asked Niles.

"I don't know. Raskob claims he saw a horseman down there."

"One man?"

Raskob shrugged. "Seems there were some men afoot, but it was too dark to see clearly."

The wind swept dust about them and rolled tumbleweeds against the guardhouse. A recruit swallowed hard and looked about uneasily. It was Tantz, a kid from Pittsburgh.

"There he is!" said Raskob triumphantly. "I knew I saw him."

"A trooper," said Offut.

The horse had appeared in a small clearing. The rider sat straight in the saddle. Suddenly there was a quick movement in the brush and the bay buck-jumped and started quickly up the mesa trail. Niles stared at the rider. Possibly a courier from Fort Bowie. Yet why would he come in at that time?

Here and there about the fort men appeared. It was a few minutes before First Call. D'Angelo was blowing softly into his trumpet to warm it up.

The bay topped the low rise and headed straight for the gate, his rider swaying stiffly. Niles stared. "By God!" he said. "I'll swear that's Sergeant Gorse."

The rider came closer.

"It's him, all right," said Offut. "He must be worn out."

The bay increased its pace. The brim of the dirty campaign hat flopped back and an uneasy feeling came over Niles as he saw the staring eyes and the ashy white face. The bay slowed to a trot and approached the gate. "Christ," said Raskob, "old Gorse looks like he's been on a two-week drunk."

"Looks like he's put on some weight, anyways," said Trooper Norris.

Niles walked forward. "Gorse!" he called. The rider came on silently. D'Angelo slowly lowered his trumpet. "Gorse!" called Niles.

The bay slowed to a walk fifty feet from the gate and then stopped twenty feet from Niles. Gorse sat bolt upright. Niles stared at him curiously. He started forward. The bay shied and turned. There was a lattice-work of branches across Gorse's back and shoulders, lashed to his body, down to the saddle, and worked into the straps. Sticking out from the back was half a dozen arrows. "For God's sake," said Offut. He ran forward. The bay shied violently. Gorse sagged to one side. Offut caught him. His shirt fell open in front. Niles turned away quickly as he saw the hideous sight. The recruit Tantz suddenly retched and threw up over his boots.

"Cut him loose," said Niles.

Offut was cursing softly as he drew his clasp knife and slashed the lashing from the branches. He lowered the dead man to the ground. From across the river came a coyote call, followed by another, and then a faint derisive hooting. A dark figure stood up on a rock, stared at the fort, and then turned to slap at his haunches in an insulting gesture. The man was too far away to be seen clearly, but Niles would bet Dandy against a burro that it was Asesino. The Chiricahua was gone like the morning mist. There was no use in chasing him.

"Get him into the guardhouse before anyone else sees him," said Niles. "O'Hallihan, get Surgeon Blanchard."

"'Tis too late, is it not, sorr?"

"Damn it, go get him! Pull out those arrows, Offut!"

They carried the corpse into the guardhouse and placed it on a bunk stripped of blankets. Niles looked down into the drawn face. The eyes were wide open. What horrors had they seen?

Orville Blanchard pushed through the staring men, carrying his instrument case. His was the precise face of the man of science, set into a mold by the teachings of Edinburgh. He looked down at the dead man. "Too late for healing," he said, "but interesting just the same. Stand back, men." He pulled back the shirt, revealing the abdomen. It had been slit from sternum to groin, filled with unspeakable things that stank to high heaven, and then roughly sewn together with gut. Blanchard drew out his scalpel and slit the lashings. The skin drew back and Niles felt a sour taste in the back of his throat. Some of the men left the room as the effluvia flooded out. Blanchard, seemingly impervious to the foul stench, picked up a billet of wood from the fireplace and poked through the mass in the abdominal cavity. "Neatly eviscerated," he said quietly.

"When did he die, Blanchard?" asked Niles.

"Last night, I'd say." Blanchard began to strip the clothing from the body, cutting through the boots to free them from the swollen legs. More men left the room as the body was revealed in its mutilated nakedness. "Jesus, Joseph, and Mary," said O'Hallihan. "There is hardly any hide to the man!"

Thorpe Martin gagged, clapped a hand to his mouth, and rushed from the room with eyes of horror.

"Offut," said Niles, "tell Sergeant Ershick to detail men for digging a grave. Tell Major Dane I'd like to have him come here."

Dane arrived in a few minutes smelling faintly of pomade and after-shave powder. His face paled as he saw Gorse, "Asesino?" he asked.

Niles nodded.

Blanchard drew a blanket over the hideous sight. "Diabolical," he said. 'They flayed him just enough to keep him alive for hours. Squaw work."

Dane smashed a fist into his other palm. He looked at Niles. "What have you to say about Custer now?" he asked.

Blanchard wiped his scalpel and looked curiously at the two officers. Dane turned on a heel and left the room. Niles walked back toward his quarters with Blanchard.

"Very interesting," said Blanchard.

"How so?"

"It will make an interesting addition to my treatise on the endurance of the human body under torture. The

Medical Journal will probably appreciate my work a great deal more than I anticipated."

"Good God," said Niles.

Blanchard paused to light a cigar. "I'm a man of science, Niles. You are, too, as a soldier. I've seen the work of some soldiers at Fredericksburg, Chancellorsville, and other gay places. Don't look on *me* with disgust, my friend." Blanchard walked toward his quarters.

It was late morning when Niles was summoned by Major Dane. The commanding officer was booted and spurred. "I'm taking out a patrol of ten men, Ord," he said, "Sergeant Forgan will go along."

"Might I ask where you are going, sir?"

Dane raised his eyebrows and smiled faintly. "After Asesino, of course!"

"With eleven men?"

"Why not? Do you want me to take the whole troop?"

"It's suicide, sir."

Dane drew on his gauntlets. "Come, come. We'll be all right."

"You don't know the country, or the Apaches, sir."

"I've fought Indians."

"Not Apaches, sir!"

Dane shifted his pistol belt. "They're all alike. Don't try to parade your knowledge of this country to me."

Niles held his temper. "The Apaches *use* this country, sir! They wear it like a cloak of invisibility. They're guerrillas. They don't fight in the open, like the Plains tribes. They ambush and run away. Strike and disappear, only to reappear miles away and strike again. They can outrun a horse on the side of a mountain; ride a horse farther and faster than any white man. They know every water hole and spring for miles. It's like playing a game of blind man's buff with a rattlesnake."

Dane shook his head. "No wonder they're sending new blood out here. You officers have been frightened by shadows." He opened the door and strode to his horse.

"We'll be back in two or three days. Keep Boysen confined to his quarters."

Niles watched the small party ride past the gatehouse. The man was a headstrong idiot. As he walked toward the corral he saw Sylvia Dane watching him from a window of her quarters.

During the long day Niles kept busy. Now and again he looked toward the small post cemetery, ringed with scrubby weeds, where the mound that marked the last bivouac for Millard Gorse, Sergeant, U.S.A., stood out fresh against the lower, almost indistinguishable mounds of those who had gone before him. The thought had always been in his mind that he would occupy a similar place someday, rather than the family plot back in Illinois, but the thought of resignation hovered in his mind like an unclean spirit.

Baird Dobie took over the guard that night. Niles was in his quarters, leaning his elbows on the window, looking toward Dane's quarters. Marion Ershick was with Sylvia. Now and then he could see one of them pass between the window and the lamp. He wondered what they were talking about. He shrugged and got up, walking toward the quarters of Elias Boysen. The Captain had had the horrors that day and Blanchard had given him a sedative. Niles tapped lightly on the door. There was no answer. He tapped again. The door swung open. The quarters were dark. Niles stepped in and listened for Boysen's breathing, but the place was as quiet as the cemetery. Niles snapped a lucifer on his thumbnail. The bunk was empty except for the rumpled coverings. Niles cursed. He ran around the front of the low adobe and toward the sanitary sinks. There was no one there. Boysen had vanished.

Niles headed for the guardhouse. He hated to do it, but Boysen had to be found. He passed Sergeant Ershick's quarters. The smash of glass came distinctly to him from the darkened building. He stopped and stepped beneath the *ramada*. The door was ajar. He knew First

Sergeant Ershick was working late on his records. Feet scuffled on the floor. There was the sound of deep breathing. Niles eased himself through the doorway and stood in the dark living room. Feet scuffled in the back room. Niles crossed to the door.

"You little red bitch! I'll get you yet." The voice of Elias Boysen came to Niles.

Niles scratched a lucifer against his belt buckle and held it up. In the wavering light of the candle he saw Little Deer, crouched against the back wall, stripped, holding a broken bottle in her hand. Her dress lay at her feet, torn to shreds.

Elias Boysen blinked in the light of the match. His face dripped blood from four deep parallel scratches. He stared stupidly at Niles. "Getta hell outa here, you!" he croaked.

Niles cursed as the lucifer seared his fingers. He dropped it and lit another, igniting the wick of a harp lamp. Boysen wiped the blood from his face.

"Has he harmed you, my sister?" asked Niles quietly in Apache.

She shook her head. Her eyes never left the bloated, bloody face of her attacker.

Niles looked at Boysen. "Get back to your quarters," he said.

Boysen spat, "Don't give *me* orders, Ord. I'm your superior officer."

"You were under arrest in quarters. I'm in command of the post until Major Dane returns. Get back to your quarters!"

Boysen shrugged. He picked up his forage cap. He eyed the naked girl and licked his lips. "I'll see you again," he said.

The door in the living room creaked open. Boysen suddenly lunged at Niles. His fist skidded along Niles's left cheekbone. Niles swung from the waist and drove Boysen back against the wall. Boysen yelled in anger. Someone came across the living room and stopped behind Niles. Boysen rushed Niles, only to meet a right jab that stopped him cold. For a second he swayed there and then he went down with a crash. He lay still. Niles turned to look into the saturnine face of Sergeant Jared Ershick.

Ershick eyed the naked girl. She snatched up her torn dress and fled from the room. Niles lifted the unconscious officer. "Give me a hand," he said. They carried the officer to his quarters and placed him on his bunk. "Detail a man to stand guard here," said Niles.

Ershick nodded. "This looks bad for you, Mr. Ord," he said.

"What do you mean?"

"Striking a superior officer."

"Damn it, man! You know he was trying to rape that girl!"

Ershick tilted his head. "So? Maybe she *invited* him there, the Apache slut."

Niles raised a hand.

"Would you strike me too, sir? I can prefer charges, Mr. Ord."

Niles closed his hands tightly. "Get out of here!" he said. "We'll settle this tomorrow."

Ershick shrugged and left. Niles crossed toward Dane's quarters. A slim form came toward him. It was Marion Ershick. "What is it, Niles?" she asked.

"Captain Boysen is drunk again. God knows how he got the liquor. I found him in your quarters attacking Little Deer. Go to her."

She placed a hand on his sleeve and then hurried through the darkness.

"Niles!" The voice came from the dark *ramada* in front of Dane's quarters. It was Sylvia. Niles hesitated.

"Niles! What is it? I'm frightened!"

Niles walked into the shadows. The fragrance of her perfume came to him. He could almost feel her warmness through the dark. She gripped his arm and pulled him into the darkened living room. In the faint light from a partly opened door he could see her, clad in a flowing negligee, her blonde hair cascading over her slim shoulders. "Marion was helping me with my hair," she said. "What has happened?"

"Nothing."

"Was it Elias?"

"Yes."

She came close. "Is he drunk again?"

"Yes. Where is the lamp?"

She put her hands on his shoulders. "Why? Are you afraid of me in the dark? You never were before, you know."

"I've got to leave, Sylvia."

She drew him close and held up her face. Niles felt the old passion sweep through him like an engulfing flame, roaring in his ears, closing his throat. His hands rested on her hips, feeling the soft flesh beneath the flimsy material.

"Niles," she said softly. "At last!"

Something scuffled the hard earth outside the quarters. Niles pushed her back and turned to the door.

"Niles!" she called.

Niles opened the door. The gun cracked across the parade ground. A second later it cracked again. Niles sprinted toward the row of officers' quarters. Men shouted through the darkness. Doors banged and a lantern flared into life and bobbed up and down as the bearer ran toward the sound of the shots.

A light flared up in Elias Boysen's quarters. Niles pushed past two troopers and hurried to the noise. "What is it?" he demanded.

One of the men, Trooper Gamier, raised his head. "Captain Boysen, sir. He's been shot."

Niles walked into the stuffy room, stinking of powder smoke. Elias Boysen sat on his bunk, his back against the wall. Blood had soaked through his undershirt. Sergeant Bond was near the window, looking down at a short-barreled nickle-plated Wells-Fargo Colt that was just below the window. Boysen suddenly fell over sideways. His eyes were wide open. He was dead.

Surgeon Blanchard came into the room. "What the hell is this, Niles?"

"Suicide, Orville,"

Blanchard lowered the dead man to the bunk. "Get the men away from here," he said over his shoulder.

Joe Bond barked orders. The men reluctantly left, talking among themselves in low voices. "He finally did it," said Mulligan loudly. "I knew it was just a matter of toime."

Blanchard worked swiftly. Sergeant Bond examined the Colt. "There was two shots," he said.

"Missed the first time," said Blanchard. "You know how shaky he was."

Niles lit a cigarette to calm himself.

Blanchard turned, holding a slug in his Blasius pincers. "Caliber thirty-one." He dropped the slug to the floor and bent over the dead man. Suddenly he jerked his head and looked queerly at Niles. He turned and held up another slug. "Two," he said quietly. "In the same hole." He stood up and wiped his hands. "This isn't suicide, Niles. It's murder."

Niles dropped his cigarette and stared at the surgeon. Blanchard tilted his head toward the dead man. "Shot at close range. Not more than a foot or so away. Shirt is charred."

Bond hefted the Colt. He glanced at the window. "A long-armed man could have leaned through the window," he said, "held the pistol close to Captain Boysen, and fired twice. Dropped the pistol by accident and then skited out of here."

Blanchard nodded. "You'd have made a good Pinkerton man, Bond."

Tattoo floated across the parade ground. The three men looked at each other. "But *who?*" asked Niles softly.

Blanchard shrugged. "I gave you my post-mortem. You're the C.O. here. It's your job, not mine, to find him.

Poor Elias. Well, he's better off this way." The surgeon left the room.

Sergeant Bond drew a blanket across the still form. "He wasn't popular, sir, but I don't know of anyone around the post who hated him enough to kill him."

Niles had a cold feeling in his gut. He remembered the lean face of Jared Ershick and the look on it when he had seen Niles standing over the unconscious form of Elias Boysen.

CHAPTER EIGHT

The Apache sat his white horse on a promontory that thrust itself out from a butte like a great lion's paw, grooved with gullies and stippled with thorny brush. On his head was a war bonnet made of the skin of a strangled fawn from which protruded two steer horns stained yellow. His upper body was clothed in a soft deerskin battle shirt decorated with the symbols of the sun, moon, stars, lightning, water bug, and spider, to which the wearer could pray in time of need. A short buckskin kilt was about his waist, and his thigh-length, button-toed desert moccasins were folded about his knees. A lance was slung behind one shoulder, made of strong cane, strengthened at points of stress with the uncut whole skin from the leg of a deer, fitted tightly down the shaft and bound with rawhide. The lance head was made from the flattened bayonet of a Mexican soldier. A stubby Spencer repeater lay across the naked brown thighs. A brass-bellied cap-and-ball Colt was thrust through the broad girdle, from which depended a buckskin bag of powdered *galena,* the potent *hoddentin* medicine of the Men of the Woods.

It was the face that caught attention. Broad and high,

the eyes narrow slits, the thin mouth drawn down at the corners, the chin protruding pugnaciously. The deep marks of smallpox pitted the brown skin. This was Inda-yi-yahn, He Kills Enemies, of the Akane or Willow gens of the Chiricahuas, the Big Mountain People, known to the Mexicans and the Americans as Asesino, the Assassin.

His horse stood patiently at the very brink of a sheer two-hundred-foot drop. The two of them were like a carven statue, only their breathing giving away the fact that they were alive. The wind rushed softly from the heights moving the tail and mane of the horse, through which bits of colored rags had been woven. Far below them, winding in a single file through a deep canyon, was a line of troopers. Twelve men. The sun glinted from their metal equipment and a plume of dust rose high behind them to be tattered by the dry wind.

Asesino uncased his field glasses and studied the little figures, picking out the face of the *nantan,* who rode ahead on a spirited bay. It was not the skillful Na-txe-ce, Never Still, he of the red face and reddish beard and the hard gray eyes who had captured Little Deer and stampeded the Chiricahua horse herd weeks before. It was not the tall officer known to the friendly Apaches as Tzitjizinde, The Man Who Likes Everybody, who fought nearly as well as Never Still. Nor was it the untried officer Eclatten, Raw Virgin Lieutenant, who would have been forced by Chiricahua tribal law to carry the cane-drinking tube and head-scratching stick until he had proved himself a man among men.

Asesino studied the handsome face of Major Dane. This man was a fool to come into the country of the Men of the Woods with such a small command. Asesino grunted. He thudded his heels against the flanks of the white horse and vanished into the brush like a brown wraith. Only a puff of dust showed where he had been standing.

Asesino took a brightly polished metal mirror from the folded top of his right moccasin and flashed it to the west. He flashed it to the northeast and then rode down a long slanting draw to gather the Apaches whom he had just alerted.

It was mid-afternoon when the warriors gathered in a deep cup of rock that held a *tinaja* or water pan, the brown scummy water thick with wrigglers. The horses drank thirstily while the warriors filled their horse-gut canteens, slinging the greasy tubes over the withers of their mounts.

Some of them munched on mesquite-bean cakes or bits of jerky as Asesino spoke.

"The white-eyes ride into a trap," he said. "Eleven men, led by a new *nantan.* They ride toward the Canyon of Big Stones. On the sides of that canyon are sandy slopes. We will ride there swiftly and conceal ourselves. Round Hat will close up the rear. Lame Deer will close up the exit. I will stay with those in the canyon. Look to your weapons. There will be no shooting until I have fired twice with my *besh-egar.*"

"This thing we will do," said the warriors almost as one.

"Enju!" said Asesino. He had twenty tried warriors and seven untried youths, still carrying the head-scratching stick and the water-drinking cane. He swung up on his horse and led the way through the brush.

———

It was late afternoon when the Chiricahuas set their trap. Lame Deer posted his men at the far end of the canyon among the great rocks. Round Hat hid his warriors in the brush near the canyon entrance, waiting for the white-eyes to pass through so that he might stopper the entrance. Asesino smoked his pipe, watching his men work swiftly, digging holes in the soft earth of the slopes. When they were done they slid into the holes with their weapons and water bags. Asesino himself covered them with gray blankets and sifted earth and bits of brush over the blankets. When he was done there was no indication that fifteen warriors lay in ambush. Asesino walked up the slope to a rock cleft and settled himself in it, puffing steadily on his pipe, watching the entrance for the troopers.

The troopers came an hour before dark. Asesino had already noted that the Coyotero scout Nato was not with them; otherwise he would never have set the trap, for the Coyotero had the senses of a lobo and would have smelled them out.

The troopers made their camp beside a rock pan, picketing the big bay horses, setting out three sentries. Fires glowed as they placed spiders over the coals and cooked their hog meat and beans. The odor of *tu-dishishn* wafted up to Asesino. He loved the black water known as coffee to the white-eyes, but he bided his time, knowing full well that soon he would gather the hard brown berries from among the bodies of the soldiers.

The new *nantan* sat on his saddle, eating slowly from a tin plate. When he was done he lit a slim cigar and lay back on his blankets. A big trooper with the three chevrons of a sergeant talked earnestly with the *nantan,* pointing toward the heights, but the *nantan* laughed and waved him away. The sergeant eyed the heights and patrolled through the brush, passing within fifty feet of some of Asesino's men. The camp settled down, the men making their beds, beating the brush with sticks to drive away the snakes. The fire died down, emitting a thread of blue smoke.

Asesino raised his Spencer and levered home a round. He rested the repeater on a rock and sighted on the *nantan.* The sights swam about and settled on the blue coat. Asesino took up the slack and squeezed off. The Spencer bellowed, driving back into Asesino's shoulder.

He fired again. The *nantan* dived for cover. The powder smoke drifted off on the wind. All along the sandy slopes the rifles of the Chiricahuas spoke, the flashes dotting the gathering darkness. Here and there a trooper went down. The horses screamed and jerked back on their picket ropes, ripping them from the soft earth. The picket pins lashed about, striking the excited troopers. Their carbines flashed at targets they could not see.

The multiple reports of the rifles slammed back and forth between the canyon walls. Seven of the troopers were down. Most of the horses stampeded toward the end of the canyon where the men of Lame Deer awaited. The big sergeant snagged a horse from the rush and swung up on it. He reached down and gripped the *nantan* by the shoulder. The *nantan* jerked free and drew his Colt, firing futilely into the shadows. The sergeant raised his pistol in a short chopping motion and slugged the *nantan*. He got down and heaved him up over the withers of his horse and then mounted, spurring the big bay back toward the men of Round Hat.

The canyon was a hell of rifle shots and drifting smoke. A slug smashed into the smoking fire and scattered the coals into the dry gamma grass. Fire leaped up and worked its way swiftly with the wind, sending up a pall of bitter smoke. Through this the big sergeant drove his sweating bay, firing with a pistol in each hand to clear the way.

Asesino churned his Spencer dry and leaped to his feet. He whooped tremulously, drew his war club, formed of a round stone encased in tightly stitched rawhide, and bounded down the slope. His men rose from their cover like brown demons rising from the pits of hell and surged down toward the scattered troopers. Clubs and rifle butts rose and fell among the wounded and dead, crushing skulls so that the spirits of the dead would not pursue the Chiricahuas to wreak ghostly vengeance. Asesino stood amidst the wreathing smoke holding his bloody war club, the light of battle in his liquid eyes. His men gathered up the weapons and food. Lame Deer drove five bays back down the canyon. From the position of Round Hat there came a sputter of fire and then the steady tattoo of beating hoofs.

Round Hat came up the canyon. He had no prisoners.

"Where is the white-eyed *nantan?*" demanded Asesino harshly.

"His *chalchihuitl* was good," said Round Hat quietly. "Our bullets were turned aside. They have escaped."

Asesino raised his war club, matted with blood and hair. For one awful moment he looked as though he would strike. Then he lowered the club. Round Hat was slow of wit but a good fighter. He had many relatives who would bring even the doughty Asesino to a bloody accounting, one duel after another until Asesino would die. *"Dan juda"* he spat.

Round Hat hung his head. He turned away and savagely smashed his carbine butt down on the head of a young trooper who was pierced by half a dozen slugs. The Chiricahuas worked swiftly, stripping off the uniforms, gathering the fine weapons and the stores of food. They disemboweled the naked bodies and Asesino drew his *besh,* a fine Spanish knife. He described a circle around the fine blond hair of Trooper Shaver, and popped the scalp free. He hung it at his belt to make medicine, and gestured to his men. They waited for the horses to be brought up by two of the untried braves. Asesino gestured. "Burn all trash," he said.

The Chiricahuas threw whatever they didn't want onto the smoldering fire. They mounted their ponies and rode slowly to the northeast, leaving a stench of burning leather and wool behind them as the sun went down, plunging the canyon of death into deep shadow. Ten sprawled bodies lay staring up with unseeing eyes. Coyotes howled from the dark slopes as they gathered for an unexpected feast.

Asesino nodded in satisfaction. This was war the

Chiricahua way. A quick ambush with no losses. Many prizes of war. Ten dead enemies. A spanking of nettles; the war path. *"Hoo. Hoo. Hoo. Ahoo"* he chanted into the darkness.

"Hoo. Hoo. Hoo. Ahoo" echoed the warriors of Asesino as they left that place of silent death.

CHAPTER NINE

It was just after Reveille when Niles heard the hoarse challenge at the gate and then an excited yell of the officer of the guard. Niles sprinted from the officers' mess toward the gate. A lone bay stood with bowed head. Big Sergeant Tim Forgan was easing Roland Dane down from the bloody saddle. Dane's fine gray shirt was ripped and bloody. A filthy bandage was about his right shoulder. Niles came to a stop. "Where are the men?" he asked.

Forgan's bloodshot eyes steadied on Niles. "Dead," he said harshly, "in Big Stone Canyon. Asesino. Caught us in bivouac last evening. Never had a chance. I wanted to camp high, but the Major refused."

Dane opened his eyes and gripped the stirrup leather of the bay. "Shut up, Forgan," he said. "You're broken as of now!"

Forgan spat. "You damned idiot!" he said. "You killed ten men! *You're* the one that should be broken! You damned mewling swine!"

Niles turned. "Corporal Schimmelpfennig! Place Forgan under arrest. Confine him in the guardhouse. Walzik! Get a stretcher from the dispensary for Major

Dane. Tantz! Take the bay to the corral. The rest of you back to your posts."

Dane leaned against the guardhouse wall. "I'll have that scum drummed out of the service," he said.

Niles looked into the drawn face. For a moment he was tempted to speak, and then he took the wounded man by the arm.

Dane shook free. "Let me alone," he said. "I've been wounded before. And wipe off that damned I-told-you-so smirk!"

Walzik came up on the double with a stretcher. They placed Dane on it and took him to the dispensary. Niles followed slowly. Surgeon Blanchard had on his rubber apron. He worked swiftly, extracting the slug from the wound, holding it up with the *Darmschere*. "Fifty-six-fifty-six caliber. Conoidal. Spencer slug, I'd say." He dropped the slug into the pan of blood-tinted water. "Souvenir of Asesino, Major Dane."

Dane opened his eyes. "Damn you, Blanchard! Keep your petty professional remarks to yourself."

Blanchard shrugged as he cleansed the wound. The odor of blood and carbolic filled the small room.

"Where's my wife?" demanded Dane.

"In her quarters," said Niles.

"Damn her! She could at least come to see me."

Blanchard looked over Dane's head and shrugged again. "Anderson!" he called to the medical orderly. "Get Major Dane to his quarters. Warm soup for his first meal."

Blanchard watched as Anderson and Walzik eased the officer onto the stretcher. They carried him from the room. "The swine," said Blanchard. "Too damned bad that slug didn't hit him in the other shoulder about six inches down."

Niles shook his head. "Ten men!" he said. "For the love of God, Orville. Why? *Why?*"

Blanchard stripped off his apron and scooped the

contused slug from the pan of water and slipped it into his waistcoat pocket after wiping it dry. "Souvenir for *me,* anyway, Niles. Look in that case. Interesting exhibit." The surgeon placed a hand atop the case. "Bit of rope from a noose that tightened around the neck of Trooper Kastine at Fort Bowie after he shot his sergeant in the back from a range of two feet. Skull of Yellow Snake, a Tonto who got the *keshke* and tried to kill a whole squad in a single-handed raid at Fort Apache. Spurs of Blackjack Moran, who killed three Mexicans in a brothel at Gila Bend. Take a look. There are other interesting items." Blanchard opened the door of the case and placed the slug among the grisly exhibits. "Professional interest," he said with a cool grin.

Niles looked out the window. Sylvia Dane was standing beside the stretcher. Her full body shook a little as she looked down at her husband. Sergeant Ershick was beside her, speaking to the Major.

Niles left the dispensary and went to the guardhouse. Tim Forgan was seated on his bunk while Corporal Schimmelpfennig finished bandaging a slash on the big Irishman's right thigh. Niles jerked his head and the German left the cell. "Well?" he asked Forgan.

Forgan shook his head. "Ten good men. That damned fool camped us at the bottom of the canyon. If we'd had Nato with us, we'd have been wise. At least, I *think* we would have. But we were no match for Asesino."

"You're sure it was him?"

"Christ, yes! I saw him as plain as I can see you now, sir."

Niles gave the trooper a cigar and lit it. He lit one for himself. "Why did he break you?"

Forgan spat. "I'd been broken before, sir. For drinking and fighting. But I saved his insignificant life, sir. Scooped him off the ground and he didn't want to leave. I had to slug him." Forgan grinned. "That lump on his skull is one satisfaction I've got, anyway."

Niles puffed at his cigar. "Keep your mouth shut,

Tim. You're too good a man to be broken like this." He stood up. "I'll get your stripes back."

Forgan shook his head. "No. Not now, anyway. I'll be a dogface in the rear rank of B Company until that man is dead." The hard eyes held Niles's. "And he *will* die, sir. I've got the second sight from me old mother. The spalpeen will die... in black disgrace. I know."

Niles went to headquarters. Ershick was at work. Niles spoke quietly. "Troopers Shaver, Garmer, Knowles, LeRoy, Quinn, Whitson, Yerby, Gottschalk, Highboy, and Patterson, from Duty to Killed in Action."

Ershick's lean face was expressionless. "Forgan, Timothy P., from Sergeant to Private. Who gets his stripes, Mr. Ord?"

"Let it wait."

"Yes, sir." Ershick dipped his pen into the ink. "How long will that squaw be in my quarters, sir?"

"Not long. Has she given you trouble?"

"The men keep hanging around the place."

"Tell them I'll buck and gag any of them who annoy her."

"Maybe she likes it, sir."

Niles bit his lip to prevent a sharp retort. Apache women were chaste to extremes, but this fool didn't know that; the thought had been engendered in his evil mind.

"Did you send the courier to Fort Lowell," he asked, "with the report of Captain Boysen's death?"

"Not yet, sir."

"Write out a report on this massacre and include it." Niles left the stuffy office and glanced up toward cemetery hill, where the white headboard of Elias Boysen stood out in the rising sun. There would be hell to pay when *that* report reached headquarters, and Dane's doomed patrol wouldn't make pretty reading. There would be an inspecting officer at Fort Bellew before long. Niles looked in at the window. "Ask for reinforcements

also, Ershick," he said. "State that Asesino is raising hell
and no one knows how far this thing will go."

Baird Dobie went to morning mess with Niles. Niles
just took coffee. Baird helped himself liberally to the
mush and bacon. "Eat," he said. "You've got a damned
canker sore in your mind. No matter what happens, Mrs.
Dobie's little boy always fills his belly."

Niles shoved back his cup. Quartermaster Jim Ashley
came in and sat down. "Well, what now?" he asked. "The
Major sure lost face on this patrol. Ten men. My God!
Just like that!"

Niles lit a cigar. "I've a feeling that headquarters will
blast us straight to hell. Whether we had anything to do
with it or not, our service careers are finished right now."

Dobie rubbed his lean jaw. "You're in command now,
Niles, until Dane gets on his feet. What will you do?"

Niles shrugged. "We've hardly enough men to hold
this post if Asesino gets it into his warped mind to come
down on us. What a coup that would be for him! Taking
a post away from the Army. It hasn't been done in the
Army's history of fighting Indians west of the Mississippi, and for a good many years east of the Mississippi.
Not from regulars, anyway. I can't send out a patrol to see
what he's doing. We're on the defensive as of right now."

Ashley filled his plate. "What about reinforcements?"

"Dane asked for them when he first took command,
weeks ago. Have *you* seen any of them?"

"No."

"I've requested them again."

Dobie drained his coffee cup and set it aside. "What
are your orders?"

"Concentrate the horses in one corral. Post an extra
guard in the stables covering the corral. We might place
all the women in the same quarters, where we can watch
them easier."

Dobie grinned. "Sylvia will like having Little Deer in
with her. Not that I'm sure which is the *lady* of the two."

"Shut up, Baird," said Niles sharply.

Thorpe Martin came into the mess and sat down. "Do we go after the bodies, sir?" he asked quietly.

Niles shook his head.

Martin flushed. "You mean we leave them out there for the coyotes?"

"What would you do, Thorpe?" asked Dobie. "Risk living men to go after the dead?"

"It just isn't right," said Martin. His handsome face grew bitter. "We should show Asesino we can take care of our dead."

"Good God!" said Jim Ashley. "Listen to him."

Martin turned angrily. "A whole post afraid of a few half-naked savages? At least we can give those men a decent burial."

Dobie refilled his coffee cup. "Maybe you'd like to do it?" he suggested.

"Damn it! Certainly I would!"

Dobie yawned. "You couldn't get near that canyon with a squadron now," he said. "It'd be just like Asesino to wait for you."

"I'll cut my way through!"

"Sir Lancelot speaketh," said Baird with a grin.

Martin looked at Niles. "Will you let me go, sir?"

Niles shook his head. "I can't send men out to bury the dead," he said.

"Let him go," said Ashley dryly. "He'd look nice buried up to the neck with a trail of wild honey leading from his face to an anthill."

Dobie nodded. "Or bound in a green hide and placed in a nice sunny spot. When the hide tightens... *sqoooosh*. You're jelly."

Ashley took up the thought. "How about being staked spread-eagled and naked in the sun with eyelids cut off?"

Niles slapped a hard hand down on the table. "Damn it, I've heard enough."

"Just joshing, Niles," said Baird, looking quickly at him.

"You're out of line with that talk."

"Sorry."

Thorpe Martin threw back his head. "I know what they're driving at," he said. "It's because I haven't been off the post on patrol. Well, I'm ready to volunteer any time and I'm not afraid of your silly talk. Besides, Ashley, *you* don't get off the post, counting your bags of beans and flitches of bacon. You can't kid me!"

Ashley flushed. "So? At least I'm not chasing after the commanding officer's wife."

Niles stood up. "I've heard enough!"

Thorpe stood up and eyed Ashley. "Maybe you'd like to step outside and say that?"

"I'll say it *here!* Every man on the post knows about it. Kissing her under the *ramada* last night on your guard rounds!"

Martin's hand cracked across Ashley's face.

Niles gripped the junior officer by the arm. "Damn it! There are enlisted men in the kitchen hearing every word of this! Get out to morning stables!"

Martin's face was set and white. He strode from the mess room. Niles placed both hands flat on the table. "Now hear me, you two, and hear me well. I'll say this only once. Keep the post's dirty linen to yourselves. It isn't like either one of you to talk like this."

"We were only joshing," protested Baird Dobie.

"Maybe you were, but Jim went too far."

"I saw him!" said Ashley. "And I'm not the only one. He's like a hound dog hanging around a bitch in heat."

Niles placed a hand on the quartermaster's shoulder. "We know all about it, Jim. I'll talk to him later. Take it easy."

"I didn't like that crack about counting beans and bacon."

"We all know you're as good a field soldier as any of us, Jim. Besides that, you've got the natural ability to handle the quartermaster's job."

"Plumber, mason, carpenter, architect, storekeeper,

transport man, bookkeeper, and engineer," said Baird Dobie. "We love you, Jim."

Ashley left the mess room. Niles watched the chunky officer cross to his quartermaster building. "I never saw Jim flare up like that," he said quietly.

Dobie glanced at the kitchen door. He leaned close to Niles. "Not until the lovely Sylvia came down from Heaven to grace Hell's Acre," he said.

Niles glanced quickly at his bunkie. "You don't mean..."

Dobie nodded. "That leaves Surgeon Blanchard and myself who are as yet unstricken by the devastating Sylvia. I don't know about dear Orville, but this lad would rather cuddle up next to a grizzly than the gorgeous wife of Major Dane."

"Well, I'll be damned!" said Niles.

They left the mess room and walked across to their quarters. Baird suddenly stopped. "Look!" he said. To the east a thin plume of smoke wavered up in the clear morning air. A twin column rose to the north. Niles whirled. To the west, on Cuchillo Peak, the highest point of the Escabros, which allowed an observer atop it virtually to look down into the mess kits of the men at Fort Bellew, rose a third column of smoke.

A cold feeling grew in Niles's belly. "Asesino," he said, "getting ready for the kill."

Baird Dobie filled his pipe. "Let me take a dozen men up in those hills, Niles. On foot, wearing moccasins and with repeating rifles, with Nato as scout. No fires. We'll cut him up."

"Sure! Sure! You'll cut him a bit, but not a damned one of you will get back here alive."

Dobie shrugged. "For this we are soldiers, Niles."

"There are a little over sixty men on this post, counting officers, troopers, quartermasters, medics, and Nato. I can't spare a damned one of them for a hopeless sally like that."

Dobie lit his pipe. "As our esteemed commanding

officer once said, surely one U.S. cavalryman can handle a dozen Apaches?"

Niles cut his right hand sharply to one side. "He didn't prove it. Lost ten without even creasing one warrior. Baird, see to the orders I gave you. Have the bullet-proof shutters placed on all the buildings. Have extra weapons issued to the women. Have Sergeant Bond show them how to use them. I want all the fire buckets full to the brim. We'll need a roving patrol after dark. Say five men and a steady noncom."

Their eyes met. "I'm relying heavily on you, Baird," said Niles.

Dobie nodded. "I'm glad I'm serving with you, Niles."

Niles crossed to headquarters. Sylvia Dane sat in the shade of the *ramada,* petting her small dog. "Niles!" she called.

Niles stopped beside her and took off his cap. "Yes?"

Her clear blue eyes, which could look so damned innocent, studied him. "Roland is asleep. Will you do something for me?"

She stood up and came close. "Take me away from here! Tonight! I've got enough money for both of us."

"Our affair has been over for five years, Sylvia."

She tilted her head to one side. "So? You remember the night poor Captain Boysen died? You were with me, weren't you?"

"Yes."

"Rather compromising, wasn't it?"

He flushed. "It was you that planned it."

She nodded. "Teresa was outside. She heard and saw everything. She threatened to tell Roland, whom she admires. It's cost me plenty to keep her mouth shut. If I stop paying her, she'll tell him."

"So?"

She smiled. "Roland is a deadly pistol shot, Niles. He was saber champion of his class at West Point, and competed against some of the finest blades in Europe two years ago. He won. Do you follow me?"

A bitter hatred grew in Niles for the beautiful scheming woman in front of him. "Perhaps Thorpe Martin might be interested in hearing that," he said. "Or haven't you told *him* yet?" He turned and left her. He could almost feel the rancor in her eyes as he crossed the sunlit parade ground.

CHAPTER TEN

Kevin Maddox, a lean trooper who had learned to ride as a boy in his native Ireland and had been an officer in the Inniskilling Dragoons until he had killed a fellow officer in a drunken brawl, was detailed as courier to Fort Lowell by Niles. Niles stood at his stirrup leather as the trooper slung the dispatch case over his shoulder. "You've got a horse that will outrun any Apache mount on the straightaway, Maddox. It will be rough going until you get out of the pass. Take it easy on the flats and run like hell if you see them."

Kevin Maddox's face broke into a grin, revealing the even white teeth beneath the jet-black mustache. There was the soft tone of gentle-born Irish in his speech. "Dragoon will get me through, sir." He patted the flank of the rangy bay. He touched the butt of the Spencer beneath his thigh. "With this and two revolving pistols, sir, I'll hold my own."

Niles walked beside the courier as he rode toward the gate. "They'll be watching you. There's no need to deceive you. The hills are full of them."

Maddox waved a gauntleted hand. "They'll not get *me*, sir. You can depend on it."

"I would have sent Nato with you, but he's vanished like the snows of yesteryear."

Maddox touched his rakish campaign hat. "Tis all right, sir. We Irish have always had the odds running against us."

"The Wild Geese, eh, Maddox?"

The blue eyes steadied on Niles. "Aye," the trooper said softly, "the Wild Geese. Good-by, sir."

The hoofs beat a tattoo on the baked earth of the river road and a drift of dust came back on the dry wind. Niles watched the lone horseman for a moment and then turned back.

"There is death breathing in the dark shadows," said a low voice just behind Niles.

Niles turned to see the bitter face of Tim Forgan looking at him from the window of his cell. "So?" he said. "You've got the second sight again, Forgan?"

Forgan looked at the lone trooper splashing across the ford. "There's one for sorrow," he said. "It's the Irish in me that knows."

Niles passed his tobacco in between the bars. "Maybe you'll give me a reading of the tea leaves," he said. "Or would you rather use the cards, Forgan?"

Forgan took the tobacco. "Is it all right to speak freely?"

Niles waved a hand.

Forgan rolled a smoke and lit up, drawing the smoke deep into his lungs. "Aye, the weed is good, sir."

"Get on with it, man!"

Forgan rested his elbows on the sill of the window. "The hills are full of the wild people. The Major wears an Apache slug in his shoulder. Ten good men lie with blue faces in the wilderness. Millard Gorse lies up there with his poor torn corpse. Captain Boysen is dead with two slugs in him and no one to know who did the deed. The woman Ana is dead in the camp av the woodcutters, and they speak of dark vengeance against the Major!"

Niles started. "What was that you said?"

Forgan blew a ring of smoke. "The breed woman is dead."

"How do you know?"

Forgan grinned crookedly. "The Lieutenant insisted that I give him a reading."

"Who told you?"

"Nato came by here on his way down the river. He knows."

Niles whirled on a heel and strode toward head-quarters.

"There is death breathing in the dark shadows, Mr. Ord!" called Forgan. He laughed harshly.

Roland Dane was sitting propped up in bed. Sylvia had come to the door. "What is it, Niles?" she asked.

Niles looked past her, not caring to look into her face. "Major Dane, sir, may I see you alone?"

Dane glanced at Sylvia. She flushed and closed the door behind her. Still her presence seemed to be in the room as Niles crossed to the big bed. The faint clinging odor of her perfume; a pile of dainty underthings on a chair, a wardrobe door gaping open, revealing some of her dresses.

Dane raised his head. "What is it, Ord?"

"The woman Ana is dead, sir."

"Ana?"

"The woman at the woodcutters' camp."

"What is that to me?"

"The rumor is that you killed her, Major Dane."

Dane stared at Niles. "It was nothing more than a flesh wound."

"In any case, she's dead, and the woodcutters blame you."

"I was performing my duty. You'll bear witness to that."

"I personally know it was an accident, but those men don't think so."

"I'll make restitution."

Niles shook his head. "Some of those men have Yaqui

blood. Ana herself was part Yaqui. It's said that Porfirio himself is the son of a chief by a Mexican woman."

"So?"

"The Yaquis and the Apaches are cousins. The Yaquis have a saying: 'The *yori* killed your father. The *yori* killed your grandfather. The *yori* killed your mother. Kill the *yori*. Never trust the *yori*.'"

Dane shook his head and laughed. *"Yori?"*

"Foreigners. The white people."

"I didn't know you were such a student of ethnology that you'd annoy a wounded man with your tales from the hills, Mr. Ord."

Niles flushed. "I came to warn you, sir."

"Those skulking peasants won't come on the post. I'll have them run off."

"They'll wait and wait, sir. Someday when you least expect it, they'll strike."

The dark eyes studied Niles. "I actually think you came to warn me in good faith, Ord."

"What do you mean, sir?"

Dane glanced at the pile of underthings on the chair and then at an oil painting of Sylvia, in all her blonde beauty, that hung over the fireplace. "Nothing, Ord, nothing at all. Thanks for your concern. I'll keep a loaded pistol handy. You sent the courier to Fort Lowell?"

"He left twenty minutes ago, Major Dane."

"I've asked for two more companies of cavalry and a company of infantry to guard the post while my new squadron roots out Asesino. In addition, I requested a pair of Gatlings."

"They won't be of much use in these mountains."

"With mule packs? We could cut them to ribbons!"

"If they wait long enough for you to unpack the guns and set them up."

Dane reached for a cigar, wincing a little as the strain told on his wounded shoulder. Niles took the smoke from a humidor and lit it for the officer. Their eyes met over the flare of the lucifer. "You're a good man, Ord," said Dane. "Too bad we'll never see eye to eye."

Niles left the room. Sylvia stood by the front door. She glanced at the closed door leading into the bedroom. "Have you reconsidered, Niles?"

He shook his head.

She came close and twisted her fingers in the collar of his shirt, trying to draw his face down to her. He gripped her wrists and gently disengaged them. "Your husband needs you," he said.

She came close. "Niles! For God's sake, help me!"

A door creaked at the far side of the room. Niles looked past Sylvia. The dark face of Teresa showed at the edge of the partly opened door and then she was gone, closing the door softly.

Niles broke away from the woman before him and left the dwelling. He crossed to his quarters. A detail of men was busy adjusting bulletproof shutters on the barracks. Another detail was filling water buckets from the tank wagon that had come dripping from the river.

Baird Dobie came toward Niles with Marion Ershick. "Any more orders, Commander?" he asked.

"Sergeant Bond was to instruct the women in the use of firearms, Baird."

Baird nodded. "I promised Marion the use of my Wells-Fargo Colt, Niles."

Marion laughed. "I don't believe he has one, Niles. I think he just wanted to talk to me."

Baird looked pained. "How you talk, Miss Ershick! Niles will tell you I *do* have one. Mother-of-pearl grips. Hand-honed action."

Niles shook his head. "It's really my handgun, Marion," he lied. "Baird has used it as a lure before."

Baird raised a hand. "My best friend," he said. "All right, Niles. You give it to her. I'm off to inspect the Pentagonal Redoubt. I doubt if anyone's been in there in the past year."

Marion watched Baird Dobie walk toward the low

swell of ground to the south of the fort. "The Pentagonal Redoubt?" she said. "Are you thinking of using that?"

Niles rubbed his lean jaw. "No. But Baird reminded me about it."

"It hasn't been used since just after the war, Niles."

"There may be an inspector general out here any day. He might check it."

She turned to face him. "That's another lie, Niles. Is the trouble with Asesino serious enough for you to have to depend on the redoubt to defend the fort?"

He took off his hat and looked up at the hazy hills. "Not yet. But we might need it."

"But cavalry is mobile, not to be used penned up behind earthworks and walls. We'll never defeat Asesino waiting for him to come here."

Niles smiled. "You would have made a good soldier, Marion. But from all indications, Asesino outnumbers us now. He captured and killed Millard Gorse. He trapped Major Dane as neat as you please. We haven't enough men now to maintain offensive patrols and defend Fort Bellew at the same time. Until we get more men, we're in the infantry category. We fight where we stand."

Joe Bond came out of the quartermaster building carrying several carbines and revolvers. Marion placed a hand on Niles's arm. "I'll have to hurry. Joe is ready to instruct the Amazons."

Niles walked into his quarters and took Baird's Colt from a drawer. It was a beautiful weapon with a silk-smooth action, the barrel and cylinder chased with silver. Niles took a box of cartridges and turned toward the door. She was standing there. He stopped in mid-stride, for he had never seen her look at him like that before. "What is it?" he asked softly.

"Oh, Niles, I want to help you so!"

He came close to her. "What do you mean?"

She looked up at him. "You're so all alone now."

He grinned. "On a post with sixty men?"

She shook her head. "That's not what I mean. So

many of us depend on you alone. Since that woman came here, this has been an unhappy place."

"It was never a health resort, Marion."

"Yet in your hands we felt safe. You know this country and the Apaches. The men trust you, and the officers swore by you. Now..." She raised her arms and dropped them helplessly by her sides.

"I've never seen you like this before. The fighting heart!"

She touched his sleeve. "Major Dane hates you. Sylvia Dane is a web of schemes, with an eye for every officer on the post. She has turned the head of silly Thorpe Martin, and even Jim Ashley isn't the same. I'm afraid, Niles. There's something else. My father talked in his sleep last night. Something about a secret report to be sent to Fort Lowell."

"Yes?'

"There's something in it about the death of Captain Boysen. Something about a suspicion that *you* killed him."

An icy finger seemed to trace the length of Niles's spine. "Who wrote it?"

"Major Dane, from information given him by my father."

"You believe it?"

"Of course not! Someone must have been with you when he was murdered."

"Yes."

Her eyes met his. "They'll testify for you, Niles."

He looked away. "Yes. Yes."

"Who was it, Niles?"

He handed her the gun and cartridges. "You'd better hurry," he said. "A good solider is prompt."

"Who was it, Niles?" There was an urgency in her voice.

"I can't say just yet."

"Was it her? Mrs. Dane?"

Niles took her by the arm. "Hurry," he said.

She walked to the outer door. "It was her then. I know," Marion said. She hurried across the sun-beaten parade ground. Her shoulders shook a little.

Niles stood under the *ramada* and saw Sylvia Dane, Teresa, Marion, and Mrs. O'Boyd gather about Sergeant Bond under a brush sun shelter built on the firing line of the pistol range. First Sergeant Ershick came across the parade ground and saluted. "Sir, a word with you."

Niles was watching the dry wind flutter the skirt of Marion Ershick about her long slim legs. "Yes?"

"My daughter sir. I saw her come out of your quarters. As her father, sir, I strongly protest!"

Niles looked into the bitter face of the man. "I merely gave her a handgun to use at practice, Ershick."

"Perhaps."

"What the hell do you mean?" demanded Niles.

Ershick stepped back a little. "There's enough talk of scandal on this post now, sir, without my daughter's being involved."

The impulse to smash the man down swept over Niles, but the iron discipline of the frontier soldier gripped him. "I assure you, Sergeant Ershick, that your daughter is not involved in any scandal, nor will she ever be, as far as I'm concerned. Does that satisfy you, Ershick?"

For a long moment their eyes held steady on each other and then Ershick saluted. "Yes, sir. Perfectly, sir. Will you sign the morning report at your convenience, Mr. Ord?"

There was a thump of pistol fire from the range as Sergeant Bond emptied a Colt. The smoke drifted across toward the corrals. Niles followed Ershick to headquarters and silently signed the report. He left the taciturn first sergeant to his duties and walked through the heavy heat across the mesquite-dotted area beyond the fort to the swell of ground where the redoubt squatted, overlooking the post proper. Baird Dobie was seated on a crumbling parapet, smoking his pipe. "A mess," he said.

The parapets had fallen into the interior. There had originally been five gun embrasures, one to each side of the pentagonal fortification, but three of them were filled with drifted sand and tumbleweeds. Sand had been swept into the interior, raising the floor level almost two feet in places, so that a rifleman would be chest and shoulders above the level of the parapets. "Do you think we'll really need it, Baird?" asked Niles as he lit a cigar.

Baird Dobie stoked his pipe. "It covers the post well enough. But if we're holed up in here, the Apaches can reach the post buildings at night and fire them. We could protect the corrals well enough in the daytime with carbine fire, but after dark there would be nothing to stop them from stealing every damned mule and horse on the post. It isn't practical, Niles."

Niles nodded. His eye caught a thread of dust rising across the rushing Rio Bravo. Maddox, perhaps, forced back by the Apaches.

Dobie relit his pipe. "The men are jittery, Niles, seeing the shutters going up and the women practicing shooting."

"They'll be a hell of a lot more jittery if Asesino begins creeping about here at night with his band of cutthroats."

"Do you think we'll get those reinforcements?"

"We'll have to! Right now Asesino has the country under his control. He can raid from here to the Gila and west to the San Carlos without any interference from us."

Dobie eyed Niles through the wreath of tobacco smoke. "He won't, though. Not Asesino. You made him lose face by driving off his herd. He's out for blood now, not for loot. We're the bait, Niles."

A lone horseman splashed across the ford and urged his mount toward the post. It was Nato. The Coyotero trotted his horse across the parade ground. Niles stood up and waved his hat. Nato rode toward them and swung from his horse. He came slowly up the slope and leaned on his long Sharps rifle. "My brothers," he said.

"Greetings, my brother," said Baird in execrable Apache.

Niles eyed the foam-flecked bayo coyote. "You have ridden far and fast, my brother?"

"Very far."

"There is a *nahlin* perhaps you like somewhere?"

The Apache did not smile, but there was a glitter in his eyes. "Yes. But Nato did not go to see her."

"You killed another panther, perhaps?"

Nato squatted beside the parapet and accepted a cigar from Niles. He lit it and puffed steadily for a time. The two officers waited patiently. Nato touched the breech of his Sharps. "The long *besh-e-gar* spoke three times near the Place of Twisted Trees this day."

"So? You missed a rabbit, perhaps?"

Nato shook his head. He reached into his pouch and brought out a handful of curious-looking lumps covered with a whitish substance.

"My God!" said Baird, taking his pipe from his mouth. "Human ears!"

"Salted," said Niles dryly.

Nato puffed at his cigar. "The men of Asesino followed the tall dark soldier. Three of them. Nato saw. The *besh-e-gar* spoke twice. Two of them went to the House of Spirits. The third tried to get away. The *besh-e-gar* reached out with a long arm and broke his back. He rides also to the House of Spirits. The tall man is safe now for his long ride."

"*Enjul*" said Niles.

Nato reached out his hands toward Baird. "The Man Who Likes Everybody would like these for his wickiup?" There was a trace of laughter in the Coyotero's voice.

Niles grinned at Baird as the tall officer drew back a little. "It's a great honor, Baird."

Baird handed Nato his tobacco pouch. "Keep them, Son of Stenatliha. Here is *Nato*. I honor a great warrior."

Nato gravely accepted the tobacco pouch, and placed it and the ears in his own pouch. "I thank you, my brother." He looked at Niles. "There are many warriors in the hills watching this place."

"We are ready for them, my brother."

"En-thlay-sit-daou." Nato picked up his rifle and went to his horse.

"Place him in the corral, Nato!" called Niles. "Tell the *coche* sergeant to feed you!"

Baird watched the Coyotero lead his weary horse to the corral. "What did he mean, Niles?"

"En-thlay-sit-daou?" Niles relit his cigar. "He who abides without moving. One who is calm, clearheaded, and courageous in the face of events."

"He's worth a whole platoon to us, Niles." Baird studied Niles. "Somehow he seems to know you better than any of us."

Niles stood up. "I hope to God he's right, Baird. He's more sure of me than I am of myself."

"Amen, my brother, amen."

They went down the slope together.

CHAPTER ELEVEN

The day after Trooper Kevin Maddox left Fort Bellew, Niles came across the parade ground just after the sun seemed to drop behind the hills. A cool wind crept through the draws and rustled the brush. Niles stopped beneath his *ramada* to see Nato squatting beside the wall, his stubby unlit pipe in his mouth. Niles silently handed the Coyotero a cigar and Watched the strong brown fingers shred it and then cram the leaf into the pipe. Niles lit the tobacco and a cigar for himself. He squatted beside the scout. Minutes drifted past. Then Nato spoke, as though speaking to someone right in front of him, as though Niles weren't there. "Inda-yi-yahn goes to the holy place to make medicine, Never Still."

"The holy place, my brother?"

Nato pointed to the west. "Near the tall peak there is a hidden canyon. There great medicine is made for the Chiricahuas."

"You have been there of late?"

The Pinal Coyotero shifted a little and placed his hand on the *chalchihuitl* that hung from his neck. "No! It is forbidden to me. Only the Chatterers, the Chiricahuas, can go there."

"It is a strong place?"

"Very strong. There is but one way in."

"A box canyon?"

"Yes."

Niles smashed his right fist into his left palm. "Damn! If I had one more company, I'd try to trap him!"

Nato shook his head. "Asesino goes alone. One man, no more, might get in there and kill a dog. A man as silent as a soaring hawk. A man who could climb like a goat. A man who could strike swiftly like the snake and then vanish like the morning mist when the sun shines on it. You are the man, Never Still."

In the silence that followed, there was a burst of laughter from the company barracks. A trooper ran out of the building and was pursued by another. The two of them wrestled savagely as though to maim each other and then separated to laugh heartily at each other. Nato eyed them. "The white-eyes are strange," he observed. "They laugh and then fight hard, then laugh again. Why? Do they not hate each other to fight like that?"

Niles shook his head. "It is horseplay, my brother."

Nato shoved back his greasy hat and scratched his head. "Play of *thlees?* I do not understand."

Niles waved an impatient hand. The thought of finding Asesino and killing or capturing him occupied his whole mind. "You will show me this place, Nato?"

Nato puffed at his pipe. "Once, many grasses ago, Nato went there, hunting. While I slept, Nau-u-kuzze, the Great Bear, appeared to me in a dream, and spoke with words of warning. I awoke to feel strange things. The sky was dark. The wind was cold, and moaned through the trees with the voices of the long dead, who sat their ghost ponies. They had come from the House of Spirits to warn me also, but were too weak to help me. I got up and left that place. I ran swiftly with winds about my legs."

"But you actually saw nothing."

Nato turned his head. The wise eyes studied Niles.

"Tell me, my brother, what is it man fears most? That which he can see, or that which he cannot see?"

Niles nodded. He himself, in his years on the frontier, had received many subtle warnings in time to avoid danger.

"Asesino goes to take the *ta-achi,* the sweat baths, to purify himself and have visions of what he shall do in his war against the white-eyes."

"How do you know these things, my brother?"

Nato sucked at his pipe. He touched the fetish that hung from his throat. "As a boy I chose wisdom rather than war, to be a *diyi,* a medicine man. I went to the bear to get it. But the *chillacoges,* the damned Chiricahuas, attacked my camp many grasses ago. My wife and two children, my boys, died under the knife of Asesino. I left the way of wisdom and followed the way of war. Yet the wisdom remains to guide me. Therefore I know Asesino goes to the holy place."

There was no use in trying to find out how he actually knew Asesino was going to make medicine. "How far is this place, wise one?"

"Nah-kee."

Two days of travel. Niles shifted and relit his cigar. "You will show me?"

"I cannot, Never Still."

"Perhaps I can find it alone?"

"No."

"Then this is the talk of fools!"

Nato removed his pipe from his mouth and spat. "No. There is one who can lead you there."

"Who?"

"The woman Little Deer."

Niles glanced toward Ershick's quarters. Yes, she would know of that place. But would she show him?

"She will go, Never Still," said Nato quietly.

Niles started. It was almost as though the Coyotero had read his thoughts.

"I will have a horse for her in the long draw behind the red rocks to the west of this place."

Niles stood up. "By God, I'll do it!"

Nato looked across the parade ground to the brightly lit quarters of the Danes. "You will not ask the *nantan?*"

Niles studied the gambit. Dane wouldn't let him go, he was sure of that. Yet the profit in saved lives would be worth the risk. He would go. Niles spoke to the Coyotero. "Wait here." He went into his quarters and put on his field uniform, drawing on the thigh-length moccasins. He took his Henry rifle and put out the light. Nato followed him like a shadow as he went to the corrals and got his bay. Nato took the horse and led it away.

Niles went to the back of Ershick's quarters and tapped softly on the door of the lean-to shed where Little Deer slept. There was a rustle of feet on the packed-earth floor. "Who is it?" asked the squaw.

"Never Still. Come out."

She opened the door and looked up at him. She must have been sleeping naked, for she held a blanket about her rounded shoulders. The odor of dried flowers and mint came from her warm flesh.

"Nato has told me Asesino has gone to the holy places, two days' travel to the west," said Niles. "I would go there, little sister, to slay or capture him."

There was a sharp intake of breath from the girl. Niles well knew she hated the man who had taken her as his squaw. For she was a Tonto, and beyond that he had violated an ancient law, for they were of different clans, not considered compatible in marriage.

Little Deer looked up at Niles. "I know of the holy place, but I cannot go in there."

"You will take me to it?"

"Yes, Never Still. But it will be dangerous. The trail is hard. The Chatterers will guard the way. Perhaps we will not come back."

"You will be safe enough, little sister."

"It was not of myself I thought," she said quietly.

Niles placed a hand on her shoulder. The blanket had slipped to one side and he touched the warm smooth flesh. He withdrew his hand quickly. "I will wait for you," he said. "Do not tell Marion."

He heard her move about in her little room. In a few minutes she reappeared, dressed in her deerskin clothing, wearing her desert moccasins.

"Marion will be told," he said, "but only after we have left. Go to the place where the long draw is, behind the red rocks to the west. I will be there shortly."

The girl vanished into the darkness. Niles went back to his quarters and wrote a note to Baird Dobie. He left it on the desk and then went out and circled behind the post, walking silently in his moccasins. He found Nato with Little Deer. The two horses had morral bags slung from the saddles. "Food," said Nato. He watched them as they mounted. "I will watch the men of Asesino," he said. "*Ya-dalanh,* Never Still!"

"*Yadalanh,* Tobacco!" Niles touched the bay with his heels and rode up the long draw toward the west. At the top he glanced back at the post. The yellow lights showed sharp and clear through the darkness. A mule brayed from

a corral, and somewhere across the river, the long-drawn, melancholy wail of a coyote drifted out.

They rode slowly until the faint light of the moon filled the eastern sky and then rode steadily at a faster pace. It was midnight by Niles's repeater watch when he called a halt. They led the horses into a brushy offshoot of the long canyon in which they had been riding. Niles took blankets from the horses and handed the girl a shelter tent. She worked swiftly, placing the canvas across the tops of some bushes. She spread the blankets beneath it as Niles got out the food. They ate ravenously of the food that Nato had provided. Dried meat, hard bread, and dried *hoosk,* the delicious red fruit of the prickly-pear cactus. They washed it down with water. Little Deer repacked the leftover food in a morral. She drew off her moccasins and loosened her tight belt. She looked up at the moon and spoke softly, casting a pinch of *hoddentin* toward it as she spoke her prayer. "Be good, Oh Moon; Night, be good. Do not let me die. *EM"* Then she placed her slim body on the blankets and covered herself.

Niles picketed the horses and went back to the little camp. He filled his pipe and smoked, sitting with his back to a rock, watching the rising moon. The girl was already asleep. Her soft breathing came to him. He eyed her beneath the shelter tent. He had kept her close by his side when they had been in bivouac, on the return from the patrol on which she had been captured, causing some off-color remarks from his orderly, Trooper Mulligan. But then it had been different, for the men of the patrol had been all about them. Now they were alone, in a wilderness, miles from any other humans. Niles shifted uneasily. He was dead tired and wanted to sleep, but something kept him from lying down. He finished his pipe and pulled off his moccasins, removed his gunbelt and hat, and crawled in beside the sleeping girl. He placed his Henry rifle close at hand and rested his head on one of the morrals. He closed his eyes.

The faint odor of mint came to him. The girl moved and Niles shifted. She was young, but she had known what it was to be the wife of a war chief. Suddenly he remembered the night he had discovered Elias Boysen in the act of attacking her. She had been standing, slightly crouched, with her dress lying at her feet, the soft light of the match showing her full breasts and rounded thighs. Niles shook his head. He tried to think of anything else, but the picture persisted until he cursed under his breath and sat up, taking a blanket from the bed and carrying it out into the brush. He returned for his rifle and looked down at the girl. He shook his head and went to his lonely bed.

———

THEY LEFT their fireless camp in the faint light of the false dawn, following the great trough in a northwesterly direction, climbing higher and higher through a strange land, which changed from a slaty gray color to reddish brown. In the great walls towering on either side of them were curious mottlings of lobster red, chrome yellow, and sky blue. Thorny growths stippled the talus slopes, intermingled with stunted trees that thrust twisted branches upward like the beseeching arms of a tortured man. Puffs of clouds, each perfect in itself, drifted across a sky that was almost a frost blue. A dry wind searched through the great canyon, billowed the fields of brush, dried the sweat on their bodies and the yellowed lather on the horses. There was no sign of life, no sound other than the steady clopping of the hoofs and the creak of leather, and always the ceaseless rush of the wind.

The heat grew intense at noon, the sun striking their bodies like blows from a heated saber. They watered the horses at a shallow *tinaja,* where the fluid had to be strained through cloth to clear it of the animal droppings and green wrigglers. They drank from one of the four canteens Nato had provided. Niles picketed the horses in a draw, and Little Deer and he stretched themselves in the dubious shade of a great shattered rock. Niles watched the light change curiously on the canyon wall across from them. Far to the west a darkening of the sky was apparent.

Little Deer touched Niles's arm. "We will be near there at midday tomorrow, my brother."

"Is the trail hard?"

"Danjuda. All bad. We must climb very high."

The sky was darker now. The wind increased. Far to the west, above a hazy line of serrated mountains, lightning lanced down toward a high peak.

"I wonder how Nato knew of Asesino's going to the holy place, Little Deer," Niles said.

The girl shivered a little. "He was once a *diyi.* A strange man. When I was a little girl, he used to visit our *rancheria* at the time the *gan,* the masked dancers, would perform. He That Is Just Sitting There, we called him. A strange and silent man. Then he would do works of magic."

"So?"

"Once I saw him pull out his intestines, saying he had no need of them. Many feet of them, Never Still! It was a wondrous thing."

Niles nodded. He had once seen a Walapai do the same trick. The secret lay in tightly rolling a ball of sinew and attaching one end to a small twig inserted between the teeth. After the heat and moisture had softened and expanded the sinew a man could draw out yard after yard of it. "A wondrous thing," he said.

"Once he lit a pipe holding both hands high in the air. There was much covering of mouths in awe when he did it."

Niles turned away to hide a smile. Nato had a small burning glass in his pouch. It would be easy to focus the glass on the tobacco.

"You do not believe me, Never Still! Yet it was that way!"

Niles nodded. Despite all of Nato's tricks of magic and the explanations for them, there was no way of knowing how the Coyotero had found out that Asesino was going to the holy place.

They went on after an hour's rest. The sky was totally dark now. The wind was cold. A spit of rain came. Then a slow drizzle started. The lightning lanced down again and again. Somewhere far to the north, thunder rumbled like the beating of an ox-hide drum. Little Deer cast her *hoddentin* and prayed to the lightning to spare them. She drew a blanket about her shoulders as the rain came down in shifting, wavering sheets that cut visibility to a few yards. After an hour's soaking ride the girl pointed down at the floor of the canyon. Water was rising slowly. The rain lashed down, stippling the flood waters. Niles knew what was coming. He led the way up a talus slope until they were high above the canyon floor, which was now a shallow river. Niles tethered the horses beneath an overhang and found a shallow cave not far away. They carried in their gear and watched the waters rise.

A dull roaring noise came to them from up the canyon. Suddenly a wall of water appeared, bearing brush and rocks in its frothing maw. It crashed and leaped with a spume of dirty yellow foam cresting it. In the racing water were the bodies of animals, brush, trees, and small rocks. The flood poured along the bottom of the talus slope. A cold wind searched through the cave. Niles and the girl huddled in their blankets, gnawing at jerky. There was no dry wood for a fire. Niles shivered a little. "The glory trail," he said aloud.

"I do not understand, Never Still."

He grinned. "The warpath, Little Deer. A spanking of nettles. As The Man Who Likes Everybody says, 'It is nothing. For this we are soldiers.'"

She smiled and handed him a piece of meat. He watched her even white teeth as they cut through her piece of tough meat. She was a primitive, yet there was about her an animal magnetism that almost made him wish he had left her behind and tried to find the holy place of Asesino by himself. It would be a long night for Niles Ord.

CHAPTER TWELVE

The rain beat down after dusk with a steady persistence, warning of an impassable trail the next day. Niles and Little Deer huddled beneath their blankets listening to the roaring of the flood waters below them. Now and then a flash of lightning revealed the tawny tide that swept down the canyon floor, carrying everything with it. Niles at last dozed off.

A cold hand touched Niles's face. He awoke with a start, reaching for his rifle. "It is I, Little Deer." The voice came to him in the darkness of the cave.

Niles saw the dim form of the girl close to him.

"The rain has stopped at last," she said. "See? The moon tries to come through the clouds."

Niles stood up and dropped his blanket. He walked to the cave entrance. The moon showed dimly behind ragged clouds. He looked at his watch. It was four A.M. He turned toward the girl. She was huddled in her blankets. He knelt beside her. "You are cold, little sister?" he asked.

She nodded. He got his blanket and placed it about her, holding his right arm about her shoulders. She leaned close to him, shivering violently. He drew her closer. She stopped shivering. They sat there for a long time and then she rested her head on his shoulder. A warmness came over him. She snuggled close to him. Niles adjusted her blankets and his left hand touched the fullness of a breast beneath the damp deerskin dress. She looked up at him in the dimness. Her lips were slightly parted. Niles drew back a little, but his hand remained at her breast.

Niles dropped his right arm and Little Deer gripped him by the front of his shirt. Suddenly it was no use; he could not draw away. He kissed her. With a soft sigh she relaxed in his arms while he covered her face with kisses. The blankets dropped back and he gripped her slim body hard, drawing her close. She placed her arms about his neck and thrust her body close to his. There was no sound in the cave other than their hard breathing.

One of the horses whinnied softly. Niles kissed Little Deer on the forehead. The horse whinnied again and Niles came back to harsh reality. He stood up and placed a hand on the girl's soft mouth. He picked up his rifle and eased himself out of the cave. He padded along the rock ledge to the place where the horses were. He looked down into the canyon. The moon had come out from behind the clouds. A splashing noise came faintly to him. He leaned his rifle against a rock and gripped the wind-pipes of the horses. The splashing noise grew louder.

Niles looked down into the muddy canyon, stippled with pools of water. A lone horseman urged his mount through the slippery footing. Niles felt a ball of ice form in his gut. *Apache!* He could clearly see the horned war bonnet and the brown face banded with stripes of white clay. There was no mistaking Asesino. The war chief flogged his horse mercilessly. He passed just below Niles and then was gone, almost like a wraith. It had happened so quickly, and mysteriously, that if it were not for the horse tracks plainly seen in the yellow mud, Niles would have been convinced he had seen a ghost.

Niles led the horses to the cave. He stepped in. The moonlight revealed Little Deer. Her deerskin dress lay crumpled at her feet. A blanket was about her naked shoulders, hanging partly open, revealing the deep cleft between the full breasts. Her lips were parted and her eyes were on Niles.

"Asesino," said Niles. "Riding west."

She stood still, waiting for him.

For a moment Niles almost went to her, and then the iron discipline of the frontier took over. "We must follow him, Little Deer. Now!"

For a moment she seemed bewildered, and then she turned aside with a face of shame. Niles left the cave and got his rifle. When he returned, she was fully dressed and was packing the gear. Without a word she placed the gear on the horses and led her own mount down the slope. Niles cursed softly as he followed her. At the bottom of the canyon she mounted and set off swiftly toward the north as though nothing had happened.

———

THE TRACKS of the war chief's horse were still plain when dawn filled the great canyon with cold light. They had been climbing steadily. The sun came and the ground steamed for a time and then the air became humid, and still the tracks went on, sometimes straight as a die, sometimes following the windings of the great trough. They came to a place where the canyon widened and Little Deer slowed her horse, circling him on the fore-hand. She spoke for the first time since they had left the cave.

"The great peak," she said quietly. "See? The sun touches it. It is the home of Stenatliha, the virgin goddess who gives birth to warriors. That is the place, my friend." It was the first time since Niles had brought her to Fort Bellew that she used the expression "my friend," instead of the more familiar "my brother." Niles knew then how she had changed in her feelings for him.

The naked peak thrust itself up from a serrated mass

of mountains. The rising sun had tinted it a warm rose color. "That is the place, my sister?" asked Niles.

"Yes. Below that peak. It is a long trail."

Niles followed the girl. Soapweed and manzanita covered the canyon slopes. The light changed from yellow to tan and then to hazy purple on the mountains. Pines and stunted junipers began to appear. The canyon narrowed and twisted in a great S shape. Little Deer slid from her mount. "From here we go on foot," she said quietly.

Niles picketed the horses in a small box canyon within easy reach of a *tinaja* filled with rain water. They ate and drank and then the girl set off tirelessly through a jungle of shintangle brush. Niles noted that were were no more tracks in the soft earth. "There is another way in, Little Deer?" he asked.

"Yes. But there will be guards. This is harder, but we will be safe from Asesino's warriors."

She turned aside from the trail and began to climb a great fault that angled down the canyon wall. Now and then the rotten rock would give way and tumble far below, almost beneath their feet.

It was midafternoon when at last Little Deer disappeared from sight around a curve, saying, "We are almost there."

Niles followed the lithe girl. She had stopped in the shadow of a shattered pinnacle of rock. "Look," she said quietly.

Spreading out before them, shadowed by the great naked peak, was a deep *barranca*. The floor of the great trough was at least a mile across, broken and rough. To one side a line of stunted greenery betrayed the course of a stream. The sun beat down into the area not shaded by the peak and shimmering heat waves rose from the valley floor. Now and then a wind devil rose, whirled about in its wild rigadoon, swirled swiftly across the baked surface of the earth, and then vanished as mysteriously as it had come. Then Niles saw a thin wisp of bluish smoke rising from beside the stream. There was something human down there. Asesino.

Niles unstoppered his canteen and offered it to the girl. She swallowed a little water. It was then that Niles realized how tired she must be. "You will wait here," he said.

She shook her head. "No. I will go on with you. You might need help."

"Is this not a holy place?"

"Yes, but I am not afraid."

Niles shrugged. She led the way down a barely perceptible trail. There was a harsh scream overhead and an eagle soared past them. Little Deer kept on, finding her way with a sureness that amazed Niles. The heat was intense when they reached the bottom of the *barranca*. Niles checked his weapons. "You will stay here," he said.

"No!"

Niles handed her his heavy revolving pistol. "Yes," he said quietly.

For a moment she looked as though she would argue with him, and then she bowed her head in submission. Niles walked part way into the brush. She stood there with the heavy weapon in her brown hands, watching him for a moment, and then she turned away.

The heat hung like a heavy blanket in the great valley. There was no sign of life other than the thin tendril of smoke, now hardly distinguishable against the base of the peak. Niles's feet were masses of burning pain. Even the wood of the gun was hot to the touch. It took him an hour to get to a point where he could see the source of the fire. He uncased his glasses and studied the place. There was the smoldering fire with its streamer of smoke. But there was no sign of man about it. Niles shook his head. He studied the stunted trees and brush near the fire. Nothing moved. He scratched his bristly chin and turned to look back. Then he saw a thin wisp of dust half a mile behind him and a terrible thought came over him. He cased his glasses and started back at a shambling run, every step a torture.

He was within two hundred yards of the place where Little Deer was hidden when the rifle bellowed from the brush, awakening the sleeping echoes. A puff of smoke rose from the brush. The slug whispered past Niles's head. He hit the dirt and levered a round into his Henry rifle. The gun spoke again and the slug threw dirt into his face, blinding him. He dropped his rifle and clawed at his eyes. There was a yell of triumph and then the beating of hoofs. Desperately he wiped at his streaming eyes, dimly seeing a horseman bearing down on him. He groped for his rifle and couldn't find it. He darted behind a clump of brush. The horseman came on, riding low. A lance was pointed in front of him. Within fifty yards of Niles, Asesino shifted, dropping his reins. He raised his lance overhead in both hands and drummed his heels against his horse's ribs. Niles ran around the brush clump. He could see fairly well by now.

The horse swerved. The lance head shone in the sun. Then a gun spoke from the brush. The horse faltered in its stride. Asesino turned his head. Little Deer stepped out of the brush and held the heavy Colt up in both hands. She fired again. Asesino yelled in pain as the slug skidded across one shoulder, drawing blood. He turned the pony.

"Run sideways!" yelled Niles to Little Deer.

"Get your long *besh-e-gar!*" she called. She did not move. She raised the heavy pistol as her husband bore down on her. It misfired. She made no effort to get away. The lance head caught her low under the breastbone and drove her back. She went down like a bundle of rags and Asesino jerked the deadly weapon from her fallen body. Blood streamed brightly from the long blade.

Niles snatched up his Henry rifle and fired. The shot was too hasty. Asesino bent low on his mount's back and hammered toward the brush, disappearing just as Niles fired again. The Chiricahua was heading for a far part of the valley.

Niles ran to the girl. She lay on one side, pressing a bloody hand over the wound. Her eyes were closed, but she opened them when Niles knelt beside her. There was a look of death on her pale face. She coughed, and a froth of blood formed on her lips. "You... must... leave here, Never Still."

Niles cradled her upper body in his arms. His right hand touched the warm wetness of blood on the back of her dress. She had been run clear through. He shook his head. There was a sour taste in the back of his mouth.

She moved. "He is... like the... gray wolf. He saw us," she said.

"Do not speak, my sister."

For a moment her free hand gripped his sleeve with surprising strength. "You must... get away. I was... wrong to... bring you here. The *Kan*... were... against ... us." Her eyes closed.

She breathed harshly for a time and then opened her eyes again. "Never Still," she said softly, "why did you ... not come... to me... this morning... in the cave?" Niles bowed his head.

She touched his face. *"Yadalanh,* Never Still." She sagged in his arms. She was gone.

———

IT WAS dark when Niles finished piling rocks in the cleft atop the body of Little Deer. He wiped the sweat from his face and bowed his head. He spoke a short prayer and then picked up his rifle. He started up the dim trail, a lean lath of a man, with cold hate moiling in him. There would be no rest for him now. There would be no turning back.

He stopped at the top of the trail and looked down into the deep darkness of the great *barranca.* But it was not the darkness he saw; rather the oval brown face and great liquid eyes of a little Apache girl who had died deliberately because of her hidden love for him.

The thin wail of a coyote drifted across the great trough. Niles Ord trudged up the trail. A part of his life lay cold and stiff beneath the rocks far below him.

CHAPTER THIRTEEN

Two days after the disastrous experience with Asesino, Niles Ord reached Fort Bellew at night. He was saddle-weary and full of bitterness. He expected a verbal blasting from Major Dane, but there was no fear of the commanding officer in Niles's mind. He had made his decision. If Dane censured him, he would resign, hunt down Asesino, and then leave for Mexico to start a new life. The very simplicity of his plan had cleared his mind of all doubts. Simple in plan, but not in execution.

Niles tethered his weary bay behind his quarters and walked in. Baird Dobie was seated at his desk. He turned to look at Niles. "Christ, Niles!" he said as he jumped to his feet. "I'm happy to see you, but I have a good mind to thrash you within an inch of your life for the worry you've caused me."

Niles threw his stinking campaign hat on the cot. He looked into the mirror. The planes of his angular face were sharper than ever; his eyes were darkly circled; his reddish beard was thick with dust. "I won't fight back if you do," he said quietly. "What did Dane say?"

"He doesn't know you left."

Niles turned. "What do you mean?"

Baird grinned. "Blanchard and I cooked up a story. Our esteemed surgeon told Dane you were slightly ill with what he thought might be the preliminaries of a contagious disease, and said that you'd best be kept in quarantine for a while."

Niles tilted his head to one side. "Then he really doesn't know I was gone?"

"Not unless some loose jaw has told him. Jim Bond knows, and he made damned sure no trooper would talk."

"What about Little Deer? Was she included in this fabrication?"

Baird poured a drink. "I talked with Marion. She reported that Little Deer had run off."

Niles sat down and looked at the liquor. "Little Deer is dead."

"For God's sake!"

Niles slowly told the story of his failure. "She saved my life. Actually she gave her life for me." Niles looked at his friend. "Baird... she didn't *want* to live."

Dobie looked down at his boots in embarrassment. "I had a feeling she loved you, Niles."

Niles downed his drink. He gripped the glass tightly in his big hands. "I have a feeling of doom about this place. Tim Forgan once said, 'There is death breathing in the dark shadows.' He said he had the second sight. I almost believe him now."

"Superstition, Niles."

"Little Deer is dead, and as sure as I'm sitting here, I took her to her death."

Baird placed a hand on Niles's shoulder. "Get, cleaned up. Dane has been wanting to see you. Do you want me to tell Marion about Little Deer?"

"No. I'll do it. What about Maddox?"

"There has been no word about him."

Niles nodded. "Forgan said he was one for sorrow." Suddenly the glass shattered in Niles's powerful grip. He dropped the shards and looked stupidly at the blood that dripped from his hands. "Blood," he said quietly. "The place reeks of blood and hate!"

Dobie shook his head and left the room.

Niles cleaned up and crossed the parade ground. His clean-shaven face was still stinging from his close scraping. He rapped on the commanding officer's door. Sylvia let him in. "Niles," she said softly.

Niles glanced at the bedroom door. "I'd like to see the Major."

For a moment she eyed him. "Back from the trail," she said. "Where is the little savage? Did she run away from you, Niles?"

For a moment Niles almost lashed out at her, before curbing his raging hate. "The Major," he said quietly.

Roland Dane was propped up in bed staring moodily at a map spread across his legs. He looked up. "So! You're all right now?"

"Yes, sir."

Dane slapped a hand down on the map. "You've let an ignorant savage bluff you, Ord. Staying close to the post, preparing for a defense instead of an offense. Your patrol is long overdue. However, let that wait until I'm on my feet. Maybe some of the fresh men that reinforce us will be better for an offensive patrol. I'm sure my new officers will bear me out in the theory that cavalry is best used on the offensive, *never* on the defensive."

"Yes, sir."

Dane studied him. "You don't look very ill, Ord."

"It was just a precaution, Major Dane. We can't afford to quarantine other men now, sir."

Dane grunted in his throat. "Well," he said testily, "it can't be helped. Now, let me alone. I'm learning this damned jumbled-up country from this map."

Niles left the room. Sylvia sat in a chair reading under the mellow glow of a harp lamp. She eyed Niles. "Congratulations on your recovery, Niles."

The lamp brought out the highlights in her golden

hair. Her full body reminded Niles of a sleek tigress in repose.

"Drink?" she asked.

"No, thanks."

She glanced at the bedroom door. "He's been drinking too much," she said. "More than usual. It does strange things to Roland."

"You'd better cut him off, then."

She shrugged. "I really don't care, Niles. He lets me alone when he drinks a lot."

"Good night, Sylvia."

She eyed him for a moment. "You haven't changed your mind about me?"

"No, and I never will."

She smiled. "Maybe you will. If *you* don't, there are others around here who might do as I want them to."

"I have no doubt about that," said Niles dryly. He left the room.

———

IN THE FEW days that followed, Dane's words rankled in Niles. Smoke signals stained the clear skies. Niles kept a half-dozen mounts saddled at the guardhouse in case Maddox might be cut off in his attempt to reach the post. It would be Asesino's way to show his disdain for the troopers. Thorpe Martin and Jim Ashley had stopped speaking to each other except in line of duty. Jim Bond was forced to take Trooper Argyle behind the corrals to teach him respect for his superiors via the skinned-knuckle route. Trooper Visby was confined to the guardhouse after he attempted to remove Corporal Cassidy's head with a honed saber. The men grew sullen and quiet because of the extra duties required of them. And always there was the menacing signal smoke drifting up in the skies.

It was late afternoon on the sixth day after Maddox had left that a spiral of dust rose on the road across the

Rio Bravo. Trooper Reelfoot gave the alarm. Corporal Cassidy turned out the guard. Niles studied the road with his glasses, A lone horseman appeared across the river, spurring his flagging horse. Now and then he looked back across his shoulder. The bay faltered in its stride as it reached the river. Half a dozen Apaches appeared out of the dust and lashed their ponies after the lone cavalry- man. Niles turned to Cassidy. "Boots and Saddles!" he yelled to him.

Cassidy led the five troopers hell for leather toward the ford. Niles studied the dusty face of Kevin Maddox, streaked with sweat runnels. Maddox splashed across the river and turned in his saddle to empty his handgun at his pursuers. The smoke obscured him. Cassidy's men hit the ground and scattered through the bottom brush to open fire, the horse-holder leading off their mounts. A spatter of carbine fire broke out. The Apaches broke for cover. One of them, mounted on a spirited Appaloosa, nocked an arrow to a heavy hunting bow. The bowstring snapped. The shaft arched, glinting, through the air. Maddox was bent low in the saddle, urging his mount up the trail. The arrow struck hard. Maddox swayed and then regained his seat. He reached the gate as Cassidy's men drove the warriors back up the road.

Niles helped the tired Irishman from his bay. Maddox grinned. "The way was long and hard," he said. He gripped the shaft behind his back. "And now, Mr. Ord, if ye'll be so kind, I'd be obliged if ye'd pluck this knitting needle from my back."

The shaft had penetrated the dispatch case, skinning the trooper's side. Blood flowed freely. "Another inch or two, Maddox," said Niles quietly, "and you'd never have made it." He inspected the sagittate flint.

Maddox hopped to a rock and sat down. He slit his right trouser leg with his clasp knife and ripped back the dirty cloth. There was a deep cut in the heavy muscles of his right thigh. He squeezed the wound. Blood dribbled from it. "Point got me here," he said quietly. "Deep."

Niles sent for a stretcher.

Cassidy's detail hammered up. He mopped his red face. "Got one of them, anyway," he said with a grin. "That was Asesino himself who pinked you, Kevin."

"God rot his black soul," said Maddox. He handed Niles the dispatch case. "The news is not good, sir."

Niles took the dispatch case to Dane in his quarters. Dane read the flimsies swiftly. His face fell. Niles knew then how much the wound had weakened the man. "Nothing," said Dane. "Nothing at all!"

"What do you mean, sir?"

Dane slapped the dispatches to the floor. "No reinforcements! No Gatling gun!"

"But why?"

"Colilla Amarilla! Yellow Tail, damn his heathenish name, has crossed the border from Sonora with a hundred *broncos*. He has raided as far north as the San Simon. Columns from Fort Bowie, Huachuca, and Lowell are converging on him. Not a trooper can be spared! In addition, we are to send a strong patrol south to the headwaters of the San Simon to watch his movements in case he eludes his pursuers!"

"It can't be done."

Dane grinned crookedly. "No? But it *will* be done! How many men can we spare?"

Niles calculated quickly. "Fifteen men, perhaps. But we'll be terribly weakened."

Dane poured a drink. "They say Asesino is a minor factor in the whole mess. How many warriors would you say he has?"

"Between a hundred and a hundred and fifty. He may have more by now."

Dane downed his drink and refilled his glass. "Detail fifteen men and an officer."

"I'll send Thorpe Martin with them. Nato can scout part of the time for them." Niles bit his lip. "I can't spare Sergeant Bond, but Cassidy or Schimmelpfennig can go along. Both of them are due for sergeantcys."

Dane shook his head. "Keep Martin here. Send Dobie."

"We can't spare him, sir."

"Send Ashley, then. He's been in that damned warehouse too long as it is."

"It would be a good experience for Martin, sir."

The dark eyes studied Niles. "No," said Dane quietly. "He'll get his experience here. I'll see to that. Send Ashley." Dane glanced down at the scattered dispatches. "When the campaign against Colilla Amarilla is over, you'll have to report down to Fort Lowell for an investigation."

"I don't understand."

Dane emptied his glass. "There have been charges placed against you for the murder of Captain Elias Boysen."

"That's absurd!"

"Is it? You fought with Boysen before he was taken to his quarters. You were defending that Apache doxie. It was well known about the post that you hated Boysen for the drunken sot he was. You are to remain on duty until things clear up. Then you will be sent, under officer guard, with all witnesses, to Fort Lowell for the investigation."

A clock chimed softly in the living room. Niles raised his head. "You had better place me under arrest now, then, sir."

Dane unsteadily filled his glass. Niles had never seen the man drink like this before. "Just where *were* you when Elias was killed? Providing you didn't kill him?"

Niles flushed.

"Well?"

"I did not kill Captain Boysen."

"So? You didn't answer my question, Ord."

"I'll answer that when the time comes, before the proper authorities."

Dane drained his glass. "I think I know," he said quietly. "The whole damned post probably knows."

"What do you mean?"

Dane wiped his mouth. "You were with Sylvia! I have proof. I knew you two would get together. It was inevitable. Not that I blame you. She always does attract men. Admit it! You *were* with her, weren't you?" The bloodshot eyes steadied on Niles.

"Yes," admitted Niles. "She knew there had been trouble over at the Ershicks'. She wanted to know what it was about."

"With the lights out?"

Niles flushed. "It was late. Major Dane, I assure you, sir, my association with your wife ended before she even knew you existed."

Sylvia came into the room. She glanced from one to the other of them. "Roland," she said, "you've excited yourself."

"You've excited yourself," he mimicked. "You damned doxie! Swaying your rounded hips at every officer on the post. Can they pay for your clothing and your jewels and your fripperies? Maybe Thorpe Martin can, at that. Damn you, you've tried hard enough to make that fool want to!"

Niles turned. "I'll leave now, sir."

Sylvia bent to pick up the dispatches. Dane gripped her wrist. "Will you appear in court to clear *him!*" he demanded.

"Roland! You're hurting me!"

He slapped her hard across the face. "You'll be hurt a lot more before I'm through," he rasped. "I'll spoil your scheming life, you she-devil!"

Niles left the quarters. The sun had died in agony behind the Escabros in a welter of rose and gold. The bedroom scene had sickened him. He went to Ashley's quarters. "Jim," he said, "you're to take fifteen men and patrol south toward the headwaters of the San Simon. Colilla Amarilla has raided across the border from Sonora again. You're to watch his movements if he escapes from the pursuing columns. If he presses north, fall back before him."

Ashley took his pipe from his mouth. "Why not send the cub?" he asked.

Niles shook his head. "It's your detail. Dane's orders. I'll let you have Nato for a time."

"No. You keep him here. You'll need him more than I will. This is insanity, Niles! You can't hold this post with the handful of men you'll have left. I may be gone for weeks."

Niles shrugged. "It's the Army, son. Leave after morning mess. Nato will scout for you as far south as the Gila. You can send him back then."

Ashley relit his pipe. "I'm sorry to go," he said quietly. "Beware of that woman, Niles. I have a feeling all hell will soon break loose in more ways than one."

"Just get back as quickly as you can. I wish I were going with you."

Niles went to his quarters. Baird Dobie listened as Niles told him the latest news. "Who *did* kill Boysen?" he asked.

"I wish I knew, Baird. There's only one thing for me to do now."

"So?"

"Resign. Pull out of here. Head south or west, and to hell with Dane and his trumped-up charges."

Baird straightened up. "You can't do that. We depend on you too much."

"It's been hell here at the fort ever since Dane reported in."

"You mean since Sylvia showed up, don't you?"

"Yes. I can stand him. He's not a bad soldier. But Sylvia is determined to have her own way. She wants me to take her away from here."

"She's mad! It would ruin your career. She'd use you and then drop you as she did before. Besides there's Asesino. What a plum to fall into his greasy hands! A white woman, wife of the commanding officer, and you, the man who has done more than any other to keep him at bay."

Niles poured a drink. "Get out and see that the night post patrol is ready. Tell Cassidy to form a patrol for Ashley. He'll go along. You help Jim pick the men. Nato will go with them and turn back at the Gila. Then I want him back. I have some plans for Asesino in which Nato figures."

Dobie left the room. Niles went to Ershick's quarters. Marion came to the door. "You've come at last to tell me about Little Deer," she said.

Niles took off his cap. "Yes. She went with me to trail down Asesino. She died saving my life. It was a foolish thing to do."

"It took a very brave man."

He shook his head. "It cost the life of a woman braver than most men. Marion, the whole thing seems to have destroyed any hope in me for the future."

"What will you do?"

Niles shrugged. "Dane has pressed charges against me for killing Elias Boysen. You know that."

"At the instigation of my father."

Niles rubbed his jaw. "It doesn't really matter any more. Little Deer might have helped me a little, testifying that Boysen tried to rape her and I defended her. Still, your father would say that I struck Boysen."

She bit her lip. "You were with Mrs. Dane. Can't that be brought out?"

"What an unholy mess that would create. Innocent or not, it would make me look like a rotter in the eyes of every officer and enlisted man in Arizona."

"You can tell the truth, Niles. You must face them! We all depend on you."

Niles smiled. "Yes, and I depend on all of you. Marion, if anything happens, I want you to know I had intended to ask you to marry me as soon as I received my captaincy."

She came close and looked up into his face. "Does

rank matter? If you were a private in the rear rank I wouldn't care, Niles."

He shook his head. "Sometime, perhaps. When things are different. Good night, Marion."

She turned quickly away and ran into her quarters. Niles heard a muffled sob as he walked away.

He went to his room and sat down at his desk. He took paper and pen and composed a letter of resignation. He dressed in his field uniform and took his field gear. He placed it behind the quarters and went to get his bay. The sentry at the corral asked no questions. Niles saddled Dandy, his own property, and led him to the quarters. He loaded his gear and led the bay through the mesquite east of the fort until he reached the river trail. He mounted the bay and rode north toward the camp of Porfirio Armendez, the woodcutter. Porfirio had always been his friend. Perhaps the woodcutter would bring his men to the fort to help protect it.

Niles spurred the bay through the shadows with his Henry rifle across his thighs. He felt as though the best part of his life had been left behind him at lonely Fort Bellew.

CHAPTER FOURTEEN

Porfirio Armendez listened quietly as Niles told him of his resignation. The liquid eyes showed no emotion as Porfirio filled glasses with good Bacanora mezcal. "Would it not have been wise to remain on duty until your resignation was acted on?" he asked in his own tongue.

Niles nodded. "Yes, but I could not stay, *amigo*. There is a sickness in me."

"The Major, he is still there?"

"Yes. He was wounded in a fight with Asesino."

"He will live?"

"Yes."

Porfirio smiled. "That is good. There is a reckoning he must pay for the death of the woman Ana."

"It was an accident, Porfirio."

"So?" Porfirio raised his glass and studied the liquid in the light of the guttering candle lanterns. "There is a debt to be paid. There will be soldiers leaving the post tomorrow?"

"How did you know?"

"The woman Teresa came here. She has told me."

Niles drained his glass.

Porfirio gave Niles a cigar. "There are not enough soldiers to defend the post, then, if Asesino attacks?"

"It would be a close thing, Porfirio."

Porfirio shifted. "I have twenty men here who could make the difference, Niles."

"Will you take them to the camp?"

"No. Unless I can make a trade."

There was a cold feeling in Niles. "What do you mean?"

The woodcutter leaned forward. "Deliver to me the Major. In return I will take my men to the camp."

"It can't be done."

"You are my friend. I have many friends at the fort. I am willing to help them, but not unless Major Dane is given into my hands."

"You ask the impossible!"

"So? I am part Yaqui. Ana was part Yaqui. We do not forget a blood debt if it takes us a lifetime to have it paid off. That *yori* up there, he must die!"

Niles lit his cigar. "Forget it. The soldiers would hunt you down, Porfirio."

The Mexican laughed. "In my own country? I am going back to Sonora for the winter. No one can touch me there."

"Perhaps your camp will not be safe from Asesino."

The dark eyes studied Niles. "Has he ever attacked my men or my camp?"

"No."

"Have you never wondered why?"

"I have thought of it."

"Years ago I knew Asesino in my own country. The soldiers of Mexico caught him. They tortured him. I saved his life. He has never forgotten."

Niles looked out the open door. The Mexicans were seated about their fires, eating their tortillas and frijoles. Roland Dane would live a long time before he finally succumbed to their skilled torturing. There was no further reasoning with Porfirio.

Niles stood up. "There is a place for me tonight?"

"Take the jacal of Ana."

Niles picked up his gear and went to the jacal. He lit the fire in the beehive fireplace and dropped on the rumpled bedclothes. He could still see Elias Boysen lying on those same covers, drunk and dirty. Niles closed his eyes and fell asleep.

A rapping on the door awoke Niles. He sat up. The jacal was dark. The glow of embers showed in the fireplace. Niles took his Colt and padded to the door. *"Quien?"* he asked.

"Niles, it's Marion. I must speak with you."

Niles opened the door. Marion came in, throwing back the hood that covered her head. "You must come back," she said.

"Who sent you?"

"Baird. Major Dane doesn't know you've left. Niles, you can't leave like this."

Niles threw some mesquite branches on the fire. "You know you took a terrible chance coming here," he said quietly.

Her eyes held his. "You know why I came. This isn't like you, Niles."

"I can see no other way out."

She gripped his arms and drew him close. "Come back for me," she said. She kissed him.

His arms went around her and he crushed her close, searching for her lips. They clung together. "Come with me," he whispered. "We'll make a new life. In Mexico."

She drew back and looked up at him. "No! Every time you saw a trooper or the flag you'd regret ever having thrown away your career. You're Army, Niles, and so am I. They depend on you at Fort Bellew. You must come back."

He drew her to the bed and they sat down. He held her close. "I can't go without you," he said. "I know that now." She rested her head on his shoulder.

There was a movement outside the door. Porfirio looked in. "There is another woman here, Niles," he said.

Sylvia Dane walked past the woodcutter and looked at Marion and Niles. "Very touching," she said.

Niles stood up. "What are you doing here? Don't you realize the danger?"

Sylvia smiled. *"She's* here. Is it a rendezvous? The honorable Lieutenant Ord meeting an enlisted man's daughter secretly?"

Niles flushed. "She came to ask me to come back."

Sylvia threw back her head and laughed. "So? Well, *I* didn't! Niles, this is our chance. Roland doesn't know either of us is off the post. I have money. Take me away with you. To Mexico. Anywhere."

The firelight glistened on her blonde hair. Porfirio eyed the lush body. He faded from sight. Niles pulled on his boots. "I'll take you both back," he said. "Before God, this is a mad business."

Niles walked to the door holding Marion by the arm. The Mexicans leaned against the huts. Most of them were breeds, half white and half Tarahumare or Opata or Apache, or perhaps, worst of all, Yaqui. The firelight glinted on their weapons.

Niles jerked his head. "Get to the horses," he said quietly to the two women.

They started forward but were swiftly encircled by the silent woodcutters. Porfirio came forward. "What is this, Porfirio?" asked Niles.

The woodcutter glanced at Sylvia. "The wife of the officer at the post will stay here," he said quietly, "until he himself comes to us."

"This is madness."

"No. She will be safe until he comes. I will give him until dawn."

Niles's hand closed on his Colt.

"Do not try anything, my friend. You are safe."

Niles eyed the quiet men. One of them began to sing softly. Niles recognized the tune as *"La Raza de Bronce Que*

Sabe Morir." "The Bronze Race That Knows How to Die."
It was a song written by the Mexicans, honoring the
brave and obstinate Yaquis, Tarahumares, and Opatas.

Porfirio lit a cigar and studied Niles over the flare of
the lucifer. "The two women will stay," he said. "If Major
Dane does not appear by dawn, delivering himself
unarmed, we will take the two women to the camp of
Asesino. I hardly need tell you what will happen.

Niles cocked his Colt. One of the Mexicans moved
like a striking snake. A whip lashed out, and wound itself
about Niles's wrist with shocking pain. The Colt flew
from his grasp.

"Go," said Porfirio.

Niles cursed. He turned to Marion. "Don't try to
escape," he said. "I'll get you out of this." He walked
through the crowd of woodcutters, who gave way before
him. He reached Dandy and looked back. Porfirio was
taking the women to the jacal of Ana. Niles swung up on
Dandy and spurred him toward the river trail. There was
a coldness in him not engendered by the chill of the low-
lying river mist.

The guard passed Niles in. He rode to headquarters
and swung down, knocking on Dane's door. The door
swung open under his hand. Roland Dane sat in a leather
armchair, staring at Niles. A half-empty decanter stood
by his elbow. He was stripped to the waist, the whiteness
of the bandage on his right shoulder contrasting with his
dark hair and eyes. His Castellani saber lay across his lap,
glittering in the lamplight.

"Major Dane," said Niles, "your wife and Marion
Ershick are in the hands of Porfirio. He will not release
them until you surrender yourself to him."

"So?" Dane raised his head. Niles suddenly realized
the man was drunk.

"Let me take a detail down there and surround the
camp."

Dane poured a drink. "You left the camp without
permission," he said. "You're under arrest."

"You fool! Those women will be placed in the hands of Asesino if we don't act before dawn!"

Dane leaned back in his chair. "You had your chance, Ord. Sylvia was willing to go with you. She has money. Why didn't you go? You still love her, don't you?"

"We haven't time to argue."

"Yes, we have. Maybe it's better this way."

"If you don't care about Sylvia, I care about Marion."

Dane laughed. "Beloved of women," he said. "Why? A lowly first lieutenant doomed to a life of hell on the frontier. No money other than your Army pay. How long do you think Sylvia would stay with you?"

Niles cut his hand sideways. "I'll take command, then!"

"No. I've already sent Ashley off with his patrol. The post is undermanned now. You can't take any men from here."

Boots thudded on the hard *caliche*. Thorpe Martin came into the room. "Niles! Where is Sylvia?"

"At the camp of Porfirio."

"My God!" Thorpe Martin gripped the handle of his saber, slung at his side. "Let me go and get her, Niles."

Dane stood up slowly, swaying a little. *"I'm* in command here," he said, "you damned sneaky shavetail! Chasing after my wife!"

Martin eyed his commanding officer. "What did you ever give her?" he demanded. "Cruelty. Bringing a woman like her, used to the best of everything, out to a place like this."

Dane laughed. "She's worked her witchcraft on you, too. I could have left her in Washington, but I would have spent every night wondering who had bedded with her."

Martin cursed. He whipped out his saber. Niles turned to stop him. The sabre came up and the heavy stud at the top of the haft caught Niles a stunning blow on the temple. He went down hard.

Dane thrust out his saber, point down, in his left

hand. "Shut the door, Martin," he said quietly. "Let's settle this now."

Martin's face was set and white. "I won't take advantage of a wounded man."

"You puppy! See? In my *left* hand. En Garde!"

Niles staggered to his feet, but Dane was too quick. He slashed sideways. The flat of the blade caught Niles alongside the head. As he went down, he heard the first clash of blades, and then he lapsed into unconsciousness.

The ring of steel came dimly to Niles. He opened his eyes and tried to get up. Hoarse panting came above the clash of blades. He sat up. Thorpe Martin was behind a couch, fending off the lightning thrusts of Roland Dane. Dane's face was like that of a demon from hell. Sweat dripped down his naked chest. He easily parried Martin's clumsy blows. Niles pulled himself to his feet just as Dane drove the junior officer into a corner. Dane stepped back. "How do you want it, Martin?" he asked coldly.

Martin rushed in and Dane turned aside his wild attack. They circled. Then Dane came in fast. He forced Martin back against the door. A quick twist and Martin's blade flew across the room and clattered against the wall. The officer went pale as Dane raised his blade. "I'll scar up that pretty face of yours, Martin," he panted, "and all your money won't set it to rights."

Niles picked up a heavy poker and circled softly behind Dane. The Major whirled. Niles smashed down, but missed the slim Castellani blade. Dane cursed. He jumped to one side and thrust hard. Niles kicked a stool against Dane's legs. Dane grunted in pain. Niles brought the poker down again, driving the saber from the Major's hand. He swept the poker in swiftly, striking Dane on his wounded shoulder. Dane bent forward, gripping his shoulder, and fell to the floor. Blood stained the bandage. "Ahhh..." he said, and then he passed out.

Niles dropped the poker. "Get out of here!" he said to the panting junior officer.

"You had no right to interfere in an affair of gentle-men," said Martin angrily.

Niles raised his head. "He had you cold," he said. "Get out of here."

Martin came close to Niles. "She loves me," he said. "You lured her down there."

Niles's hand lashed out, backhanding Martin across the mouth. "You ass," he grated. "She tried to use you as she has everyone else. Now get out there and soldier. Try to make a man out of yourself, because you'll need all the guts you've got within twenty-four hours."

Martin picked up his saber, eyed Niles for a moment, and then turned.

"Keep your mouth shut," said Niles.

"I'm a gentleman," said Martin.

"You're a damned fool!" said Niles.

Niles picked Dane up and carried him into his room. He inspected the wound, rebandaged it, and then lashed the unconscious major's wrists together. He tied his ankles to the bedposts and put out the light. He straightened up the living room and hung the Castellani blade above the fireplace. He closed the outer door behind him.

A dark shadow came toward him. It was Teresa. "Where is the Major?" she asked quietly.

"Asleep."

"I will stay with him."

Niles gripped her by the arm. "Listen," he said harshly. "You've caused enough trouble here. Spying and carrying stories. Get off the post."

She laughed. "The blonde woman is in the camp of my father," she said. "She will die horribly, Lieutenant Ord."

He jerked his head. "You love the Major?"

"Yes. Before God, I did it all for him!"

"Go to him, then. Stay with him. But if you cause any trouble, now or at any time, I'll have you locked up."

She went into Dane's quarters. Niles crossed the parade ground. Baird Dobie came out of the shadows.

"Niles? Thank God! You damned fool! I heard about Sylvia and Marion leaving the post. What's to be done?"

"Has Nato left?"

"I kept him here."

Niles told the tall officer what had happened.

Dobie paled. "We can't leave the post, Niles."

"Send Nato to me." Niles went to the wash house and bathed the blood from his face.

Nato came silently in behind him. "My brother," he said.

Niles turned. "Where is Asesino?"

Nato shrugged. "Many of his warriors are in the Canyon of the Hawks across the river, watching the fort."

"And Asesino?"

"I do not know. His trail leads to the east. There are twenty warriors with him."

"Go to the camp of Porfirio and watch it. The two white-eyed women are there. The squaw of Major Dane and the *nahlin* of the Sergeant Ershick. At dawn Porfirio will attempt to take them to the camp of Asesino. If he tries to take them before that time, you must warn me at once. Do you understand?"

"It is understood."

Niles watched the Coyotero vanish into the darkness. He went back to Baird Dobie. "How many men do we have?"

"Ashley took fourteen troopers and Corporal Cassidy. Officers and men counted, we have forty-five men for duty."

Niles cursed. "Asesino's men are watching us. If I take men from the post, we'll be seen. And I can't weaken the garrison."

Baird filled his pipe. "I've a plan, Niles. It's a long shot. They know we've been working on the Pentagonal Redoubt, obviously for a defense of the post. Yet there is a better defensive position, which no Apache would expect us to use, by their own reasoning."

"Keep talking."

"Follow me." Dobie led the way through the darkness and up the slope just behind the corrals to the lonely post cemetery. "We've got a clear field of fire up here. I've had a detail digging here since dusk."

In the dimness Niles could hear the hard strokes of mattocks and the husk of shovels against the dry earth. The voice of Corporal Schimmelpfennig came to them through the darkness. "Throw up the dirt, boys. Dig deep. You, O'Hallihan! Lean on that shovel yedt."

" 'Tis a sin," said O'Hallihan, "diggin' in the holy place. No good will come of it, mark me words."

"You damned Irisher! You wandt them bushy-haired devils to come through the posdt like a dose of saldts? Dig, you dunderhead! Dig!"

Baird grinned. "You've seen the Apaches hide in holes with blankets over them and then rise from the earth itself to attack. I took a leaf from their own book. We can sweep the corrals from here and cover most of the post as well."

Niles nodded. "But if they attack at dusk or dawn, you'll have a hell of a time seeing them."

Dobie held up a long forefinger. "The estimable Farrier Sergeant Mick O'Boyd came through with an idea. Follow me."

Niles followed Dobie down the slope. O'Boyd's big frame showed dimly in the darkness. The quartermaster detail, under quiet Sergeant Ransom, was hard at work. They were laying a trail of forage around the field-stone corral. The odor of kerosene came to Niles. " 'Tis almost done, sorr," said big Mick O'Boyd. "The hay is piled along the backs o' the buildings and about the corral. One match and we'll loight this place loike a Brock's benefit."

Dobie kicked at the odorous hay. "The blaze will give us enough light to shoot hell out of them," he said.

Niles gripped Dobie's shoulder. "I've got to go after those women," he said.

"It's too damned risky, Niles."

Niles walked back to his quarters. "I've got to go," he said quietly.

Baird Dobie watched Niles change into his field uniform, drawing on the desert moccasins. "How many men will you need?"

"Give me a squad."

"It's insanity."

Niles looked at his friend. "Would you go under the same conditions?"

"Not for Sylvia Dane."

Niles picked up his Henry rifle. "I'm going for Marion," he said.

Baird nodded. "Take Corporal Pierce. He's a good man."

"I'll take Tim Forgan."

"You'll take neither," a quiet voice said from the doorway. "I'm going along, Mr. Ord."

Both officers turned quickly. The thin face of Jared Ershick studied them. Ershick came into the room. "My daughter is up there," he said. "I'm going, sir, and there's no use trying to stop me."

Dobie glanced at Niles. Niles shrugged.

Ershick looked at Niles. "She followed you," he said. "I've never liked you, Mr. Ord. You've often wondered why. I'll tell you. You've never heard me speak of Marion's mother. She was a lot like Marion. Pretty and young, too damned young for me. There was a handsome captain in my company during the war. Marion's mother had come to our bivouac in Tennessee with young Marion. We were in winter quarters. One night she left the baby with me and ran away with that officer. I never saw her again. I heard he deserted her in Chicago. I never bothered to look for her. I wanted Marion for myself. But she loves you. That's why I've *got* to go with you."

Niles gripped the taciturn noncom's hand. "Get seven men. Mulligan. Raskob. Fletcher. Vassily. Argyle. O'Toole. Norris. They're all good men. Veterans. One hundred and fifty rounds of carbine ammunition. Fifty for the handgun. Cantle and pommel packs. Extra canteens."

"Yes, sir!" Ershick left the quarters.

Dobie gripped Niles by the shoulder. "I would never have believed it."

"He'll be all right." Niles looked into Baird Dobie's eyes. "I don't know who has the worst detail," he said, "you or me."

Baird shrugged. "We're a good team," he said quietly. "Niles, if anything happens, I want you to know I've enjoyed your friendship. Without you I might have cracked up long ago."

They gripped hands and Niles left the room. Ershick was rounding up his men. In a few minutes Fletcher led the saddled bays onto the parade ground. The men appeared and placed their packs on the bays. Ershick saluted Niles. "We'll be ready in fifteen minutes, sir."

Niles walked to his bay and thrust his carbine into its sheath. He could hear the thud of mattocks and shovels up at the cemetery. He looked across at the lighted quarters of Major Dane. Teresa passed a window. He knew now she loved the man. What an unholy mess!

Ershick led up his detail. Niles mounted and led the way to the river trail. A cold wind blew down from the brooding heights. As he passed the guardhouse he saw the bitter face of young Thorpe Martin watching him.

CHAPTER FIFTEEN

There was a girth-high mist hanging along the river bottom. The slightest sound seemed to be magnified in the brooding quietness. They were within half a mile of the woodcutters' camp when a dark form seemed to grow up out of the mist like some mysterious plant. Ershick cursed and reached for his handgun, but Niles gripped his wrist. "Take it easy," he said. "It's Nato."

The Coyotero rode toward them and drew rein. "The women are gone," he said.

Ershick leaned forward in his saddle. "That swine Porfirio," he said. "Let's wipe him out, sir. We'll stay on his trail until hell freezes."

Nato looked curiously at Ershick and then spoke to Niles. "The *Nakai-yes* are still in their camp, but the women are not there. I do not think that they know they are gone."

Niles turned in his saddle. "Let's go," he said. He spurred Dandy and the detail strung out along the dark trail, riding hard. There was an unholy haste in Niles. He led the men right into the camp and turned to Ershick. "No shooting," he said, "unless there's trouble. Mind you, Ershick!"

Porfirio Armendez came to the door of his jacal, draped in a heavy *serape*. "Lieutenant Ord," he said. "Where is the Major?"

Niles slid from his horse and walked stiff-legged toward the big Mexican. "You damned swine," he said. "Where are the women?"

Armendez leaned against the side of the doorway. "They are here." The dark eyes studied the hatchet-faced troopers. "My men are behind walls, *Teniente*. Your men are covered."

Niles raised his head. "You won't open fire. If one trooper is so much as scratched, you'll be hunted down clear to Durango."

The Mexican smiled. "To Durango? You overestimate the power of your army."

Niles held the Mexican with hard eyes. "I'd come alone, Armendez. You'd die worse than a Yaqui prisoner, whimpering for mercy."

Armendez shook his head. "They know enough to aim for you first, *Teniente* Ord."

Niles nodded. "That is so."

Armendez fumbled in his shirt pocket for tobacco, but his brown fingers did not withdraw it. Niles's Colt muzzle was deep in the Mexican's armpit. The brown eyes were wide.

Niles smiled thinly. "But now *you* are first, Senor Armendez."

In the silence that followed, a trooper bumped his carbine barrel against his saber scabbard. A piece of wood in the fire snapped in two.

Armendez slowly withdrew his right hand from his pocket. "The women are in the jacal of Ana," he said. "I will go and get them for you."

Niles smiled coldly. "We will go together, Porfirio."

Armendez shrugged. He walked toward the jacal. "You understand, *Teniente,* that I had no intention of giving the women to Asesino. It was what you *yanquis* call the big bluff."

Niles nuzzled Armendez' side with the Colt. "I believe you, Porfirio."

"I do not want the trouble with the soldiers. I do not wish to be kept from this country. You will not report this?"

"When the women are safe I will see."

"*Gracias!* It was a foolish thing to do. The tequila fogged my brain. I meant no harm to the women." Porfirio tapped on the door of the jacal. "Ladies, the *Teniente* Ord is here. May we come in?"

There was no answer.

"Perhaps they are asleep," said Porfirio.

Niles kicked the door open. A candle guttered in the neck of a mezcal bottle. A thread of smoke rose from the dying fire. The room was empty. Niles turned slowly. "Well?"

"Before God, *Teniente!* They were here but an hour ago. I brought them food." Porfirio turned. "Bartolomé! Jorge!" he yelled.

Two Mexicans came from the shadows. They halted in front of their *patrón.*

"Where are the women?" asked Porfirio.

"Are they not here?" asked one of the men.

"Pig! Dog! Drunken swine!" The big man's hand lashed out, smashing against the face of the nearest man. Blood flowed from his mouth.

"We were hungry!" cried the other man.

Porfirio whipped out his knife and started for the frightened men. Niles stepped in between them. "Forget it," he said. "I believe that they were here, Porfirio." Niles turned. "Nato!"

The Coyotero padded forward. Niles ran around to the back of the jacal. Nato followed him. The Apache scanned the ground. "Light," he grunted. A Mexican brought a brand from the fire. Nato bent from the waist and walked slowly toward the scrub willows of the river. "Two women," said Nato. "See? Here they walked softly, placing the toes first and then the ball of the foot. Then, near the willows, they ran swiftly. Here they stopped, to listen perhaps." Nato read the faint messages of the trail as though perusing a book. He vanished in the mist, his presence known only by the eerie flickering of the torch. Niles followed him. Nato crouched by the stream. There was a pile of dung there. He raked quick brown fingers through it. "The dung is from a *thlee* of the Tinneh," he said.

"Or a Mexican or perhaps a *yanqui*," said Porfirio scornfully.

The brown eyes of Nato held the big Mexican steadily. "No. The *thlees* of the *Nakai-yes* are fed with maize, the *thlees* of the white-eyes with grain. There is gramma grass alone in this dung. The Tinneh."

Niles went cold all over. "You are sure, my brother?"

Nato stood up. He held out his hand. In it was a headband of calico. "Asesino's warriors wear these, Never Still. Four warriors."

Porfirio cursed. "Bartolome said he saw four of the Assassin's men near here this afternoon. He thought they came to steal mules for meat."

Niles looked toward the river, hung low with trailing mist. He had seen the fate of white women in the hands of the Tinneh. Death or insanity usually resulted from their brutal treatment, and then there were always the Apache women, worse than the men. "Porfirio, send a courier to the post. Have him report to Lieutenant Dobie. Tell him we are on the trail. That the women are in the hands of Asesino."

Porfirio turned and spoke rapidly to Bartolome. the Mexican nodded and ran back to the camp. Porfirio shook his head. "Kill me, *amigo!* See, here is my *cuchillo!* Bury it in my breast!"

Niles cut his hand sideways. "Forget the dramatics. I'm following this trail. At dawn send out some of your men. Send them west into the hills as though looking for new timber. If they see Asesino, or any of his men with the women, they must report to the fort at once."

"Si! This I will do. I will go myself."

Niles trotted back to the camp. He looked at the hard trooper faces beneath the hat brims. "There are two women in the hands of Asesino," he said. "Sergeant Ershick's daughter and Mrs. Dane. I'm going after them. The odds are against us. The deck is probably stacked. I'll need every one of you, but I want volunteers."

Not a man moved. Mulligan raised his head. "What the hell are we waitin' for, sorr? Beggin' the Lootenant's pardon!"

Niles rammed a fist into his other palm. There were no words to be spoken. They knew each other. Mulligan, the Irish tosspot, with the sly, lecherous wit. Raskob, the steady soldier. Fletcher, the lady-killer, who did not speak of his conquests about the bivouac fires, but only smiled. Vassily, with his flat Slavic peasant face and his mind mechanically adjusted always to obey without question. Argyle, with a book of Browning or Shelley always in his saddlebags, and the eternal polish of a gentleman, despite a secret past. O'Toole, the snowbird, who had enlisted in New York on a cold winter day to get three squares and warm blankets, planning to desert at the first chance. Norris, the veteran trooper of Brandy Station, Orange Tavern, and Trevilian Station. Nato, with the inscrutable dignity of his race, and his loyalty to the white-eyes, who had given him bread and salt. But, standing out from them, with a soul-searing bitterness in his hard gray eyes, was Jared Ershick, whose wife had betrayed him and left him with a female child to raise in a world of dust, heat, and sudden death. A female child, now a woman, for whom he had hated officers for what one shoulder-straps had done to him.

Niles spoke. "We'll leave those damned sabers here."

Ershick spoke quickly. "No, mister! I'll draw Asesino's blood with mine! Pint by pint, so that he screams for the death thrust. No hot lead for me, sir. Steel!"

"All right! All right!" barked Niles. "But muffle them! Muffle every damned bit of jingling metal!"

Hoofs thudded on the river trail. Niles drew his Colt. A trooper appeared in the swirling mist and urged his bay up the rise. It was Giovanni D'Angelo, the trumpeter. He slid from his horse and saluted Niles. "Meester Dobie sends his compliments, Meester Ord," he said. "Patched Clothes, the Arivaipa scout, came in froma the hills. The Indians hasa skedaddled, he says. Maybe the fort ees safe for a time, he says."

Niles nodded.

D'Angelo hesitated. "The Lieutenant has a few men. Perhaps I coulda go weeth you, sir?"

Niles rubbed his jaw. He could use a dozen more like the smiling Italian. "All right, D'Angelo."

Ershick saluted. "Time is wasting, sir."

Niles swung up on Dandy. "Let's go," he said. Nato kneed his bayo coyote toward the river trail. With a thud of hoofs on the hard earth and a creaking of saddles, the little command followed Niles. The mist drifted about them. Nato followed the trail to the north beside the swift-rushing river.

———

IT WAS four A.M. by Niles's repeater watch when he called a halt. The men were hunched in their cold saddles. Nato had vanished into the darkness like a questing hound. Three times during the night he had found traces of the passage of the Apaches. The last sign had been a strip of cloth at which Ershick stared with wide eyes. "Marion's dress," he said. "I saw her make it a month ago."

Nato grunted. "Chatterers move fast." He made the sign of a bird, signifying swiftness.

Niles glanced back at the men. "An hour's rest, Ershick," he said. "Make fires. Coffee and food."

Ershick's face clouded. "We haven't time, sir!"

Niles thrust out an arm. "When will you learn that *I'm* paid to command, Ershick? I'll rip those damned chevrons from your arm if you try to contradict another order!"

Ershick held Niles with hard eyes for a moment and then led his horse back to the men. In a few minutes they had gathered squaw wood and started a fire in a natural rock bowl. Vassily placed the spider over the blaze and heaped it with bacon. O'Toole filled the coffeepot and smashed the coffee beans with the butt of his Colt. Nato accepted a cigarette from Niles and held it between his thumb and four fingers as he smoked it. "Chatterers cross river soon, going east," he said matter-of-factly.

"You are sure, my brother?"

Nato nodded. "There is a ford just ahead."

"Why east?"

"'To join Asesino."

"Patched Clothes said the Chiricahuas had left."

Nato spat deliberately. "Patched Clothes," he said contemptuously. "Arivaipas! The Girls! Sees a trail and does not follow. He is a fool! Asesino is across the river."

"How do you know?"

Nato sucked at his cigarette and then touched his *chalchihuitl.* "Nato knows."

Niles smoked quietly until Mulligan brought him a tin plate of bacon and hardtack. The troopers ate swiftly, cleared their plates with river sand, and drained their coffee cups. Ershick prowled back and forth like a caged animal until the hour was up. Niles passed the command. As they mounted, he noticed that the faint gray light of the false dawn was in the sky.

Nato stopped at the ford and examined the ground. Plain to be seen were a number of unshod pony tracks. He glanced at Niles and then urged his bayo coyote into the cold rushing water. On the far side of the river the hills rose steeply, leaving an opening that ascended sharply up a track paved with rounded stones. The hoofs of the horses rattled on the stones like beans in a gourd. Nato halted at the top and showed Niles a place where the herbage at one side of the trail was bruised and bent.

He tested it with a finger. "Chatterers pass here not too long ago, Never Still," he said. "See? The stems have not sprung back yet and the juices are still in them."

Niles got down to examine the herbage. The men eyed him. Beyond the rise the hills tumbled together in a chaotic mass. Niles knew what was in their minds. It was a perfect place for an ambush of the type so well employed by the enemy. It was the time of day when spirits are lowest, when a man's misbegotten past rises like a gibbering ghoul to haunt him, when the aches and pains of the accumulated years seem to ally themselves in an effort to overthrow the body they infest. Tired eyes looked at Niles. After all, they seemed to say, we are only eleven men, looking for well over a hundred of the best guerrilla fighters in the world. We're all alone with hundreds of miles of loneliness and danger crowding in on us.

Ershick placed a hand on the butt of his carbine. He looked from one man to the other as though expecting an argument, but there was none, just the uneasy looks, the eyes that lifted to look at the lightening heights that crowded in on them.

Niles swung up on Dandy. "All right, Nato," he said.

The Coyotero trotted his bayo coyote up the trail. The troopers followed. The eastern sky was lighter now. A cold wind swept down the defile. "I'd trade me soul for a wee drap o' the crayture," grumbled Mulligan.

Fletcher spat. "You traded your soul long ago, Mulligan," he said, "and there's no jawbone up here."

Niles could taste the bitter coffee in his mouth. He thrust a hand into one of his saddlebags and touched the neck of the bottle in it. He wanted a drink, but he withdrew his hand. There was just enough for a good slug for each of them when the time came.

The sun tinted the eastern peaks as they rode, outlining the sharp edges. Rounded bulges of rock shouldered into the narrow winding trail. The clatter of their approach echoed back and forth. The sun tipped the peaks and the first rays touched the upper hills, but it was still cold and shadowy in the defile. Nato rode steadily, watching the trail, as though no Chiricahua were within fifty miles. The sun had dipped into the narrow canyon when he halted. He looked at Niles. "Stay here, Never Still." He urged his bayo coyote around a bend in the trail.

The men dismounted and dropped on the hard, rocky earth. Niles squatted and lit a cigar after sipping a mouthful of water.

O'Toole shivered. " 'Tis a cold place," he said. "Freeze at noight, fry during the day. 'Tis no place for a man."

Norris scratched his ear and grinned. "Did you ever hear of the trooper who died at Fort Yuma and went to hell, O'Toole?"

The Irishman shook his head. "At least he was warm enough."

Norris tilted his head to one side. "The night after he died, his ghost appeared before the quartermaster sergeant with a request."

"So?" said O'Toole. "And what did he want?"

Norris grinned. "He came back to draw his issue blankets. The drop in temperature was too damned much for him after Yuma."

Niles joined in the laughter. O'Toole shrugged. " 'Tis probably thrue."

An hour drifted past and then Nato reappeared. He slid from his mount. "The Chatterers left the trail a mile ahead, Never Still."

"Heading north?"

Nato shook his head. "South, my brother."

Niles rubbed his bristly jaw. Asesino's warriors had been in the Canyon of the Hawks, which was almost directly southeast of Fort Bellew across the Rio Bravo, but Patched Clothes had reported that they had left the area. Niles stood up. "Boots and Saddles," he said.

They mounted and followed Niles. Norris was softly whistling, "Goober Peas." The sun was flooding the defile now and Niles was acutely aware of the odors of sweat-soaked wool rising about him. He thought back on his days at the Academy, when he had had dreams of leading a squadron in hell-for-leather charges behind the guidons, against a mounted enemy. It had been a bright picture of glory without the stink of sweat-soaked wool and leather, without the saddle weariness and the irritation of a dirty body. Sergeant Feeley had once said, "Polished brass and silk-stitched flags don't make an army, Mr. Ord. A soldier in a dirty shirt can fight as well as one in a full-dress uniform. Maybe better, at that, for he can be so damned mad at his filthy way of life that he'll lick his weight in Minie balls."

Niles felt the first trickles of sweat run down his upper body. He scratched vigorously under his left arm, grinning as he heard the irrepressible Mulligan speak in a low voice. "Don't tell me that the officers get them little beasties too."

A ragged buzzard floated high over the defile like a scrap of charred paper. A bright lizard eyed the horsemen for a moment and then flashed out of sight. The odors of juniper and mesquite, warmed by the hot sun, floated over the column, mingling with the stronger odors of the men and horses.

Somewhere in that jungle of rock to the south of them were two women riding with fear as a running mate. Somewhere in that chaotic wilderness was bloody Asesino, planning a master stroke against the white-eyes.

CHAPTER SIXTEEN

I t was noon when they saw the Apache. It was Nato that gave the alarm from where he was riding, ahead of the column. He thrust up an arm and then pointed to a bald butte to the west. There was no need to call out a command. The troopers slid from their mounts and led them into cover. Niles let Mulligan take Dandy and then uncased his glasses. The lone Apache swam into view. He was looking to the north. There was no doubt he was a Chiricahua, for Nato had taught Niles how to tell the difference between the tribal divisions by the indefinable tilt of the headband. Even as Niles watched him, he seemed to fade off into the brush.

It was after two o'clock when they had the first sight of one of the women. Four Apaches showed up on a rocky slope far below them. Riding among them was a cloaked figure on a sorrel. Ershick accepted the glasses from Niles. "That's Marion," he said quietly.

Niles took back the glasses and cased them. He wiped the sweat from his face. Where was Sylvia Dane? Despite her character, Niles felt an emptiness within him. Perhaps it was the thought of what the Chiricahuas would do to any white woman. More likely it was the thought of her full white body and what she would experience in the hands of the *broncos*. Niles led his small command through a canyon filled with heat as though a great issue blanket covered the trough in which they rode. Norris and Vassily rode point with Nato. Niles was with Mulligan, Argyle, O'Toole, and Fletcher. Sergeant Ershick brought up the rear with Raskob and D'Angelo.

It was just after they sighted Marion Ershick that the rifle spoke flatly from the brushy heights and dropped Vassily from his saddle. There was no use chasing the ambusher. Any well-trained Apache could outrun a horse on those craggy slopes. Vassily had been dead when he hit the ground, with a bluish hole in his low forehead.

"One down, ten to go," said Mulligan as he stripped Vassily of his weapons and canteen. "Poor Stan never had a chance."

They kept on the rough trial. On and on, up and up, through thickets of shintangle and juniper. Higher and higher until at last they reached a plateau where they could see the loops of the Rio Bravo far below them like a silver ribbon on a carpet of mingled green and yellow. Dust wreathed up from the far side of the plateau. It was the Chiricahuas and Marion Ershick.

Niles felt thirst claw at his throat. The pebble he held in his mouth did little to alleviate his thirst. By four o'clock the trail dipped downward again. Along the trail they found another scrap of Marion's dress. They followed a narrow ledge that trended down through a jungle of rock and brush. Raskob's bay broke a leg and Raskob shifted to Vassily's led horse. The report of his Colt boomed flatly from the heights as he finished off his own horse. There was no use in secrecy. The Chiricahuas knew they were on the trail.

The long shadows were gathering when they reached the bottom of the treacherous trail. Nato was nervous. Time and time again he looked up at the heights. *"Dan juda,* Never Still. All bad. Very bad," he said quietly.

Niles ordered a rest. He squatted in the shade of his bay and rolled a smoke. The men were wearing thin. His own nerves were wire taut. "Where does this trail lead, Nato?" he asked.

"There is no way out. Dead end, as you would say, my brother."

"Why would they come in here?"

"Who knows? Yet they are here."

Niles looked up at the heights, somber and brooding in the lengthening shadows of late afternoon. A feeling of foreboding came over him.

They caught sight of the Apaches again half an hour before sunset. They were on a faint trail that led up out of the canyon. The horses seemed suspended in mid-air. The dark cloak of Marion Ershick stood out against the naked rock. The troopers drew rein far below them. "They can hold that trail with one man," said Norris quietly.

Niles took out his glasses. The Apaches were at the top of the trail. Marion dismounted. As Niles watched, she turned. His heart skipped a beat. Suddenly she took off her cloak and looked down into the canyon. It wasn't Marion Ershick. It was a flat-faced Apache squaw. She made an obscene gesture toward the troops. A warrior stepped forward and raised his arms. He laughed out loud and then turned, slapping his haunches in an exaggerated gesture. The other warriors busied themselves among the rocks. A boulder suddenly rolled over the edge of the canyon and smashed against the narrow trail. A slab of rock broke loose from the trail and crashed far below in a cloud of dust.

"Damn them!" yelled O'Toole. "They're breaking up the only way out av this hole!" He set spurs to his bay and raced for the trail.

"O'Toole!" yelled Niles. "Come back, you damned fool!"

But the Irishman had his dander up. He reached the bottom of the precarious trail. The bay faltered but O'Toole seemed to lift him on by sheer force of will. Another boulder caromed down, shearing off another slab of the decomposed rock. It fell with a shuddering crash. The Chiricahuas yelled. Argyle and Norris opened a long-range fire to drive them back, but the distance was too far for the stubby carbines. Another boulder arced through the shadows. It struck just ahead of O'Toole. For a moment the Irishman and his bay were poised on the brink of the fall, and then with horrifying slowness the whole trail seemed to slide downward. O'Toole yelled once, tried to turn the bay, and then shouted hoarsely as the solid rock dropped beneath his horse. The trooper and his mount disappeared in a cloud of dust. There was a scream like a frightened woman's from the horse and then nothing but the dry rumbling of the falling rock and the thick cloud of bitter dust that enveloped the troopers. When it cleared they could see that the trail ended a hundred yards above the floor of the canyon. The Chiricahuas had vanished like the morning mist when the sun routs it.

Niles slid from Dandy. Asesino's men had led them up a blind alley. There was nothing to do but backtrack all the weary, thirsty miles to the ford of the Rio Bravo.

It had been a clever ruse, disguising an Apache woman in Marion's cloak. Asesino had outsmarted Niles to a fare-thee-well.

"That goddam mick!" said Norris. "What the hell did he do that for?"

"Typical," said Argyle softly. "The Celt who always seems to fight for the lost cause."

"What the hell are ye jabberin' about?" yelled Mulligan. "He was me bunkie, was O'Toole!"

"Shut up," said Norris.

Mulligan started stiff-legged toward the veteran trooper. His eyes were glazed. "I'll tear him apart with me bare hands, Norris."

"You'll shut up and act like a soldier!" barked Norris.

Mulligan reached out with clawed hands. Norris swung from the waist and clipped the crazed Irishman alongside the jaw. Mulligan went down and bounced up again, clawing for his Colt. Niles stepped in, jerked his Colt free, and neatly buffaloed the raging Mulligan. He stepped astride the fallen trooper. He twirled the cylinder of his revolving pistol. The whine of steel sounded loudly in the stillness. "Enough," he said.

The men looked at each other. Niles sheathed his Colt.

"Fletcher! Take care of Mulligan. The rest of you men unsaddle your horses. Raskob! Start a fire. Get some food in the spider. Nato! Come with me."

The crisp words of command steadied the troopers. Niles led the way through the shintangle brush to the west. It was hard going, and once he thrust his booted foot into a clump of jumping *cholla* that sent waves of numbing pain through his foot. In twenty minutes they stood at the brink of the racing Rio Bravo. Eddies of foam swirled beneath their feet. The river here was deep, rushing over its rocky bed with a sullen murmur. Niles studied the far shore. "Where are we, Nato?" he asked.

Nato spat. "Two miles downstream from the fort, Never Still."

"What do you think Asesino plans to do?"

Nato rolled a smoke and lit it, eying the brown flood at their feet. "He has led Never Still into a trap. The one he fears most."

"So?"

Nato lit his smoke. The flare of the lucifer showed against his liquid brown eyes. "We cannot cross the river here. The fort is short of men. Asesino has many warriors. Three miles south of us is an easy ford. He can cross there at his leisure. He will make the attack tomorrow."

Niles felt an icy finger trace the length of his back. Suddenly he was acutely aware of his extreme weariness. "And all the time he was leading us into a trap. Oh, it was neat! God damn his bloody soul!"

Nato shrugged. "So the fort falls. The women die. We're alive, Never Still. In time we will track him down."

Niles eyed the rushing flood. He had eight men. Perhaps not enough to forestall Asesino's plans, but enough to attempt something that had formed in his mind. He rose and walked back toward the camp. The fire reflected from the gaunt walls of the canyon. The odor of frying bacon and strong coffee came to him. Ershick sat beside the fire, slowly smashing one fist into his other palm. Raskob was scooping the bacon from the big spider. Mulligan sat holding his battered head in his hands. Fletcher stood at the base of the collapsed trail with his carbine in the crook of his left arm. Argyle sprawled beside the fire, perusing a leather-bound volume. D'Angelo was carefully polishing his trumpet. Norris was inspecting his bare feet with the preoccupation of the old veteran.

Niles squatted by the fire. "We'll cross the river at dawn," he said quietly.

"It's impossible, mister," said Norris.

Ershick stopped his fist-smashing. He looked at Niles. "By God!" he said. "It never occurred to me, mister. You earn the difference in our pay, all right."

"Danjuda," said Nato as he filled his battered pipe.

"Douse the fire, Raskob," said Niles. "Leave some embers. Before dawn we start a fire up again. Two men will stay here and move around as sentries. Mulligan and Raskob. The rest of you will tumble out with me. Leave your blankets with brush under them as though there were men asleep."

"It's a long shot," said Ershick. His gaunt face was alight with new hope.

" 'Tis mad!" said Mulligan.

Niles ran his tongue across his furry teeth. "None-theless, we cross the river," he said. "We'll put another leaf in Asesino's book."

"Danjuda," said Nato.

CHAPTER SEVENTEEN

Niles Ord lay with one arm across his eyes, thinking hard. Now and then he heard the sentries move a little. The night was dark. The air was still bitter with the dust from the collapsed trail. A coyote howled from the heights. A picture of long ago came to Niles. The flat fields beyond his father's farmhouse, stretching to the icebound river. The moon shining on the soft, new-fallen snow. Then the distant rumble of the local train, whistling mournfully for the crossing, carrying to Niles. The sound had always chilled and fascinated him. The two loneliest sounds in the world, he thought, were the whistle of a night train and the cry of a prowling coyote somewhere in the Western night.

Boots crunched close to Niles. "Mr. Ord! 'Tis almost daylight." It was Mulligan.

Niles sat up and pulled on his stiff boots. He shivered, and not only from the cold air. Mulligan went to the banked fire and poured coffee into a tin cup. He brought it to Niles. " 'Tis sorry I am for that outbreak last noight, sorr," he said.

Niles waved a hand. "It's not easy to see a bunkie die, Mulligan."

Mulligan awoke the others. They grumbled beneath their breath as they got ready. Argyle and Norris led the horses to the river. The men drank the bitter coffee. Swiftly they formed dummies of brush and rocks beneath their blankets. Niles led his detail through the brush to the river. Mulligan piled brush on the fire. It flared up, revealing Raskob standing near the base of the collapsed trail.

Niles looked out on the dim river. It flowed along with a smooth rushing noise. It was deeper here than at most places. The rocks were rounded and slick from the scouring of the water. Niles turned. "Who'll volunteer to take a line across?" he asked.

Fletcher raised his head. "I'll go," he said. "Spade is a strong swimmer."

Niles nodded. The tall trooper pulled off his boots and hung them from his saddle. He pulled his carbine from its boot and snapped it to the sling swivel, drawing up the sling so that it held the breech of the Springfield above his shoulder. He unbuckled his gun belt and slung it about his neck. Argyle busied himself tying picket ropes together. He handed the coil to Fletcher and made the end fast to a stunted tree.

Fletcher mounted and touched Spade with his spurs. The big bay edged into the current and then hesitated. Fletcher urged him on. The bay went deeper. The current caught at the horse and then suddenly he was swimming strongly. A quarter of the way across, the bay whinnied sharply. Fletcher cursed. The line tightened. They could see the tall trooper urging the mount on. "Come on, Spade! It's only a brook, old man!"

The current began to sweep them farther down-stream. Suddenly Fletcher cursed. The bay was going down. He turned the mount back toward the bank. Niles ran down the shore, stumbling over the smooth rocks. Fletcher was fifty feet from the shore. Suddenly he cast his carbine away and dropped his gun belt. The bay was low in the water, struggling hard. Fletcher slid from the saddle and gripped the bridle, swimming strongly toward the shore. The current tore the bridle from his hands. There was a shrill neigh of terror and Spade disappeared in the darkness. Fletcher went down and bobbed up again. Niles plunged into the cold water, gripped Fletcher by the collar, went under himself, and then fought back on his heels, dragging the big man ashore. D'Angelo gripped Niles under the arms and pulled him to dry land.

Fletcher gasped. "It's hellish," he said. "Poor Spade. He was mine since I came out here, a year ago."

Niles emptied his boots and dried his handgun. "Good try, Fletcher," he said.

"Yes," said Fletcher dryly, "but what *now*, sir?"

Ershick pulled off his boots. Before Niles could stop him he had taken the line and plunged into the river. He made good headway for a time and then went under. He bobbed up again. The current in the center of the river caught him. He sank and came up again. The current swept him in toward shore and slammed him against a rock. Nato gripped him by the hair and brought him ashore. The top sergeant grunted in pain and gripped his left thigh. Niles knelt beside him. "Broken," said Ershick. "Of all the damned luck!"

D'Angelo slit Ershick's trouser leg. The bone protruded through the bruised skin. He looked up at Niles and shook his head. They carried the injured man back to a level place and propped him up. Niles got his bottle and gave Ershick a stiff slug. "We'll get you to the sawbones," he said.

Ershick wiped his mouth and looked at his swollen leg. "No," he said quietly.

Niles stood up. He walked down to the river. It wasn't any wider than the river at home, and didn't look as swift. He had swum the Clearwater many times as a boy. He stripped down to his underwear and took the line.

"Don't do it," said Fletcher.

Niles waded into the river. The current tugged at his legs. Niles made the line fast about his waist and waded out armpit-deep. The swift water flowed about him with a clinging, cold embrace. He struck out, fighting hard. There was a feeling of strong life to the water. The false dawn was graying the eastern sky. The water looked viscous and smooth, deceptively smooth. Niles reached midstream and the current fought for his body. He was carried downstream, while one of the men paid out the line. Then he was across the center of the stream, fighting to get into an eddy that would sweep him to the west shore. He went down, and when he came up he heard Argyle yell, "You'll make it, sir! You've *got* to make it!"

He was numbing fast. His arms and legs felt like logs as he thrashed on, gaining a foot and losing two. He looked back over his shoulder. Fletcher was running along the shore, paying out the line. Niles felt his bare feet hit hard, skinning his toes on the hard bottom. He went down again and shoved himself forward. The water was to his waist now. He struggled to a stunted tree that overhung the bank and pulled himself out. He dropped flat, his wind coming in great painful gulps. He rolled over and made the line fast and then stood up. "I want two men over here!" he yelled. "Fletcher and Norris!"

Norris stripped and gripped the line. He waded in and pulled himself along, the water surging over his head most of the time. Foot by foot he pulled himself along until Niles dragged him from the water. Norris dropped flat. Fletcher entered the water. The handsome trooper lost his hold halfway across the river and was swept far downstream, but Niles saw him crawl out on the shore.

Niles cupped his hands about his mouth. He could see the men on the far shore clearly now in the dawn light. "Two of you at a time now! Argyle and D'Angelo! Help each other!"

The two troopers followed the line into the stream. Argyle was behind the trumpeter. Halfway across D'Angelo went down. Argyle gripped him by the hair. Fletcher, Norris, and Niles pulled on the straining line.

D'Angelo pulled himself along, aided by Argyle. Norris looked upstream. "For Christ's sake!" he yelled. "Look out!"

Niles looked upstream and felt his gut moil. A large tree, butt foremost, was racing toward the two struggling men with the upthrust prongs of its thick roots standing up like a great clawed hand. D'Angelo had his feet on the bottom, but Argyle was directly in the path of the log. He looked up in terror and yelled once. There was a dull thud as the log hit him and carried him under. The line clung to the log and then was freed as Norris jerked it sharply. Then there was nothing but the log in the stream, wallowing a little in the current.

D'Angelo turned toward Niles. There were tears in his eyes. "Heesa giva hees life for me, Meester Ord!"

Niles looked away. He yelled across the stream. "Nato! Get Mulligan and Raskob!"

The Coyotero got the two troopers. "Mulligan!" yelled Niles. "You stay with Sergeant Ershick! Raskob! Start one of those horses into the river! We'll see if he makes it."

Raskob led a bay down to the water and started him in. The bay struck out. The current caught him. It was Norris's horse. He called out to the struggling animal. Midway the horse went under and then came up again. The current swept him into a backwater and safety.

In the next twenty minutes they lost one horse while another made the far shore away downstream. Raskob took to the water leading two of the mounts. He talked to them constantly as they pulled him along. He let go of the reins three quarters of the way across and the two horses made the shore. Nato drove two more horses into the stream. One of them went under while the other fell heavily in the shallows with a broken leg. That left two horses on the far shore. Nato's bayo coyote and Niles's Dandy. Nato swung up on his mount and took Dandy's reins. He entered the water, talking constantly to the two mounts. The current swept him downstream but he appeared leading the two horses, laden with the troopers' clothing.

It was full light now, with the sun appearing over the range to the east. Mulligan stood at the edge of the stream watching his mates. The troopers were pulling on their wet uniforms. Raskob was busy drying the weapons. "Mulligan!" yelled Niles. "Find a hideout. We'll get back as quick as we can."

"'Tis a lonely place, sorr. But I'll stay with the top kick."

Ershick looked across the river. "Look!" he called. A dozen Apaches had appeared on the trail that led down into the canyon. They were riding hard. Niles blanched. Ershick drew his revolving pistol and looked up at Mulligan. Niles could see them talking swiftly. Ershick pointed his handgun at Mulligan. The Irishman walked into the water and looked back. Ershick shot over his head. The report boomed hollowly, slamming back and forth in the river gorge. Mulligan wasted no time in gripping the line and attempting the river. Ershick cut the line when Mulligan was halfway across. The current swept the trooper downstream, but strong arms pulled him to safety.

Ershick raised his carbine and fired. An Apache went down. The others scattered.

"Damn you!" yelled Niles. "You haven't a chance, Ershick!"

Ershick reloaded his carbine. He looked across the river as the Apaches opened fire. "Get going, mister!" he called "I'm done for! You'll have to save Marion now!"

The troopers led their mounts into the thick brush. Some of them opened a long-range fire. Ershick fired twice. There was nothing Niles could do. He raised his Henry rifle and then lowered it. It would just waste ammunition, for the warriors were well hidden in the rocks. "Ershick!" he called. I'll save her!"

"I know that, sir! I'll take a few of these greasy hellions with me!"

"We'll come back!" called Niles. "Get under cover!"

There was a long silence, punctuated by two shots from the Apaches. A slug whined thinly over Niles's head. "You'd never make it, Mr. Ord!" called Ershick. "Get moving, sir!"

There was another long silence. Niles trudged up the bank and looked at the tired men. "It's no use," he said. "He's done for."

Norris spat. "I hated his guts," he said, "but he's a soldier."

Fletcher led the way up the slope. Niles stopped at the top and looked back. "A man can cancel out a lot of debts by the manner of his dying," he said quietly. "Boots and Saddles!"

They rode through the jungle of rock and brush. Shots came faintly to them. Then silence. Then a ripple of fire, in staccato fashion. "A handgun, that," said Norris softly, looking back over his shoulder.

They rode south. Niles could see Ershick's end in his mind's eye. The crippled man, backed against a boulder, shooting steadily at the elusive targets. Then the swift, tiger-like rush when the Colt had run dry. There was a sour taste in the back of his mouth as he followed his small detail. The wind rushed against his wet clothing. He shivered. "For this we are soldiers," he said aloud.

CHAPTER EIGHTEEN

Niles halted his small command a mile south of the fort when he saw Nato, on a rise, ride his bayo coyote in small circles and then point south. Nato sped down the slope and drew his horse to a halt beside Niles. "Asesino," he said. "Behind the ridge."

"How many warriors?"

"Many more than one hundred, my brother."

Niles wiped the sweat from his face. Baird would have about thirty-five men to defend a post that would strain the defensive abilities of twice that many. "What is he doing?" he asked.

"They are resting in the shade of the trees. A small scouting party is coming this way."

"Did you see the women?"

"Yes. They are with the warriors."

Niles looked about. There was a high knoll two hundred yards away. "We'll hide there," he said. "Raskob and Norris, take the horses down in that brushy hollow. If the warriors follow this trail, then the horses will be far upwind."

The troopers legged it to the knoll as the two horse-holders took away the mounts. Niles dropped flat and uncased his glasses. Nato dropped beside him. A thread of dust rose on the trail and four Apaches came into view riding slowly. Niles studied them. They wore no war paint. They were talking as they rode. "They're not planning an attack," he said quietly.

Nato scratched himself. "They will attack at dawn," he said. "Will we go to the fort, Never Still.'"

Niles lowered his glasses and rested his chin on his crossed arms. It was hard to think. He was tired, dirty, and damned hungry! Seven men wouldn't add much to the defense of the fort. Yet seven men might be able to throw a wrench into Asesino's machinery. It was the women that bothered Niles. He looked at Nato. "Those warriors who attacked Sergeant Ershick," he said. "How long would it take them to reach Asesino?"

Nato considered. "The trail from the canyon is gone," he said. "If they leave the canyon, they must go back to the trail we followed from the river, then go east, then south, then west, beyond the mountains."

"A long ride, my brother."

"Two moons."

Niles closed his eyes, forcing himself to concentrate. Asesino would have no knowledge that Niles was across the river. "Nato," he said, "can you scout the camp of Asesino without being seen?"

Nato spat.

Niles opened his eyes. "Then do so. On foot. Tell me of the women."

"It is understood." The Coyotero wriggled through the brush and vanished down the slope.

The sun was beating down into the hollow atop the knoll. D'Angelo was polishing his beloved trumpet. Mulligan was hacking away at a tin of embalmed beef. He ripped off the lid and sliced the repulsive-looking meat with his case knife. He parceled out the slices and opened another can. "Tis the last," he said, "until we sit down at Mess Sergeant Antonelli's board again."

"Providing we *get* back," said Fletcher.

Mulligan scowled. "That's no way to talk," he said bitterly.

Fletcher grinned. "Anyway the damned food in hell will be warm, Mulligan."

Mulligan spat. He handed a piece of the beef to Niles. Niles ate slowly, watching the men. They were trail-filthy. Their uniforms had dried wrinkled under the hot sun. D'Angelo had lost a boot somewhere in the crossing of the Rio Bravo, and had wrapped his foot in an extra shirt. Fletcher's temple bore a bad bruise from his conflict, with the river. Mulligan had lost his hat and had bound his yellow scarf about his red hair. The sour odor of sweat hung heavy in the hollow.

Two hours drifted past. The men were asleep under hastily rigged brush shelters. Niles heard the sibilant scout warning. *"Tsst! Tsst!"* It was Nato. He slid into the hollow. "The women are well," he said. "They have not been mistreated."

Niles felt a surge of relief go through him. "And Asesino?"

"He sits in council. There are Tontos, Arivaipas, and Chiricahuas there."

Niles handed the Coyotero some of the embalmed beef. He leaned back against a rock. Baird would be sweating, wondering what had happened to Niles. For a moment a wild urge came to Niles to make an attempt to save the women, but he expelled it from his mind. He and Nato might get close to the camp of the *broncos,* but the troopers would never make it. There was nothing to do but wait for Asesino's next move.

The long hours idled past. Niles slept for a time. He kept the men busy stripping down their weapons and cleaning them as well as they could. There were seven of them with six horses. At dusk Nato vanished again.

It was ten o'clock by Niles's repeater watch when Nato returned. "Look," he said.

The moon had risen, silvering the rocks and earth. For a moment a lone horseman showed on the ridge and then warrior after warrior rode down the ridge, following the broad trail. Niles started up for a moment as he saw two cloaked figures in the center of the main body, but Nato's hand closed on Niles's wrist like a clamp.

Niles counted them as they went noiselessly past, their ponies shod with rawhide boots. One hundred and sixty of them. They rode like phantoms, seeming to emanate from the shadows themselves. Then they were gone, as mysteriously and as silently as they had come, leaving behind nothing but the bitter smell of dust in the quiet night air.

Niles turned. "All right," he said, "get the horses. You men wait here until Nato and I come back."

Nato led the way along an arroyo. Half a mile from the fort Nato halted. Niles squirmed up beside him. They could overlook the fort. The yellow rectangles of light from the guardhouse showed clearly through the night. The moon shone palely on the yellow adobes. A mule bawled from a corral, the bray echoing from the silent hills. Niles looked down the slope. The downslant was stippled with mesquite, cactus, and long-stemmed *pitahaya*. Then he saw them, huddled beneath dun blankets. Scores of warriors, lying in spidery patience, waiting for the right time to attack; the time when man's morale is at the lowest. The dawn. The time of the war god.

The moon was high in the heavens when Niles returned to the hollow, leaving Nato to watch the warriors of Ase-sino. They muffled all metal and bound their horses' hoofs with strips of cloth. Niles led them to within a quarter of a mile of Asesino's position. They scattered into cover. From where Niles was hidden he could see the broad trail leading south. From his elevation he could see two humped hills, low and rounded. Between them was a narrow defile leading down to the river, which shone brightly in the moonlight. Niles studied the position and pondered.

The moon waned and died. Darkness covered the earth. The silence was occasionally broken by the distant howling of a coyote. There was no sound from the Apaches waiting on their slope.

Niles slept for a time and awoke shivering when Nato shook him. "Look," the Coyotero said quietly. He pointed east. There was the faintest suggestion of light in the eastern sky.

Niles shivered. He crawled to D'Angelo and awoke the veteran. D'Angelo wrapped his arms about his body. "I leava sunny Italy for thees, meester. You think I'm crazy ina head?"

"No doubt," said Niles. "Joe, I want you to do something."

"Yes?"

"Go to the river and upstream to the ford. Asesino's warriors will attack in a short time. When you hear the shooting getting heavy, I want you to blow the Charge and any other damned trumpet call you can think of. Put some spit into it!"

D'Angelo looked queerly at Niles. "You feela all right, Meester Ord?"

"Yes, damn it!"

"I take the horse?"

"No. Leg it. I'll need all the horses."

D'Angelo stood up and touched his trumpet. "I'da rather stay here, Meester Ord."

Niles grinned. "You'll be playing the part of a whole damned squadron." Niles rubbed his jaw. "On second thought, take a horse. While you're trumpeting, drag a pile of brush up and down the flats."

"I see! I see! D'Angelo is a squadron. One man, weeth trumpet, and on a horse, is a *squadron!*"

D'Angelo got a horse and led him south.

Niles called his men together. "Asesino is getting ready to attack," he said. "We'll sit tight up here until we can hit him where it hurts the most."

"With six men, mister?" a dry voice said in the darkness. It was Fletcher.

"With six men," said Niles.

"God help us," said Mulligan.

Twenty minutes drifted past. Nato came up the slope. The eastern sky was lighter but the area near the fort was still in darkness. "Soon, Never Still," said Nato.

A cold feeling came over Niles. He could just distinguish his tiny command in the dimness. The stink of the uniforms and the bodies was more distinguishable than the faces. This was the frontier trooper, the warp and woof of faded blue and dirty yellow that could be woven into the tight fabric of discipline. Niles looked down the slope. In a short time the ball would open. In a short time he would throw his infinitesimal command into the scales of battle and either go down fighting or tip the balance in favor of victory.

CHAPTER NINETEEN

Down the slope overlooking the sleeping fort was He Kills Enemies, known as Asesino, the Assassin, to the white-eyes, and aptly named. Below his horned war bonnet the hard eyes stared at the fort garrisoned by a handful of the men with long knives. The white bands of bottom clay crossing the beaklike nose gave the broad face a devilish appearance in the dim light. The white-eyes were soft for killing, like the small party his men had trapped on the other side of the river the day before. Never Still, he of the hard gray eyes and the reddish beard, would be lying amidst his stripped and disemboweled men, with his skull crushed and his hands and feet lopped off. This was good medicine.

Asesino stood up and looked to right and left. The white-eyed women were under the guard of two trusted warriors. They had not been touched, for the best of reasons. If the fort was too tough a nut to crack, Asesino would use them as hostages to make the white-eyes treat with him. If they were driven back—and Stenatliha would not allow *that*—the white women would feed the lust of the warriors and then be turned over to the squaws for their amusement. It would be pleasant to see the full white bodies straining against the rawhide bonds as the keen knives and burning brands turned the white-eyed women into pitiful screaming animals before they died.

Asesino padded down the slope. From among the mesquite and *pitahaya* his picked warriors arose. The cream of his *broncos,* the men who would hit the corrals first and take the mules and *thlees* away from the sleep-drugged troopers. This was war as practiced by the Men of the Woods. Asesino cast *hoddentin* toward the east, muttering a swift prayer to the oncoming dawn. The corral was a hundred yards away. Asesino skirted wide around the Place of the Dead on its low hillock, muttering a prayer and clutching his *chalchihuitl.*

The corral was close now. A tarry smell came to Asesino's keen nostrils. He hesitated, trying to identify it. Suddenly, as his men gathered about him, a tongue of flame licked up near the corral and then swiftly leaping flames soared up, illuminating the painted warriors. From the Place of the Dead a volley crashed out, driving stinking smoke down toward the *broncos.* Three warriors went down, thrashing in agony as 45/70 slugs ripped through muscle and bone. Asesino shrieked in anger and fired his repeater toward the Place of the Dead.

Niles saw the ring of flames encircle the corral. Horses neighed in terror and the noisy mules bawled out their fright. In the yellow glare of the burning hay and straw Niles could plainly see Asesino's men scattering for cover, leaving a dozen warriors lying still or thrashing in pain. Niles grinned. Baird Dobie's plan was working.

The firing grew heavy, echoing flatly from the hills. Flashes of carbine fire rippled along Cemetery Hill. Niles could almost see, in his mind's eye, the grins on the faces of Dobie's motley command of troopers, medical orderlies, quartermasters, and officers.

Asesino's warriors fell back. The warriors on the slope began to fire down toward the cemetery. A smoke pall drifted up into the graying sky. The firing sounded as though a boy were dragging a stick along a picket fence.

Nato fumbled in his pouch. He withdrew paints and a small steel mirror. Carefully he painted his broad face. He put away his paints, carefully tested the edge of his knife and his short reserve knife, and then drew the load from his long Sharps, reloading it with a fresh charge and a new cap on the nipple. Niles checked the magazine of his Henry rifle and twirled the cylinder of his Colt. In the hollow the troopers checked their weapons and loosened their sabers in the scabbards.

The firing was heavy now, like the ripping of heavy cloth. Then suddenly, like a diamond scratched across a pane of glass, the faraway notes of the Charge rose above the sound of firing. The sky was light now, revealing the warriors on the slope. Dust threaded up into the quiet air near the ford. D'Angelo gave tongue to Recall, followed it with Boots and Saddles, and then lipped again into the thrilling notes of the Charge.

Asesino stared toward the ford, at the dust. He screamed orders to his men. They fell back. The boys and untried braves brought up the horses. Dust rose from the pounding hoofs. At least thirty warriors would ride no more on the war trail. The Apaches mounted. Many of them quirted their horses in panic toward the trail leading south. Asesino yelled at them, but fear rode their bare backs. Asesino and a knot of twenty warriors followed the main body. The two women were among them.

Niles turned. "Boots and Saddles," he said. "Sheath your carbines. Hold your pistol fire until I fire. Then into them with the sabers."

"For the love av heaven," said Mulligan. "'Tis madness!"

"Write your Congressman," said Norris.

Fletcher swung up into his saddle with a smash of leather. " 'Bout time you earned your keep, Mulligan," he said.

Niles mounted Dandy. He looked back. Nato, Fletcher, Norris, and Raskob and Mulligan riding double.

The glory trail. He set spurs to Dandy and raced down the slope. They were within a hundred yards of Asesino's fleeing men before the warriors saw them. Rifles spat. Raskob grunted, swayed, and straightened up. A slug whipped into Niles's saddle. The startled faces came nearer. Niles raised his handgun, sighted, and fired. A warrior shuddered and slid from his pony. Colt fire crashed out. The heavy slugs chewed into the milling Chiricahuas. Niles fired four times and thrust his Colt beneath his belt. His Solingen blade came out with a steely slither.

Then the troopers were in among the shrieking braves. Almost chest to chest, the troopers closed in with the *broncos* in a wild kaleidoscope of whirling horses and glittering blades. Fletcher went with a hoarse sobbing cry. Raskob, his face white and set, thrust deep into the back of a yelling warrior tastefully painted in yellow and blue polka dots. The blood added to the garish coloring. Mulligan shifted to the warrior's pony.

A lance was thrust at Norris's chest and Niles slashed down hard, shearing the ash neatly. Norris grinned. "Owe you one, mister!" he yelled, and spitted a potbellied brave neatly, withdrawing swiftly to split a young warrior's face in half.

Niles ducked the sweep of a clubbed rifle and saw Marion Ershick. She had dismounted to snatch up a fallen brass-bellied Colt. It barked twice, driving a screaming brave back on his haunches. Then Niles saw Sylvia Dane, screaming shrilly, her red mouth squared like that of the Greek mask of tragedy as a warrior dragged at the riata looped about her slim waist. Niles pulled the trigger but the handgun misfired. The warrior led the plunging pony that bore Sylvia Dane down the defile toward the river. A rifle butt thudded against Niles's gut, driving the wind from him. Nato killed the warrior with a pistol shot fired point-blank.

Marion fired again, missed, and was dragged from her feet by Asesino, who bent low from the back of his appaloosa and scooped her across the horse. He lashed the horse down the defile. Niles, fighting for breath, set the steel to Dandy. The bay reared, caught a knife slash intended for Niles from a dismounted warrior, and then lashed out with his hoofs to cave the warrior's face in like a dropped pumpkin.

Mulligan parried a knife thrust and smashed a warrior's face with the stud of his pommel. He bent forward, grunting in pain as a war club crashed against the side of his head, driving him from his saddle into the churned dust.

A man yelled at Niles. He turned to see Roland Dane, at the head of a score of troopers, his Castellani blade thrust forward, crashing into the rear of the panicky warriors. Then Niles was off down the defile after Asesino. He reached the end of the slot and saw Sylvia Dane being led south along the river trail. Asesino was at the edge of the stream. He turned to see Niles. He dropped Marion like a bundle of rags and quirted his pony toward Niles. Niles felt for his Colt. It was gone. He thrust out his Solingen and raced toward the warrior. Asesino waited until the last possible second and then slammed his war club down on the saber. It shattered, numbing Niles's hand. He hurled it at Asesino, ducked a vicious blow of the war club, and leaped from his saddle, clutching at the greasy body of the war chief. They went down hard into the wet sand of the riverbank.

Steely fingers clawed at Niles's eyes. He turned his head and drove telling punches into the lean gut. Asesino gasped and broke free, feeling for his reserve knife. A left hook staggered him and a right drove him to the water's edge. Marion screamed as the reserve knife traced a course down the right side of Niles's face. He gripped the knife wrist with his left hand, pulled it up, and then thrust his right arm under Asesino's arm to lock his right hand on his own left wrist. He bore back hard and the arm bone snapped. Asesino gasped. Niles hit him with a driving right. Asesino fell back into the water and Niles landed atop him, gripping the Chiricahua's throat with steely fingers. He held the head, still with its horned bonnet, beneath the cold rushing waters of the river. Blood ran down his face. Asesino struggled hard, weakened, and then lay still. Niles looked down into the bulging eyes beneath the clear water. The bonnet drifted off and the long black hair wavered in the swift current.

Niles stood up and flicked the blood from his face. Suddenly his gut moiled and he retched hard, spewing sour vomit into the waters of the Rio Bravo.

He turned toward Marion. She ran to him and gripped him tightly. "Niles! Niles! Niles!" She cried.

"Where is she?" The hoarse voice came from behind them. They turned to see Roland Dane, on foot, holding his crimsoned blade. His eyes were wide in his thin handsome face. Niles looked down the river valley. The warrior who had Sylvia was standing beside his fallen horse. Four other warriors were cutting in toward him. Sylvia Dane sat her horse, looking toward the white men.

"Not a chance," said Niles quietly. "You'll never catch an Apache in a stern chase."

Nato limped down the slope trailing his long Sharps. Roland Dane looked back up the defile. The troopers had vanished, chasing the remaining warriors up the ridge. Dane threw down his saber. For a moment he stared at his wife. Then he jerked Nato's rifle from his hands. He rested the heavy rifle on a boulder. The trigger finger tightened. Then the Sharps roared. Sylvia Dane went down under the impact of the heavy slug. Niles knew she was dead.

Roland Dane handed the smoking rifle to Nato and looked at Niles. Then he turned and plodded up the slope.

CHAPTER TWENTY

They ascended the defile as the sun peered above the eastern ranges. Marion clung to Niles's arm. She talked steadily in a low voice about her experiences, but Niles had no ears for her. He impatiently wiped the blood from his face, watching Roland Dane return to the trail. The troopers were forming in the trail. A dozen Apaches lay scattered about. Pistols barked as Norris and Mulligan finished off the wounded.

"Enough!" called Niles, but it was too late. Trooper Fletcher lay across a dead Apache, his fingers gripped about the warrior's throat. The handsome trooper's eyes were wide open. He had died as he finished off the Chiricahua. Raskob lay back against a rock, his bloody fingers twisted in his blood-soaked undershirt. His face was set. Even as Niles went to him the veteran died.

Mulligan had a lump the size of an egg alongside his head, bulging out the yellow scarf he wore as a head covering. Norris had a knife slash along his left forearm. As Niles looked at the filthy leavings of the fight, he wondered how any of them had come through it alive.

Nato walked down the road. As Niles watched the Coyotero, he skillfully scalped a fallen warrior. He cut some hairs from the reeking scalp and burned them on the ground to purify himself.

Dane swung up on his horse and rode silently back to the post. Niles turned to Sergeant Bond. "You're first sergeant until your orders promoting you are made out, Bond."

Bond wiped the sweat from his red face. "Where's Ershick?" he asked quietly.

"Dead. Take our dead back to the post. Get my horse."

Niles mounted Dandy and pulled Marion up behind him. He glanced down the defile at the body of Asesino, half awash in the river, and then kneed the bay into the trail.

Troopers near the cemetery were pulling the scattered bodies of the Apaches into a heap. Here and there a trooper lay silent in death. Calhoun of the quartermasters lay with a shattered leg beside Second Lieutenant Thorpe Martin. Martin's left arm had been smashed at the elbow by a heavy slug.

Surgeon Blanchard wiped his bloody hands and stood up. "You'll lose that arm, son," he said. "Take it as part of the game."

Thorpe Martin looked quickly away, his face muscles wire-taut.

Baird Dobie came over to Niles. "You crazy fool," he said. "You trying to win a Congressional? By God, Niles, you sure pulled the snapper on them."

Niles held his scarf to his slashed face. "They damned near snapped it back on us," he said quietly.

Baird Dobie looked at Roland Dane, walking slowly to his quarters. "He insisted on leading the foray, Niles."

"He's a soldier, Baird."

"Where's Sylvia?"

Niles shook his head. "Dead. It's for the best, Baird."

Dobie eyed Niles closely. "So?"

"Get the men ready for burial. Send out a detail to get those Apache corpses out on the trail."

"Sure, Niles." The tall man's thoughtful eyes studied Niles as he walked away.

Marion bathed Niles's cut in her quarters. He had told her of her father's death. "He died a man and a soldier," he said.

"We were never close," she said. "Sometimes I think he kept me away from you because of his fierce jealousy of officers. But he was good to me, Niles."

"We'll recover his body."

She finished taping the bandage. "No," she said. "Bury him there. A lonely grave for a lonely man." She kissed him.

Niles walked to the window and looked across at Dane's quarters. "He wasn't the only one on this post," he said. "How did the Apaches treat you?"

She shrugged. "Not bad. Asesino seemed like an incarnation of a devil, but he saw to it that we were protected."

"Meaning to use you as hostages."

"Yes. I'm sorry for those people, Niles."

"With Asesino gone, killed like any mortal, which he claimed would never happen to him, they will return to the reservation."

She came to stand by his side. "What do you intend to do?"

"Face my trial at Fort Lowell and then resign if I'm cleared of Boysen's death."

She leaned her head against his shoulder. "Who *did* kill him, Niles? My father hated him."

"He didn't do it."

"How do you know?"

He looked down at her. "Your father wouldn't kill like that, Marion."

She kissed him. "I was worried thinking that you might have thought so."

"Why did you leave the camp of Porfirio Armendez?"

She tilted her head to one side. "Sylvia talked me into

it. The Apaches caught us at the river. We didn't see them until they rose out of the mist like phantoms."

"You should have waited for the troopers."

Her grave eyes held his. "She was afraid, Niles. I had to help her."

"Why?"

"She said you still loved her, and that you planned to resign and take her away."

"It was far from my mind. Why did you believe her?"

She came close. "I did then, but I know better now,"

"She never really knew what she wanted."

"She loved you in a way, Niles."

"Perhaps. In any case it's all over now." The guard tramped by, raising the yellow dust. A trooper attached the flag to the swivels and hoisted it to the top of the warped flagpole. The dry wind snapped it out. From the farrier's shop came the steady clanging of metal on metal. The odor of bacon drifted across the parade ground. Suddenly Niles knew he could never have any other life.

CHAPTER TWENTY-ONE

Retreat, lipped by Trumpeter D'Angelo, shattered its notes against the hazy Escabros. The little brass cannon near the flagpole boomed flatly, echoing and re-echoing across the rushing Rio Bravo. The flag slid down.

"Pass in review!" barked Niles from the head of B Company. He glanced back at his command, in company front, the guidon fluttering, dress helmets leveled with the eyes of the hatchet-faced troopers. The company, now under the command of First Sergeant Jim Bond, passed in review and came into platoon column, passing before Roland Dane. Then B Company rode toward the stables.

Niles walked toward Marion Ershick. In the weeks that had passed since the defeat of Asesino, he had found it difficult to think of anything else except his impending marriage, and a long leave with his bride.

She reached up and touched the partially healed scar on his tanned face. "You're not as handsome as you were, Niles, but somehow I like you better this way."

Roland Dane came toward them, his thin face shadowed by the cowl of his dress helmet. "Mr. Ord," he said quietly, "I'd like to speak with you in my quarters." He turned and walked away, stiff-legged, with straight back, as though nothing would ever disturb the bearing of Roland Dane.

Niles followed his commanding officer. Baird Dobie was leaning against the mantelpiece in the Dane parlor. He nodded as Niles came in. Dane hung his helmet from a hook and poured brandy into glasses. He looked at Niles. "Well, mister," he said, "my orders have come through."

"Orders, sir?"

Dane swirled the brandy in his glass. "I requested duty elsewhere shortly after I was assigned here."

"Sorry to see you leave, sir," said Niles politely.

Dane smiled thinly. "I have no doubt about that," he said dryly. "I have recommended you for promotion to captain, Ord. I know it will go through. Fort Bellew will be under your command when you return from leave."

Niles sipped his brandy. "The Major forgets that I am to report to Fort Lowell for a court of inquiry into the death of Captain Boysen."

Dane shook his head. "Elias Boysen died by his own hand."

Niles stared at the man.

Baird Dobie straightened up. "There were two slugs in his body, sir."

Dane waved a hand. "I have a written statement in my files. From Sergeant Ershick. He hated you, Ord, because you might take Marion from him. Yet he prepared a statement to clear you."

"So?"

Dane drained his glass. "Ershick was with Boysen when it happened. Boysen turned his handgun on himself and pulled the trigger. The first charge was faulty but strong enough to lodge a bullet in the barrel. The second shot drove the first bullet into Elias' body, followed by the second. The powerful recoil tore the gun from his grasp. It was a strange thing. Ershick seized on it to use it as a method to destroy you. You're clear of all charges,

Ord." Dane held out his hand. "I'm sorry for the trouble I caused you. Forgive me."

Niles took the proffered hand of the strange man before him.

He and Baird left the quarters. Long shadows crept down from the Escabros. Dobie paused to light a cigar. "God help him," he said. "There's one for sorrow, as Tim Forgan would say."

"Where is he going?" asked Niles.

"Fort Abraham Lincoln, near Bismarck, North Dakota. Custer's Seventh is there, getting ready for an all-out campaign to wipe out the Sioux. Custer requested Dane as a special aide."

Niles looked back at the commanding officer's quarters. "I hope he finds the glory trail there, Baird."

Baird Dobie puffed at his cigar. The glow brought out the sharp planes of his face. "He will, Niles. His feet are set on a one-way road, but sorrow will ride always with that man."

Niles left Baird and walked slowly toward Marion's quarters. He glanced back at Cemetery Hill. So many good men lay there. So many good men lay dead in the brooding hills. Young Thorpe Martin lay in the post hospital at Fort Lowell, with his left arm gone at the elbow, contemplating a life of ease, with money to burn, as the only heir to a fortune. Jim Ashley was far south with his weary patrol, helping to drive Colilla Amarilla back to Sonora. Orville Blanchard, post surgeon, was patiently wiring together the skeleton of Asesino, to add to his gruesome collection of oddities. Each to his own, said Niles to himself.

Marion met him at the door. Her lips searched for his in the darkness.

"My captaincy is coming through," he said. "I'll probably stay here to command Ford Bellew, unless my bride wants to forsake all this for civilian life in the East."

She threw back her head and looked up at him. "And have you rearing like a charger every time you hear a trumpet or see Cavalry yellow and blue? No! Wherever you go, I go too. We're Army, Niles. For better or for worse."

He kissed her. Beyond the post he could hear the steady murmur of the Rio Bravo as it rushed toward the desert, far below.

BUGLES ON THE PRAIRIE

FOREWORD

The "California Column" passed on in history with few records to mark its passing. The huge armies in Virginia and Tennessee emblazoned history's pages with the roaring battles of Shiloh and Chickamauga, Antietam, Gettysburg and Cold Harbor. Lesser theaters of war were almost unnoticed. But the California Column did the job for which it was intended. It opened up the Southern Overland Road and helped drive the Confederates from Arizona, New Mexico and West Texas. The Californians fought the fierce Apaches and Navajos.

The California Volunteers built Fort Bowie in dangerous Apache Pass. They garrisoned obscure posts in Arizona and New Mexico. They traversed a desert country in the deadly summer heat. Two thousand troops and eighteen hundred animals made the long journey. Nothing could stop them. They were fine young men, splendidly equipped and led by capable officers. General James Henry Carleton was a strict disciplinarian, and there were times when his men almost rebelled at his orders, but he got his command through and accomplished his mission.

The skirmish at Picacho Pass was the only real fight between Union and Confederate troops in Arizona.

Mangus Colorado was actually wounded by Private John Teal of the California Volunteer Cavalry. Teal was part of a detachment of couriers sent back from the pass. Teal's horse was killed by Apaches led by Mangus Colorado, but Teal coolly foiled up and drove them off, severely wounding the giant Mimbreno chief. Then Teal walked eight miles through the desert, carrying his saddle, to join his comrades.

The credit which the California Column never received in the pages of history is expressed in the words of General Carleton. "The march of the column from California in the summer months across the great desert, in the driest season that had been known in thirty years, is a military achievement creditable to the soldiers of the American Army, but it would not be just to attribute the success to ability on my part. The success was gained only by the high physical and moral energies of that peculiar class of officers and men who composed the column from California. With any other troops, I am sure I would have failed."

CHAPTER ONE

The setting sun stained the sky rose and gold over the brooding Diablitos. A cold wind crept out of the hills and rustled softly through the brush as Ross Fletcher picketed his bay in a draw to the north of the abandoned mission of San Cayetano del Tumacacori. He studied the mud-colored ruins as he drew his Sharps from its boot, half-cocked it, and placed a fresh cap on the nipple. He eased his Colt in its sheath and padded through the swaying mesquite for a closer look at the ruins.

There was no sign of life. An abandoned *carreta* sagged in the center of the weedy patio, banked with tumbleweeds. The dying sun tinted the white dome a pinkish hue. The cross atop it hung at an awkward angle, almost ready to fall. The mission had been abandoned in 1849, thirteen years ago. Now even the peaceful Pimas had given it up, for the Federal troops had evacuated Arizona, and the Apaches held full sway from Durango, far to the south, clear up to the Mogollon Plateau.

Ross padded softly down an eroded draw, a lean lath of a man, with crow's feet etched by the suns of the Southwest about his hard gray eyes. His long face and square jaw gave him the appearance of a man who had been longer on the earth than his twenty-five years. His soft tread was surprising for a man of his size. There was but the faintest whisper of sand beneath his flat-heeled boots as he worked his way forward. There was a suggestion of unleashed power in the broad shoulders and the long, flat-muscled legs. The gray eyes seemed to be on an endless search as they picked out each possible place of cover, checked it, and passed on. For a man did not live long in Apacheria if he missed a possible ambush.

Ross stopped at the solid wall which enclosed the burial ground, the Campus Sancti. His left hand slid inside his buckskin jacket to touch the faded diagram in his shirt pocket. He stepped up on a rock and stood there for a long time, testing the dusk with his senses. The cold February wind soughed through the openings in the old church and scrabbled dryly through the mesquite.

Somewhere in that church Phillip Rand and his daughter Isabella had spent their last night on earth. There was a hidden crypt in the ruins. In the crypt was supposed to be the deed for the Sahuarita silver mine. The diagram showing the location of the crypt had been brought by messenger to John Fletcher, Ross's older brother, early in January. A week later there had come the news of the death of Phillip Rand at Tumacacori, and the disappearance of his daughter. As usual, John Apache had attended to the bloody details.

Ross pulled himself up on the wall and dropped lightly into the cemetery. Three sagging wooden crosses stood at the heads of rock-covered graves. Across the expanse of weedy *caliche* was the rounded chapel, and behind it rose the walls of the church. The empty bell tower etched itself against the dusk sky. It was a place of the dead.

Ross crossed to the door of the sacristy. The sky was now an amethyst color and the light was clear enough for him to study the diagram. The crypt was in the baptistry, just to the east of the vestibule at the south end of the ruins. Ross climbed over a pile of fallen adobe bricks into the sacristy. The old walls were sooty. The floor was a filthy litter of ashes, rags, battered utensils and bat dung.

Ross wrinkled his nose in disgust as the stench of human waste rose about him from the mess. "Bastards," he said softly.

A feeling of utter loneliness came over him as he walked into the sanctuary. Time and vandals had allied themselves in an orgy of destructiveness. The place had been gutted.

The gilded reredos had been torn down. The carving about the deep niches had been battered into shapelessness. The five altars had been demolished. Deep pits had been sunk into the floor and the earth beneath it. Ross looked up at the deep niche above the altar where the statue of Saint Joseph had once stood with hands held out in the act of blessing. The niche was hacked and battered, revealing the burned adobe bricks beneath the thick plaster. High overhead in the dimness Ross could see the plaster palm fronds which signified martyrdom. It was fitting that they, at least, should still be untouched by desecrating hands.

His skin crawled as he walked the long length of the nave, skirting the gaping treasure hunter's pits. The fourteen Stations of the Cross had been defaced, leaving a litter of plaster and adobe on the floor. The wind sighed through the gaping doorway of the church and swept a small tumbleweed against his legs. He stopped beside the door and looked out across the churchyard. It was deserted.

Ross walked into the baptistry, marveling at the wall which was at least nine feet thick. The old Jesuits had built well. The walls had been covered with a wash of pure gypsum, affording enough reflected light for Ross to scan the diagram again. He looked along the wall for a niche. He tapped the plaster with the butt of his carbine. Three feet to the left of the niche he detected a rougher area of plastering. He tapped it with the carbine, detecting a faint hollow sound. He slugged at it with the carbine butt. The plaster fell about his feet. Then he took out his heavy sheath knife and worked around the big adobe brick he had uncovered. It gave a little as he worked. Carefully he pried it out and reached inside the hollow. His hand touched a tin box.

He took the box to the deep window and opened it. A handful of Tubac cardboard money, *boletas* marked with the images of pigs, roosters, horses and bulls, lay on top of the contents of the box. There were a few gold coins beneath the cardboard money. He took a folded parchment from the box and unfolded it. He translated slowly from the ancient Spanish lettering and a feeling of relief came over him. It was the deed. John had been right. The deed had not been taken to Mexico with other records when the Mexicans had left Arizona, nor had it been on the body of Phillip Rand.

An oval object wrapped in silk rattled against the side of the box. Ross unwrapped it. The dying light showed an exquisite ivory miniature. The lovely face of a girl, framed in dark hair, looked up at him. It must be Isabella Rand, a young woman whose beauty had been talked and sung about around the campfires of Sonora and Arizona even when she was barely in her teens. Her beauty was a perfect blending of her father's Anglo-Saxon handsomeness and her mother's pure Castilian beauty. It was an alloy of such exquisite perfection that Ross whistled softly. Somewhere, deep within him, something was lost forever to the girl of the miniature which he held in a big brown hand.

Ross slid the miniature into his jacket pocket. Suddenly he whirled like a great cat, snatching up his Sharps. Above the rustling of the brush he had heard an alien sound. He walked back into the nave and looked out across the churchyard. The sun was almost gone now, dying in a bloody welter of fleecy clouds. Ross waited with the patience of an Apache.

A hawk circled slowly on motionless pinions low over the desert to the south. Suddenly it veered off on the strong wind and flew swiftly out of sight. Ross full-cocked his carbine and padded back through the nave, into the dark sacristy, and then out into the Campus Sancti. There was urgent haste in him as he went across the cemetery and climbed the back wall, for Ross Fletcher never liked to be caught within four walls. Out on the desert, or in the lonely mountains, he was at home.

He trotted up a rise and stopped beside a velvet mesquite to look back at the brooding ruins. He was sure he had heard the faint whinny of a horse, but there was still no sign of life about the shell of Tumacacori.

Ross leaned on his carbine, studying the ruins. The massive structure was slowly reverting to the native soil from which it had been built. The Jesuits who had built it, and the humble Franciscans who had taken it over, were long gone, moldering in forgotten graves. An aura of tragedy had come to roost at San Cayetano del Tumacacori. Even the bones of Father Gutierrez, buried beneath the floor of the sanctuary, had been unearthed by greedy vandals. Ross turned and walked away in the garnering dusk. His father had once said a man left a small part of himself wherever he traveled. Ross left a small part of himself as an offering to the unutterable tragedy of San Cayetano del Tumacacori. But he touched the box in his pocket, thinking of the girl who had been another part of the tragic history.

MOHAVE nickered as Ross bent to loosen the picket pin. Then the big bay snorted. Ross whirled. Something shadowy moved in a mesquite thicket. Ross hit the ground and thrust forward his carbine. A rifle crashed in the thicket, driving a billow of smoke ahead of it down the draw. The slug sang thinly over Ross's head. He rolled over and snapped a shot through the center of the smoke, and was rewarded with a muffled curse.

Feet grated on the gravel. Ross snapped down the lever of his carbine and slid another linen-covered cartridge into the hot chamber. He raised the lever, shearing off the tough base of the cartridge. He capped the nipple as he ran at a crouch alongside the draw. He dropped into a hollow and watched the rifting smoke. There was a thrashing noise in the brush. Ross fired again. He reloaded and waited. Minutes later he heard the steady drumming of hoofs near the Santa Cruz.

"Son of a bitch," said Ross to Mohave.

The bay whinnied. Ross fed him a lump of coarse sugar. *"Gracias,* you old bastard," said Ross. "You've got ears like a mule."

Mohave jerked his head.

Ross grinned. "I'm sorry," he said.

Ross mounted and kneed the bay out of the draw. He rode toward the Tucson road, hunching his jacket collar higher on his neck against the cold, searching fingers of the night wind. It was forty-eight dangerous miles into Tucson. John Fletcher would be worried.

Moonlight covered Tucson, the Old Pueblo, with a silvery wash, as Ross reached the outskirts after his long ride from Tumacacori. He snapped open the cover of his watch. It was half after two o'clock in the morning. The big bay was tired, but he had steel springs in his muscles, and a spirit that would have kept him going until he dropped dead if Ross had ordered him on. Ross looked to the south. Each clump of mesquite might have concealed a Chiricahua buck or a thieving Sonoran, but the ride had been as peaceful as a canter in the park.

Ross uncapped his Sharps and let the hammer down. He slid it into its sheath and swung down from the bay, feeling the tingling flow of blood into his stiffening legs. He led the bay through the narrow, filthy streets. A mangy cur scudded for cover. Pigs slept near piles of rotting garbage casually tossed from front doors into the stinking streets. Sagging adobes and *jacals* sprawled unevenly to form the winding alleyways called streets by the people of Tucson. From somewhere in the Plaza de Armas, a drunk was singing hoarsely.

Ross turned into the street where John had rented an eroded adobe. A man stood in the shadows of a deep doorway. Ross slid his right hand down to the butt of his Colt. There was no mistaking the man. The steeple sombrero, heavily crusted with coin silver ornamentation, was the trademark of the huge man who wore it. Nick Maxwell, partner of Matt Risler, who ran Tucson in his own way, and to hell with the opinions of anyone else.

Maxwell yawned and flipped a cigar almost at Ross's feet.

Their eyes met, hard gray and feral green. Ross didn't nod to the big man as he passed, but there was an itchy feeling between his shoulder blades as he felt the green eyes bore into him. Ross skirted the rotting carcass of a pig and glanced back. Maxwell was sauntering toward the Plaza de Armas. In a few minutes Matt Risler would know that Ross Fletcher had returned to Tucson.

Ross led the tired bay into the lean-to shed behind the adobe. He unsaddled him, rubbed him down, covered him with a blanket, and then walked to the back door of the adobe. He tapped three times, then twice, then three times again.

Feet grated inside the adobe. "That you, Ross?" called out John Fletcher.

"Yes. Open up."

The door swung open. Ross went in and waited until John closed and barred the door. John Fletcher relit the stinking candle lantern he had snuffed out. He placed a four-barreled Sharps pistol on the table. "You had me worried sick," he said quietly.

Ross carelessly slapped the dust from his clothing. "I got near there early yesterday morning and hid in the hills until dusk last night." He placed the tin box on the table. "There it is, John."

John Fletcher opened the box with his right hand. The left sleeve of his black frock coat was pinned to the breast. John Fletcher had lost his left arm at Chapultepec fifteen years before. The lantern light revealed the gray that shot his dark hair. Although he was only fourteen years older than Ross, he gave the appearance of a man much older than his thirty-nine years.

John took out the deed and flattened it on the table. "It doesn't seem possible that we should have such luck. The diagram was right then?"

"I had no trouble finding the crypt."

John studied the dusty face of his brother. "I knew you could find it, if it *could be* found. Did you have any trouble?"

"There were smoke signals near Twin Buttes yesterday. I stalled around until dusk. I figured no Apache in his right mind would enter a haunted place like Tumacacori at night."

"You always figure such things out."

Ross grinned. "It's kept me alive, John."

"Yes," said John Fletcher dryly, "but for how long?"

John sat down. "There's food in the cabinet. What did you think of the old mission?"

"Lonely. Tragic. I find it hard to forget."

"Yes." John tapped the deed. "This establishes our claim to half-ownership of the mine, without a doubt."

Ross made a thick sandwich of bread and dried meat. "If Isabella Rand is dead, we now own the whole damned mine."

"You don't think she is? Her father was found near Tumacacori with three arrows in his back. Surely she must have met the same fate."

"Her body was never found."

John slapped a hand on the table. "She must be dead!"

"Her scarf and coat were found near her father's body. She was young . . . and beautiful. She might be an Apache squaw even now. Unless—" Ross let the thought die on his lips.

"Go on."

Ross wiped his mouth. "They might have had their way with her."

"She could still live through that."

Ross eyed his brother. "I've seen what some of those

bloody bastards can do to a white woman. They're chaste as all hell with their own woman. But a white woman is part of their loot; no more, no less."

"We must have proof that she *is* dead, Ross."

Ross shook his head angrily. "Damn it! How can we get it? She could be anywhere within hundreds of square miles of Apacheria. How in hell's name could a white man find out, John?"

John opened a bottle of Bacanora mescal and filled two glasses. "Phillip took her down to see the mine against my wishes. He was insistent. You know the rest. The soldiers had gone from their forts. Tubac was abandoned. Phil's Mex employees deserted him. He hid the deed in the crypt and sent a Pima to let me know where it was by means of the diagram. Phil meant to take Isabella to her mother's people in Sonora. He never made it. I have lost the best friend I ever had, Ross."

Ross finished his sandwich and drained his glass. He refilled it. "Well, the mine is ours. Every damned centavo we had is invested in it. Thanks to Phillip Rand, we're not paupers."

John nodded. "I sent for you from California because I knew you could find that deed."

Ross grinned. "I'm good for something then, John?"

John Fletcher looked up. "You make me feel old, Ross. I wonder if I ever felt as you do?"

Ross shook his head. "No. You were mature when you were a kid." Ross leaned over and took his brother's silver cigar case from his pocket. He took out a cigarillo and lit it, watching the smoke drift about the guttering lantern. "You've always given me plenty of free advice, John, most of it good. You were the leader. Now I'm telling you what to do. Get out of Arizona!"

John eyed his brother. "What are you driving at?"

Ross leaned forward and tapped John on the arm. "There's a good rumor that Confederate cavalrymen are riding west from New Mexico to take possession of this area. We're known to be Union men. This place is getting to be a hotbed of secessionism. Now that you've got the deed there's no reason for you to stay here."

John unwrapped the delicate miniature. "We must think of this girl."

"Is she really as beautiful as that?"

John looked at the smoldering embers of the pinon wood in the beehive fireplace. "Yes. This miniature doesn't do her full justice. Isabel was a beautiful child."

Ross rubbed his bristly jaw. John had used the short form of her name. He had never married. A strange thought came to Ross, but he knew it couldn't be true. John Fletcher must be a good twenty years older than the lost girl.

Ross stood up. "Take my advice; get out of here tonight. You can make the Pima villages. You'll be safe there until you can get to Yuma."

John Fletcher's head snapped up. *"Me?* You're going with me, if I go."

"No."

The older man stood up, "I give the orders here, Ross. Now listen to me! First, I'm not leaving here until I know that girl is alive, or dead. Second, I'm not leaving without you!"

Ross's mouth tightened. "I want no quarrel with you, John. You seem to forget that I'm not a clumsy kid anymore."

"What do you intend to do?"

"There's one person here in Tucson who might know about Isabel Rand."

"Who?"

Ross grinned. "Luz Campos."

"Damn you! Are you out of your mind? She's worse than some of the men who live in this hole."

"Perhaps. But there isn't much that goes on that she doesn't hear about."

"A woman of the gambling halls! Why, the man she works for, Amadeo Esquivel, is one of the worst Border scum in the country. She's nothing but a whore, Ross!"

Ross picked up his hat and placed it on his head. He drew the *barbiquejo* up under his chin. "Amadeo reminds me of something that crawls away when you lift up a rotting log, and I wouldn't trust him any further than I can throw him. And as for Luz Campos . . . you seem to forget I've been around quite a bit, John, in places where you wouldn't soil your linen."

Tight lines etched themselves on the face of John Fletcher. Ross had always listened to him. But the big man who had come from California at his request was almost a stranger to him. "I'll go with you," he said quietly.

Ross laughed. "You? You wouldn't look right in Esquivel's place."

"Meaning that you do?"

Ross nodded. "I've seen the elephant," he said.

"Be careful, then. Matt Risler has been working openly to arouse these people against the Union. A story has been circulating that we're Union agents."

"That's a new angle."

"You always did take things too easily. Still, I don't know what I would have done without you."

Ross gripped his brother's shoulder. "Maybe the family black sheep is useful for something."

"I never held that view. Father planned my career for me in law. He planned a career in medicine for you."

"He didn't get far," said Ross dryly.

"No."

"There were too many hills to look over."

John nodded. He touched his left sleeve. "Perhaps if this hadn't happened I might have looked over a few hills myself."

Ross shook his head. "No. You've built a career for yourself. It was your judgment that bought us our half-interest in the Sahuarita."

"Yes—just as war broke out. If the rebels invade Arizona the deed won't be worth the paper it's written on."

There was a deep, dangerous look in Ross's eyes as he unbarred the door. "If the rebels do invade Arizona they'll get the damnedest fight they ever had. Keep your pistol handy, John."

"Are you sure you had no trouble at Tumacacori?"

Ross turned. "Why do you ask?"

"Just a feeling." John Fletcher sat down and drew his pistol close to hand. The light reflected from the silver-chased barrels of the .30-caliber multishot. "Do you really think there is any danger for us here?"

"Nick Maxwell was watching this house when I entered the street. By this time Risler knows I'm back. I still wish you'd pull out of here. I can meet you at the Pima villages."

John pulled back on the hammer of his pistol and pressed the button which allowed the four barrels to slide forward. He checked the loads. "I'm staying," he said quietly. "It seems as though you won't take orders from me. By the same token, I'll not take orders from you. We're in this together as brothers."

"And partners."

There was a slow smile on John's face. "Yes, Ross." There was an odd premonition in Ross as he opened the door. There was none of Ross's recklessness in John, but there was a steadfastness in him which called for a high quality of courage.

———

Ross stopped beside the house and drew out his cap and ball Navy Colt. He checked the caps and slid it back into his holster. He peered through a slit in the dingy cloth which covered the small window. John Fletcher was looking at the picture of Isabella Rand. A small worm of jealousy seemed to form in Ross's mind; he shrugged it off as he padded down the street. But he knew now he could never leave Tucson until he found out what had happened to the girl.

The moonlight lent a soft glamour to the streets of Tucson which the harsh light of day would never allow. Ross eased his holster farther forward on his thigh. Tucson in 1862 was a den of lawlessness. There was no recognized authority since Federal troops had evacuated Forts Breckinridge and Buchanan. Ross had been at the diggings in Calaveras County when he had received John's letter advising him of the investment John had made in the Sahuarita. The mine had originally been the property of Dona Ynez Padilla Rand. Rand had been in need of ready cash, and had agreed to take John and Ross in as partners. John had handled Phillip's legal matters for some years prior to that time. But the actual possession of the mine had presented difficulties. When the Mexican authorities had left Arizona after the treaty of Guadalupe-Hidalgo, they had taken most of the old records with them. Valuable properties had been taken over by lawless Border scum who used knife and pistol to assert their claims. There was no denying them, for without the deeds, the properties seemed to belong to the strong.

Ross had come to Tucson in answer to John's request to help locate the deed. In the few weeks Ross had been in Tucson, he had fit into the life of the tough town much more easily than had John. John had been a man of peace since the Mexican War, where he had received a bellyful of blood and fighting. But Ross had learned to use his wits and speed in lawless towns from Santa Fe to Calaveras County.

Ross stopped in the Plaza de Armas and relit his cigar. It was at least three hours after midnight, but there was no curfew in the Old Pueblo. Ross had wanted to leave Tucson, but now he wasn't so sure. The dark beauty of Isabel Rand had etched itself in his mind. He had never met a woman he could really love, but now he wasn't sure. He shrugged and walked across the littered plaza toward Esquivel's gambling hall.

CHAPTER THREE

A rush of warm, smoke-laden air met Ross as he opened the door of the gambling hall. The mingled odors of smoke, greasy food, liquor slops, cheap perfume and sweat, wrapped about him like an old, familiar cloak. Roulette wheels whirled. Faro dealers hunched in the slot. Glasses clinked along the zinc-topped bar which ran the length of the south wall. Eyes swiveled toward Ross as he walked to where Amadeo Esquivel perched like some evil bird on the stool pigeon's high chair. Esquivel was watching his dealers like a hawk. Sweat trickled down his oily face. His hair shone with grease. A nicotine-stained cigarette was pasted in one corner of his mouth.

"You have come back I see, Senor Fletcher," said the Mexican, without taking his eyes from a monte dealer.

"You've got eyes in the side of your head."

"You do not fear the Apaches nor the Sonorans? Your business must be important for you to take such a risk."

"Perhaps. Is Luz Campos in?"

Amadeo jerked a thumb toward the back of the hall. "She is not dealing tonight. She is resting."

"Thanks." Ross walked around the hall owner.

Esquivel placed a greasy hand on Ross's arm. "I said that she is resting, senor."

"I heard you."

There was a dangerous light in the yellowish eyes of Amadeo Esquivel. "I have heard it said that you and your brother will soon leave Tucson. Is that true?"

Ross brushed the hand from his sleeve.

Esquivel shrugged. "It is said that the Tejanos are riding here under the flag of the Confederacy."

"So?"

"A word of caution, Senor Fletcher."

The yellowish eyes watched Ross as he parted the dingy curtain which screened off the dimly lit hallway from the rest of the building. The Mexican's lips seemed to form a word. *Gringo!*

Ross rapped on the end door.

The door swung open and Luz Campos smiled at him. "My Californian. Come in. It is good to see you."

The room was large for Tucson. The stolid face of an Indian-carved *santo* peered out of a whitewashed wall niche. Rich perfume drifted to Ross as Luz Campos came toward him. Her shapely body was clad in a thin white *camisita* which left her smooth brown shoulders bare and her full breasts unhampered. A bright skirt, flesh-tight over her hips, flared out just above her knees. Her dark, smooth helmet of hair was drawn into a tight knot at the back of her narrow head, and held with a silver comb. As he reached for her he noted the silver cross which hung about her neck and between her breasts. Beneath the paint and rouge there were still traces of the girlish beauty she had used to good advantage in following her profession as a gambler.

"Wine?" asked Luz Campos.

Ross nodded. He drew her close and crushed her soft body against his. Her mouth met his with lips partly open. Her smooth arms crept about his neck and gripped him with surprising strength. Then she broke away as swiftly as she had come to him.

Luz took a bottle from a cabinet. Ross watched her slim fingers, bedecked with many rings, as she opened the bottle. "I have come to ask you something, Luz," he said.

"I have been lonely for you. We will talk of many things."

"I have been to Tumacacori. What do you know of the death of Phillip Rand and his daughter?"

She hesitated and then looked up at him. "What should I know about it?"

Ross sat down and took a full glass from her warm hand. "You know of many things, Luz. There is not much going on here that you don't know about."

The Indian was strong on her expressionless face as she watched him over her wine glass. Ross had often wondered where she had come from. There was Indian in her, and also a trace of good blood. Some Spanish don had planted good seed in old Mexico generations before.

"What is it you wish to know?" she asked.

"Is Isabel Rand dead?"

She sipped her wine and crossed her shapely legs. She swung the top one back and forth in a tantalizing arc. Ross felt warm all over, and he hadn't yet had enough to drink. "How should Luz Campos know?" she demanded. "She may be a squaw in an Apache rancheria. Her bones may be whitening in some arroyo. Perhaps she is in a Sonoran brothel."

"Come! You know more than that." Ross took out his wallet and tapped it against his thigh.

"Damn you! I don't want money from you!"

"Then tell me."

She stood up and crossed to him with a swish of her full skirt. She kissed him quickly and then stood by the door listening. "It is said that Phillip Rand was lured from Tucson," she said quietly over her shoulder.

"What do you mean?"

She came to him and placed a hand on his shoulder. "It is said that he had much money."

He looked up at her. "You know why my brother and I are here. We own half of the Sahuarita. If Isabel is alive she owns the other half. That's something we don't know. But we think someone was after the deed. Phillip Rand did not have it on his body when he was killed."

"So?"

"Whoever did the job wanted that deed. The mine would have been theirs without question."

"It is said they were killed by the Apaches. What would they do with a deed? It means nothing to them." Ross emptied his glass and slid an arm about her waist, drawing her close. "Who really killed them, Luz?"

She ran a hand through his hair. "I do not know. Why do you ask?"

"Was it Matt Risler? Nick Maxwell? Amadeo Esquivel?"

She paled beneath her paint. "Mother of God! You are mad!" She glanced nervously at the door. "Do not talk like that in this place! Even Luz Campos could not save you!"

"Then you *do* know!"

She bit her lip. "So?"

"Whoever possesses the deed, possesses a fortune."

She leaned close. Her unhindered breasts were in full view beneath the thin *camisita*. The inviting, womanly odor of her lithe body worked on Ross. "You have that deed, my Californian?" she whispered.

"I did not say so."

She broke away, whirled and dropped into his lap, twining her arms about his neck. "You found it at Tumacacori?"

"Tumacacori is in ruins, a place of the dead. Besides, I came here to ask *you* questions, Luz Campos."

She pressed wantonly against him and softly laughed. "That is not the only reason you came, my man. You wanted to feel the arms of Luz Campos about you before you left for California." She kissed him. Her throbbing warmth seemed to beat against him. He pushed her back to look into her eyes.

She stood up. "Why must you talk of these things? I have been so lonely for you, Ross." She refilled the glasses. The flickering firelight brought out the warm tones of her bare flesh.

Ross went to her, placing big, rough hands on her smooth shoulders. She turned and slid her arms about his neck, pulling him down toward her. He kissed her and carried her to the couch. He passed his hands over her and kissed her again and again. The fire crackled. The room was warm and alive with the vitality of Luz Campos. Ross snuffed out the candle.

She drew him down to her in the shadows.

————

ROSS OPENED his eyes to darkness. His head thudded like an oxhide drum. He ran a thick tongue over his gummy lips. His stomach moiled with white worms; his brain was queasy with alcohol. He bent and pulled on his boots, wincing as his steamy brain felt the rush of blood. "Jesus," he said thickly. "Jesus God!"

He buckled on his gunbelt and settled it about his lean hips. He weaved his way to the water olla and drank deeply, splashing some of the water on his heated face. He reached for his jacket, swaying uncertainly, and then shrugged into it. The hallway was dark as he felt his way along to the gambling hall. He pulled the curtain aside, wincing shakily as the foul air clogged his nostrils. There was a sour sensation in the back of his throat.

The room was still crowded. The roulette wheels whirred incessantly. Rifts of bluish smoke wavered in the drafts. Luz Campos sat at her table. She was dressed in sober black silk, the very picture of a lady, with a silver cross dangling against the high-fronted gown. Nick Maxwell sat beside her, his chair tilted back against the scabby wall. His heavy sombrero was slanted back from

his broad face. Sweat glistened on his low forehead. He
eyed Ross and then looked away.

Amadeo Esquivel came through the crowd. "A drink,
amigo?" he suggested. "Brandy? Wine? Mescal?"

Ross nodded. "Mescal."

Esquivel took a bottle from the bar. Ross gulped
down the fiery liquid. It seemed to settle him a little.
"What time is it?" he asked thickly.

"It is almost dawn."

Ross placed the bottle on the bar. "*Gracias.*" He
walked slowly toward the outer door.

Matt Risler came in as Ross reached the door. He was
neat in black broadcloth and fresh linen. He was a tall
man with a pallor beneath his light tan. "Hello, Fletcher,"
he said easily.

"How are you, Risler?"

"Fine." The gambler took a cigar case from his
pocket. "The Texans are twenty miles from here," he said
conversationally. He clipped his cigar and lit it, eying
Ross over the flare of the lucifer with dark eyes.

"Meaning?"

"I'm not sure of your politics, Fletcher, but this will
be a mighty uncomfortable place for Union men before
long."

"I don't follow you."

Risler drew in the smoke. "You'll probably have to
swear allegiance to the Confederate States of America
before long, or be imprisoned."

Ross shrugged and walked outside. The cool gray
light of the false dawn met him. He was sure now that he
had been drugged like a greenhorn. Chloral hydrate,
probably; he had once seen the crystals in her room. He
had always been a good man with a bottle. His gut was
lined with copper. He had taken about eight glasses of
wine—nothing unusual for him—but now he felt as
though he had mixed a dozen different drinks. John
would be on the prod, and Ross couldn't blame him. John
never allowed liquor or women to interfere with business.

Ross walked unsteadily across the plaza. He nearly heaved as he passed the decaying body of a pig. He weaved down the narrow street and hammered on the back door of the adobe. The door creaked open under the impact. He walked in and felt in his pocket for a lucifer. His left foot kicked something under the table as he reached for the lantern. He lit the lantern and gripped the edge of the rickety table to steady himself.

"John!" he called out.

There was no answer. Then he focused his eyes on the couch. John was lying on the floor beside it. His eyes stared unseeingly at Ross, almost as though to accuse him of negligence.

Ross cursed thickly as he knelt beside his brother. The white face was cold. He rolled the body over. The white shirt was soaked with blood and stained with filth from the floor. Ross stood up. While he had been drinking and riding the two-headed beast, his brother had been murdered.

———

Ross wiped his lips with the back of his hand. He reached for the mescal bottle and drank deeply. Tucson swarmed with men who would kill for a handful of Tubac *boletas* or a paste stickpin. Ross looked about the room. The tin box stood on the table. It was empty. He looked under the table. The ivory miniature lay there. That was what he had kicked when he had come in. He picked it up and put it into his pocket.

Ross wiped the cold sweat from his face. He picked up John's body and placed it on the couch, covering it with a serape. Then he drew out his Colt and twirled the cylinder. The noise of the whirring steel sounded loud in the stillness. The drug seemed to be burned away in the hate which flooded through him.

CHAPTER FOUR

The faint sound of shouting came to Ross as he finished packing his gear. A gun cracked flatly. Ross placed his saddlebags by the rear door and shut it behind him. He walked toward the Plaza Militar. Men were running through the winding, dusty streets. Ross stopped when he reached the plaza.

A column of dusty horsemen was threading its way into the plaza. At a barked command they wheeled awkwardly into an uneven line. Some of them wore faded gray shell jackets trimmed with yellow braid. Most of them wore parts of uniforms mingled with civilian clothing. All of them wore floppy, wide-brimmed hats. Single- and double-barreled shotguns were carried by many of the troopers. Others had battered muzzle-loaders hanging by slings from their backs. Cap and ball six-shooters were carried by some, while others had single-shot percussion pistols. All of them had heavy, straight-bladed sabers, and bowie knives in rawhide sheaths. At their head was a lean, bearded man wearing a gray uniform. Three bars glittered on his collar, and his sleeves were decorated with intertwined trimming of gold braid.

"It's Captain Sherrod Hunter of the Texas Mounted

Rifles!" yelled a drunk. "We're under the blessed flag of the Confederacy at last! Hooray!"

Hunter held up a gauntleted hand. In the silence that followed, the dry wind snapped out the company swallow-tailed guidon with its single white star on a field of red. The officer drew a paper from his coat and read it in a loud, clear voice.

The gist of the proclamation was that all of the Territory of New Mexico lying south of the 34th Parallel of North Latitude would hereafter be known as the Confederate Territory of Arizona. Tucson, as part of Dona Ana County, Territory of New Mexico, was now to be considered as part of the newly conquered territory. The seat of government was to be La Mesilla in New Mexico, and the governor, Colonel John Baylor, C.S.A. It was dated August 1st, 1861.

A roar went up from the assembled spectators as Hunter finished. A red-shirted miner emptied a pepperbox pistol into the air.

When the echoes died away against the buildings, Hunter again raised his hand. "We can prove to you loyal men," he shouted, "that we can back up this proclamation! Sibley's Texas Brigade decisively defeated the Yankee Regulars at the Valverde Fords the twenty-first day of this month! You can shortly expect to hear of the occupation of Santa Fe and the capture of mighty Fort Union near Las Vegas! General Sibley will, in all probability, march west through Arizona for the eventual conquest of California! With the deep-water ports of the Pacific in our hands, as well as the gold diggings, the Confederate States of America cannot fail to win the war!"

Ross spat. The Texans were young men, for the most part; the guidon bearer was hardly more than a kid. Big talk, he thought, for a ragtag, bobtailed, draggle-assed parcel of wet-nosed Texicans.

"There's a Yankee," said someone close to Ross.

It was Nick Maxwell. Beside him was a strange character known only as Yaqui. His flat face was impassive, and his eyes were as cold and deadly as those of a copperhead. Men walked quietly when he was around. It was said that he walked freely into the rancherias of his mother's people, the dreaded Yaquis, and that the Chiricahuas accepted him as a blood brother because of some relationship with them. He was never very far from Maxwell or Risler.

A miner squinted at Ross. "You better light a shuck outa here, Fletcher," he warned. "These Texas boys might rawhide you."

Ross dropped a hand to his Colt. The town had always been dangerous, but he had made a few acquaintances at the bars. Now the place was full of hostility. "I'll leave when I'm ready," he said flatly.

Maxwell picked at his front teeth with a dirty fingernail. "Cocky, ain't you?" he asked. "I woulda thought you'd learned a lesson by now."

Ross turned slowly. "Meaning?"

Risler pushed his way through the crowd. "Shut up, Nick," he said quietly. He looked at Ross. "Get out of town. These boys won't bother you."

Nick grinned and slid a hand inside his coat.

Yaqui moved swiftly. "Wait," he said in his flat voice.

Ross looked at Risler. "Why are you taking my part?" he asked.

"I like fair play."

I'll bet you do, thought Ross. He walked around the crowd and stopped not far from Captain Hunter.

A man was talking swiftly to the rebel officer. "Sylvester Mowry, down to the Patagonia Mines, will help you out, Cap'n Hunter. You can get food supplies up north at Pima villages and Ammi White's Mill. God, but we're glad to see you."

Ross faded into the crowd. It didn't serve his purpose to be singled out among the predominantly rebel crowd. He stopped by the adobe of Bartolome Diaz, an undertaker, to arrange for the burial of John. He stood for a long time at the edge of town looking across the irrigated fields to the green line of the Santa Cruz. He had failed John. John had feared no man, but had never really been fitted for the frontier. Ross had watched him like a hawk. But a few minutes of carelessness on Ross's part had cost John's life.

"Luz Campos," said Ross between his teeth. His big hands clawed out as though to feel her smooth throat between them. He turned on a heel and headed for the gambling hall. The sun warmed his back, but there was a ball of ice in his belly and a deep hatred in his soul.

———

ESQUIVEL'S WAS ROARING. Liquor flowed like a freshet. This was the biggest day the filthy hole had seen since the town had turned out in a body and strung up Fourfinger Ochoa for knifing a fifteen-year-old prostitute. Toasts were flung back and forth—toasts to Sherrod Hunter's Company A, toasts to John Baylor, toasts to Jeff Davis, toasts to the whole Goddamned fighting, victorious Confederacy.

Amadeo was at the end of the bar. His veiled eyes studied Ross. "She is sleeping," he said.

Ross pushed past him.

"She is sleeping, gringo!" snapped the Mexican. He gripped Ross by the arm. Ross placed his right hand flat on Amadeo's and pressed it hard against his arm. The painful pressure brought the greasy sweat out on the owner's face. "Before God," he said in a hoarse voice, "I mean no harm."

Ross let him go and hurried down the hallway. He pushed open the door. She was asleep on the couch, partially covered by a serape, one bare arm hanging down to the floor. Her black silk gown lay in a careless heap beside the black stockings and the rose-decorated garters.

"Luz!" said Ross harshly.

She opened her eyes and looked uncertainly at him. Then she sat up quickly, dropping the serape from her breasts. "It is you. Back so soon for more love, my big Californian?"

Ross kicked the door shut. "Why did you keep me here last night?"

She stretched lazily. "Did you not want to stay?"

He stood beside the couch. "Was that vino drugged?"

Her eyes widened in innocence. "The wine? You are talking loco! Why do you ask? Why are you here?"

He gripped her wrist and pulled her close. "My brother was murdered last night, while I was here."

Her free hand crept up to her throat. "No! It is not possible!"

"What do you know about it?"

"You are hurting me!"

He twisted her wrist savagely. Quick tears came into her eyes. He threw her back against the wall and straightened up. She covered herself virtuously with the serape. "I know nothing about it," she said defiantly.

The door banged open. Nick Maxwell stepped in with a cocked Colt in his right hand. "Get away from her," he said. "I don't need you, Nick!" snapped Luz.

Nick grinned. "Sorry to bust in on a lady like this, but Amadeo said Fletcher was making trouble here."

Luz thrust slim bare legs into her slippers. Maxwell eyed them in appreciation. She frowned as she draped herself in the serape. "Get out of here, pig!" she screamed.

Maxwell shook his head. "Not until he goes."

Ross looked at Luz. "I'll go."

She touched his arm with a shaking hand. "Before the Virgin, I know nothing of what you said."

Maxwell spat into the fireplace. Suddenly he twisted his left hand in the front of Ross's shirt. "God-damned Yankee," he said.

Ross slapped his right across the brutish face and clamped his hand down on the gun wrist, twisting it out and sideways. Maxwell cursed. Ross drove in a jolting right that shook the big man to his heels. Maxwell grunted as Ross smashed a fist to the gut just above the big belt buckle. Ross ripped the Colt from his opponent's hand and dropped it.

Luz screamed as Maxwell tried for the groin with a hard knee. Ross sidestepped, thrust his left leg under Maxwell's rising leg and threw the big man off balance. Maxwell turned away. Ross clasped his hands and smashed them home at the base of the thick neck. Nick went down, clawing at the wall. He rolled over, shielding his face, and came up like a whale from beneath the small vanity table. Rouge, paint, powder and perfume cascaded about him amid a shattering of glass.

Luz ran into a corner, dropping the serape. She snatched up her silk gown and buried her face in it.

Maxwell charged to meet a left that straightened him up. A right snapped against his jaw, reeling him back against the wall.

"You smell like a cheap whore, Maxwell," said Ross. "Keep away from me."

A chair collapsed under the big man. Something nudged Ross in the middle of the back. "Maybe we'll make you smell worse," a slurring voice said behind Ross. It was Yaqui. Ross hoisted his arms, feeling a warm trickle of blood run down his sweating back.

Matt Risler pushed past Ross. "What happened, Nick?" he demanded coldly.

The big man wiped the blood from his mouth. There was a faraway look in his mad green eyes. "Get outa my way, Matt," he said thickly.

"Damn you! I asked you a question!"

Nick looked past Risler at Ross. There was bloody death in his eyes. "He was after Luz. Tore the clothes off her. I heard her scream."

Luz thrust out a clawed hand. "He lies!"

"Get out," said Risler.

Ross turned. Yaqui was just behind him. All the way

into the gambling hall Ross expected the hard thrust of the *cuchillo*. Cold sweat worked through his shirt.

"There's the only Yankee left in town," a drunk shouted. "Heat the tar and get the feathers!"

"Hell! String him up and get it over with," another said.

Risler came into the hall. "I warned him to leave town," he said. "Why did you ignore me, Fletcher?"

Ross looked at the hostile faces. "My brother was murdered this morning," he said. "Stabbed in the back."

"Now ain't that too bad," said Maxwell. "One less blue-belly to kill off."

Ross whirled in raging hate. He shoved Yaqui to one side and clipped Nick against the jaw. Maxwell grunted. He spat on his hands and shuffled his big feet. "Don't stop me this time, Matt," he warned.

Risler opened his mouth.

"Shut up!" yelled a miner. "He's Maxwell's man!"

The crowd formed a circle, eyes alight with the coming carnage. Maxwell fingered his jaw and then spat blood. Then he came on, thick arms pumping like pistons. A right crashed against Ross's jaw, a left sank into his lean gut. He backed away, blocking with elbows and forearms, but the punishing blows rained on him like a battering ram. Someone shoved him toward Nick in time to meet a whistling hook. He staggered back. Maxwell grinned. A left sank into Ross's queasy belly, a right thudded over his heart. Ross rolled away and countered with a fair right to the jaw.

Nick retreated and thrust out a leg. Ross gripped it and upended the big man. Maxwell thudded down on his shoulder blades. He rolled free and gripped Ross about the knees, dragging him down on the filthy floor.

Nick growled like an animal. He had the brute strength and vitality of a grizzly. He gripped Ross about the rib cage. Ross felt his breath leave him. A rib cracked. He got both hands up under the blocky jaw of Maxwell and shoved with all his remaining strength. Maxwell weakened. Ross kneed his groin. Maxwell turned a little and got to his feet with a surge of strength. They swayed back and forth dripping sweat. The foul air clogged Ross's lungs—the drug had taken more of a toll than he had realized. Nick gasped as the big hands shoved his head farther back. He threw Ross back and hit the bar. Glasses and bottles jumped over the far side and smashed on the floor.

Nick bounced from the bar and cut at Ross's eyes with open hands. Ross went back over a chair and got up in time to meet a sledge-like blow that drove him back through the open door into the street. He hit the hard *caliche* with a thud.

Nick came on like a tiger. Boots thudded against Ross's ribs, a spur raked the side of his face. He rolled away, sick and weak, and got to his feet. A fist lanced against his jaw. Another staggered him. He went off balance, making the kill easy for the big man. Maxwell put all his weight into a hook. Ross went down on a knee. A boot smashed against his rump and sent him flat. The earth abraded his face. Blood spotted it from his mouth and nose. He lay still, his breath harsh in his throat.

The crowd flowed out into the street with the killing fever on them. Nick spat on his bloody hands and drew his case knife, flicking open the long blade. He tested the edge with his thumb. Then he gripped Ross by the gunbelt. "I'll fix this Yankee rooster so that he don't bother any more women," he said.

"Hold it! Put up that knife!" a crisp voice snapped.

Ross looked up at a rebel officer wearing the two gold bars of a first lieutenant on his collar. Five troopers, trailing carbines, were behind the officer.

"That's enough," said the officer in disgust. "The man is beaten."

Maxwell spate deliberately. "Who the hell are you?"

"Lieutenant Jenkins. Texas Mounted Rifles."

Maxwell grinned. "Now ain't that nice, soldier boy? What do you hombres say?"

"Dehorn him," a gaunt man snarled.

Yaqui nodded. His eyes never left Maxwell's knife. Risler leaned against the wall of the gambling hall with folded arms, watching the play.

Jenkins lifted his holster flap. "What has this man done?"

"Attempted rape," said Nick. "We got a cure for that here."

Jenkins shook his head. "Captain Hunter has appointed me provost marshal. Tucson is under martial law."

"Tucson is a free town," said Risler.

Jenkins shook his head. "You're wrong. And even if it was a free town, I'd stop this brutality, sir!"

"Takin' a lot on yourself, ain't you?" asked Nick.

Ross eased his hand down to his Colt. His head had cleared a little, but the drug and the bloody fight had taken a lot out of him.

"Move along! All of you!" ordered the officer. He drew a big LeMat pistol. "I've got nine forty-four slugs in this handgun, and a twelve-gauge charge in the lower barrel. I can make quite a mess with this weapon."

The troopers cocked their carbines. The crowd drifted back. Some of the men went back into the gambling hall.

Maxwell slowly stood up. "To hell with this! I ain't takin' orders from a pup in a gray suit!"

Jenkins flushed. He cocked the big LeMat.

Ross got to his feet and placed his hand on his Colt to back the Texan's play.

Risler caught Nick's eye. "Git!" he said sharply.

For a moment the big man stood like a mad dog, wanting to face down the opposition. His eyes traveled from the LeMat along the line of carbines and stopped at Ross Fletcher. There wasn't death in the eyes of the soldiers; there *was* death in the eyes of the badly beaten man standing at the end of the line. Nick Maxwell wanted badly to win the showdown; it was in his blustering nature. But he didn't want to take a chance on dying to show these people who was the biggest hog in the Tucson pond. Nick spat deliberately to one side and swaggered off, flexing his thick muscles. Yaqui followed him like a ghost.

Jenkins looked at Ross. "I don't know your political beliefs, mister, but in this town every man will, swear an oath of allegiance to the Confederate States of America by sundown or go to prison. What started this fracas anyway?"

"My brother was murdered early this morning. I was trying to find the killer."

Jenkins lowered the hammer on his pistol. "From the looks of that mob you would have joined your brother before you found out, sir. You'd better jump up some dust getting out of here."

Ross nodded. *"Gracias,"* he said.

———

THE STREETS WERE PEOPLED ONLY by dirty Mex kids who curiously watched the big gringo swaying along. His face was swollen and bloody and his clothing ripped and torn. It wasn't anything unusual to see a gringo like this. When they weren't fighting Mexicans or Apaches they were fighting each other. *Ay de mi!* How the gringos loved to fight!

The human locusts had been hard at work in the adobe while Ross had been gone. Mohave was gone, and so was all his saddle gear. Ross looked for his carbine, but that had been taken with everything else. John's body had been taken away. Ross walked outside and leaned against the wall.

"Went down to Jericho and fell amongst thieves," he said dryly.

A frightened face poked around the corner. It was Bartolome Diaz, the undertaker. "Before God, Senor Fletcher," he said, "you must leave Tucson!"

"Have you taken my brother, Bartolome?"

"Yes. Yes. All is well."

"He must be buried today."

"It will be done."

"When will you be ready?"

"Soon. Soon. It is not your intention to attend, Senor Fletcher?"

"Certainly I'll be there!"

Diaz slid around the corner. "There is much talk at Esquivel's gambling hall. Nick Maxwell plans to wait for you after you leave the cemetery. Holy Mother, do not come there, senor. I will take care of him. There will be words said over him, I assure you."

Ross touched his bruised face. The Mex was right. It would do no good to go. John was past helping. "I need a horse," he said. "Who stole Mohave?"

Diaz thrust out his hands palms upward. "I came for the corpse. Everything was gone. This is a den of thieves, as you well know."

"Can you get me a horse?"

The Mexican paled. "If they should find out, they will beat me. I have seven children, senor. You see how it is?"

Ross nodded. He took out his wallet and paid the Mexican.

"Vaya con Dios," said Diaz as he vanished around the corner.

Ross went into the house. There was a long chance the deed might have been secreted by John. Time was running short and he was out on a limb; if he stalled around much longer he'd cut off the limb between himself and the tree.

CHAPTER FIVE

R oss finished searching the adobe. He had found nothing but two inches of mescal in the bottle which had been kicked under the table. He had wasted his time. The deed was gone with the snows of yesteryear. He downed the mescal and opened the front door of the adobe.

Hoofs thudded down the street. A lone horseman was guiding a rangy dun past the piles of garbage. There was no one else in the street. The horseman wore a brass-buttoned blue shell jacket and a blue forage cap on his head. The sun flashed from the crossed sabers on the cap and from the linked brass shoulder scales.

"Hey, friend!" the trooper called out. "Where's head-quarters in this hole?"

"For Christ's sake!" said Ross. "Get off that horse! Lead him around the back!"

The trooper slid from his saddle and led the dun behind the adobe. He looked curiously at Ross as he opened the lean-to door.

"Get that dun in here," said Ross.

The trooper slid his hand down to his pistol. "Who the hell are you?"

"Ross Fletcher, from California. The rebels occupied Tucson this morning."

The trooper whistled. "Jesus God! I didn't know they was anywhere nearer than La Mesilla."

"There are no Federal troops closer than Fort Craig on the Rio Grande, and I'm not so damned sure about that now." Ross closed the door behind the dun. "Anyone see you?"

"Damned town looked like it was empty. Leastways where I came in. I'm Sam Ogden of the First California Volunteer Cavalry, with dispatches from Fort Yuma."

Ross peered through a crack in the door. "I'm the only Union man here in Tucson, Ogden. You'll have to get out of here in a hell of a hurry!"

"My horse is wore out. I've got dispatches for all troops in this vicinity to cooperate with the advance of the California Column."

Ross turned. Sweat ran down his body. This complicated matters. Ogden and his blue uniform would stand out like a lump of raised bread in the bright sunlight. "We'll have to sweat it out here until dark. You can't go through those streets now."

Ogden wiped the dust from his face. "There was some Pimas with me. They was supposed to scout ahead for me. They pulled foot last night. I came on alone."

"What's the news from the Coast?"

"Colonel Carleton has formed a column of California Volunteers to re-enforce Canby in New Mexico. Colonel West is already at Fort Yuma, strengthening the works. When we're ready we'll go through Arizona and New Mexico like a dose of salts!"

Ross spat. "Sibley has already defeated the Federals at the Valverde Fords. Santa Fe may have been taken by now. Texas troops are occupying Arizona from here to the New Mexico line. The Apaches are raising pure hell all over. You'll get a bellyful of fighting while you're administering those salts, Ogden."

Ogden paled. "I didn't know it was as bad as all that."

"I've been in trouble already. My brother was murdered this morning."

Ogden scratched in his short beard. "You said you was Ross Fletcher. Would your brother be John Fletcher?"

"Yes."

"I was told to look for him if I got into a scrape."

"Too late, So I'll have to help you. I'll be damned if I know what to do, though."

Ogden yawned. "I'm beat to a frazzle."

"Lie down on that straw. They may come looking for me. If they do we've got to shoot our way out of here."

Ogden nodded. He took his Sharps and checked the load, capped it and left it at half-cock. He placed his Colt on a box and dropped to the straw.

"There's an old adobe at the edge of town," said Ross. "The Mexes say it's haunted; they won't go near it. We'll try for it after dark. Until then we sweat."

"You sweat. I'm sleeping."

———

THE LONG HOURS DRIFTED PAST. Once a Mexican looked about the adobe. Ross gripped the dun's windpipe until the Mex drifted off. Now and then the fresh wind brought the sound of shouting and an occasional shot as Tucson celebrated in frontier style. Ross couldn't figure it out. Why had they left him alone?

Late in the afternoon feet grated on the *caliche*. A lean young Texan trooper came along the side of the adobe. Ross eased through the doorway.

The Texan eyed him. "Mr. Jenkins sent me to find you, sir. He spread the word around town you was gone. He figgered he'd better warn you to jump up some dust outa here if you was still around. Everybody's been taking the oath of allegiance. The townspeople been watching the show. They been gettin' likkered up considerable. I expect you'd better pull foot, sir."

Ross flipped the trooper a gold coin. "*Gracias.*"

The trooper fingered the coin. "You ain't a bad hombre, for a Yank. I got nothin' against you. If you was to have one of them bluebelly suits on, it would be different."

Ross grinned. "Maybe I will have one on some day."

"Suit yourself. Next time you see me I'll come a-shootin'." The trooper hesitated. "I seen them bury your brother, sir. Trooper Dobie said a few words over him. Dobie is an elder from the Baptist Church. It were a right nice service."

Ross looked away. "Thanks."

"Forget it" The trooper wandered off.

———

WHEN THE STREETS filled with velvet shadows, the two hunted men left the lean-to. They reached the abandoned adobe, an old warehouse, without incident, and led the dun inside. Ross barred the door.

Ogden wiped the sweat from his face. "Now it's getting me," he said nervously. "Let's hit the road."

Ross tensed. He had heard the grating of feet against the hard earth. He cocked his Colt. Ogden picked up his Sharps. Ross peered through a gaping shutter. A group of men stood at a corner a hundred yards from the adobe. One of them came silently toward the warehouse with a pistol in his hand. It was Yaqui. Ross held a hand against Ogden and shook his head. Ogden turned away and banged his carbine against the wall. Yaqui jumped to one side and fired toward the shutter. Pistols flashed in the darkness and slugs smashed against the adobe.

Something slapped through the thin wood of the shutters. Ogden grunted and gripped his belly. "In the gut," he said faintly and then pitched forward and hit the floor.

Ross knelt by the trooper. Ogden coughed thickly. Bloody foam flecked his lips. "I ..." he said, and then his eyes widened and his jaw went slack.

Ross snatched the dispatch case and ran toward the back of the building. The front door crashed open and guns flashed in the darkness. Ross dived through a window and rolled into a ditch. A man rounded the warehouse. Ross jerked out his Colt and fired, resting it on the lip of the ditch. The man staggered and went down.

Ross scrambled out of the ditch and raced toward *a jacal* with slugs keening from the hard earth behind him. He vaulted a fence and landed ankle-deep in filth. He raced across a littered patio and hurled himself over the far wall. He ran down a twisted alleyway with his breath harsh in his throat. Men yelled from the warehouse. A man ran in front of Ross. Ross drove into him with a shoulder and sent him down, hurdled him, and darted between two buildings and across the next street. The human hounds were in full cry down the next street.

Ross circled a wagon, ran down an alley and stopped behind Esquivel's gambling hall. It was a long chance, but he had no choice. His chances of surviving in the streets Were almost hopeless. He opened the rear door of the hall and stepped into the dimness. He tapped gently on Luz Campos's door.

"Quién es?" she called out.

"Luz! It's Ross!"

"Madre de Dios!" She opened the door and pulled him in. She clung to him as he shut the door. "I thought they had killed you! Thank the Blessed Virgin that you are safe."

Ross wiped the sweat from his face. "That's a matter of opinion," he said dryly. "Can I hide here?"

She pushed him back and looked at him. Tears cut grooves in the thick powder on her face. "But of course! There is no other place for you! They are hunting you like a rat!"

Ross picked up a mescal bottle and drank deeply. He leaned back against the wall with the sweat of exertion and fear running down his body.

"No one will come here. You can leave before dawn."

Ross let the hammer down on his Colt. "But can I trust you, Luz Campos?"

"Yes! Yes! Who else can you trust?"

"You've got me there." He sat down, watching her strip to the skin and slip into her petticoats and silk dress. Swiftly she sheathed her fine legs in stockings and slid her gaudy gaiters over the smooth silk. She thrust a comb into her thick hair and ran to the table. She repaired the damage to her make-up and applied her perfume. Then she turned and held up her face for a kiss. He got up and kissed her.

She held him close. "Thank the Blessed Virgin," she said. "I will act tonight, Ross. No one will ever know. Go with God!"

Ross closed the door behind her and reloaded his Colt. He placed a chair against the door and dropped onto the couch with his Colt in his hand.

CHAPTER SIX

The hand gripped his shoulder and shook him awake. Ross looked up into the shadowy face of Luz Campos. "Quiet!" she hissed. "It is an hour before dawn. You must leave. I thought you might be gone."

"Have you heard anything?"

"But naturally. A Union soldier was killed in an old warehouse at the edge of town. They know you were with him. One of the men who followed you is dead with a bullet in his belly. They have been searching the fields and streets for hours. There are Tejano patrols on all the roads."

"I'll go. Too dangerous here."

"Yes! Matt Risler and Nick Maxwell are even now with Amadeo in the gambling hall. They will notice I am gone from my table." She kissed him hard. "I am afraid for you, my man."

"You saved my life, Luz."

She held him close. "Before God, I did not know they planned to kill your brother. Now I must go. You will come back to Luz some day? Yes?"

Ross gripped her by the arms. "Who planned to kill John?"

She pulled away. "I don't know!"

"You do!"

"Perhaps it was Nick or Yaqui. I do not know. Get out of here!"

She whirled away and left the room.

Ross opened the rear window and pushed aside the shutter. Faint moonlight washed the alleyway. He would need money. He opened the dressing-table drawer. His hand closed on the butt of a pistol. He held it up. It was a silver-chased, four-barreled Sharps, the initials J. F. engraved on the brass backstrap. John Fletcher. An icy feeling came over him. Hastily he pawed through the drawer. He found some gold coins in a small jar. He put them in his pocket and then looked at the door.

She *must* have been involved in John's death.

"I'll be back, Luz Campos," he said softly.

Something grated in the hallway. He climbed out into the alley and ran across to a deep doorway. A head appeared at the open window. Nick Maxwell looked up and down the alleyway. Ross almost raised the Sharps pistol, but then he lowered it. His time would come.

When Maxwell disappeared, Ross fastened the dispatch case to his belt and made his way through the alley toward the north. The moon was almost gone. He skirted dry, half-filled wells, piles of refuse and decaying carcasses of animals. The town was quiet. In a few minutes he was at the shaky northern wall of the town. He climbed over it and dropped into the mesquite. Hoofs rattled on the nearby road like beans in a gourd. The horseman drew even with him. There was no mistaking the horse and the man. Mohave and Yaqui.

The breed was alone. Ross slipped back over the wall and behind a long building, stopping just short of the street. He drew his Colt and reversed it. Yaqui rode past. Ross moved like a great lean cat. He slid a hand under the breed's belt and slashed at the head with his gun barrel. The breed grunted and slid sideways, aided by a hard pull on the belt. The breed broke loose and turned. "Fletcher," he said.

"Yes, you bastard!"

Ross closed in. He slashed with the Colt. Yaqui was swift. He whipped out his long-bladed knife. Ross backhanded him with a left. He gripped the knife wrist and drove it up hard. They met chest to chest. Ross swung his Colt, but Yaqui twisted and took it on a shoulder. He butted Ross with his head, and Ross dropped the Colt.

They strained together silently. Ross twisted away, dragging down on Yaqui's left arm, thrusting his left hip into the lean belly of the breed. Yaqui gasped and jerked back his head. Ross slashed the exposed throat with the edge of his hand. The breed gagged and went down, dropping the knife.

Ross snatched up the knife as Yaqui thrust a hand inside his shirt and drew out a derringer. Ross swiped at the gun hand with the knife. He raised the blade and ripped at the flat face. The knife struck at the corner of the left eye and raked downward deeply to the point of the jaw. Blood spurted against Ross's face. Yaqui grunted and gripped his ripped face.

A door crashed open, flooding them with yellow lamplight. A Mexican stared at them. "The Yanqui gringo!" he yelled. "Pedro! Jorge! Come! There is a reward for him!"

Ross picked up his Colt and swung up on the big bay. He rammed his heels into Mohave's sides and turned the bay toward the road. The Mexican darted out into the street. Ross kneed the bay to one side. The Mexican went down under the big hoofs, screaming in agony. Ross bent low in the saddle and let the big bay out. They passed the town hall and hit the open road, heading north to freedom.

His Sharps was in its boot. The canteen was full. He looked back. Men shouted in the streets. But Mohave had a good lead and steel springs in his loins. It would take a damned good horse to catch up with him.

————

THE SUN TIPPED the Catalinas as Mohave drove on at a steady, mile-eating pace. There was no dust on the Tucson road behind them. Ross looked ahead. The nearest Union troops were at Fort Yuma, two hundred and fifty miles away, across Apache-infested country.

By noon the bay was tiring as they climbed toward Picacho Pass. To the northwest loomed the somber purple hump of Picacho Peak. There was a faint thread of dust miles behind Ross. He turned the bay from the road and dismounted, leading Mohave into a deep draw. Half a mile from the road he dropped the reins and grasped his Sharps. Three wagons showed on the road. Ross wiped his face. They were probably some of Hunter's Texans heading for the Pima villages and Ammi White's Mill for supplies.

White was a staunch Union man. Ross had heard that he had been forwarding information to California about rebel activities in the Tucson area. White received newspapers from La Mesilla and sent them on to Fort Yuma.

Ross stayed in hiding all afternoon, resting the bay. It gave him time to think. His whole world had collapsed about his ears in Tucson. The loss of his brother had now come fully home to him. Risler, Maxwell and Yaqui had probably had their dirty hands in the murder. Luz Campos was the enigma. She was mixed up with the scum, and Amadeo Esquivel was part and parcel of them too. Yet she had saved his life when every man's hand was against him. Yaqui would have told them of Ross's escape from Tucson. It might set them to thinking. Luz Campos would be treading on dangerous ground.

He slept for a time and then took out the miniature. Where was Isabel Rand? John had wanted to find her. Ross studied the oval face framed by the dark hair. John could have dismissed her as dead and kept the mine with Ross but it wasn't his way. Ross wondered if his brother could possibly have been in love with a woman twenty years his junior.

Ross looked out across the desert to the changing light on the mountains. He felt responsible for John's death. He had a big task ahead of him—to find Isabel Rand, and to avenge the death of John Fletcher. The latter would be the easiest. If Isabel Rand were still alive, he had to find her in a land where death ran riot.

CHAPTER SEVEN

In the days that followed his escape from Tucson, Ross traveled by night and rested by day. He skirted the Pima villages and reached the Gila. His beard grew and his body thinned out from lack of food. The sun lanced down steadily. In four days he reached Elk Wash and rested there for a full day. A lone Pima had sold him food and told him he had seen no federal troops. Two days after leaving Elk Wash he saw the dim Gilas hump themselves up out of the hazy southwest.

He had seen no marauding Apaches. Carelessly he rode on after dawn one day, looking for water. The big bay was in bad shape. A shallow *tinaja* in a big wash held inches of brown water. The sun was not up yet. A cold wind searched through the mesquite as he strained the gamy water through his scarf. The bay drank thirstily. Ross looked through his saddlebags for a scrap of food.

Suddenly a shot blasted the quiet. The slug whispered over his head. He jerked his Sharps from its sheath and slapped the bay on the rump. He hit the dirt and cocked the carbine. A rifle rang out. The slug rapped into the saddle.

Ross rested the Sharps on a rock and searched the brush with his eyes. Smoke drifted on the wind. A man raised his head from behind a rock, a calico headband holding back the thick black hair. Parallel lines of white bottom clay lined the hawklike face. Apache!

Ross squeezed off. The Sharps rammed back against his shoulder. Ross reloaded as he ran at a crouch to another position. The warrior was thrashing in the brush. Ross snapped a shot at a running buck. The slug keened off the Apache's rifle barrel. Mohave was down the draw. Ross whistled shrilly. The bay raised his head and then trotted toward him. A rifle spat. The bay snorted and reared. A worm of blood crept down his dusty flank. Ross swung himself up into the saddle and sank home the steel.

Three warriors lashed their mounts out of a hollow and raced to cut him off. Ross downed a horse. More Apaches came up from behind, spreading out into the dreaded pursuit crescent. The bay was tired but he drove on, spurred by the slug in his flank. Ross was in for it now; nothing to do but fight it out and save the last shot for himself.

They crossed a hard flat. A mesquite-covered knoll was ahead. Mohave staggered, almost done. Ross freed his feet from the stirrups and hit the ground running as Mohave went down in a welter of dust and sand. Ross plunged into the thicket as a crackle of gunfire broke out behind him. He dropped behind a rock and slid his Sharps forward, cursing at the sweat which clouded his vision. He reloaded and drove a slug into another horse. The Apaches vanished into a hollow, leaving a veil of dust and powder-smoke to mark their passage.

The warrior whose horse had been downed rolled out of a mesquite bush. His upper body jerked in a hopeless struggle against the paralysis which bound his lower legs from a broken spine. Ross spat and then took out his Colt, placing it on the rock. The buck stopped thrashing, but the early morning wind fluttered his clothing.

Minutes drifted past. The bay got to his feet and stood there, with his legs spread wide and his head hanging down. Blood dripped from his mouth. Then he fell sideways and lay still. Ross looked away. It seemed as though everything he loved was slated for violent death.

The brush rustled at the far side of the knoll. A moccasined foot showed beneath a bush. Ross sighted about where the rest of the Apache should be and squeezed the trigger. The brush thrashed and then was still except for the swaying wind.

Smoke puffed from behind a rock, followed by a bellowing discharge. The sand spurted over Ross. Damned Indians never could shoot worth a tinker's dam. Ross rolled over and reloaded. He bellied fifty feet along the earth and lay down behind a rock ledge. A curious gecko lizard eyed him and then darted for cover.

A rifle barrel slid out from the brush. Ross fired too quickly, and the rifle vanished. Ross checked his Colt and replaced a lost cap. He reloaded the Sharps and looked back over his shoulder. A shallow draw meandered off to the north. A bird called from the brush and was answered by another. The Apaches were moving in.

Ross crawled to the draw, slid into it, and then ran softly along it. Feet slapped against the ground, followed by a quick rush of gravel. Ross whirled. A warrior was thirty feet from him, closing in swiftly. The Sharps crashed from hip level. The gut-shot buck pitched forward and released his soul to the House of Spirits.

Ross raced up the draw. He was beat, but fear lashed him on with raking spurs. Six warriors broke from the brush and closed in. Ross slid a cartridge into the carbine and closed the breech. He capped it. Out of water, out of food, no horse. Salt, pepper and gravel in the grease. But a man could always die fighting.

The Apaches spread out, rifles raised, watching the big man who crouched behind a rock. They had lost too many men to let this white-eye get away.

Ross felt cold sweat work down his body. A sudden calmness seemed to steady him. There was no use in looking back for help. He drew cracked lips back. "Come on," he said softly. "Let's make a real Donnybrook out of this, you stinking bastards."

Hoofs drummed behind him to the west. More of them. Ross took out John's multi-shot and placed it on a rock.

The warriors were looking off to the west. One of them yelled. They quirted their ponies down the draw, hell-bent and to hell with the hindmost. Ross turned. A dozen horsemen in glorious dusty blue were hammering toward the draw with carbines resting on their hips. Ross grinned, wincing as his lips cracked afresh. He shot offhand at the last warrior. The slug creased a paint pony. The Apaches yelled as though the devil whipped them on. Dust whirled up from the draw.

The troopers opened fire. They crashed down into the draw and spurred their big horses after the swifter ponies. A big trooper slid to a halt near Ross. Sergeant's chevrons were on the sleeves of his jacket. "Just in time, mister," he said with a dusty grin. "Just in time."

Carbines rattled out on the flats. Ross shoved back his hat and wiped the cold sweat from his face. He said hoarsely, "Now I know what an angel looks like."

The sunburned non-com slid from his big dun. "Never been called an angel before. I'm Sergeant Mike Duncan, of Cremoney's Company B, First California Volunteer Cavalry."

Ross gripped the big hand.

Duncan looked out across the flats. "We heard the firing and saw you skite like hell into the brush. It was a close one, mister."

Duncan was a big-bodied man, with short, bowed legs, designed to grip a McClellan. His muscular thighs seemed ready to burst through the material of his trousers. His face looked as if it had been roughhewn out of a solid block of mahogany, with his beak of a nose slanted jauntily to one side from some tremendous blow of the past. His light-gray eyes were startling against the tan of his face.

"Who are you?" asked Duncan. "And what in hell's name were you doing out here alone holding off them Apaches?"

"The name is Fletcher. Ross Fletcher, of California. I was riding from Tucson to Fort Yuma. They caught me at the only damned waterhole I found for thirty miles. They got my horse. I was cold-decked."

Duncan looked down at the cocked Sharps. "Quick way out, eh?"

Ross nodded. He let down the hammer of the pistol. "I've seen what they can do to a prisoner."

Duncan eyed his men gathering at the lip of the draw.

"We're on patrol from Fort Yuma. Camped at San Cristobal Wash last night." He eyed Ross shrewdly. "Tucson, eh? Any secesh there yet?"

"Yes. A full company of Texas Mounted Rifles. Seems like I'm the only Yankee between here and the Rio Grande. Leastways, I *was*."

Duncan looked at the dispatch case. Ross unhooked it and handed it to him. "You'd better take charge of this. Private Sam Ogden of the Second California was killed by secesh in Tucson. I got away with this."

Duncan took the case. "Poor bastard. He was so damned sure he'd make it. He started out with four other troopers. Guess the Mohaves or the Apaches got them."

A corporal stood up in his stirrups. "Got two of them, Dunc! The rest scattered!"

"Form over here." Duncan shoved back his forage cap. "Ross Fletcher? We were told to look out for you and your brother. Colonel wanted to see your brother."

Ross picked up his weapons. "John was murdered by secesh in Tucson."

"Too bad. Colonel West wanted to commission John in our artillery section. We heard he had quite a record in the Mex war."

Ross nodded. "One of the best."

"What's doing in Tucson?"

"There are about a hundred Texas Mounted Rifles there. Captain Sherrod Hunter's Company A."

Duncan spat dryly. "We're concentratin' two thousand men at Fort Yuma for the march east to New Mexico. You'll be able to get a horse at Yuma for the rest of your trip."

Ross grounded his carbine. His hard eyes held Duncan's. "I'm going back—with the California Column, or alone. I've got a score or two to settle."

"You know that country?"

"Yes. I prospected there before the war."

"We can use good scouts."

"I'm on, Duncan."

"Bueno! One of the boys can ride you double. Captain Cremoney will be glad of what you have to tell him about Tucson."

"Cremoney? Would that be the man known to the Apaches as Iron Belt?"

"Yes. He was with Kearney in New Mexico. He knows the Apaches better than any white man I ever met."

"He'll need his knowledge. They're raising hell and stoking the fire."

Ross swung up behind a little trooper, and looked back at Mohave. Already a *zopilote,* a great land buzzard, was circling high overhead waiting for the troopers to clear the way for the forthcoming feast.

The little trooper spoke over his shoulder. "You got anything on that horse you want?"

"No."

"Rough. Losing a horse is worse than losing a woman."

A lean trooper grinned. "What the hell would you know about that, Ed? You ain't ever had a good woman."

"Up your butt, Slim!"

Corporal Owsley held up an Apache belt studded with turquoise. "Got me a remembrance," he said.

"Lucky you didn't get a slug in your rump," said Ed.

Ross looked back at the site of the scrap. He thought

of Cremoney, the tough soldier who had ridden right into the camp of Mangus Colorado, wearing four Colts at his belt, a man who spoke fluent Apache and who had once claimed Red Sleeves as his friend. He would be a good commander with whom to go to war.

Company B was bivouacked near the great wash. The tanned troopers eyed Ross curiously as he slid from the horse and walked with Duncan to the small tent before which fluttered the company guidon.

Cremoney was a well-built man. He listened silently to Ross's story, refilling the whisky glasses from time to time. Cremoney had grayed a great deal since the last time Ross had seen him in Monterrey. His eyes were sharp and fearless, with a hidden touch of laughter in them as though he enjoyed some vast secret joke at the world's expense.

Cremoney lit up a cigar as Ross finished. "So John is gone," he said quietly. "I knew him in San Bernardino some years ago. We had hoped he would join up with us as an artillery officer."

Cremoney looked out on the sunlit desert and spoke around his cigar. "Big things are going to happen, Fletcher. Colonel Carleton has a fine force of the best men in California. We were originally recruited to open up and guard the overland mail, but when the news of Sibley's invasion of New Mexico came to California we were diverted here by Wright. He's the commanding officer of the Department of California. We have detachments marching from Los Angeles. Quite a few camped at Warner's Ranch. Fort Yuma is being strengthened and garrisoned by others—two thousand Californians ready to blow Sibley and his damned Texans back to San Antone."

Ross puffed at his cigar and watched the smoke drift out of the tent. "It won't be easy. There's been a drought. The summer heat will soon be here. The waterholes are dry now."

Cremoney waved a hand. "Carleton is a driver as well as an organizer. He'll get us through."

"I'd like to enlist, sir."

"As a soldier?"

"Duncan said you needed scouts."

"We do. Are you interested?"

"Yes. I know the country. Besides, I have some personal affairs to settle in Tucson."

Cremoney studied the hard-bitten man across from him. He had smelled hell lately. "About John's death, I take it?"

"And some other matters."

"You'll be damned busy scouting."

"The California Column may be damned busy too, sir. Sibley has already whipped Canby at the Valverde Fords. He is supposed to be pushing on to Santa Fe and Fort Union. Captain Hunter claimed the secesh easily whipped Canby's regulars."

Cremoney spat. "Secesh propaganda! If anyone was beaten at Valverde Fords it wasn't the regulars. We know the bulk of Canby's force is composed of Mex *paisanos* who dirty their baggy drawers if you mention a Tejano."

"I saw Hunter's men. Young and hard in the prat. They have the damnedest assembly of weapons I ever saw, but they seem to know how to use them."

Cremoney pulled back the tent flap. His men were lining up for breakfast at their mess fires. "See them? Most of them are miners from Calaveras and Amador Counties. Easterners and Middlewesterners. We have skilled teamsters, wagon bosses, blacksmiths, farriers, cooks and roustabouts. We have vast stores of compressed potatoes, dessicated vegetables, pork, bacon, ham, flour, beans, rice, tea, coffee, sugar, molasses, vinegar, pickles, candles, soap, salt, lime juice, whisky, medical supplies, dried apples, black pepper and pemmican."

"Sounds like the inventory of a general store," said Ross dryly.

"It is. We've even got trading materials for the Indians we encounter."

The odors of coffee and bacon came to Ross. He suddenly realized how hungry he was.

Cremoney refilled the glasses. "We'll return to Fort Yuma tomorrow. You can enlist there. I'd like to have you in this company, Fletcher, but I warn you I intend to draw first blood from those rebels in Tucson."

Ross drained his glass. "I might beat you to that, sir."

Cremoney stood up. "Any news about the Apaches?"

"I've heard it said that Mangus Colorado and Cochise might ally themselves."

Cremoney picked a piece of tobacco from his lower lip. "So? I don't like the sound of that."

"The column can take care of them."

Cremoney looked east. "I'm not so sure. Each of them is dangerous enough alone. The only way we whites have ever been able to handle Indians is because we ally ourselves and fight long after we are supposed to be whipped. Now that the troops have evacuated many of the frontier forts in Indian country, the hostiles might get sharp enough to join together. Then there will be hell to pay, Fletcher."

Ross left the tent. Cremoney watched him as he ate at a squad fire. He'd be a welcome recruit, but there was more than a desire to win the war in that hard-pratted bastard. There was a coldness deep in his gray eyes. The coldness of impending death for someone. . . .

That night huge raindrops lashed the desert in a frenzy, while the Thunder People plied their great bows and shot their lightning arrows through the wet murk. Ross lay in his tent and listened to the rain slash against the canvas. It was a sure-enough male rain. The water crept in rivulets across the earthen floor. Before dawn the washes would be filled with roaring, turgid floods which would sweep everything before them. Ross listened to the cursing troopers as they shifted their blankets. The water wouldn't bother him. He hoped to God it would pour down in a heavier flood. It would delay the march of the column for a time, until the roads dried, but it would also fill the waterholes and the shallow rivers.

He went to sleep. For the first time in days he felt that his luck had changed.

CHAPTER EIGHT

F ort Yuma squatted on the western bluffs above
the muddy Colorado. Below the fort was the
little adobe settlement of Jaegerville with its big
ferryboat. The view from the fort was breathtaking, but
the men of Companies B, H and I of the First California
Volunteer Infantry, and Cremoney's Company B, First
California Volunteer Cavalry, had been there since
November, after having relieved the Sixth U.S. Infantry.
They were getting damned sick of building fortifications
to protect Fort Yuma, a million-dollar investment of
government funds.

Colonel Joseph Rodman "Dandy" West had his
hands full strengthening the post, keeping a wary eye
on the war between the Yumas and the allied Mari-
copas and Pimas. Dandy West wanted to go east and
boot the Texans out of Tucson. Colonel Carleton was
pushing men and supplies on from Camp Warner in
California. Private Ross Fletcher of Cremoney's
Company B practiced right and left moulinets with his
shiny new saber, swung a pick and shovel in the three-
hundred-and-fifty-foot fortification west of the fort,
rode in fours with the rest of the company, and got
damned sick of soldiering at Fort Yuma while his

enemies drank mescal in Amadeo's gambling hall in Tucson.

The Thunder People played hell with Arizona and California, sluicing down male rains which swelled the roaring Colorado, prevented the shallow draft river steamers from bringing up transshipped supplies from the Gulf of California, and turned the desert roads into quagmires.

The barracks leaked. The earth fortifications melted and ran down into the gullies. The parade ground *caliche* turned into a whitish paste. The Californians turned out for duty in their waterproof talmas and cursed the rain as only Californians can. But the eastern washes were full. The waterholes overflowed. Once the rain stopped there would be nothing to prevent the eastward movement against Tucson and New Mexico. They had to have patience.

But supplies were piling up steadily as Carleton worked like a queen bee in a hive, keeping his blue-clad drones hard at it. Fort Yuma received quantities of saddles, bridles, harness, carbines, sabers, revolvers, ammunition, knapsacks, haversacks, horseshoes and horseshoe nails, charcoal for blacksmiths' tires, nosebags and hobbles, rope, water kegs, bedding and cooking utensils and all the vast impedimenta required by a civilized army involved in uncivilized warfare.

Ross left the mess hall one watery morning and splashed his way across the barracks, eying the water which almost surrounded the post. He stopped under the ramada and shook the water from his talma. A tall man was dismounting from a sorrel in front of headquarters. Ross went cold inside. There was no mistaking the spare figure of Matt Risler. The gambler tethered his sorrel and walked into headquarters.

"What are you staring at, Ross?"

Ross turned to see Sergeant Duncan.

The sergeant stared at him. "By Christ," he said. "What did I say to rile you?"

Ross shook his head. "Nothing."

Duncan glanced at the sorrel. "That man one of them?"

"Yes. Matt Risler. Gambler. Kingpin in Tucson."

Duncan took his pipe from his mouth. "Now don't get any ideas, soldier. You've got no proof he was involved in your brother's murder."

Ross gripped big fists. "No," he said quietly, "but I'd copper the bet. What the hell is he doing here?"

Duncan shrugged. "There are a lot of queer birds flying about this war, Ross."

"Vultures."

"That may be. Tell you what. I've got some paper-work over at headquarters this cheerful morning. I'll keep my off ear peeled and see what I can learn."

"*Gracias.*"

"The company is to stay in barracks and furbish up their weapons." Duncan turned his pipe upside down to keep the rain out of it, and then started across the parade ground. He turned. "I know what you're thinking," he said; "you're a soldier now. Keep away from him until you're sure he's involved. Hear?"

Ross nodded. He watched the burly non-com cross the soaked parade ground and enter headquarters. Duncan knew every latrine rumor in the service. There wasn't much going on that he didn't know about. Ross would have to play his cards close to the belly until he knew what Risler had in his mind.

———

ROSS WORKED at his weapons while the rest of the platoon did the same. Sharps carbines, Navy Colts and Chicopee sabers were cleaned and polished while the minutes dragged on.

Little Eddie Neiderdecke shifted his chew of spit-or-drown. "Hear tell Captain McCleave and two of his men was captured at Ammi White's Mill last week."

Slim Hause looked up. "Where'd you hear that? In the sanitary sinks?"

"Hell no! I was orderly last night at headquarters. A breed Pima came in with the news. Seems as though Captain Sherrod Hunter was asleep in White's house when McCleave showed up with two men. Hunter's men bagged them."

Corporal Owsley yanked his pull-through out of the barrel of his Sharps. "Turned the damned tables," he said. "That was McCleave's job. To capture Hunter."

Eddie nodded. "That ain't all. Hunter declared White's chickens and hawgs as contraband and took 'em. Wrecked the flour mill and doled out three hundred thousand pounds of flour to the Pimas after maken' 'em promise they wouldn't give us any."

"That's Company A," said Slim wisely. "Walking into a trap. Now if that had been B Company ..."

Eddie grinned. "We would have been strung up by Hunter."

Slim hefted his Chicopee. "Oh, I don't know. What do you think, Ross?"

Ross had been only half listening. He looked up. "We could go through Hunter's men like a dose of salts."

"Jesus," said Amos Bracken, a miner from Calaveras County, "you sure are getting bloodthirsty, Ross. You never were like that at the diggings."

"Times have changed, Amos." Ross got up and walked to the door and looked across at headquarters.

"He's got some kind of bitin' bug up his butt," said Eddie.

Duncan appeared at the door of headquarters and splashed across to Ross. He jerked his head. Ross walked to the end of the ramada with him. Duncan handed him a super. "Swiped it from West's desk," he said.

Ross lit up. "Well?"

Duncan looked about to see if anyone was near. "Risler and West are as thick as thieves," he said quietly.

"Seems as though Risler brought in a detailed report on rebel activities in Tucson."

"You're joshing!"

"Damn it! No! Risler is a federal secret agent."

Ross took the cigar from his mouth. "For Christ's sake!"

Duncan leaned against the wall and stroked his battered pipe. "Where does that leave you?"

"It hasn't changed anything. My brother was murdered."

"Maybe Risler was playing a part?"

Ross looked at the dripping sorrel. "That cold-gutted shark is out for no one but himself, Mike. I'd stake my life on that."

"Well, you'd better keep your mouth shut, then."

"Why?"

Duncan took his pipe from his mouth. "It seems as though Matt Risler ain't just *Mister* Risler. Colonel West is going to swear him into the service."

"I'd like to see him in this company."

"You won't. He'll be Captain Matthew Risler, Staff Officer."

Ross stared at Duncan. "Jesus! Is West mad?"

"No. Risler was in the army before the war. He's come back to the fold, for better or for worse, until death do us part."

Ross threw down his cigar and ground it under a boot heel. "When do we leave this hole?"

"Who knows? When the rains allow the troops at Warner's ranch to collect here. Remember what I told you? Keep away from him until you're sure he's involved. When you're sure you can take care of him."

"I will."

Duncan grinned. "Shots can go wild in battle, Ross. I've seen more than one man, or officer, accidentally shot by his own men."

Ross looked into the hard eyes of the veteran. "No," he said quietly. "When the time comes I want Matt

Risler to *know* who killed him." He turned on a heel and walked into the barracks.

Duncan knocked out his pipe. "I wouldn't want you thinking about me that way, Ross," he said, "or I'd already be numbering my days."

Matt Risler left Fort Yuma that afternoon with the mail party riding west to Warner's ranch. Ross did not know if Risler knew he was at Fort Yuma. It was just as well, for Ross had to bide his time. There was an unholy haste in Ross to get back to Tucson. There was the unsettled matter of Nick Maxwell and Yaqui. There was also the matter of Isabel Rand. Gradually she had begun to take up more and more of his thoughts.

CHAPTER NINE

The Pima scouts were restless. Their hide sandals husked on the hard earth as they flitted through the mesquite, eying the thread of yellow dust which rose near Picacho Pass. Ross swung down from his dun. He slanted his forage cap low over his eyes and studied the dust. There were no federal troops ahead of Calloway's advance command. The only sign they had seen of Hunter's Mounted Rifles had been some burned haystacks near the Pima villages.

Sergeant Mike Duncan kneed his horse close to Ross. "What do you make of it?" he asked.

Ross shook his head. " 'Paches, maybe. The Pimas hate their guts."

"They afraid of them?"

"I don't think so."

A Pima stood up on a sandy knoll and stared eastward. The wind fluttered his cotton breechclout and the sun shone on the barrel of his muzzle-loading rifle.

Duncan slid down to the ground and uncorked his canteen, handing it to Ross. "You've been a helluva lot more sociable since we left Fort Yuma," he said.

Ross sipped the water and swilled it about his mouth. "I don't like drilling."

"But you like scouting?"

Ross grinned. "If you hadn't asked for me as scout with Calloway's detachment, I swear to God I would have gone over the hill and followed that bastard Risler."

Duncan sipped from the canteen. "You silly bastard," he said. "They would have caught you, shaved your hard head and drummed you out."

"Poor old soldier. Poor old soldier. Lashed and shaved and sent to hell, because he wouldn't soldier well."

"You hit it, sonny."

Two miles behind them, Calloway's command of his own Company I, First Infantry, a detachment of Company A, First Cavalry under Lieutenant Jim Barrett, Company D, First Cavalry, and a detachment of Company K, First Infantry under Lieutenant Jeremiah Phelan, and two mountain howitzers, waited in a dry wash while the scouts investigated the mysterious trailing dust.

Duncan looked back toward the west. "Calloway is nervous," he said.

"He's been nervous ever since we were ordered on to Tucson."

"He ain't spoiling for a fight like you are."

"Up your butt, sarge," said Ross disrespectfully.

"You'll never make a soldier!"

"It isn't my main ambition, if that's what you mean."

One of the Pimas flitted through the brush like a prowling coyote.

"Here comes the 'bitter man' to report," said Ross.

"What the hell does that mean?"

"Christ, but you're ignorant. How'd you ever get those stripes?"

Duncan rubbed his right chevrons with his left hand. "Shined my buttons. Always showed up at reveille, drunk or sober. Kept my bowels and ears open and my mouth shut."

"That figures," said Ross dryly.

"You didn't answer my question."

"The bitter man is a war leader."

"Can he speak English?"

"Better than you."

"Go to hell!"

Ross watched the lithe Pima come through the brush. In the few days they had been on the way from Fort Yuma he had worked with the Pimas. He had a knack for languages, and between his learning some of the key Pima words, and the knowledge of English that most of the Pimas had acquired from long friendship with the whites, he had got along well.

The bitter man stopped in front of the two white scouts. "Soldiers," he said.

"Ours?" asked Ross.

"Pinyi maach."

"What the hell is that?" asked Duncan.

"He said he didn't know. It figures they must be Texans. We haven't any of our men out there."

Ross touched his uniform. "Do they wear this color?" he asked.

The Pima shook his head. He reached over and touched Ross's gray undershirt where it showed through his duck cavalry shell jacket. "So!"

"Rebels," said Ross.

"How many?"

Ross held up his hands. "How many?"

The Pima wiped the sweat from his broad face. He held up one hand three times and then held up two fingers.

"Seventeen," said Ross.

"My," said Duncan sarcastically, "you *do* speak the language like a native."

Ross grinned. "Comes easy to a man of intelligence."

"My God!"

"What do we do?"

Duncan swung up on his horse. "Stay here. I'll report to Calloway."

"Do hurry, Sergeant."

Ross eyed the Pima. The Indian was muttering incantations. He had been picked to be the bitter man because of his courage and unwillingness to give in to the enemy, as well as his ability to make incantations which would take away the enemy's power.

The Pimas were peaceful farmers, like their cousins, the Papagos, or Bean People. They hated war but were not afraid to fight their hereditary enemies, the predatory Apaches. The bitter man carried a muzzle-loader by a leather sling. At his waist hung a hardwood club shaped like a big potato masher.

His thick black hair was bound at the nape of the neck by a string, and he had thrust a stick, painted in primary colors, through the hair knot.

The bitter man made a motion as though smoking. Ross gave him a dry cigar and watched the warrior light it and bathe himself in the smoke to purify him. It was in his mind that he was going into battle.

The rest of the Pima scouts were watching the dust. It did not seem to move very fast. Ross checked his Sharps and Colt. He did not even look at the damned cumbersome Chicopee saber, which hung, razor-sharp, in its sheath beside the saddle.

Dust rose to the west. Duncan hammered up with Lieutenant Jim Barrett and his twelve troopers from A Company of the First Cavalry.

Barrett drew rein. "What is it, Fletcher?" he asked.

Ross stood up. "Seventeen rebels, Mr. Barrett."

Barrett smiled. "Captain Calloway has ordered me to flank them while he brings on the rest of the detachment. You and Duncan will accompany me."

"It might be only a picket detail," said Ross. "There might be more of them than we know about, sir."

Barrett drew his Colt and checked the caps. "You're not worried, are you?"

Ross flushed. "I don't believe in sticking my neck out, sir."

Some of the troopers grinned behind Barrett's back

nervously, thought Ross. He swung up on his dun and followed Barrett in a wide detour through the brush. The Pimas, with the exception of the bitter man, had vanished as silently as coyotes.

———

THE BIG BULK of Picacho Peak loomed over the pass. The dust was thicker now, roiling up from the brush. The sun glinted on metal. Ross saw a mounted man through the dust. His floppy hat bobbed up and down. Texan. There was a curious uneasy feeling in Ross as he drew rein behind Barrett.

Barrett turned. "Check carbines and revolving pistols," he said.

Metal rattled as breechblocks were lowered on carbines and Colt cylinders were twirled. Some of the troopers eased their big sabers partway from their sheaths and slammed them back with a ring of metal.

"Forward, ho!" yelled Barrett as he set the steel to his big horse.

They clattered forward over the rough ground. Now they could see the Texans, riding hard away from the Federals. Barrett's face was set as he led the pounding pursuit. The bitter man was left behind in the thick veil of dust.

The low buildings of Picacho Station showed through the dust. Barrett thundered on, followed by his jangling little command. Duncan looked at Ross and shrugged.

A carbine popped from the Texan ranks. Barrett freed his pistol and cocked it, urging on his horse. Then there was a sudden rattle of firing from the Texans who had turned to stand at bay. Slugs whispered over the heads of the Californians. Ross bent low in his saddle and swung his carbine forward on its sling, unsnapping the swivel.

Quickly the gap closed. A Californian grunted and threw up his arms, sliding from his saddle to be lost in the moiling dust. Another yelled and pulled aside, gripping a bloody arm. Barrett ignored his losses. Duncan fired his carbine and slung it, ripping free his Colt.

They were close now. Carbines and pistols rattled through the smoke and dust. A Texan raised a muzzle-loading musketoon and fired point-blank at Barrett. The officer shuddered with the impact of the heavy slug and then went down, hitting hard and rolling over on the ground.

Ross fired. A Texan turned his horse away, gripping his left shoulder. The fight became a whirling kaleido-scope of horses and men, circling and firing at top speed. A slug skinned over Ross's left shoulder, tearing off his scaled epaulet. He pumped out three shots from his Colt.

Suddenly the Texans pulled foot, firing back as they raced off. Ross saw one of them jump free from his saddle as his horse went down. Ross spurred toward him and thrust his pistol forward. "Up with the hands!" he yelled. "Grab your ears!"

The Texan was hardly more than a kid. He raised his hands.

His white teeth showed against his dusty face as he grinned. "Don't shoot, Yank," he said. "You got me!"

The fight was over almost as suddenly as it had started. Duncan cantered up to Ross. "Barrett is dead," he said. "Never knew what hit him."

Ross nodded. "He was so damned anxious to have a fight. He got it."

Duncan looked at the retreating Texans. "We lost Barrett, and two troopers killed. Three wounded."

Ross looked down at his prisoner. "I wounded one of them."

The Texan nodded. "Two of the boys was hit."

Four Californians flushed two more prisoners from the brush. The dust was settling, but the sun glinted on metal near the position of the Texans. They were still ready to fight.

Ross swung down from his dun and reloaded his Sharps. A skinny Californian spurred his horse through the dust, yelling like a Comanche, brandishing his big saber. "They killed my bunkie!" he yelled hoarsely. He raced toward the prisoner Ross had captured.

The Texan paled. "Jesus!" he said. "He's gonna kill me, Yank!"

Ross shoved the Texan behind the dun. The Californian raised his saber for a blow, kneeing his horse savagely to one side. The saber swept down. Ross thrust up his Sharps and parried the vicious blow. Steel rang on steel. The trooper sagged from the saddle with the effort of the blow, dropping the saber from nerveless fingers. He pawed at his Colt with his left hand. Ross reversed his carbine, stepped in close, and thudded the steel-shod butt home behind the Californian's ear. He dropped to the ground and lay still.

Duncan cursed as he disarmed the unconscious trooper. "Too damned close for comfort," he said.

Ross nodded. The saber had cut into the Sharps barrel, inches from his left hand. He looked at the shaken Texan. "Where did you come from?"

"Pima villages. We was confiscating provisions they was goin' to send to Fort Yuma."

"Who was in command?"

"Lieutenant Jack Swilling. We're from Hunter's Company, Texas Mounted Rifles."

"How many Texans are there in Tucson?"

The captive licked his cracked lips. "Couple hundred. More on the way from the Rio Grande. You'd better jump up some dust outa here. We aim to run you Yanks plumb back to Fort Yuma."

Duncan spat. "You little rebel craphead," he said, "the war is over for you. Don't talk so God-damned big!"

Dust moiled up from behind the small party of Californians. The sun reflected from metal.

"Calloway," said Ross.

Duncan nodded. He waved his arm to gather the members of the detachment. "Corporal," he said, "take care of the wounded. Get the dead together. Round up the stray horses."

Ross jerked his head at the kid. "Get over there with your friends," he said.

The detachment jingled up from the west. Two stubby howitzers bounced along the ruts. Calloway drew rein. Duncan reported to him. The officer was nervous. He focused his field glasses on the Texans.

"They're leaving," said Lieutenant Baldwin. "Shall I pursue them, sir?"

Calloway shook his head.

Baldwin flushed. "I can catch them, sir."

"No!"

The officers gathered near Calloway, glancing at the body of Jim Barrett. Their faces were set beneath the dust. Lieutenant Jeremiah Phelan looked at the distant Texans. "Let's get them, Captain," he urged.

Calloway didn't answer. Precious minutes ticked past. Ross led up his dun and waited for the order. The Californians kept looking at the irresolute Calloway. The officer lowered his glasses and cased them.

"Give me the word," said Baldwin.

Calloway shook his head. "We'll return for reinforcements."

"Jesus Christ!" said Ross.

Calloway looked at him. "If I hear any more from you, soldier," he said, "I'll have you bucked and gagged!"

Duncan saluted. "Shall I go ahead and scout, sir?"

Calloway bit his lip. "Stay here in the pass with your men. If there are no signs of pursuit you will return to Stanwix Station. If there are signs of pursuit, you will harass the enemy to the best of your ability, send a courier on after us with a full report as to the number of the enemy, and escape as best you can."

Duncan saluted again.

Calloway looked at the bodies of the men. "Poor Barrett," he said. "He was so damned anxious to get his share of glory. See that they are buried, Mr. Phelan. We will remain here, resting the horses, until after the service for the dead."

Ross and Duncan rode east followed by five troopers who had been designated as scouts. They drew rein a mile from the main body. The Texans had pulled foot.

"If there are no signs of pursuit," said Ross sarcastically, "you will return to Stanwix Station."

Duncan shrugged. "You're in the army now," he said philosophically. "You might as well get used to the ways of officers."

"Too damned bad Barrett was killed. He'd have gone on and taken all of them."

Duncan spat. "Don't get any ideas of chasin' them Texicans alone, Ross."

"Calloway could have gone on and bagged Hunter and his men. We'd have Tucson by the rump."

"Dandy West will soon be up. He won't fool around. Be patient, damn it! You'll get to Tucson yet."

"Since I've put on this damned blue suit it's been nothing but wait, wait, wait! I'm sick of it, Mike."

Back in the pass they buried Jim Barrett and his two men. Then Calloway, like the legendary Duke of York, after having marched his men up the hill marched them down again, while Swilling's fourteen men, as scared as Calloway, cut the wind for Tucson.

CHAPTER TEN

The morning of May 20th dawned bright and clear. The men of Company B, First California Cavalry, stood to horse watching the four infantry companies slog off through the dust east on the Tucson road. Their knapsacks bobbed and the sun flashed from their bayonets.

Colonel West waved a hand to Captain Emil Fritz. "You may move on when ready," he said.

Ross and Sergeant Duncan stood by their horses. There was an eagerness in Ross as he waited. In the long weeks since he had left Tucson, alone and harried, he had begun to think of deserting so that he could come back by himself. Since the skirmish at Picacho Pass, he had sweated blood while the Californians had worked at Ammi White's Mill, throwing up an earthwork which had been named Fort Barrett. Slowly more detachments of the column had arrived at the Pima villages. Scarcity of water had forced West to move only four companies at a time, at twenty-four-hour intervals, from Fort Yuma to the Pima villages. May 15th, Colonel West had advanced from the Pima villages, leaving the overland route at Sacatone Station, past White's ranch, through the Casas

Grandes, to reoccupy old Fort Breckinridge near the confluence of the Gila and the San Pedro.

Duncan shifted his feet. "You think the Pimas were right in saying the Rebs have more troops than we have, Ross?"

"I don't give a fiddler's damn how many they have."

Duncan grinned slyly. "They say they have a mile of rifle pits fully manned."

"Jesus! They haven't got enough Texicans to man a good-sized bar!"

Fritz moved out, sending Ross, Duncan and several other scouts ahead. Fritz was to come in on the east side of the town with the first platoon. Lieutenant Juan Francisco Guirado, with the second platoon, was to come in on the north side, while the beetle crushers were to come in on the road from the west.

Behind the scouts the trumpet sounded, forming the troopers into a column of fours. They moved out across the fields with a jangling of metal and a squeaking of saddle leather. The guidon snapped in the morning breeze.

"How's the liquor in Tucson?" asked Duncan.

"It'll keep that rum blossom you wear for a nose in the right shade, Mike."

"You've seen plenty of this country through the bottom of a glass, amigo."

"Let's cut stick. I'm tired of this damned dawdling."

"Keno!"

"Any objection to a soldier killing a few civilians by accident, Mike?"

Duncan shrugged. "Once you shoot you can't tell where a bullet will end. As the Mexes say, 'God will separate the souls.'"

Ross could see the new greenery along the Santa Cruz. Water glinted in an irrigation ditch. A *paisano* stared at the dusty troopers and dropped his hoe. He bounded over a fence and skittered like some ungainly bird for the town wall, holding his steeple hat tight on his head.

"We're making enough noise to awaken the dead," called Ross.

Jack rabbits hopped out of the brush, eyed the troopers, and then bounded off like the scared *paisano*. A gorged hawk rose almost under the hoofs of the scouts' horses and winged off slowly, leaving a ravaged rabbit carcass behind.

Ross and Duncan circled in toward the quiet town. There was no sign of life. No freshly turned earth to denote rifle pits. No sun flashing on weapons. Fritz and his men drew rein behind the scouts and waited.

Ross turned in his saddle. "Damned if I see any rebels," he said.

From the west side of town they heard the deep notes of an infantry bugle. Dust swirled up from the north where Guirado's platoon was forming a long line.

"What are we waiting for?" asked Ross testily.

"Jesus, but you're hot! All right, sonny. Here we go!" Duncan turned and waved his arm.

Fritz's platoon formed a line. Sabers flashed in the sun. Colts were gripped in left hands. Fritz bawled out his command. The platoon started forward in an uneven line. They came forward at a walk through the mesquite jungle, then changed into a trot.

Ross left his saber in its sheath and drew his Colt. They fell in at the flank of the platoon. Within a hundred yards of the houses the platoon surged forward in the charge. Dogs and cats scattered from in front of the pounding hoofs. There wasn't a soul in the dusty streets. They swept past the warehouse where Sam Ogden had been killed. Ahead of them was the plaza. Not a rifle or pistol popped. The smashing of the hoofs echoed from the silent houses. Then the plaza was right in front of them. A column of blue-clad infantry was double-quicking into the plaza from the west. Guirado's platoon hammered into the plaza from the north. Dust swirled across the barren expanse. Not one baggy-drawered/paisano nor a shawled woman showed. Nothing but cats and dogs rooting in the stinking garbage.

"We'll, I'll be dipped in manure!" said Duncan.

Captain Fritz stared at the empty plaza. The troopers lowered their sabers. "A damned ghost town," said Fritz.

"Never even popped a cap," growled a rangy sergeant.

"God-damned Rebs pulled foot," said a trooper.

Ross saw a door open a crack and then close. He slid from his dun and ran toward the adobe. He thrust a shoulder against the door and heaved hard. The door gave a little. Ross smashed against it. There was the sound of a muttered curse and something hit the dirt floor within. Ross pushed into the room. A shivering *paisano* lay on the floor, eying Ross with frightened liquid eyes.

"Where is everyone?" asked Ross in Spanish.

"Senor, I do not know."

"Get up!"

The Mexican got up. Ross gripped him by the collar and rushed him out into the street. Colonel West drew rein in front of them. "Ask him what has happened," he said.

The Mexican shivered as he looked at the hatchet faces of the dusty troopers. "Before God," he said, "everyone is hiding. The Texans said the Abolitionists would slaughter the men and rape the women."

Ross twisted the greasy collar. "Where are the Texans?"

"They left some days ago, senor. Do not kill me! I have a wife and seven children."

Ross drew the man close. "Are Nick Maxwell, Yaqui and Amadeo Esquivel in town?"

The Mexican wet his lips. "I think so. The people are in their houses or hiding in the fields." He cringed. "Many of the people have left for Sonora."

Ross looked up at the colonel. "He says the people are afraid. Many of them have left for Sonora."

West nodded. "We'll send men after them with a promise of safety." He looked at Captain Fritz. "Find quarters for the men. The horses can be corralled in the Overland yards. Run up the Stars and Stripes, Captain Fritz. You will act as provost marshal until further orders. Every person in town will be required to take the oath of allegiance. If they don't, you will place them under guard."

In half an hour Tucson was fully occupied. Patrols went through the winding streets and rounded up the people.

As soon as Ross was free he headed for Amadeo Esquivel's gambling hall with Mike Duncan. There was a coldness in him as he opened the door. The place was empty. He loosened his Colt in its sheath and padded down the hallway, followed by Duncan. He hammered on Luz Campos's door. There was no answer.

Ross raised a foot to kick in the door.

Duncan gripped his shoulder, "take it easy," he said. "We can get picked up by the provost for things like this."

"I'm worried," said Ross. He smashed against the door. It shook on its hinges. He kicked it again.

"*Quién es?*" called out Luz Campos.

"Ross Fletcher!"

She opened the door. Her face was pale beneath her powder. She held out her arms. "I knew you would come back."

Ross pushed past her. Amadeo Esquivel was crawling through the window. Ross gripped him by a leg and jerked him inside. He hit the packed earth floor with a crash. "Get up, you bastard," said Ross. "Where are Maxwell and Yaqui?"

"*Madre de Dios!* I do not know!"

"You're a God-damned liar!"

Esquivel sat up and wiped the sweat from his greasy face. "I will buy the drinks," he said.

"You're damned right you will!"

Duncan grinned as Ross shoved the cringing Mexican toward the door. He gripped him by the arm and rushed him up the hallway.

Luz Campos came close to Ross. "You are a *soldado* now! An officer perhaps?"

Ross kicked the door shut. "No. A jackass private in the rear rank."

"The soldiers will not bother the women?"

Ross looked at her. "That shouldn't worry you."

"You know I waited for you."

Ross took John's Sharps from his pocket. "Where did you get this, Luz Campos?"

She saw it in the mirror. Her hands shook as she placed the powder puff on the table. She turned. "I won it at the tables."

"You bitch! You're lying! Where did you get it?"

"Do not talk that way, *chiquito*."

He gripped her by the arms. "Talk," he said. "Or I'll make you wish you had."

"You are hurting me!"

Ross shoved her to the couch. She sat down and put her arms about his thighs. "What is wrong? You have changed so much. Do you not love your Luz?"

Ross looked down at the smooth dark hair. "Where did you get this pistol?"

She looked up. Tears cut grooves in the thick face powder. "Believe me. I won it at the tables."

Ross pulled her to her feet. "I'll fix you so that you'll never screw another miner out of his poke."

She wiped her face. "Yaqui gave it to me," she said. "He always hangs around me. Always he gives me little things."

"Like a Sharps pistol from a murdered man?"

"Before God, I never knew it was your brother's, Ross."

Ross turned away. He opened the door and walked into the barroom. Duncan leaned against the end of the counter with a bottle of mescal in front of him. Esquivel stood behind the bar. There was hate on his sweaty face.

"Nothing," said Ross. "She got it from Yaqui, she claims."

"The little *pistola?.*" asked Amadeo. "Yes, it is so. I saw Yaqui give it to her. Always he wants to go to bed with her."

"Like going to bed with a copperhead," said Ross. He filled a glass and downed the liquor.

"It is all right if I open the doors for the soldiers?" asked Esquivel eagerly.

Duncan refilled his glass. "Get out there and take the oath, greaser. Then sell your God-damned rotgut to anyone you please."

A trooper came into the gambling hall. "Sergeant Duncan," he said, "Captain Fritz has orders to close this hole. He said it was a known hangout for rebels and rebel sympathizers."

Duncan nodded.

Esquivel's lips drew back from his teeth. "Gringos," he said. "I spit on them."

Duncan leisurely reached across the bar and gripped Amadeo by the front of his jacket. His right fist shot out a foot and connected solidly. Amadeo went back against the shelving at the rear of the bar. Bottles crashed down on top of him or smashed on the floor, the pungent fumes filled the air. Duncan wiped his fist on his blouse. "Damned if I like to be called a gringo by a greaser, even if he just bought me a drink on the house."

Ross slipped the Sharps into his pocket. "Let's get out of here."

Duncan reached across and slipped a bottle of Bacanora mescal into his blouse front. "Spoils of war," he said. "Lead on, MacDuff!"

Colonel West came across the plaza. "Fletcher!" he said. "Do you know the country south of here?"

"Yes, sir."

"Good. There are Tucsonians out on that road. Take rations and ride south. Turn all of them back, if you can."

"I'd like to go too, sir," said Duncan.

"You are to take a scout detail to the east to look for signs of the Texans."

Duncan spat as the colonel walked off.

"Too bad," said Ross.

Duncan rubbed his jaw. "I heard that Maxwell and Yaqui kited out of town just ahead of us. Now you don't have any ideas of going after them?"

"Me? Why, Sergeant Duncan, you surprise me!"

Duncan eyed Ross. "I know you too well. For God's sake, Ross! Do as you're ordered and get back here with a whole skin."

Ross shrugged.

Duncan handed him the bottle. "You might need this. I'll get another bottle before I go east. Good luck, Ross."

"Vaya con Dios, Mike."

Mike Duncan watched the tall Californian walk toward the corrals. He shook his head. There would be hell to pay between Tucson and the Sonora line if Ross caught up with Maxwell and Yaqui.

CHAPTER ELEVEN

I t was dusk on the second day of Ross Fletcher's ride south of Tucson. The first day he had turned back many people who had been hiding in the brush, afraid of the blue-clad gringos, but more afraid of the prowling Apaches and thieving Sonoran raiders. Few of them had any arms other than knives and some large-bored *escopetas* which looked more dangerous to those who carried them than they would be to an enemy.

He had camped the first night out on the banks of the Santa Cruz with a large party of Tucsonians whom he persuaded to return. Yndelecio Diaz, a muleteer of Tucson, had told him that he had seen Nick Maxwell and Yaqui riding south the same day the troops had occupied Tucson. They had taken food supplies from a small party of frightened townspeople.

Ross passed the deserted hamlet of Tubac just as the sun disappeared behind the mountains. A cold wind blew down from the mountains. If Maxwell and Yaqui had gone on to Sonora, his chances of overtaking them were hopeless, for the Mexican troops along the border would turn back any Yankee soldier. His one chance was that they might have stopped at Tumacacori, as many wayfarers did. Still, they might have gone to the Mowry

Silver Mine east of Tumacacori, in the Santa Ritas. Sylvester Mowry, a Rhode Islander and a retired United States Army officer, was known to be a Southern sympathizer, and had over four hundred employees at his wealthy mine, many of them tough Sonorans. Mowry had political ambitions and had once claimed that he, with his twenty Southern employees, could whip a hundred blue-bellies. His mine buildings at Patagonia were said to be fortified and protected by a six-pounder brass fieldpiece.

A feint moon was up when Ross drew rein on the same rise on which he had viewed the ghostly ruins of the mission in February. John had been alive then. The damned deed which Ross had found had cost John Fletcher his life. Ross was sure that Yaqui had done the job. It was his type of work—the silent knife in the back.

Ross studied the ruins. The moon washed the white dome in silvery light. Then the feint odor of woodsmoke drifted to Ross on the night wind. Someone was there. Certainly not Apaches, for to them the place was haunted and to be avoided like the plague. Maybe it was Maxwell and Yaqui. Perhaps a band of frightened Tucsonians. Maybe a group of Sonorans on the lookout for horses and loot.

Ross dismounted and ground-reined the big dun in a mesquite thicket. He took his Sharps and drifted through the moonlit brush after removing his spurs. He stopped at the wall of the Campus Sancti. A horse whinnied from the shadows. Ross faded along the wall to the east. He followed the back wall of the arcaded rooms which formed the north wall of the large patio.

The wind rustled the scrub trees which bordered the river. Whitish patches of *caliche* showed in the silver wash of moonlight. An owl hooted in the trees and then flitted silently overhead as Ross climbed over the ruined east wall of the patio. He crossed to the inner patio and stood for a long time listening. The smoke drifted with the wind. It was coming from some of the half-ruined rooms along the western side of the patio.

The wind shook the branches of a fine velvet mesquite tree. From somewhere in the hills a coyote gave tongue, and far to the north an answer came faintly. Ross checked Sharps and Colt. He eyed the shadows beneath the loggia. There was no movement there. Ross passed between some cacti and halted behind an abandoned *carreta*.

Metal clinked from somewhere west of him. Then he saw a quick flare of light. A man had lit a cigar. The flare of the match revealed the hard face of Nick Maxwell. Ross followed the shadowy figure and the glow of the cigar as Maxwell padded along the west side of the patio and disappeared into a doorway on the south side.

Ross passed the *carreta* and walked silently beneath the loggia. He walked to the west end and stopped. The odor of smoke was strong now, mingled with the rich aroma of cooking beans.

Light showed briefly from a window. Ross eased along the west row of rooms and stopped short of the window. He peered into the room. Yaqui was lying on a pallet of blankets in a corner, watching a squat woman stirring a pot which sat in the embers of a beehive fireplace. The breed was toying with his knife. A bottle sat on the floor beside him. As Ross watched, the breed drank deeply.

Something grated on the ground behind Ross. He turned. A man was across the patio, carrying a load of wood. His sandals husked on the hard earth. He stepped beside the loggia and rested. Ross leaned his Sharps against the inner wall of the loggia and walked softly to where the man was. He reached an arm around a pillar and clamped a big hand across the man's mouth. His sombrero dropped to the ground. Ross dragged the little Mexican into a room.

The Mexican shivered like an aspen leaf. Ross put his mouth close to the man's ear. "Do not call out, amigo," he said.

The *paisano* shook his head.

Ross took his hand away from the man's mouth. "Who are you?"

"Jorge Madera, of Tucson."

"The carpenter?"

"Yes. Yes. I know you! You were in Tucson with your brother some months ago."

"Yes. What do you do here?"

Jorge crossed himself. "My wife Theresa and I came here from Tucson. We have relatives in Sonora. This afternoon those two men came here. They forced us to work for them. Even now Theresa prepares beans for them."

"There are only two of them?"

"Yes."

"Is there anyone else in the ruins?"

"No one but the ghosts of the old *padres,* senor."

Ross squatted beside the frightened carpenter. "I want those two men, Jorge."

"Madre de Dios! Are you mad? They are killers! I am afraid for Theresa. Already the big one has slid his hand beneath her skirts and made free with her. What shall I do?"

"Go back with the wood. Can you steal any of their weapons?"

"How? They would kill me!"

The Mex wouldn't be of much help. Ross was sure he could take either one of them separately, but together they'd be a handful for two good men.

Ross rubbed his bristly jaw. "Go back then. I'll wait until the big gringo comes back and then surprise them. Do not show your fear, amigo. When I get the drop on them you must take their weapons. You will do this?"

"I cannot."

Ross gripped him by his greasy shirt. "Listen, pig! Do you want your Theresa to have a bastard by one of them? That is how it will be, I promise."

"There are other soldiers with you?"

"No."

"You are mad!"

"They don't know that."

Jorge rolled his eyes upward. "You gringos are mad."

Ross pulled him to his feet. "Go back. You must do as I say. If you do not, I will kill you and take your Theresa. Go now!"

The shivering Mexican crept from the dark room. He picked up his wood and walked toward the room where Yaqui sat at his ease.

Ross walked back to his Sharps. Maxwell appeared and went into the room. Ross cocked the Sharps and folded back the holster of his Colt. He walked along the wall and peered in. Theresa was still at her cooking. Yaqui was still at his bottle. Jorge was breaking the branches of the firewood. Maxwell squatted with his back to the window. Tobacco smoke drifted over his head.

Ross felt the cold sweat work down his sides. It was like facing two riled diamondbacks. He wished to God he had big Mike Duncan with him. The two of them could handle Maxwell and Yaqui.

Ross stepped to the window and thrust in the Sharps, cocking it as he did so. He thrust the muzzle against the back of Maxwell's sweat-stained shirt. "Don't move, you bastard," he said, "or I'll blow a hole through your dirty guts! Stay where you are, Yaqui!"

Maxwell raised his hands. Yaqui sat still, the bottle still in his hand. Theresa turned. Her face was pale and drawn. Jorge wet his lips.

Yaqui moved a little. "It's that bastard, Fletcher," he said thinly.

Ross shoved the muzzle against Maxwell's back and stepped into the room. "Take their weapons, Jorge," he said.

"I am afraid, senor."

"Take them, you chicken!"

Yaqui watched the little carpenter take Maxwell's

Colt. "I'll remember you, Madera, when I take your wife. I'll let you watch, and then I'll kill you."

"Pig! Dog!"

Jorge turned toward Yaqui. Somewhere beyond the mission, along the Santa Cruz, a coyote howled. Ross listened. There was something unnatural about the sound. Yaqui looked toward the window. He drew out his big Remington six-shooter and handed it to Jorge, and then gave him his slim knife. Jorge grinned. He turned the knife toward Yaqui. "'Now," he said triumphantly, "Jorge Madera will show you what he does to a man who would trifle with his Theresa."

"Damn it, Jorge!" said Ross, "Keep away from him!"

Jorge shook his head. He thrust the knife at Yaqui's groin. The breed jumped aside and snatched up the bottle. He smashed it at Jorge. The bottle cracked on the little carpenter's head. Jorge dropped the knife as the mescal poured down his face, blinding him. Theresa screamed. Maxwell turned, but Ross jammed the Sharps against his back. "Don't move, Nick," he said.

Jorge screamed like an animal as he groped for the knife.

The coyote howled softly just beyond the mission. Ross went cold. There was something alien about the sound. Then from south and west of the mission he heard answering calls. He walked to the door and looked out. Dim figures moved at the far end of the patio. There was no mistaking the thick manes of hair bound by strips of cloth, nor the moccasins folded about the muscular legs. Apaches—at least ten of them.

———

ROSS JUMPED THROUGH THE DOORWAY. Maxwell laughed. Ross sprinted toward the loggia. Maxwell fired from the doorway. The slug creased Ross along the left side of the head. He crashed against a pillar and dropped his Sharps. The Apaches closed in, running softly on the hard earth.

Ross freed his Colt and fired. One of the warriors went down. Ross felt his senses spin. Blood dripped down the side of his head. Jorge broke from the room. Yaqui yelled in slurring Apache. A warrior tripped the frightened carpenter. He rolled over and over, coming to a stop in front of a brawny warrior. Jorge screamed. "Do not kill me!"

There was no pity in the cold eyes. The knife poised and then flashed down, ripping into the Mexican's throat, turning deftly sideways at the end of the stroke to almost decapitate Jorge. The corpse fell sideways with lolling head while great gouts of blood splattered the legs of his killer and stained the *caliche*.

Ross jumped behind another pillar and fired twice. The warriors scattered. Ross felt his head pound as he cocked the big Colt. The cap snapped but the charge did not explode. He slid out behind the pillar and sprinted for the far wall. A warrior jumped in front of him and went down with the barrel of the Colt laid across his broad face. Ross hurdled the buck and met another chest-to-chest. His greater weight smashed the warrior aside.

"Get him, damn it!" roared Maxwell.

Ross bent beneath another buck and thrust his body upward, feeling the slash of a knife across his left shoulder. The Apache went up and crashed down like a sack of meal. Ross dropped his Colt, speared a buck with a left and dropped him with a smashing right.

He broke free. He looked back over his shoulder. His right foot struck a low wall. He pitched headfirst into an old cistern and crashed down on a pile of dirt and adobe brick. A warrior landed atop him. Two more followed. He fought like a mad dog in the narrow space, kneeing, kicking and smashing with bloody fists. The greasy odor of the warriors flooded his nostrils.

"Take him alive!" yelled Maxwell from up above.

One Apache was down with a smashed nose. Ross felt his strength drain. He went battling back against the wall, kneed a buck in the groin and heard him grunt in agony. The warrior fell against him, knocking him down. Ross looked up into the masklike face of the last warrior. The buck swung up a war club made of a stone encased in rawhide. It whipped down and bounced from his aching skull. Then Ross slid into a darker pit, down, down until he knew nothing more.

CHAPTER TWELVE

The sun beat down like a brazen lance from a cloudless sky, reflecting from the rocks of the Santa Ritas. Ross Fletcher plodded along the rough trail. His wrists were lashed behind him and a rawhide rope led from them to the hands of a squat buck who rode a claybank mare twenty feet behind Ross, jerking the line viciously whenever Ross stumbled. Ross felt his head throb like an oxhide drum. The dust from the warriors' mounts ahead of him swirled up about his face, coating his nostrils and throat with dryness.

He had been stripped to his drawers and socks at the mission that morning, and in half-an-hour's travel the socks had shredded away, followed by the skin of his soles. Now his feet were aching, bloody masses, studded with hairlike cactus needles. Parts of his uniform had been distributed among the warriors. A hulking brave rode his dun.

Yaqui and Maxwell were somewhere up ahead, where the dust did not moil. Every one of the party with the exception of Ross suffered from a prodigious hangover, and bloodshot eyes surveyed the world about them. Ross had come to hours after he had been felled, lashed like a roasting pig in a room beside the place where Yaqui and

Maxwell had made their camp. For hours he had heard
them slopping down the large quantity of liquor which
Maxwell had provided.

It had been one hell of a debauch. Theresa Madera
had been violated by each of them, one after the other, in
endless repetition. At first she had screamed and fought.
Then she had pleaded. Then she had begun to moan until
they stuffed her mouth with a rag. At dawn they had
dumped her beside the cold corpse of her husband. The
last Ross had seen of her was a glimpse as he crossed the
patio. She had lain there in her bloody rags, beating her
fists on the hard earth in unutterable agony as her
calloused captors rode past her with hardly a glance.

There was a cold core of hatred in Ross as he planted
one bleeding foot ahead of the other on the harsh trail.
Maybe there was an excuse for the Apaches; they were
without mercy, the tigers of the human species. Yaqui
was a breed. Some breeds were worse than those of
unmixed blood. But Nick Maxwell was a white man—
white of color, black of soul.

Still, Ross had noted that the warriors had eyed him
with respect as they dragged him out into the morning
sunlight. The fight was rather vague to him. He had
wounded one of them with his Colt, and remembered
downing four or five of them in hand-to-hand fighting.
They must rate him as one hell of a *muy hombre*. His body
felt as though he had been run through a stamping mill.

Some of the warriors had broken off from the main
body far back down the trail. Smoke signals had drifted
up from the north. There were Tucsonians up north for
easy pickings. The warriors were Chiricahuas, Big Mountain People, the diplomats and toughest fighters of the
Apaches. They were the diamond-hard core of resistance
to the whites. Tougher and more vicious than the Tontos,
Aravaipas, Coyoteroes, Mescaleroes and Mimbrenos.
The Spaniards had never conquered them, nor had the
Mexicans. They raided from the Gila all the way south to
the very gates of Durango, warriors who knew every trail

and waterhole in hundreds of square miles of desert and mountain, warriors who would ride a horse to death, stop long enough to slaughter him, ripping out his long gut for a canteen, and hanging strips of meat across the rumps of their fresh mounts to dry in the sun for supplies. They could outrun a horse on the side of a mountain and would fight to the death if trapped, providing they could be trapped.

Not for the Apache was the clash of horseman against horseman out in the open. They preferred the silent ambush and the quick bloody raid with few casualties. They could find food where a white man would starve to death, and could go three or four times longer without water.

———

AT NOON they halted high on a mountain spur. The expressionless warriors sat about chewing jerky, eying Ross with their bloodshot eyes. The tired horses stood with bowed heads and foam-flecked flanks. One of them was almost gone.

Nick leaned against a rock and grinned at Ross. "Tough hombre! *Muy hombre!* You shoulda had more sense than to jump me and Yaqui here. Where the hell are the rest of them bluebellies? I thought you woulda had more brains than to enlist. Jesus, Yaqui! A soldier!"

Yaqui touched the welted scar which ran from the tip of his left ear to the tip of his jaw. There was feral hate in his flat eyes. Ross wished to God he had killed him. Twice he had had the chance and let it go by. The third time would be the charm, if Yaqui didn't get at him with his knife first. The odds were with Yaqui.

Nick jerked his head at Yaqui. "Tell one of these drunken bastards to give him a drink."

"No, Nick."

Nick spit. "Look! I don't give a damn if he dies right now. But they want him taken to Cochise."

Yaqui spoke in slurring, guttural Chiricahua. A young buck took a horse-gut canteen from his horse's withers and untied the end. He held it to Ross's mouth. The water stank and was gamy, but it helped. He swilled it about his raw mouth.

Maxwell laughed. "Ain't so bad once you get it past your nose. Hawww!"

Smoke drifted up from the mountains to the east. "See that, Fletcher?" asked Maxwell.

"I'm not blind."

"You might be before long, you bastard."

Maxwell cut a chew of tobacco and stowed it in his mouth. "Cochise and Mangus Colorado are getting together," he said; "Chiricahuas and Mimbrenos. Hundreds of 'em, gathering like buffalo gnats. You know what for?"

"I can guess."

"Yeah. You ain't got enough bluebellies in Arizona to stop 'em. Canby in New Mexico is getting his ass knocked off by Henry Sibley. There ain't nothin' goin' to stop these bushy-haired bastards."

Ross eased a raw foot. "Where do you fit in?" he asked.

Maxwell spat. "Cochise and Mangus need guns and ammunition. We hear that the bluebellies plan to issue hundreds of rifles, and wagon loads of ammunition to the Pimas."

"So?"

Nick scratched his belly. "It seems as though a certain officer might get the deal to issue those weapons."

Ross looked up. "What do you mean?"

"Mebbe you don't know it, but Matt Risler went west to get a commission in the bluebellies. Now Matt is smart enough to talk his way into taking charge of those rifles."

"I'll bet," said Ross dryly.

Maxwell nodded. "Now, supposin' he does? There ain't no assurance that the Pimas *will* get 'em, is there?"

"You're shooting off your mouth."

"Yeah. Now Yaqui here knows Cochise and Mangus like they was kissin' cousins back in Georgia."

"That figures."

"It does. Now, supposin' the Chiricahuas and Mimbrenos get them rifles and all that ammunition instead of the Pimas? You ain't got enough troops to control Arizona. They aim to go on to New Mexico and shoot at Texicans, not 'Paches. You ever think what can happen around here if these boys get all the arms they need?"

The whipsaw scream of an eagle drifted down from the heights. Ross stared at the big man. "Why are you telling me all this?"

Nick shrugged. "You won't live to tell anyone about it." He stood up and came close to Ross, looking down at him with cold eyes. "You'll scream, you Yank bastard. You'll scream and plead with Nick Maxwell to put you outa your misery. And you know what you'll get?" A big foot came up. Maxwell rammed the heel into Ross's belly and turned it hard, just above the groin.

Ross grunted in agony as he doubled up. A sour flood poured from his slack mouth as waves of pain shot through him.

Yaqui yawned as he sheathed his knife. He stood up and looked at Ross. "By Jesus, Nick," he said. "For a minute back there I thought you was getting soft."

CHAPTER THIRTEEN

The sun was low in the west as the file of warriors threaded their way through a cactus jungle. There was an excitement on the usually impassive faces of the Chiricahuas, for ahead of them rose the stronghold of their people in the Dragoons. To one man who rode with them the stronghold meant nothing but a slow, lingering death. He and the horse were both scarecrows. Ross Fletcher was a gruesome caricature of the big trooper who had ridden to Tumacacori some days before. For food they had given him some of the guts of a mule they had killed. Several sips of gamy water a day from a greasy horsegut had sustained a spark of life in him. They had finally allowed him to ride, not through any quality of mercy, but because they wanted him to live long enough to provide sport and pleasure for the band of Cochise.

Ross rode with bowed head, gripping the straggly mane of the shambling horse with weak hands. The leather thongs had cut deeply into his flesh, almost buried in the puffiness. His feet were swollen as though he had elephantiasis and the hairlike needles of cactus had infected the swollen flesh. The sun had reddened his flesh, then broken it out into large blisters which hung heavily and then burst, letting the fluids run down his back, soak into his filthy drawers and cake them against his buttocks and the sweating back of the horse.

His eyes seemed to be burned hollows in his reddened face and his lips drew back from his teeth, cracked and swollen. There had been a savage skill in the way they had let him peer into the depths of blessed death, and then had shut the doors in his face, allowing him to ride almost an instant before he went down forever, feeding him just enough to keep the vital spark in him. To them, they had broken his spirit. To him, deep beneath the torture he had undergone, his spirit was a cold, hard core. It had sustained itself by hatred which fueled the flame when it flickered its lowest.

He had almost forgotten John's murder. Isabel Rand was only a dim memory. But the faces of Yaqui and Nick Maxwell were always in his mind's eye. Any violent end he had planned for them in a smashing, bloody attack, had given away to a pure desire for cold, methodical destruction. To the warriors he was a figure of respect. It wouldn't change their minds about his way of death, but they admired him for his courage and stamina.

The entrance into the huge cup of the stronghold was a vague picture to him. The crashing reports of guns and the high-pitched, special shrieking of the women was part of the nightmare that had started some days ago.

The strident music of the fiddles and drums, with the scraping of the elk bones, sounded like music straight from the smoky halls of hell. He didn't really feel the stones which flew at him. One of them thudded against his head with a noise like someone thumping a melon. The worm of blood which ran down through his bristles and trickled into his mouth was part of the dream.

They dumped him from the horse and kicked him until he crawled into some brush and lay still. Sometime in the next hour or so a warrior came to look at him. A tall man, for an Apache, with a face which was all planes and angles. The tight jaw and compressed mouth showed no signs of mercy. But deep in the large, intelligent eyes he saw respect. Ross didn't know it was Cochise and he wouldn't have given a damn if he did know.

He was almost completely exhausted as he lay there in the cold wind of evening. High above him were the blue walls of the stronghold, through the moving branches of the trees. The many fires cast gigantic, grotesque shadows against the natural walls of the citadel as the people passed back and forth. The returned warriors feasted like gluttons. A foal had been torn unborn from its mother and stewed in the natural juices. There was sweet mule meat and the accordion pleats of dried meat. There was soup from cactus fruit. There were nuts, seeds, berries, maize and many pots of tiswin, the heady corn brew. But the captive was forgotten as he lay in the coldness of the brush.

The saturnalia went on for hours. The married women had been long in the preparation of their bodies for the return of their men. They wore their best clothing and had scented themselves with mint and crushed flowers. The widows and the divorced women had stripped themselves to breechclouts and had powdered their bodies white, rubbing crushed mint on their nipples. They had joined excitedly with the married women. They would satisfy the warriors who had no women of their own.

There was a time when Ross saw Maxwell and Yaqui staggering around with the dancing men, stewed to the gills. Later they had gone with the other men to the dark wickiups to finish off the debauch, while sober sentries patrolled their beats, and the fires flickered low.

It was then the dream came to him. He was asleep, or at least he thought he was, when the brush rustled near him. A vague figure showed in the dimness. Then the odor of smoky buckskin came to him, intermingled with the woman odor. He looked up into a shadowy face framed by thick black hair. A hand was pressed softly against his mouth. He did not move.

She bathed his face with a wet cloth, wiping the caked blood from the cracked skin. She washed the filthy accumulation of dust, blood and sweat from his upper body. Gently she pressed the swollen lips of his wounds to exude the pus, and then wiped it away.

"Who are you?" asked Ross in English.

She did not answer. She held a water olla to his lips. The blessed clear fluid trickled down into his throat.

"Who are you?" he whispered in Spanish.

She pressed a hand against his mouth and shook her head. She placed some food beside him and then stood up. The fire closest to them flared up. A wave of strange emotion swept over him as she glided silently through the brush and disappeared among the swaying trees. He had seen the oval race of a beautiful young woman. A woman he had thought dead. "Isabella," he said softly.

A warrior padded through the rancheria with a rifle across his left arm. He stopped near Ross and looked down at him. He poked him with his rifle butt. Ross stirred. The sentry nodded. No one wanted the big white-eye to die; not yet.

Ross dropped off to sleep. Hours later he woke up to see the faint moon high in the sky. He had dreamt of Isabella Rand. He moved. He felt fresher. Something was under his body. He rolled over and found a piece of cooked meat lying in the dirt. Then he knew she was alive.

The sun was peering into the vast cup of the stronghold when Ross awoke. The women were astir, feeding the many fires. Smoke hung low in the windless air. The warriors were still asleep.

A buck came across to Ross and jerked his head. Ross got to his feet and walked out into the clearing. His joints and muscles seemed to shriek deep within him as he moved. The warrior thudded the rifle butt against Ross's back, heading him toward a large wickiup which stood to one side. A tall warrior sat there, smoking slowly, contemplating the bluish smoke which drifted about him. It was Cochise.

The warrior stopped in front of Cochise and spoke. Cochise nodded and waved a hand. The warrior walked away. The sun glinted on the metal armbands worn by the famous warrior. There wasn't an ounce of fat on the rangy, muscular frame of the big Apache.

Cochise studied the gaunt man who stood before him. He looked at the swollen dirty hands. Then he stood up. He was almost as tall as Ross. He drew a slim knife from its sheath and tested the edge with his thumb. Ross did not move. Maybe it was better this way. A swift thrust and swifter oblivion. The chief held his hand and deftly slit the embedded lashings. Blood ran down from Ross's hands as he pulled them apart. The chief sat down.

"Sit down," he said in Spanish.

Ross sat down.

"Do you know who I am?"

Ross nodded. "Cochise."

"Yes."

In the silence that followed Ross could feel the first tingling of blood as it began to circulate through his wrists.

Cochise puffed at his cigarillo. "It is said that you are a brave man. Are you afraid now?"

Ross shrugged. The heady odor of the tobacco smoke raised a hunger in him. As though he had read Ross's thoughts, the chief took a cigarillo from a woven basket, placed it between the cracked lips of his prisoner and lit it with a lucifer. Ross gratefully drew the smoke deep into his lungs.

"Who are you, white man?"

"Ross Fletcher."

"It is a curious name."

"No more than Cochise," said Ross boldly.

Cochise allowed the faintest trace of a smile to light his face. "Where do you come from?"

"I am a soldier."

"Why is it you are hated by Yaqui and Maxwell?"

"I think they killed my brother."

Cochise nodded. "That is reason enough. It is said that you fought like a warrior with the *heshke,* the killing craze."

"It is so."

The calm eyes studied the battered man who sat before them. "Many men would have died from the way you have been treated."

"That I do not know."

"I know."

The odors of stewing meat drifted to them. Ross felt a little faint. He wondered where the girl was. Maybe it had been a dream. It had been many months since she had disappeared.

"There are Yanqui soldiers in Tucson?"

"Yes."

"How many?"

"I cannot tell."

"I can make you tell."

"You can try."

Again the faint smile. "You are truly a warrior. Have your soldiers come to Tucson to fight against my people?"

"They have come to fight against those who wear the gray suits."

"But not my people?"

"They will if they have to."

"They will go east?"

"Yes."

The face hardened. "Through the Big Medicine Pass?"

"Apache Pass? Yes."

"There is no such word in our language. Do you know what Apache means?"

"The enemy."

"That is so. We also call you white-eyes by such a name in our tongue. *Indah.*"

Ross puffed at his cigarillo. He felt no hatred for the tall Chiricahua. He was a man.

"You know that you are to die."

"Yes."

"I do not like to see a man die like a pig."

"Give me a weapon. Let me fight against Maxwell or Yaqui. If I win I go free."

"That is a man's way."

"It is so."

Cochise looked at the emaciated body of Ross Fletcher. "You are weak now. There would be little chance."

"I don't care. Let me die on my feet, facing an enemy."

Cochise beckoned to a woman. She brought them food on Mexican plates. They ate with their fingers. When Cochise had finished he wiped the grease on his sinewy legs. "Do you know why I did that?" he asked.

Ross shook his head.

"There is a tale amongst my people, a story of a man who always fed his belly. He was pursued by the enemy. They killed his horse. He began to run. His legs would not work. He asked them why. Do you know what they said?"

"No."

"You have always fed your belly to make it grow. We have received no food. Let your belly do your running for you."

Ross couldn't help but grin. He wiped the grease on his thighs, through the great holes in his dirty drawers.

"Enju," said Cochise.

Ross felt almost at home with the chief. He relit his cigar, helping himself to the lucifers. The eyes never left his face. There was respect in them. Ross leaned back against a tree. "When do I die, Cochise?"

"Who knows?"

"You can say when."

"It is so."

"Today?"

Cochise stood up. "No. Perhaps not for some days. It is good to talk with a brave man, even if he is an enemy. There is much that can be learned." He looked about his natural fortress. "You will not be tied. But do not attempt to arm yourself or escape. If you do, I will order the torturing to begin at once. Do you understand?"

"Yes."

"*Enju!* It is good."

There was no sight of Yaqui or Maxwell during the morning, nor was there any sight of Isabel Rand. Ross lay in the brush, moving only to drink vast quantities of water from the cool spring. The women stared at him when they thought he wasn't looking at them. The children scuttled through the brush ahead of him and peered at him from cover like so many chipmunks. The few warriors that were about watched him as he went for water.

It was early afternoon when he saw her. She was seated beside a wickiup near that of the chief. She wore a buckskin dress over her shapely body. Her hair hung about her shoulders. She did not move, nor look about the camp. Ross watched her for a long time before he passed her on the way to water. She did not look up. On his way back he spoke softly to her. "Isabella? Isabella Rand?"

There was a blankness on the lovely face which turned toward him. It destroyed part of her beauty. A cold feeling came over him as though he had felt the thick cold body of a rattler with a questing hand. She looked away. Ross walked to his place in the brush. When he turned, she was gone.

Yaqui and Maxwell appeared in the late afternoon, with bloodshot eyes. Ross watched them as they talked with Cochise. Maxwell was angry about something, and Ross knew what it was. Now and then the burly bastard would thrust out a thick arm toward Ross and argue heatedly, but the chief would only shake his head. Yaqui and

Maxwell left the camp at dusk, followed by a dozen warriors.

Ross was fed by a squaw. No one bothered him. He was reminded of a hog being fattened for the kill. They had patience—too damned much patience.

He noted the weapons in the rancheria. Double-barreled shotguns, muzzle-loading carbines, rifles and musketoons, large-bored *escopetas,* a few revolving pistols and many single-shot horse pistols. All the warriors were armed with bows and arrows as well as their war clubs and knives. The well-armed Californians could go through them like a hot knife through butter, and the artillery would make the big difference in a showdown. But if these bushy-haired bastards got better weapons there would be hell to pay along the overland route to New Mexico.

CHAPTER FOURTEEN

Ross began to feel his strength return after a few days of food and rest. He made no attempt to escape, although many times his mind scaled the rugged walls of the fortress, soaring up toward the blue, cloud-dotted sky. The odds were immense against his escaping. There were too many of them. There was only one way out of the stronghold. On foot he would be ridden down, and even if he made good his escape for a few hours or days he knew they would track him down.

Cochise ignored him. Gradually Ross grew to accept his imprisonment, studying the people about him for want of anything better to do. He had asked a warrior about Isabella. "Mind-gone-far," the warrior had grunted in Spanish.

That was why she was safe and unmolested. The children played around her as though she didn't exist. A young Chiricahua squaw took care of her, brushing the thick hair, and feeding her patiently from a bowl. In time Ross began to wonder if it had really been she who had come to him in the darkness and bathed his body.

One afternoon he watched a slim warrior clean a battered Burnside carbine. He had noticed the warrior before. There was none of the deep-chested squatness about him. He was of different blood. Ross leaned against a tree, studying him.

The buck wiped his carbine barrel with rendered fat and then rubbed it down with a piece of rag. He looked up at Ross. "Are you not afraid, gringo?" he asked in Spanish.

"More or less."

The warrior put his carbine aside and took out his knife.

He began to whet it on a stone. "Cochise is a great man," he said.

"Yes. For an Apache."

"Perhaps also for a white man."

"That may be so. You are not Chiricahua?"

The liquid eyes held Ross's eyes for a moment. "Not by birth. By adoption. I was born in Durango."

"You joined the Chiricahuas?"

"In a way. I was captured when I was a boy. I have been raised with the other boys."

Ross squatted beside him. "Have you ever thought of leaving them?"

The knife blade went *wheet, wheet, wheet* on the stone. "Why? It is a good life. Plenty of food. Women. All others fear us. I have a good wife here."

Ross shrugged. "One gets used to it, I suppose."

"One does."

"How are you called?"

"As a boy I was called Bartolome. Here I am Agoitaye, Thin One."

Ross looked about. Some of the warriors were playing lance billiards some distance from the camp. The sound of the game singers drifted to them through the trees. The women were busy about their house-keeping.

"What do you know of the white girl? The mind-gone-far one."

Thin One began to take the wire edge from his blade by whetting it on his muscular thigh. "She was found near

San Cayetano del Tumacacori many months ago. Her father was killed."

"By the Chiricahuas?"

Thin One shrugged. "I do not think so."

"Why do you say that? He was filled with arrows and found in the desert near the old mission."

"It is said that he was killed in the church. These people will not go into the church. It is haunted by the old *padres*."

Ross rubbed his jaw. "What do you mean, Bartolome?"

The warrior looked about the camp. "It is said that he was killed by white men and filled with arrows to make it appear as though the Chiricahuas had done it."

"Tell me of the girl."

"She was found near the Santa Cruz. Her mind was gone. She was taken along for ransom. Her relatives could not be reached. They say she is all alone. So she has been kept here. They will not harm her."

Ross nodded.

The warrior sheathed his knife and stood up. "I am to play at lance billiards with Yellow Bear. Tonight there will be a war dance. Stay away from it, gringo."

"They plan a raid?"

"No. It is war."

"Same thing."

"You do not know these people. War is for vengeance. Some of your soldiers killed three braves near Tucson. Big Deer lost his brother there. He has called for a war party."

"There are many soldiers in Tucson."

"So? There are many Chiricahuas. Soon the Chiricahuas and the Mimbrenos will fight against the soldiers."

"The soldiers have good weapons and are not afraid. They have wagon guns."

Bartolome shrugged. "We are to get many fine weapons soon. Maxwell and Yaqui have gone with some braves to get the first of many good guns." The Mexican walked away. Then he turned. "Why do you not attempt to escape? When they return with the weapons you will be put to the torture. You will wish then that you had died fighting, or trying to escape."

Ross looked across the clearing. Isabel Rand was seated in front of her wickiup, combing her hair. "It is in the hands of God, Bartolome."

The Mexican looked about and then swiftly crossed himself. Then he vanished into the woods. The girl stood up and walked toward the spring. Ross faded into the underbrush and circled around to the spring.

She came down the beaten path and stopped when she saw him. Her face was a blank.

Ross held out a hand toward her. "Isabella?" he asked softly.

There was no expression on her lovely face. She was like an exotic tropical flower from which the aroma had gone, beautiful but lifeless.

Ross looked about. They were alone. "I want to help you," he said. "My name is Ross Fletcher. Have you heard of me?"

She knelt by the water and cupped some of it into her hands. She sipped it and then stood up. She walked away from him. Ross followed her. "My brother and I were partners in the Sahuarito with your father, Isabella. We thought you had been killed."

There was no answer. The path dipped into a brushy hollow. She turned and spoke clearly. "You must not come near me, Ross Fletcher." There was no blankness in her dark eyes.

Ross came forward but she stopped him with a raised hand. "I am safe as long as they think I have lost my mind."

"But you are all right!"

She looked up at the big man who faced her, clad in the stained rags. A haunting sadness filled her eyes. "I am alive," she said softly. "That is all."

Then she was gone through the shadowy trees. Ross

felt strange emotions flit through his confused mind. She was a born actress. He shook his head as he thought of the days and weeks of hell she had lived through in that camp, knowing her father was dead and her chances of escape were practically hopeless. But she was mentally balanced, and he thanked God for that.

Cochise came from the lance billiard grounds, carrying his long playing pole. Behind him Ross could see Bartolome competing with a squat warrior in the hoop and pole game.

Cochise grounded the long pole. "There will be a war dance tonight, white man," he said. "For four nights my warriors will prepare for the trail of war. It will be better for you if you stay in the small wickiup near mine, and keep out of sight."

Ross nodded. "Why are you saving me, Cochise?"

"Who knows? Your time will come. When it does I hope that you will act the part of the man I think you are." The chief walked back to the camp.

Ross heard the monotonous singing of the game singers and the slithering of the poles along the packed earth. He looked up at the towering walls of the stronghold. It would be tough enough for him to escape alone. Now he had the girl to think about.

He walked to the small wickiup and crawled inside. Tattered blankets and hides lay near the back wall. He dropped on them and laced his hands behind his shaggy hair. Something prodded into his back as he moved. He felt beneath the blankets and brought out a knife. The tip had been broken off and the blade was thin from hard usage. He draped a blanket to block the doorway and set to work, grinding down the flat tip against a stone.

CHAPTER FIFTEEN

The was dancing had been going on for four days. The shaman had done the "seeing" after a purifying sweat bath. He had appeared in the center of the camp the first evening of the war dances, whirling a rhombus which gave off the eerie sound of a rush of wind-laden rain. He had walked through the camp from north to south and east to west, making his incantations. Then, weak from fasting and sweat bathing, he had forecast a great success on the forthcoming expedition.

Dried hides had been beaten with sticks. Four warriors had started the dancing by preparing for the war path. They had bound their long hair and had brought the back flaps of their loincloths through between their legs, tucking them beneath the belt and bringing the shorter flap through, under the crotch to tuck under the back of the belt. They were fully armed.

Four warriors came from the east to the great fire in the center of the camp. Four times they had circled the fire. Two of them had taken their stations on the north side and two of them on the south side. Singers had joined the hide beaters and drum beaters. Then the dancers faced each other and began to dance.

They danced toward each other, changed sides,

turned about and went back. Four times, the sacred number, this was done. Everyone had begun to sing and shout. The women gathered silently beyond the glow of the fire. The rest of the watching warriors put bullets between their fingers or in their mouths. Then the dancing had begun in earnest. The warriors swayed violently, dropped on one Knee and men sprang high into the air, firing their guns or loosing their arrows. They made a soft grunting cry as they danced. "Wah! Wah! Wah!"

There was no cessation for four nights. On the fourth night they danced as though they had not put out their full strength on the first three nights. The warriors charged imaginary enemies, scattering and killing them in elaborate pantomime. Now and then another warrior would enter the circle, thus signifying his intention of joining the war party. At every new song a new set of men would come out while the others retired to the sidelines and prayed for success.

Warriors would single out a bystander and call him out. Sometimes the warrior would join the dancers. Other warriors would hold back. There were few of these.

The leaping, posturing figures and the steady thumping of the hides and drums seemed to cast a hypnotic spell over the people. It was a demon's carnival. The women were absorbed in the frenzy. Names were forgotten. All women were now known as White Painted Lady, while the men called each other Child of the Water.

For three nights the "fierce dancing" had been followed by social dancing—the "round dance" for everyone, the "very partner" dances when the men were invited to dance by the women. They could not be refused. Each warrior must pay his partner with a gift.

Ross squatted in his dark wickiup, watching the dancers on the fourth night: Bartolome had told him what was going on, of the elaborate religion of these strange, warlike people. Bartolome was not to go, pleading that his medicine was not good.

The warriors paid no attention to Ross. Cochise himself had been called out the first night. "Cochise!" they had called out. "Many times you have talked bravely! Now brave enemies call to you to fight them! Cochise, they say to you! You! You! They call you again and again! You are a man! Now you are being called! What are you going to do when we fight the enemy?"

Cold sweat had broken out on Ross as he saw the big chief join the madness. There was an uneasiness in him.

———

LATE ON THE night of the fourth dance, a file of warriors came into the camp, dusty and dirty from a hard ride. They led seven pack mules, laden with bulky aparejos. Ross studied the mules. Then a sickness came over him. Those were gun cases on some of the mules. The other cases carried bullets and powder. He could plainly see the big U.S. stenciled on the boxes.

Nick Maxwell was there, grinning beneath the brim of his ornamented steeple hat. Yaqui was there, stripped to the waist, with his thick hair bound by a red flannel cloth. Behind him was a small riding mule. There was a woman seated on the mule. Her shawl was over her head, but there was no mistaking Luz Campos. Yaqui held the bridle in a dirty hand. Among the warriors was Amadeo Esquivel, wetting his lips and looking from side to side as though he wished he were anywhere else but in the wild stronghold of Cochise.

The gun cases were dumped in the clearing as the dancing stopped. Maxwell pried one of them open. The firelight shone dully on the greased barrels of muzzle-loading Enfield musketoons, fresh from the factory. Other cases yielded stubby, big-bored Sharps carbines. Cartridges were dumped on the packed earth. Cochise squatted beside the weapons, fingering the cartridges. The warriors stood about him. Then, one by one, he called each warrior out and issued the weapons, filling their hide pouches with many cartridges.

Amadeo slid from his mule and went into the brush, where he squatted to watch the warriors. His head jerked up as he saw Yaqui drag Luz Campos from her mule. Yaqui gripped the frightened woman by a hand and dragged her to the wickiup he had used with Nick before they had left the camp.

Nick Maxwell sat beside Cochise, drinking heavily from a bottle, talking swiftly. Cochise nodded again and again.

Bartolome came from the shadows and squatted in front of Ross's wickiup with his Burnside across his naked thighs. He spoke softly over his shoulder. "They raided a Yanqui wagon train near Tucson. It was easy. The escort had been lured away. Many soldiers were killed in a surprise attack."

"Why do you tell me this, Bartolome?"

The Mexican shrugged. "It does not matter. They will come for you soon."

Ross felt greasy cold sweat work down his naked sides. He fingered the thin knife he had managed to sharpen after many patient hours of work.

Bartolome shifted. "Kill yourself," he said quietly. "It is better."

"Why do they come tonight?"

"It is the price Cochise must pay for the weapons. Those men hate you. I tell you this, though: Cochise does not like it."

"What of the Mexican woman and man?"

"They were brought back by Yaqui and Maxwell. Yaqui claims her. The man in the brush is angry about it, but he is afraid." Bartolome looked about. "Strike me," he said quietly. "Take my carbine. Kill yourself."

"No!"

"You are a fool! You will scream to me when you are

under the knives. You will want me to kill you. Then it is too late."

Ross wiped the sweat from his face. His guts knotted and churned. There was a sour taste in the back of his mouth.

Maxwell was taking bottles from sacks which had been lashed to the aparejo of one of the mules. He passed them out to the warriors. Bottles were opened and tipped up, the strong liquor running down chins and dripping from the naked upper bodies of the sweating warriors. Yaqui joined the drinkers. The warriors got set for a debauch. Child of the Water had been good to them. They had a fine *besh-e-gar* with plenty of ammunition for their metal bellies.

An hour had passed. Ross felt the sands of life trickling low. It wouldn't be long now.

Bartolome had been silent. Now he spoke again. "Kill yourself," he said.

"No."

The Mexican shrugged. "Here they come," he said. *"Vaya con Dios."*

———

YAQUI HURLED an empty bottle into the brush. He wiped his mouth with the back of a greasy hand. He walked toward the wickiup, followed by two warriors. They were all very drunk.

Ross hefted his knife. Cochise had admired him for his courage. He looked at the chief. Cochise sat on a folded blanket. A bottle was by his side, but he had not touched it. Ross slid the knife between the branches of the wickiup. He tied a strip of blanket about his waist and crawled outside. Bartolome stood up and walked in among the trees. He turned to watch.

Yaqui staggered a little. He spat and jerked his head at his two companions. At the fire a warrior placed a long-bladed knife in the embers at one side and men looked at Ross. Another held some leather thongs in his hand. The other warriors squatted on their haunches, pulling steadily at their bottles.

Ross waited. There was no use in making a break. A bullet could easily bring him down, and he knew he could never outrun these swift bastards, whether they were drunk or sober.

Yaqui paused. He wiped his hands on his greasy trousers and spoke swiftly to his two men. They separated and closed in on either side of Ross. Ross stood with his arms hanging loosely. Yaqui closed in.

Nick Maxwell downed a drink. "Get him, Yaqui! I want to hear him sing!"

One of the warriors reached for Ross. Ross whirled. He drove a left into the warrior's lean gut, and smashed an uppercut beneath the down-coming chin. The buck crashed back into the wickiup in a mess of broken branches.

Yaqui cursed. Ross turned. He butted the second warrior in the gut and turned to meet Yaqui's attack. Drunk or sober, Yaqui was fast. He drove a fist into Ross's face and blocked a hard right. Ross jumped to one side. The second warrior closed in. Ross belted him on the jaw, staggering him against the warrior who was struggling drunkenly in the mess of broken branches.

Yaqui came on. They closed together, chest to chest. Yaqui spat into Ross's face. Half blinded, Ross brought a knee up into the breed's groin. Yaqui turned away from the knee.

The warriors stood up. Cochise called out to them. They waited.

Ross felt Yaqui's wiry power as they swayed back and forth. Then he broke free. Yaqui staggered. A warrior closed in on Ross from behind. He turned, gripped the outthrust right wrist of the buck, stuck his leg in front of the buck and pulled hard on the arm. The buck hit hard and lay still.

Yaqui yelled. He battered at Ross with both fists.

Ross blocked with forearms and elbows. Yaqui jumped back. His hair fell over his face. Sweat greased his body. Ross closed in. He drove a left to the gut. He followed through with a right to the jaw. Yaqui shook his head and whipped out his knife. Ross jumped back and fell over the first warrior.

Yaqui grinned as he came on. Ross hooked his left foot about Yaqui's right ankle. He drew back his right leg and slammed a hard kick home inside the breed's right knee. Yaqui went back. The knife flew from his hand and clattered on the hard earth. Yaqui sat down hard. Ross rolled over and got to his feet. He gripped the breed by the throat and tightened his big hands. Yaqui coughed and gagged.

Cochise called out. Feet pattered on the hard earth. Something smashed down on Ross's head. He fell forward over the stinking body of the breed and passed out.

CHAPTER SIXTEEN

Ross lay in his shattered wickiup, feeling drums thud in his battered head. Why he was still alive was a wonder to him. The camp was quiet. He moved a little.

A dark form showed at the door of the wickiup. "Are you all right now?" asked Bartolome.

"God-damned if I know. What happened?"

"Truly a miracle. I have never seen such a fight. *Madre de Dios!* Three of them against one!"

Ross sat up and felt the hammer in his head increase its tattoo beating. Caked blood was in his shaggy hair. A lump was behind his left ear. He felt it gingerly.

Bartolome looked over his shoulder. "Yaqui wanted to kill you, and Cochise would not let him. There were angry words. Yaqui refused to go on the war party."

"Have they left?"

"Yes, and Cochise has gone with them. Maxwell has promised them many weapons. They go toward the overland road. Many warriors."

Ross drank deeply from his water olla.

"Yaqui is with the Mexican woman. Listen!"

From Yaqui's wickiup came angry voices and then a stifled scream. Luz Campos showed at the door for a moment, holding the shreds of her skirt about her full figure. Clawed hands came down on her shoulders and she was dragged back into the wickiup, fighting savagely.

"Before God," said Bartolome quietly, "I have never seen such an animal! Listen to her!"

Luz Campos screamed again and again. Then there was silence. A sentry glanced curiously at the dark wickiup and then padded off into the darkness.

A strange figure sat beside the embers of the fire. It was Amadeo Esquivel, hunched beneath a blanket. His eyes were on the wickiup where Yaqui was venting his lust. Then he stood up and came to Bartolome. "Give me your gun," he said thickly.

"Get back!"

"Give me the gun!"

Bartolome cocked the Burnside. "Get back!"

Esquivel looked at Ross. "Help me," he said.

Ross spat. "You garbage," he said.

"She is my wife!"

Ross looked up at the Mexican. Disgust was in him. As long as Luz had made money for him in Tucson, no one had ever known she was his wife. Her beauty and body had been a sound investment for Amadeo Esquivel.

Esquivel walked away, stopping to pick up a heavy faggot. Bartolome started forward and then stopped. Esquivel stopped outside of the wickiup and then went in. There was the sound of heavy blows thudding against flesh. A man hurtled out of the lodge. It was Esquivel. Blood poured from his face as he staggered toward the fire.

Yaqui ran out of the lodge. A bloody knife was in his hand. Amadeo saw him. He screamed like a woman and ran toward the trees. Yaqui bounded after him like a great cat. He closed the gap. The gambler screamed again and again as he felt his doom close in on him.

Ross stood up. Bartolome turned the carbine toward him. "Don't move," he warned.

Ross spat. "Let the son of a bitch die," he said, "I only wish I could get at Yaqui."

A thin scream wavered up and was cut short. Minutes ticked past and then the breed came out of the trees, wiping his blade on his thigh. His bloodshot eyes looked at Ross. Bartolome swung his carbine. The breed eyed it and then padded toward the lodge. This time there was no sound from it.

THE GRAY LIGHT of the false dawn tinted the eastern sky. A cold wind crept through the trees and stirred the ashes of fire.

Ross watched the camp come to life. There were only a few grown warriors in the camp. The rest of them were boys and young men, untried in battle, who must carry the head-scratching stick and drinking cane on four war trips or raiding parties. Cochise had taken the pick of his men with him. Something big was brewing.

"I'd like to go to the spring, Bartolome," said Ross.

The Mexican shrugged. "Do not try to escape. Cochise has saved you from the torturing. Nothing will save you if you make an attempt to escape. Do you understand?"

"Yes."

Ross padded down the trail. Isabel Rand was there. She looked up at him. "This is a place of death," she said.

"Yes."

"You are all right?"

Ross touched the lump behind his ear. "I've got a hard head in more ways than one."

She closed her eyes. "I cannot sleep. You saw what happened to the Mexican?"

"Yes."

She looked away. "There was a time when he wanted me in his lodge. Yaqui, I mean. They would not let him touch me."

"You are supposedly touched by the gods."

Ross went to her and put his arm about her. "I'm going to try to get you out of here."

"There is no hope."

She looked up at him. Ross drew her close, feeling her unhampered body warm against his. She drew back, but he raised her chin and kissed her.

Something moved behind them on the path. Ross turned. Luz Campos stood there, shielding her naked body with a blanket. There were dark circles beneath her eyes. Her face was swollen and a vivid bruise showed on one cheek. She drew back a little and watched them. There was none of her old spirit in her now. Luz Campos had known many men, but none of them like the beast that had taken her in the stinking wickiup.

Ross stepped back from the girl. She assumed the blank look which had saved her from the fate of Luz.

Luz walked to the edge of the clear pool. Isabel walked back toward the camp. The Mexican woman knelt and began to bathe her face. Then she stood up. "There is nothing wrong with her," she said.

Ross did not answer. There was a bitter coldness in the woman.

Luz drew her blanket about her bruised body. "Amadeo is dead?"

"Yes."

There was no sorrow in her. "You will try to save the girl?"

"Perhaps."

"I know you too well. You mean to save her."

"That is none of your concern, Luz Campos."

"Listen to me, gringo! I must get away from here. I can't stand that beast tearing at me with his dirty claws!"

"There is nothing left between us, Luz."

"Perhaps. But know this: if you do not take me with you I will tell Yaqui that there is nothing wrong with that girl. Do you know what that means?"

Ross looked her up and down. "You should be at

home here. Yaqui is a fitting mate for a cold-blooded bitch such as you."

She came close to him. "Just remember what I have said. I go along, or I tell Yaqui about her. It is up to you, gringo." She walked back toward the camp, limping in pain.

————

WHEN NIGHT CAME YAQUI APPEARED. There were no more than ten full-fledged warriors in the camp. Young braves stood guard while Yaqui drank with his brown-skinned brothers.

Bartolome came to Ross. "There is danger," he said.

"Yaqui talks constantly of what you did last night. He means to challenge you."

"Let him, the son of a bitch."

Bartolome shook his head. "This will not be your way of fighting, with the pistol or the fists, but with the knife, amigo. And he is very good at it."

The debauch gained momentum. Bottle after bottle was drained. Drunken warriors staggered into the brush to relieve themselves. The women brought them food. The fires roared, casting great shadows on the rock walls.

It was almost midnight when Yaqui stood up and talked to two warriors. One of them came to Bartolome and spoke in slurring Chiricahua. Bartolome nodded.

"What is it?" asked Ross.

Bartolome turned. "You are to fight him, man to man With knives."

"Here?"

"Fighting is not allowed in the camp. There is a fighting ground near the canyon wall."

Ross wet his lips. He took a long chance. "There is disgust in you, Bartolome," he ventured.

"Yes. I do not like the way things have gone. There was a time when I loved the raiding. But Cochise is a fool to fight against the soldiers. I do not want to kill soldiers. This is a place of blood. It will get worse."

Ross looked across to where Yaqui sat. "What is it you want?"

"What can you do for me?"

Ross came closer to the renegade. "Help me get that girl out of here. Desert this band and come to Tucson, or better still, come with us. I will see that nothing happens to you when we get to the soldiers."

"It is not a good chance, amigo."

"The warriors are drunk. The guards are boys and untried warriors."

"That is so. But there is one thing you have not thought of."

"So?"

"The warriors are hungry for blood. You must fight Yaqui before you can do anything else."

Ross nodded. "Why doesn't that bastard try to kill me now? It would be easier."

"He cannot. Cochise has saved you from the torturing. He respects you. Yaqui cannot murder you for fear of angering Cochise. But he *can* challenge you. That is the law."

Ross gripped him by the shoulder. "The warriors will watch the fight. It will be your chance to get the women out of here."

Bartolome wet his lips. "I want to go. The women will hold us back."

"Would you see them treated like animals?"

"No."

"Then you must get horses."

"The horses are near the canyon entrance. There are only two guards there."

"*Bueno!* Go to the horses and pick out four good ones. If I win I will get to you and help you dispose of the guards."

"And if you don't win?"

"Then it will not matter, will it, amigo?"

"I will do it."

———

YAQUI WAS ALREADY GONE from the clearing. The rest of the warriors came toward Ross. Ross spoke quietly. "Warn the women. I leave it up to you, Bartolome."

"I'll do my best."

The warriors closed about Ross. They stank of sour liquor. They staggered as they walked him down the path to the south. A fire flared up beneath the canyon wall. Yaqui stepped back from it. He wore only a breechclout. A knife was in his right hand. The *saca tripas,* the curved gutting knife, deadly and efficient.

Yaqui was lighter than Ross, but his body was well nourished. The muscles were smooth and flat. The grease shone on his dark skin. His bloodshot eyes were expressionless as he tested the edge of his knife on his thumb.

Ross was shoved toward the circular area which had been cleared of brush. The ground was smooth and well packed. Here and there showed darker spots of dried blood. The dueling ground had been used before.

One of the braves took out his knife and handed it to Ross. It was a heavy blade, straight and sharp. The big handle fit his hand well. The fire crackled as wood was fed to it. Some of the warriors squatted to enjoy the show. They were liquored to the ears.

Ross was more solidly muscled than the breed, but his body had thinned out because of his experiences. The chips were down. Yaqui was sure of himself. This was his way of fighting, and it was well known the gringos fawned before the knife. Their way of fighting was with fists and pistols, and few Mexicans or Indians could match them in that way of fighting.

Yaqui looked about. He would show these people how a breed could fight. He had been shamed in front of them. Cochise was gone and couldn't stand in the way.

Yaqui respected this big white man. He would gain the respect of Cochise by killing Ross in a knife duel.

Yaqui's blade issued from the thumb side of his hand. Ross did not know it, but the breed was showing his scorn of his adversary by meeting him with the blade that way. That was the way a knife was used in butchering an animal, not in meeting a man. It was an insult as stinging as a whip of nettles. It meant that Yaqui meant to thrust low.

Ross held his blade down, as in meeting a man. His strength was low, but Yaqui had taken aboard a cargo of Dutch courage, and its strength in him was deceptive. Ross was alone among these wild people; there was no friendliness in them. It was an added attraction to the debauch they had embarked on when Cochise had left the camp. Perhaps he would have stopped it, perhaps not.

Yaqui spat. Then he closed in. His blade flicked out, testing Ross. Ross retreated. Yaqui grinned.

"Yaqui!" cried a drunken buck. There was no doubt in his inflamed mind as to who would win.

They circled. Ross crouched a little, waiting for the thrust at his groin. It came swiftly and he caught it just in time with a defensive cut that made the blades click together. Ross jumped back and felt a counterblow slice the skin on his right forearm. The blood ran down into his hand, making his grip slippery. Again, Yaqui came in, cutting swiftly and surely at Ross's right arm. Another cut was laid open.

Sweat began to drip off Ross. There was fear in him, deep in his body, but his hate was stronger.

Yaqui backed away, weaving a pattern of cuts and crosses as Ross followed him. He was playing with Ross, showing these expert knife men that he was a master of the deadly art.

Yaqui turned, whirling to offer his naked back. Ross swiped at it, and instead met air. Yaqui caught Ross across the left thigh, slashing through the ragged drawers but barely cutting the skin.

Yaqui backed away. "Two from one family," he said coldly. "Two brothers killed by Yaqui. Two gringos!"

Ross did not speak. He had been almost sure Yaqui had knifed John. Now he knew. It was the worst thing Yaqui could have done. Ross pressed the attack, slashing and cutting, driving the man back around the big circle. Yaqui fought well and silently, but the sweat dripped from him and for the first time he began to feel the weakening effect of the liquor in him. They broke. Yaqui flicked blood away from his left hand.

There was something in the breed's eyes now—a shadow of doubt, as the big gringo pressed him. Yaqui feinted and cut low. Ross met the sweep with his left hand. He drove in his blade at the throat. Yaqui twisted away. The knife sliced the skin. Blood flowed down his naked back. Ross slammed the blade down hard at the base of the ribs and felt it deflected by bone.

Yaqui broke away. He was breathing harshly now. Now he was fighting for his life instead of doing the butchering. He had meant to cut Ross to ribbons, let him suffer agony, and then finish him off; but the big gringo was tougher than he had anticipated. The courage of the liquor had worn off and suddenly he realized he had walked into a fight to the finish, where the odds had evened up.

Blood dripped from them, but the gouts about the breed's feet were bigger and fell more often. He staggered a little and slipped on a bloody spot. Ross charged, driving his big body in for the kill. Yaqui screamed once as he swayed sideways. Ross drove the blade in swiftly and surely. It struck at the base of the throat and went in to the base of the haft. Ross jerked it sideways and then jumped back.

He was safe. Yaqui went down on his knees. Then he rolled sideways. The *saca tripas* fell from his hand.

Ross stepped back. Sweat stung his cuts. He looked

about the circle. One of the drunks stood up and felt for his knife. An older warrior shook his head. "Cochise!" he warned.

Ross threw the bloody blade on the ground. Something had fallen from the breed's breechclout. The beautiful face of Isabel Rand showed in the firelight. Ross picked up the miniature and walked into the darkness of the trees. The warriors got to their feet and staggered after him.

There was no pursuit. The white-eye had won fairly. Yaqui had been a fool. The law was clean and clear-cut. There would be no vengeance visited on the big man who walked ahead of them through the darkness.

CHAPTER SEVENTEEN

The drunken warriors seemed to have forgotten Ross. Some of them staggered about in the woods, calling out to each other. One of them fell at the edge of the clearing and lay still. Ross felt for his knife in the wall of his wickiup and drew it out. He eased out of the wickiup and into the trees. The women and children had all gone to bed.

Ross tested the edge of his knife. There were still the guards to get past. But he'd take the chance, for in the morning the warriors would be hung-over for a master-piece of all hangovers. The white worms would be moiling in their guts, and tempers, always unstable in the Apache, would flare up quickly.

Ross crawled around the big ring of humped wicki-ups. Isabel Rand lived in one by herself, attended by a young squaw who lived next door. The fire had guttered low. Ross tapped on the rear of the little lodge. There was a quick movement within. He tapped again. "Isabel," he whispered.

There was no sound for a few moments. Then he heard her. "Come."

Ross bellied down and wormed his way to the front of

the little lodge. He went in just as a staggering buck weaved past the lodge, looking for a stray bottle.

"Are you all right?" he asked over his shoulder.

"Yes," a low voice said. *"We're* all right."

Ross turned quickly. In the dimness he could see two figures. Isabel Rand and Luz Campos.

Luz laughed softly. "You thought you'd get away without me, Ross. I'm not such a fool."

Ross almost cursed out loud. It would be tough enough getting Isabel out of the stronghold without having to get Luz out as well.

Luz crawled toward him. "Don't get any ideas about leaving me," she said, "or I'll scream loud enough to wake the dead."

There was no choice. He shrugged. Then he crawled to the back of the lodge and began to cut away the branches.

Luz touched him on the shoulder and jerked her head toward the front of the wickiup. Someone was moving out there. He saw the dumpy figure of the young squaw who took care of Isabel. The young woman dropped to her hands and knees and crawled in. Ross gripped a hand across her mouth and smashed a fist down behind her ear. He hit her once more. She lay still. He looked at Luz. "Gag and tie her," he said.

He cut away the branches and the outer covering of the wickiup and eased through the hole. There was no one in sight. "Come on," he said.

They followed him into the deep darkness of the trees. Now and then they could hear one of the drunks. Two of them sat at the far side of the clearing, sharing a bottle. Ross led the women away from the camp, toward the stronghold entrance. He slid into a hollow and turned to them. "Stay here," he said, "I'll scout ahead."

He worked his way through the brush, coming toward the horses on the downwind side. Someone was standing beside a tree. Ross gripped his knife. Then he made out

Bartolome. He whistled softly. The Mexican came toward him.

Bartolome was scared. He came close to Ross. "There are only two horse guards," he whispered. "One of them has been drinking. He is asleep."

"What about the other?"

Bartolome held up his carbine and tapped the butt. "There is not much time."

"How many guards at the entrance?"

"Two or three. I am not sure."

Ross squatted in the brush. "The women are in the woods. I'll take you to them. Stay with them. I'll go after the guards. I'll whistle three times when the way is clear. Then you must get the women out of here."

Bartolome's face was white beneath his tan. "This is a mad business."

"You can go back."

He shook his head. "I cannot."

"Then shut up about it. Do you have a hand gun?"

Bartolome pulled a Wells-Fargo Colt from his breech-clout. Ross took it and thrust it through the strip of blanket he wore for a belt. "Remember," he said, "I'll whistle three times."

"And if you are killed or captured?"

Ross stood up. He looked into the dark woods. "Kill them," he said quietly.

Bartolome crossed himself.

Ross slipped through the woods, feeling a cold wind play about him. The wind was from the pass, carrying any sound to him. The Chiricahuas had the sight and hearing of animals, and a sixth sense which warned them of danger.

It took him half an hour to locate the first guard. He wasn't more than a boy, squatting on a huge flat rock with a double-barreled scattergun across his thighs. The head-scratching stick and drinking cane of the untried brave hung at his waist. Ross slithered up behind him, inch by inch. The young Chiricahua was looking up the pass. A horse whinnied. He turned to look toward the strong-hold. A big hand shot from behind him and clamped his breath off. He jerked his head as the rough point of the knife found the soft spot to one side of the left shoulder blade.

Ross lowered the lifeless body to the ground and dragged it into the darkness of the brush. He dropped his own knife into a cleft and took the longer, keener one of the young buck. He stripped off the long breechclout and put it on himself. The kid had worn low camp moccasins which were too small for Ross's number tens.

He wiped the cold sweat from his face and then tensed. Something had moved in the brush below the big rock. A low, slurring voice spoke. Ross stood up and flattened himself against a rock wall. The voice came again. Then there was a soft rush of gravel and a squat buck appeared at the edge of the rock. His huge head looked from side to side as he tested the night with his senses. Then he squatted to look at the scattergun which lay on the rock.

Ross drew his Colt and reversed it. The warrior stood up and spoke again. Then he came toward the rock wall. He turned when he was within ten feet of Ross.

Ross crossed the gap. The warrior whirled. The Colt butt smashed home, and the warrior went down on his knees. Ross brought up a big knee, smashing it into the flat face. Then he hammered the Colt down viciously. The buck folded up.

Ross strong-armed the man into the brush and stripped off his desert moccasins, the *n 'deh b 'keh*, thigh-length, thick-soled and button-toed, designed for desert country and worth more than their weight in gold. A buck might discard all superfluous clothing if pursued, but never his *n 'deh b 'keh*.

Ross slid down into the dark pass and crossed it. He worked his way up the steep slope, planting each foot carefully. Just short of the top he squatted in the darkness and waited. Twenty minutes drifted past and then he saw a third guard. The warrior limped a little as he passed below Ross and looked across the pass. He howled softly, like a coyote. There was no answer to his signal. He stared at the far side of the pass.

Ross dropped ten feet onto the warrior's back. The buck went down hard with a startled cry. Big hands clamped on his throat. The buck whipped out a knife. Ross gripped it with his left hand, holding tightly to the corded throat with the other. He forced the knife from the weakening grasp. The buck broke free. His right hand shot upward, fanged with the short reserve knife. The keen edge ripped the bottom of Ross's left hand. Ross booted him in the face and dropped on him again. His heavier weight held the buck down. His left hand forced the knife hand down against the rock. With his right hand he squeezed the life from the weakened warrior.

Ross wiped the sweat from his face and hands. He couldn't wait any longer. He whistled three times and waited. Then he whistled again.

A soft whistle came from down in the pass. Three times. Ross slid down the slope. Bartolome was leading four horses. The two women were with him. Ross led two of the horses toward the desert. There was no sign of life in the brooding pass where three dead warriors stared sightlessly up at the dark sky.

Half a mile from the jumbled mass of the rock stronghold, Ross stopped and looked back. It was like a place of the dead. Ross couldn't help but grin as he thought of the hell Cochise would raise when he returned. He turned to the others. "Mount," he said.

"Where to?" asked Bartolome. He handed Ross a stubby carbine and an ammunition pouch. "The owner won't need them any more," he said.

"What do you think?"

"To the San Pedro. We'll need water."

"Bueno! Lead the way."

Bartolome thudded his heels against the sides of his

sorrel and led the way. Ross placed the slim Maynard carbine across his thighs and probed a hand into the pouch. Nine cartridges; not a hell of a lot, if they were pursued. But they were free of the stronghold and this time Ross wasn't going to be captured.

The wind moaned through the brush. A faint moon touched the eastern sky. To the south a coyote lifted its mournful cry, to be answered by another to the east.

Ross looked at Isabel. "Are you all right?"

There was no blank look on her lovely face now. There was fear; there was also relief. "Thanks to you, Ross Fletcher."

He touched her face with a hard hand. "You'll be all right."

Luz Campos shot them a look of jealousy. Her bruised face showed no signs of gratitude.

Ross let Bartolome pick his way through the jungle of desert growths. He looked at the girl. He had assured her she would be all right. If they were trapped, he hoped to God she'd die by a Chiricahua slug rather than one of his own. He didn't think he had it in him to do away with her.

CHAPTER EIGHTEEN

They had made the twenty-odd miles to the San Pedro in good time. There had been no mercy in Ross for the two tired women. He had lashed their horses every time they had slowed them down.

Ross would let them go ahead while he stayed to look and listen. It would be only a matter of time before the Chiricahuas would sober up long enough to realize what had happened. Four of their men had been killed. The death of one of them would have been enough to start them out in full cry. The only chance the fugitives had was to cross the San Pedro and head for the Whetstones west of the San Pedro and hole up.

It was Bartolome who gave Ross the most concern. He could break away and make faster time. But if the Chiricahuas caught up, Ross would need the renegade's help. Bartolome was riding with the clinging monkey of fear on his back.

They were in the foothills of the Whetstones at dawn. Ross halted them long enough to let the women stretch their legs. Bartolome slid from his mount and looked at the gray sky. "It's getting late," he said.

"The horses are almost beat. The women aren't much better."

Bartolome wet his tips. "I do not like this."

"Damn you! It's not a picnic for me, hombre."

The Mexican shifted his Burnside. "Let me have my *pistola.*"

Ross shook his head. "I may need it."

"It is mine."

Ross looked down at the angry Mexican. "Look," he said, "I'm in charge here. You did a good job; now don't rile me."

Bartolome looked away. Suddenly he raised the carbine and slashed at Ross. Ross fended off the blow with his left forearm, grunting in pain as it struck. He wrenched the Burnside away from the little Mexican. Bartolome went for his knife. Ross dropped the carbine and hit him alongside his jaw. Bartolome dropped as though shot. His eyes were filled with hate as he looked up. *"Bastardo,"* he said.

Ross gripped him by the arm and dragged him to his feet. He held a dirty fist up under Bartolome's jaw. "Smell it," he said thinly; "remember it. The next time I'll break your God-damned jaw." He shoved Bartolome back. He handed him his Burnside.

The Mexican shuffled back to his horse. . . .

Ross looked east. Dust threaded up beyond the San Pedro. "Get moving," he said across his shoulder. "Here they come."

The sun tipped the Big Mountains. The dust was closer now. Ross drew in his horse and yelled at the trio ahead of him. "They're gaining," he said. "Go on! I'll try to hold them off!"

Bartolome lashed at the women's horses with his quirt. Ross slid from his grullo and thrust forward the lever on the Maynard. The barrel tilted forward like a shotgun. He snapped the breech shut and placed a fresh cap on the nipple. Nine rounds for the Maynard; five shots in the Wells-Fargo.

Ross led the grullo into a hollow and then went back. The dust was closer. An Apache could get more speed out of a horse than most men, because they didn't give a damn if they ran them to death. They usually had extra horses with them, shifting from one to the other to make better time.

A trace of dust showed in the gully behind him. He dropped behind a rock and thrust the Maynard across it. He didn't trust Bartolome, but he had no choice.

The Chiricahuas were jumping up a lot of dust. They had to capture the four fugitives, for Cochise would rawhide them if they didn't.

Half a mile from the gully, the Chiricahuas halted their mounts. Ross snapped up the rear sight of his carbine.

There were seven of the red bastards. Three of them dismounted and scattered into the brush. The rest of them vanished from sight in a hollow. Ross waited. He had no cartridges to waste.

One of the bucks showed up beside a straggly ocotillo, studying the quiet hills with bloodshot eyes. Then he padded forward, carrying a long-barreled muzzle-loader. He stopped a hundred yards from Ross, still watching the hills. Ross cocked the Maynard. He settled the sights on the broad sweat-streaked chest, allowed a mite of windage, and took up the trigger slack. The buck was motionless. Ross let out half his breath and held the remainder. The carbine spat flame and smoke. Ross snapped the lever and reloaded. The empty hull tinkled on the rocks.

The buck had gone down as though he'd been poleaxed. The wind ruffled his dirty breechclout.

The echo of the shot bounced from the hills, dying away in a canyon. The smoke drifted downwind, raveling out through the brush. Ross shifted his position higher up the slope. Something moved in the mesquite. He saw a thick mane of hair bound by a dirty calico cloth. He sighted on it and then lowered his aim to hit the unseen chest. The Maynard bucked back against his naked shoulder. The big fifty slug smashed the warrior's left arm. He jerked about as he darted through the brush, gripping the bloody arm. Ross was tempted to snap-shoot but held his fire.

Ross ran at a crouch across the gully and dived into a clump of brush, cursing as catclaw ripped at his skin. There was no movement out beyond the gully.

A rifle puffed. The slug keened through the gully. Ross grinned. The bastard was shooting wild.

A bush swayed against the wind. Ross studied it. The body of it was darker than it should be. He sighted on the dark patch and fired. A warrior thrashed out of cover, tied to the earth by a broken leg.

Ross ran to the grullo and led it up the gully, slipping and sliding on the slick stones. Higher up the gully he stopped and looked back. The warriors had retreated.

The sun was beating down as he reached the top of the huge gully. A pile of fresh droppings steamed in the sun. He entered a maze of broken land and plodded on. He was about three miles from the gully entrance when he saw the two women, sitting in the shade of their horses. He stopped beside them. "Where is he?" he asked. Luz looked up. *"Quién sabe?"* Isabel pressed a slim hand to her head. "He left us here." Ross grounded his carbine. "He won't be back." Luz wet her lips. "The Apaches? Do they follow?" "I held them off, but they'll come on. We must move." The two women mounted their jaded horses. Ross led them farther west. By noon they were in a deep canyon, filled with a suffocating blanket of heat. High on the wall, in a thick cover of brush, he saw the mouth of a cave. He started up the slope, unmindful of the weary women.

Luz yelled. Ross looked back. Her mare had gone down. Ross went back. The mare had broken its left front leg. It looked up at him with piteous eyes.

"Son of a bitch!" yelled Ross. "Couldn't you be more careful?"

Luz spat. "Go to hell, gringo! You're not my lover now!"

Ross raised a dirty hand and then lowered it.

Isabel sat her tired horse, looking down at them. Ross flushed and looked away. Isabel touched her horse with her heels and urged him up the slope. Ross drew his knife. "Get out of here," he said to the Mexican woman. She sneered at him. "I am not afraid of you!"

"Get up there! I've got to finish off the mare."

"I've seen blood before."

His hard eyes held hers until she looked away. "Yes," he said, "and you'll see more."

He knelt by the mare and pulled her head back, tightening the throat muscles. Then he plunged in the knife and swiftly cut the taut throat. The thick blood welled out, splattering his moccasins. He stood up. "We'll have to cover her with rocks," he said.

"We? What about her?" Luz looked up the slope.

"She's almost exhausted."

"Madre de Dios! What about me?"

Ross laughed at her. "I've seen you gamble most of the night and last until dawn drinking and making love."

"Damn you!"

"Get some rocks, Luz. Fast!"

They gathered rocks, sweating and straining in the intense heat, piling them on the body of the mare. Ross looked up at the sky. "Damn it!" he said.

Luz wiped the sweat from her dirty face and looked up. "What is wrong now? Can nothing please you?"

A buzzard hung in the cloudless sky like a scrap of charred paper. Ross jerked a thumb at the scavenger bird. "See that? That's a sign pointing the way to those human bloodhounds down there."

She paled beneath the dirt. "Then we must go on!"

"The horses are almost done. We'll have to hole up."

Luz rubbed her abraded hands on her torn dress. "There are two horses. You and I can take them."

"Get up the hill!"

She cursed and then plodded up the hill. Ross looked up at the buzzard. He had been joined by another. Ross led the grullo up to the cave. It was deep and partially shielded by thick growths. He led the grullo inside and tethered both horses in the rear of the cave. Isabel sat on a rock with her face covered by her hands. Luz dropped to the ground and began a minute inspection of her shapely legs, picking the cactus needles out of them with long nails. She drew the torn skirt higher and higher until her full thighs showed. She glanced at Ross.

Ross squatted by the entrance. Luz was out to make trouble, and she was a mistress of the art.

"Get water," said Luz.

Ross shook his head. "We'll have to stay put until later on. I can't hold those Apaches off out in the open."

"If they come here we'll be trapped like rats."

The long day drifted past with no sign of the Chiricahuas. At dusk Ross left the cave and scouted up the canyon. He found a shallow *tinaja,* inches deep in brownish water. The stuff was ripe, but potable. He watered the horses and then led Luz to the pan. She drank thirstily and then lay back at the edge of the water-hole to look up at him.

"There is still a chance for us alone," she said.

Ross walked away from her through the brush. She hurried after him, glancing over a bare shoulder at the deep shadows, peopled by imaginary enemies.

Isabel strained her water through a piece of cloth. Her face was thin and she was damned near worn out. Ross supported her when they went back. She did not speak.

In the cave Ross squatted by the entrance, watching the first light of the moon sift down. The women were lying down near the back. The place stank of sweat and horses.

Luz came to him. She placed a hand on his shoulder and rested her head against it. "I am afraid," she whispered.

"You're in good company."

"You never seem afraid, Ross."

"Take it easy," he said. "I'm sweating blood right now."

She pressed against him. "Is it because of your brother that you hate me?"

He drew back a little. "You had his gun, Luz. You were thick as thieves with Risler, Maxwell and Yaqui."

"I knew nothing of what they wanted."

"Who killed John?"

"I do not know."

"It was Yaqui."

"I do not think so."

"You're lying. He admitted it before I killed him. Who was with him when he killed John?"

"I do not know!"

He gripped her arm. "Was it Maxwell?"

"No. He was in the gambling hall."

"Amadeo?"

She spat. "That *canalla?* He had the heart of a mouse."

"What about Matt Risler?"

She pulled away. Her torn dress fell from her outthrust breasts. "You are hurting me!"

He pushed her back against the wall and looked down at her.

Luz wet her cracked lips. "Listen," she said, "Matt Risler is behind everything that was done. He had Yaqui and Nick kill Phillip Rand. This I know, for Amadeo was badly frightened. But Matt didn't dirty *his* hands. He was watching you and John, knowing you were after the deed. He had men follow you. When you returned he paid me to drug you, thinking you had the deed. I could not find it. Then Matt took Yaqui to do the job on John."

"You knew they planned to kill John."

"No. No. Matt went with him, I know. They got the deed. I did not know he killed John. Yaqui gave me the little gun. It was pretty; why should I throw it away?"

He stepped back from her. "When I get you to safety," he said thinly, "get out of my sight forever."

Her eyes blazed. "And you'll stay with that little bitch back there!"

Ross turned away. There was the sound of ripping cloth. She had torn her dress down the front to reveal her full body. He bent beside her. "Damn you!"

She pulled him down and wrapped her arms around him. She screamed. The noise aroused Isabel. She jumped to her feet and saw them together. Luz was all but naked. She clawed Ross with long nails. "Let me alone, you pig!" she cried.

Ross broke away from her. The blood ran down his face. Isabel looked from the full body of Luz to Ross and then turned away and walked far back in the dark cave.

Ross slapped the Mexican woman hard across her face. She laughed. "See what you can do with her now," she said.

———

THE MOON WAS full up when Ross heard the footsteps behind him. It was Isabel Rand. "Let me watch," she said quietly. "You are tired."

He shook his head. Luz slept in the middle of the cave, as though she were as innocent as a child.

She took the Maynard from his hands. "I did not thank you for saving my life," she said.

Ross stood up. "You're not safe yet, Isabel."

"Get some sleep."

He hesitated. "I don't suppose you'd believe me if I told you that she had planned it to look like I attacked her?"

She looked away. "You knew her before, did you not?"

"Yes."

Then there is nothing to say."

Ross shrugged and went to the back of the cave. In a few minutes exhaustion took over and he drifted into a dreamless sleep.

Something thudded near the entrance of the cave,

and Ross stirred. Then he heard the thud of unshod hoofs on the earth. He rolled over and freed his Colt, jumping to his feet. Moonlight flooded the cave entrance. Isabel lay on the floor. A worm of blood ran down her pale face. Ross sprinted for the entrance. Luz Campos was down the slope, leading the grullo. She turned to see Ross and then swung up on the grullo like a *vaquero,* the moonlight shining on her white thighs as the dress hitched up.

Ross plunged after her, but Luz hammered her heels against the grullo and shot down the slope, winding in and out of the rock formations. She laughed as Ross stopped. Then she was far down the slope, riding to the west.

Ross went back to the cave. He took the girl in his arms. She opened her eyes. "I did not see her," she said. "I could not move when she took the horse."

"Let her go."

"But there is only one horse."

"We can ride together." He bent and kissed her.

They wasted no time. Ross led the horse from the cave and helped her up. He checked the Maynard and replaced a missing cap on the Colt. Then he led the horse down the slope. The steady thudding of hoofs came to them from up the canyon, as Luz Campos urged the grullo to greater speed.

CHAPTER NINETEEN

The gray light of dawn found them beyond the highest point of the canyon on the western slopes of the Whetstones, with the Santa Ritas looming before them. Ross plodded on, keeping in the gullies and behind the ridges.

It was the girl who first noticed the sound. "Listen," she said.

Ross stopped. The wind swept about them, billowing her torn skirts, and rattling the stalks of the brush. Then the sound came to him—the thin scream of a woman. He dropped the bridle and climbed up a slope. Three warriors were closing in on Luz Campos. She was lashing the jaded grullo with a thick stick. She came toward Ross. Ross looked down the slope. Isabel had dismounted. He slid down to her and handed her the Colt. "Ride up the gully. Get at least a mile away before you hide."

"What is wrong?"

"They are after Luz Campos."

She paled. "What will you do?"

He lifted his carbine. "Maybe I can help her."

"They'll kill you too."

He raised his head. "It won't be long until they're

after us."

She fingered the hand gun.

"Do you know how to use it, Isabel?"

"Yes."

He raised her chin with his free hand. "Listen to me. If they are about to catch you, you must save a shot for yourself. Do you understand?"

"Yes."

He kissed her. "Four bullets for them. The last for yourself. *Vaya con Dios,* Isabel."

She swung up on the horse and looked down at him. "I believe you about last night," she said. "I do not think you would lie to me."

She rode up the gully and then stopped. "I love you, Ross Fletcher," she said, and then she was gone.

Luz Campos screamed again. Ross dropped in the brush. He thought wryly of the hell he had raised about not seeing action while at Fort Yuma. He had his belly full now and the pot wasn't out of the fire yet. "Salt, pepper and gravel in the grease," he said as he checked the cap on the Maynard. Six rounds.

The Maynard spat at a hundred-and-fifty-yard range. The accurate little breechloader rolled a paint pony ass over tea kettle. The warrior hit the ground and stared at the puff of smoke coming from the brush. Luz turned toward the smoke. Ross reloaded. His second shot struck a warrior in the head. He hit the ground and the gray shot off through the brush as though all the imps of hell were riding it. The third Chiricahua was close behind Luz now. Ross couldn't shoot. She screamed throatily.

Ross looked to the west. Half a dozen warriors were sweeping down a long rise. There was no chance for Luz Campos now, with those hung-over bloodhounds after her. He sighted on her, but she swerved into the brush. He cursed. It was all he could do for her. Then the grullo was down and Luz Campos was running through the brush, half naked, the needles ripping at her white flesh.

Ross dropped a shot at the oncoming warriors and

wasted it. Three rounds. He slid down the long slope and
legged it up the gully. The wind picked up the thud of
hoofs and the yelling of the bucks. Then a scream was
torn from the throat of Luz Campos. They had her.

Ross hurdled a rock and plunged on, heedless of
catclaw and prickly pear which slashed against his legs,
turned aside by the thigh-length mocs. Sweat poured
from his body and greased his hands where they clutched
the hot Maynard.

He reached an elevation and shot a glance over his
shoulder. Some of the bucks were gathered around something which thrashed about under their greasy hands.
Something white and shapely, stripped to the skin, with
streaks of blood on its smoothness. He saw five warriors
lashing their ponies up the slope, not more than a quarter
of a mile behind him.

Ross plowed through the brush and came out on a
cactus flat. There was no sign of Isabel Rand. He cut to
the north, racing like a greyhound. He was at the far side
when the four warriors crested the rise and saw him. He
turned and knelt, raising the Maynard. It moved up and
down with his heavy breathing, but he forced himself to
hold his breath. His first shot missed. He levered open
the breech and slipped in another round. This time he
was on target. A buck went down in a scattering of
gravel. Ross loaded his last round.

The two bucks in the lead veered off. Ross fired at
one of them and sent his pony down. The others scattered and disappeared down the slope. Ross slogged
down a rocky slope and jumped into an arroyo which
wound north. He pulled out all the stops and ran.

The sun was high in the pitiless heavens when he
dropped the useless Maynard in a cleft. Somewhere in
the blasting desert was Isabel Rand, alone, providing the
Apaches hadn't found her too, to deal with her as they
had Luz Campos.

There was no wind on the heat-shimmering flats. The
mountains swam in a haze that hurt the eyes. Here and

there was the tinted glaze of mirages, pools of clearest water, which he would never reach, fading away from his tortured eyes as he neared them. His brain seemed to sizzle in its bony helmet. His skin was dry. Dehydration had set in, first from the upper part of the body, then from his legs, then from the deeper tissues. Soon his bones would dry out.

The earth burned through the thick soles of his moccasins. He thought of the heavy rains which had flooded the western deserts earlier in the year. He thought of the cool spring in the Chiricahua stronghold. There was only one other thought in his mind. Where was Isabel Rand?

He slogged on, heading northward. The overland route should not he too far away. Rincon Peak showed clearly, and the overland was at the foot of the mountains. He hoped to God she had run into some white men, rebels of Sherrod's command or troopers from the California Column.

The heat became hellish. He crept beneath the dubious shade of some brush and tried to rest. But the thought of the girl alone out there would not let him rest.

————

IT WAS dusk when he caught the odor of woodsmoke drifting to him on the hot wind. Then he saw the dim light. He stopped and studied it. The light showed in a rectangular shape. A lighted window. As far as he knew he was nowhere near any habitation. He stood still for a long time. He heard the distant whinnying of horses. Then he padded forward with his knife in his hand.

The wind swayed the brush. He stopped on a rise. Below him were mounded rocks and a few scrubby trees. A low group of buildings showed in the dimness, with some of the windows showing light. There was a sudden flare of light, and Ross saw the bearded face of a white man, lighting his pipe.

Ross worked closer. A man passed in front of one of the lighted windows. There was no mistaking the blue blouse and slanted forage cap with its brass saber ornament. Ross rubbed his forehead in relief. He walked closer to the station, carefully, so that no nervous bluecoat would pump a slug into him. There were a dozen horses in a corral. The place looked like a stage station.

Then he heard a familiar voice. "God damn it! Cover them windows with blankets, you bastards! You want an Apache to shoot through them? Before God, I wish I had been assigned some real soldiers instead of you half-assed militia!"

"Mike Duncan," said Ross. It was like a voice from the long distant past.

Ross circled the station and bellied along until he was near the door. There was a sentry not a hundred feet from him. A big man stepped out into the darkness and looked about.

"Mike," said Ross.

Duncan whirled, clawing for his Colt.

"For Christ's sake, Mike! It's Ross! Ross Fletcher!"

Duncan had his Colt out and cocked. He flattened himself against the wall. "Get up on your feet, whoever in hell you are! Ross Fletcher is dead."

Ross stood up and held up his hands.

Duncan came forward and stared at him. "Jesus God! Is it you or a ghost?"

The sentry closed in at the double with ready carbine. "Get back, you stupid clodhopper," said Duncan. "Here's a man crawls right up to the God-damned station while you're enjoying the beauties of nature." Duncan gripped Ross by the shoulders: "Where in hell have you been?"

Ross grinned. "Can I get a drink first?"

"Hell yes!"

Duncan led him into the abandoned stage station. Troopers looked up from their food. They stared at the filthy apparition with their sergeant. "Jesus," breathed little Eddie Neiderdecke, "it's Fletcher, or his ghost."

"A ghost don't stink like that," said Slim Hause.

Ross picked up a canteen and emptied half of it. For a minute he thought he was going to get sick. Then he sat down on a battered chair. "How's the war going?" he asked weakly.

Duncan squatted against the wall. "Last I seen of you, you were hell-fired anxious to go south looking for stray Tucsonians."

"I found them," said Ross dryly. "I also found some Apaches. I've been visiting with Cochise in the Dragoons."

"There," said Eddie triumphantly, "I knew the bastard was dead."

"Shut up," said Duncan. He studied Ross, eying the scars, the drawn face, the mat of shaggy hair, and the hell which showed out of the gray eyes.

"You hungry, Ross?" asked Amos Bracken. "We got Mex strawberries and sow bosom." He held out a filled plate of beans and bacon.

Ross shook his head. He looked at Duncan. "Where are you heading?"

"Nowhere. We're to stay here at La Cienega Springs to guard it and patrol the overland road. There's been hell to pay. 'Paches raiding the wagon trains."

Ross drank again. He swilled the water about in his mouth and swallowed. "Have you seen a white woman?"

"Out here? You loco?"

Ross took the miniature from his breechclout. "Her?"

Duncan stared at it. "This is the girl who was supposed to have been killed by 'Paches."

Ross shook his head. "She's alive. I got her out of the Cochise stronghold in the Dragoons. She'd been a captive there since early this year. I lost her early this morning. Good God, Dunc, she's out there alone!"

The troopers looked at each other and then at Ross.

"I've got to find her!"

"Not tonight, soldier. You're in no condition to go anywhere. You try it and I'll have you put under guard."

Ross glared at the burly non-com. Duncan slid his hand down to his Colt. "Get cleaned up. We'll forage up some clothes for you. No funny business, mind."

Ross felt a great weariness in him as he went outside and cleaned up. Duncan brought him drawers, socks, a worn pair of trousers and a buck shirt. "You'll have to wear them mocs until we can get the rest of your outfit."

Duncan leaned against the wall and watched him dress. "You've got lives like a cat," he said. "You find what you were looking for?"

"I found the girl."

"How about the others?"

"Yaqui is dead. I killed him. Maxwell is as thick as a thief with Cochise. They're getting guns from somewhere."

Duncan nodded. "There was a small train raided some time ago. Had rifles and carbines for the Pimas. Lost every damned one of them. Looked suspicious to me."

"Why?"

"Your friend Captain Risler was in charge of the escort. They were missing when the Chiricahuas struck the wagons. He said he had been chasing some raiders. Wasn't one damned teamster left alive. Risler got hell about it, but they let him off with a reprimand."

Ross hacked at his shaggy hair. "Cochise and his Chiricahuas are allying themselves with Mangus Colorado and his Mimbrenos. They plan to close Apache Pass to Union troops."

"They're a little late. Colonel Eyre, of the First California Cavalry, has already passed through there on his way to New Mexico with a hundred and forty men."

Ross looked up. "And no trouble?"

"No. They expected it, but nothing happened."

"Seems odd."

"Maybe you heard a cock-and-bull story."

"No. Cochise himself told me it was their Big Medicine pass. He wasn't telling me any story, Mike."

"You've been having a hard time. Nothing will happen."

"The rest of the column has to go through there."

"We can take care of Cochise and old Red Sleeves."

"Maybe. Can I go into Tucson tomorrow?"

"Not until I get orders concerning you."

"Hell's fire!"

Duncan offered him a cigar. They lit up. "You might as well know, Ross," said Duncan quietly, "that General Carleton is ruling this command with an iron fist. He rounded up all the Tucson scum and shipped, them off to Fort Yuma for imprisonment. The old bastard even levied a tax of a hundred eagles a month on all the gambling houses. One hundred a month for every table in the joint. Every bar owner has the same tax. He's been strict as hell with us as well. He's even arrested Sylvester Mowry. Carleton is absolute ruler of Arizona, sonny. Besides, you've been listed as a deserter."

"You're loco!"

"Damn it! You always *were* shooting off your mouth about going over the hill if there wasn't any fighting. That stupid statement was remembered when you vanished."

Duncan inspected his cigar. "Another thing. I don't know whether or not Risler had anything to do with the raid on the wagon train, or if he's a rebel sympathizer as you say. But I do know this: he'll be showing up here any day. It's his assignment to keep this road open. If he comes here you'd better mind your manners, or that son of a bitch will put you where you'll learn some in a hurry!"

Ross shook his head. "I've got to see Carleton. Dunc, Cochise and Mangus Colorado will be like fire and flood if we go through that pass with wagons."

"You're like every other jackass private in the rear rank, thinking you can run the war better than the generals. Take my advice. Keep your big mouth shut. Otherwise you'll sit out the war in the calabozo at Fort Yuma with a splendid view of the Colorado river country."

"Go to hell!"

Duncan grinned. He placed a thick arm about Ross's shoulders. "Damn it, though. I missed that ugly face of yours. We got some fighting to do before this war is over. Now tell me the whole damned story from beginning to end. This place is driving me loco."

Later, as Ross lay in his blankets in the station, he debated on whether or not he should skip out over the hill with one of the platoon horses to find Isabel. But if she had made it to safety, he wouldn't do her much good if they caught him. Carleton had a campaign to fight and win, and according to Mike Duncan, the stern officer wouldn't stand for any monkey business that would bother him while performing his duty.

CHAPTER TWENTY

The stage station at Cienega de Los Pinos sweltered under the June sun. Wind devils rose on the flats beyond the station and whirled aimlessly, to disappear as mysteriously as they had appeared. Two threads of smoke hung in the sky from separate peaks to the east. There was a metallic haze on the heat-soaked mountains.

The twenty men of the second platoon, Cremoney's B Company, First California Volunteer Cavalry, watched the smoke through slitted eyes. A detachment of nine troopers had passed through the area not five hours before, carrying dispatches for Eyre's command in New Mexico—if he had reached New Mexico.

Sergeant Mike Duncan loosened the collar of his undershirt. "What do you think, Ross?" he asked.

Ross leaned against the station wall, studying the smoke. "I told you Cochise was going to raise hell. Nine men! Jesus! That red bastard is anywhere and everywhere. You should have kept those men here, Dunc."

"You think I'm in command of the Column? I'm just a three-striper in command of an undermanned platoon."

Ross grinned. "Maybe you think they ought to make

an officer out of you? I've seen them make officers out of lousier material."

Duncan spat. "Sometimes you try me."

Ross squatted and picked up a handful of gravel. Idly he flicked the pebbles out of his hand. "You've got orders to keep all of your men here if things get tough."

"Yeah."

"They're tough now, is that it?"

"It ain't exactly an excursion out here, sonny."

"I'm not in your platoon."

"The hell you ain't!"

"I'm listed on the company roster as Fletcher, Ross, Duty to Desertion. You told me so yourself. If I'm listed as such, theoretically I'm not even here."

Duncan dashed the sweat from his face. "I can smell you, Johnny Raw." He grinned. "You're here all right."

Ross flipped a pebble. "Now if I were to volunteer to mosey out there to see what happened to that detachment, I think it would be according to regulations, being as how I'm not on the platoon active roster."

Duncan raised his eyes to the blazing sky. "Dear Lord," he said, "deliver me from Johnny Raws, saddle-galled horses, rusty carbines, beans and bacon. But above all, deliver me from a damned guardhouse lawyer with a mind that ain't quite right."

"I can go out there, Dunc, and settle the whole thing. Give me the fastest horse in the platoon and I'll get out there and back."

"Stop flipping them damned pebbles!"

"Yes, Sergeant!"

Duncan shook his head wearily. "All right. Before God, I think this damned sun has addled me."

Ross stood up and yawned. "Oh, I don't know. You had a head start thataway, Dunc."

"*Sergeant* Duncan!'"

Ross braced himself and saluted smartly. "Sergeant Duncan—sir!"

"Jesus!"

Ross went into the station and got a Sharps. He swung his belt about his lean waist and settled it, checking the big Navy Colt.

Corporal Owsley eyed him. "Where do you think you're goin'?"

"Scout east, Owsley."

"Alone?"

"Yes."

"You're loco."

Ross shrugged. He took his borrowed gear out to the corral. Farrier Corporal Mooney eyed him. "So it's a horse you'll be wantin'?"

"I don't aim to walk, Timothy."

Mooney spat a dollop of spit-or-drown. It struck the hard earth with the sound of a wet towel. "No. Tis not a walkin' country, me bhoy."

Ross looked at the horses. "Pick one out, Tim."

"Take Nellie. She's got no manners, but she's been around. Lookit the gleam in her eye!"

Ross walked to the dun mare. She nickered. She had good eyes. He passed a hand down her legs. No shortened tendons. No galls. He picked up a saddle and placed it on her. Her hips were plump, coiled with frictionless power. She'd do.

Ross slung his gear, adding two full canteens, and mounted the dun. She broke wind as he kneed her toward the gate.

Mooney grinned. "I said she had no manners."

Duncan waited for Ross. He looked up at him. "If there's trouble, don't stop to fight. Get back here. Jump up the dust."

Every man in the platoon gathered in the hot shade to watch Ross.

Duncan came close. "Forget about the girl, Ross. Don't take off to look for her. If you do, by God, I'll swear you went over the hill again. And this time, you'll get no jawbone on tick from me."

Ross spurred the mare out onto the rutted overland

road. To hell with Mike Duncan and the California Column. If *she* was out there in that hot hell, he meant to find her.

———

THE SUN PASSED its zenith and began the long westward slide, but the heat was worse. The mare fell into a long lope.

The smoke signals had been raveled out like coarse hair on a piece of blue linen. Five miles from the station, the smoke was a faint smudge on the sky. At the nine-mile mark he splashed across the shallow San Pedro, eyeing the fire-gutted stage station which looked at him with blank windows.

Beyond the brush of the San Pedro, the road was fairly smooth and hard packed. Nellie moved along like a machine. Ross rested her a mile beyond the river, where the brush had thinned out. He led her for half an hour, looking ahead through the hazy air. There was no sign of life. The rattlers and lizards had more sense than to expose themselves to the heat. Only man was stupid enough to travel in hell.

Beyond the San Pedro was Dragoon Springs Station, Swell's Station, and then Apache Pass, key stations on the once great Southern Overland Mail.

Ross rode slowly for a time. Now and then he looked south toward the brooding Dragoons. He wondered if Cochise had returned yet. There would be hell to pay when he did return. He wouldn't be likely to forget Ross Fletcher.

Ross decided he'd go on for a few miles and then cut back through the desert to cross the San Pedro, then through the Whetstones to look for Isabel.

There was something alien to the natural features of the desert. Ross drew in the sturdy mare. He unslung his Sharps and half-cocked it, placing a cap on the nipple, feeling the complete silence of the windless land. The sun shone on the dry flats far ahead, giving them the look of a clear lake.

Ross shifted in the saddle. There was something to the right side of the road among the mesquite. He slanted his forage cap low on his eyes and studied it. Then he knew what it was. The nine-man detachment.

He touched the mare with his spurs and kneed her off the rutted road. A hundred yards from the men, he stopped. They were lying in a rough circle, naked feet touching the feet of the man on the opposite side of the circle. Three dead horses lay there, swelling already in the blazing sun.

Ross went forward, scanning the still brush with slitted eyes, ready to spur Nellie to hell out of there if the brush erupted with shrieking Chiricahuas.

He drew rein fifty feet from the silent circle. They had been stripped to the buff, slashed and battered beyond human recognition. Their heads had a curious lopsided look. The Chiricahuas had smashed the skulls to keep the souls of the dead from pursuing them.

Ross felt a sour taste in the back of his mouth. Nellie shied and blew as she caught the odor of death. The desert was empty of life. All around the circle of death were the imprints of *n 'deh b 'ken,* the desert moccasins of the People. Arrows bristled from the battered corpses.

The first signs of life he saw were the circling buzzards high overhead.

The detachment had sold out dearly. Their shoulders were reddened from the stiff recoil of their Sharps carbines. Ross circled the silent detachment. Here and there on the trampled sand, he saw blotches of black where Chiricahuas had done some bleeding. How many of them had gone to the House of Spirits?

Ross returned to the road. There was nothing he could do there. Tonight the nocturnal prowlers would come to further the hasty ripping work of the vicious buzzards.

He headed west. Nellie moved along easily. To the

south he saw a smudge of dust near the rugged Dragoons. At the San Pedro he watered the mare. The dust was traveling parallel to the road, west, as he was traveling west. They had seen him or his dust.

Parallel to the Whetstones the dust rose, a deadly warning of the Chiricahuas. To go into those silent hills would be to sign his death warrant, and Ross Fletcher wanted to live to see Isabel Rand again.

He saw the dust on the overland road three miles beyond the San Pedro, dust to the south and to the west. Something glinted through the dust to the south. He spurred Nellie into a dry wash, and raced her up it two hundred yards. He spurred her up the rise. A shot flatted off in the stillness.

Ross slid down into the wash. He reined in and heard the steady thudding of hoofs on the hard earth. He rode south. Then he heard a yell. A horseman showed up on the edge of the wash. A carbine blasted off. Nellie jumped as the slug creased her flank. Ross turned and yelled at the horseman: "God damn it, soldier! Can't you see blue!"

The trooper reloaded. Ross kneed Nellie around. Then suddenly a half-dozen troopers lined the edge of the wash, holding carbines on him. A rawboned sergeant slid his gray down into the wash with a rush of gravel. He held a cocked Colt on Ross. "Private Fletcher?"

"Yes."

"You're under arrest."

Ross stared at him. "What the hell are you talking about? I was scouting the overland road."

"In a pig's eye, soldier. You're listed as a deserter."

"For Christ's sake!"

"I'm Tankersley of the Second California."

"Did you come from Cienega?"

"Yes."

"Mike Duncan sent me out."

Tankersley spat leisurely. "Yeah. I know. My officer sent me after you."

"Who?"

"Captain Risler. They've been looking for you, soldier. Risler swears he'll have Mike broken."

Ross handed over his weapons. "The whole damned army is loco."

Tankersley shrugged. "You would say that. You're in a mess, Fletcher."

They rode across country to the road and then west to the station. An officer stood in the shade of the station, watching them. It was Matt Risler, immaculate in fine blue broadcloth. There was no recognition of Ross in his dark eyes.

Tankersley saluted Risler. "We found him off the road, sir. He was heading for the mountains. We had to shoot at him to make him stop, Captain Risler."

"He's a damned liar," said Ross, "I saw dust on the road, and pulled off of it until I could see who it was."

Risler smoothed the front of his blouse. "Your eyes must be failing if you can't see a blue uniform, Private Fletcher."

Ross flushed. "There's no army regulation stopping an Apache buck from wearing a blue uniform."

Tankersley scowled. "Say *sir* to an officer, damn you!"

"*Sir,*" said Ross quietly.

Risler looked to the east. There were no traces of the smoke signals. "Did you see any traces of the courier detachment, Fletcher?"

"Yes, sir. They're all dead. About five miles beyond the San Pedro."

"Killed by rebels?"

"No, sir."

The dark eyes held Ross's slitted eyes. "You don't mean to stand there and tell me nine well-armed troopers have been massacred by Apaches?"

Ross cut a hand sideways. "What the hell do you think I mean? They had been stripped and their skulls had been crushed. I'll admit the Texans are rough fighters, but I'm damned if I'll believe they'd mutilate the dead."

Risler turned to Tankersley. "Place this man under guard in an outbuilding."

"On what charges?" asked Ross.

Risler inspected his neat fingernails. "Desertion on two counts. Deserting at Tucson; deserting here. Resisting arrest. Reporting false information as to the fate of the courier detachment. Insubordination to a superior officer."

Mike Duncan stepped forward. "Private Fletcher was ordered to leave Tucson, Captain Risler. He reported here of his own free will. I sent him out to see if he could find out what happened to the courier detachment."

Risler waved a hand. "Fletcher is your friend; you'd stand up for him. The man is a known troublemaker. Even now he's spreading a false story about Apaches attacking the courier detachment."

"Sir," protested Duncan, "the man is a skilled scout who knows this country and the Apaches."

Risler looked up. "So? We have detailed reports that Cochise is in Sonora with most of his men."

Ross smashed a fist into his other palm. "Damn it! Cochise is planning an alliance with Mangus Colorado of the Mimbrenos. The two of them plan to close Apache Pass to the California Column. Cochise isn't in Sonora; I saw him less than a week ago. General Carleton should be notified at once. The Chiricahuas are well armed, and are getting more weapons."

The enigmatic eyes studied Ross. "You seem to know quite a bit about it. I looked up your record before I left Tucson. There are a few entries about extra duty being given to you for making remarks about the inactivity of the troops at Fort Yuma. You were a dissenter and troublemaker. You seem to be following the same pattern here, spreading rumors about Cochise allying himself with Mangus Colorado."

"It's the truth!"

"I've always suspected you were a rebel agent. It would certainly be to the advantage of the Texans to have a rumor spread that the Mimbrenos and Chiricahuas are joining hands."

Ross stepped forward. "I'd like to ask you a few questions, you cold-eyed bastard!"

Tankersley shoved his Colt muzzle into the middle of Ross's back.

Risler jerked his head. "Lock him up," he said.

Tankersley shoved Ross toward the outbuildings. Ross yelled over his shoulder, "How is it that guns intended for the Pimas are in Chiricahua hands? What kind of dirty work is Nick Maxwell up to, Risler?"

Ross was pushed into a heat-filled room, and Tankersley barred the door behind him. He looked in at the little window. "You loco son of a bitch," he said. "You sure got yourself in a mess now. You'll spend the rest of the war in a cell at Fort Yuma."

"Go to hell!"

Ross stood at the window. Risler had come to the station with a score of troopers and four heavily laden supply wagons. The wagons were lined up to one side of the station, and a single trooper lounged against one of them as guard.

Mike Duncan came to the improvised cell. "You sure as hell didn't try to get along," he said angrily, "Now Risler is sending me back to Tucson tonight while he goes east to scout the road."

Ross stared at him. "How many men are going to stay here?"

"Owsley will have his squad."

"Jesus!"

Duncan shrugged. "It's Risler's orders."

Ross looked about. There was no one else in sight. "For God's sake, Dunc! Report to Carleton about Cochise. I swear to God he intends to close that pass."

"I'll report it."

"What's in those wagons?"

"Rifles and ammunition. Some medical stores. Bullet molds and bar lead. Mostly ordnance stuff."

"What's it doing here?"

Duncan shrugged. "I suppose they plan to make a supply depot out of this place until they can transport the stuff to New Mexico. Why?"

A cold feeling came over Ross. One squad to garrison the station. The hills full of some of the best guerrilla fighters and raiders in the world. A rich prize of weapons and ammunition sitting there before their greedy eyes.

"What about me?" asked Ross.

"I've got no orders about you."

Ross wiped the sweat from his face. Risler's detachment had formed fours in the road. "I don't like this, Mike. Risler is practically giving those supplies to the Chiricahuas."

"I'm beginning to think you're right about the two-faced bastard."

Risler looked back as his detachment rode toward the San Pedro. Then he was gone, leaving the lonely station with its small garrison.

Duncan wet his lips. "You think the 'Paches will hit us?"

"The odds are with them. They're watching this station. They can see Risler right now. If you pull out they'll know there is only a handful of men here. You know the rest. Maybe that's why Risler made sure I'd stay here. The dead can't talk."

Duncan rubbed his jaw. "What the hell can I do about it?"

Ross came close to the small window. "Pull out. Ride until after dark. Before the moon comes up, turn around and come back."

Duncan was puzzled. "I don't get it."

"I'll write it on the wall for you. I'm willing to bet Risler ordered you back to Tucson and went on to the San Pedro for one reason! He's in cahoots with Maxwell, and Maxwell is working with Cochise. That's why Risler is leaving this station practically undefended. He'll be in the clear. Cochise will wipe out Owsley's squad and take the wagons. It's a cinch."

"Jesus!"

Ross jerked his head. "Let me out. I'll work with Owsley. We'll empty those wagons after dark and load every damned one of those rifles. We can cut extra loopholes covering those wagons. When Cochise comes down we'll punch a one-way ticket straight to hell for him with lead slugs."

Duncan grinned. "Sometimes I think you're loco. But you know something, Ross? We'll try it!"

———

DARKNESS HAD SETTLED about the lonely station. Duncan had pulled out in full view of the prying eyes in the hills beyond the station. Owsley's squad emptied the gun cases and took the rifles into the station. One detail loaded them while another cut loopholes in the thick adobe walls. Sweat streamed down the working men. Owsley lashed them on with the whip of his tongue.

An hour before the moon rose, Duncan's detachment showed up at the station, leading their mounts. Every bit of metal which might make a noise had been wrapped with rags. Duncan's men led their horses into the big common room of the station. The only horses in the walled corral were those of Owsley's squad.

Duncan inspected the work that had been done. "*Bueno,*" he said. "You didn't do bad for a rebel agent, Ross."

Owsley wiped the sweat from his homely face. "What do we do now?"

"Wait," said Ross. "He won't disappoint us."

"Who?" asked the corporal.

"Cochise," said Ross with a wry smile.

CHAPTER TWENTY-ONE

The moon was but a faint suggestion in the eastern sky. The odors of horses and cooked food hung over the stage station. The searching eyes in the brush on the low ridge behind the station studied the dim buildings and the white-tilted supply wagons. Most of the white-eyes had gone east toward the San Pedro. A smaller group had gone west toward Tucson. There were only eight horses in the walled corral. The soldiers were not in sight. The place was soft for the killing.

The soles of the desert moccasins made no sound as the shadowy figures came down from the ridge. The wind moaned softly about the darkened buildings. Smoke drifted from the station chimney.

Ross peered through a loophole. Each trooper had been told to stay back from the loopholes. Owsley had his squad in an outbuilding which was at right angles to the main station building. The carbines could cover the corral and the four wagons. A man moved in the darkness and Mike Duncan cursed softly. The embers in the big beehive fireplace flared up a little. Ross could see the glistening faces of the men.

Minutes ticked past. Then he saw the first movements-shadowy flitting figures which closed in on the wagons. Other warriors flattened themselves against the corral wall. Still others padded toward the station with ready rifles. Some of them crossed the road and then came in toward the thick door of the station.

Ross counted eight of them at the wagons, six at the corrals, ten in front of the station. There might be others. Cochise would take no chances. Apaches liked heavy odds. It was their way to make sure of the trap and then pour on the coal. The bucks in front of the station were carrying a heavy timber to batter in the door.

A night bird whistled softly from behind the corral. Another answered it from near the wagons. Then, after a pause, the call came from in front of the station. This would be easy. The soldiers were asleep, with full bellies, dreaming of the women in Tucson.

Ross raised his carbine and rested it on the lip of the loophole. The troopers followed suit. Ross looked about the dark room. Heavy breathing came from the tense men.

The night bird called again. Moccasins scraped softly on the hard earth. The warriors at the front of the station eased their pistols and knives for quick drawing and then maneuvered the heavy timber in line with the door. All was ready.

Ross sighted on the broad chest of a buck near the wagons. He cocked the Sharps. Then he squeezed off. The roar of the Sharps nearly deafened him. Bitter smoke blew back into the room. The buck went down and lay still. Then the night was filled with the crashing roar of carbines. A leaden sleet poured out of the two buildings. In the gunflashes the Apaches were scattered about like bloody rag dolls.

The Sharps were emptied. Long-barreled muzzle-loaders were grabbed up and fired into the yelling raiders. The noise was deafening, and the thick smoke hung in the room. Ross emptied two rifles, tallying for each slug. There was an animal sound in the shrieking of the

raiders, torn from their throats in bullet-shattered agony.
Hardly a slug missed. It was like shooting fish in a barrel,
and the men of the platoon kept at their deadly work
until each of them had emptied at least four guns.

Then the firing died away and the troopers looked at
their bloody work. "Jesus," said Slim Hause, "it'd make
me sick to my gut if they'd a been white men."

Mike Duncan fired his Colt through a loophole. A
downed warrior jerked as the slug smashed the back of
his head. Here and there through the brush were flitting
figures, racing away from the hell which had poured out
on them from the silent building. The white-eyes had
pulled the snapper on them and had smashed some of the
best warriors of Cochise into bloody, writhing pulp.

High on the ridge stood Cochise, beating his fists
against his naked chest. He had seen the dark building
suddenly blossom with deadly red and orange flames. It
should have been so easy. The silent approach, the splin-
tering of the big door, the swift deadly work in the darkness with knife and pistol on the blanketed bodies of the
white-eyes.

It was a day of fortune for Nick Maxwell, for if he had
been there, Cochise would have struck him down like a
dog. The few survivors ran to their ponies and lashed
them up the draws toward the haven of the mountains.
They were still stunned with the smashing defense of the
station. They had paid in blood. The face of Cochise was
dark with blood as he followed his demoralized men.

———

FAR TO THE east an officer touched his horse with his
spurs and rode on after his detachment. He had waited to
hear the shooting. Cochise had done well; there had not
been much of a fight. There was a cold smile on the face
of Matt Risler as he rode toward the rising moon. He
hoped Ross Fletcher had lived through the attack to die
slowly under knife and flame in the Chiricahua strong-

hold. He had cheated the torturers once by winning the respect of Cochise. The chief had plenty of weapons now, not only for himself, but for mighty Mangus Colorado as well.

Risler lit a cigarillo. The flame of the lucifer lit up the planes of his cold face. The Federal troops would never get through Apache Pass. There would be horses and weapons for the taking. Arizona would be prostrate under the heel of the strong man who could control Cochise. Chiricahuas, Sonorans and the tough American outlaws of the Southwest would flock to the side of the man who could lead them on an orgy of raping and looting. That man was Matt Risler.

CHAPTER TWENTY-TWO

Buzzards dotted the hot blue sky to the south of Cienega de Los Pinos, circling in a great ragged wheel which dipped lower and lower toward the deep draw where eighteen warriors of the Chirichuas lay in purpling, sweet-rotten death beneath the blazing sun.

There was little talking among the men of Duncan's platoon. It was one thing to cut down Apaches with hot lead, it was quite another to drag the bloody bundles of human clay out into the desert. Many soldiers would rather fight than do fatigue work. But the big trooper who had returned to the platoon after escaping from Cochise had insisted on dragging the bodies out there.

Mike Duncan wiped the sweat from his broad face. "The boys are riled," he said. "They think it would have been easier to dump them red bastards in that old well behind the station."

Ross shook his head. "Cochise was so damned sure of himself. Let him look on those bodies. Let their rotten-ness stink in his nostrils. There won't be any victory cele-bration in his camp. We've shaken his confidence, Mike."

"We? You did it, Ross. It's a pleasure going to war with you. Still, I think Cochise will sweat blood until he gets his revenge. Jesus, what a comeuppance we gave him."

"An Indian is like an Oriental—face is important to them. Well, Cochise lost his damned face at Cienega."

"I'd better pull out of here," said Duncan. "If Risler comes back and finds me here, he'll have me court-martialed. Still, I hate like hell to leave this place with only a squad as garrison."

Ross grinned. "Go ahead. Cochise has had a bellyful. The sight of these buildings is enough to give him a headache."

Duncan nodded.

Ross scratched his jaw. "You'll have to see West or Carleton and warn him about the ambush planned in Apache Pass. If you ever did any talking, Mike, this is the time to speak with a golden tongue."

Duncan looked east. "Whether or not Risler had anything in mind when he left the station almost unde-fended, he'll have a helluva time explaining why he did it."

Ross nodded. "There's one more thing you can do in Tucson, Mike."

"I know. Isabel Rand. You think there's any chance of her still being alive, Ross?"

"They gave her up for lost once. I found her alive. She's got to be alive, Dunc."

Mike placed an arm about Ross's shoulders and gripped him tightly. "I think she is, Ross. My mother had the second sight, and I'm the second son of a second son. I say she's still alive."

"*Gracias,* Mike."

Mike led his detail west just before noon. The dust rose on the overland road. Ross looked toward the hazy purple hills. Cochise had burned his God-damned paws at the station. It wasn't likely he'd be after more chestnuts.

It was late afternoon when dust rose to the east. Owsley came to Ross. "It's Risler," he said.

Ross nodded. "Lock me up, Jimmy."

Owsley looked queerly at Ross. "Why?"

"I'm a prisoner."

"Jesus Christ! You saved his damned wagons for him, didn't you?"

"Yeah. But Matt Risler is a stickler for discipline. He wouldn't like to see me walking about a free man."

Owsley shrugged. He eyed the big man who stared toward the east with icy eyes. There was more going on than Mrs. Owsley's son knew about, but he was willing to back Ross Fletcher's play any day. If it hadn't been for the big man, Jimmy Owsley and seven troopers would be lying out in that noisome draw, instead of the Chiricahuas, looking up at the sun with eyes that did not see.

Ross was in his improvised cell when Matt Risler topped a rise and drew rein to look at the station. Smoke drifted up from the big chimney. Two troopers were currying their mounts. A line of baggy gray drawers hung on a taut picket line stretched between two buildings. A sentry stood at the front of the station, buttons sparkling and boots polished.

Risler looked up at the brooding hills. He had seen the buzzards after the detachment had crossed the San Pedro— but the big scavengers were working on something else besides Owsley's squad.

Owsley's squad had been well coached by Ross. They had been told to play dumb, as though nothing had happened. It hadn't been hard to get them to enter into the spirit of the thing. They knew the cold-eyed son of a bitch who wore captain's bars had left them to the tender mercies of the Chiricahuas. Risler was the type of officer who earned neither respect nor love, and an officer lacking either was half a man in the eyes of his subordinates.

The stage had been set and the curtain was up. The bloodstains had been covered by loose earth. The rifles had been cleaned and returned to their cases. The squad went about their boring routine as though they were still back at Fort Yuma.

Risler dismounted and glanced toward Ross's cell. Ross looked right back at him. Everything was the same, except that Ross had an issue Colt in the cell with him.

Owsley saluted. "Did you learn anything, sir?" he asked.

"Those men were killed by rebels," said Risler as he drew off his gauntlets. He looked into Owsley's eyes. "Is everything all right?"

"Quiet as a churchyard," said Owsley cheerfully.

Risler turned. "Sergeant Tankersley! Have those horses rubbed down and then mess your men."

"Yes, sir!"

Risler walked about the station and looked at the wagons. Ross couldn't help grinning. The officer looked at the buzzards. There were only a few of them airborne. The rest of them were at work ripping and tearing at the soft parts of the piled bodies.

Ross turned aside to hide a grin. He'd like to probe into Risler's mind to see the turmoil fermenting there. Christ, how Risler wanted to ask questions.

The only thing that worried Ross was that Risler might not be involved with the Apaches. Maybe it was Nick Maxwell who was behind the gun raids, but Ross was willing to bet Maxwell didn't have the gray matter to handle such an involved deal.

Risley walked back to Owsley. "I heard shooting last night," he said.

Owsley jerked his head. "Oh, *that,* sir? Some 'Paches tried to jump the station. We drove them off."

"Damn it! Why didn't you tell me?"

Owsley flushed. "I meant to, sir. Plumb forgot."

Risler looked at the buzzards. "Did you kill any of them?"

"Yes, sir! We hauled the bodies over to that draw south of here."

Risler slapped his gauntlets against the palm of his

left hand. He swung up on his horse and set the steel to it. Owsley looked at Ross and grinned. . . .

Risler was gone for an hour. When he came back to the station his face was pasty-white beneath the tan. His hands shook as he dismounted. He shot a feral glance toward Ross' cell. "Sergeant Tankersley!" he called.

The rangy non-com saluted. Risler spoke quickly. "You'll remain here with Corporal Owsley. I'm returning to Tucson."

"Alone, sir? The Apaches may be watching the road, Captain Risler."

"I'll be all right," said Risler testily. "One more thing. Get that man Fletcher out here. Bind his wrists. I'm taking him back with me."

Tankersley came to the cell. Ross slid the Colt inside his shirt and beneath his high waistband. Tankersley opened the cell door and took a length of line from his pocket.

Corporal Owsley stood by the cell with his carbine across his left arm. The men of his squad had silently gathered near him. Every one of them was armed. Risler's detachment was in the big common room of the station eating their embalmed beef and hardtack.

"What's wrong, Corporal?" asked Risler.

Jimmy Owsley jerked his head at Ross. "I don't like seeing a man tied up on a ride like that, sir. If the Apaches attack he won't have a chance."

"God damn it! Are you questioning my orders, you damned militiaman?"

Owsley flushed. "I'm a volunteer, sir—not a militiaman."

"Then get to hell out of here before I place you under arrest."

Owsley stood his ground. Tankersley looked from the determined non-com to the angry officer. "I don't like to question your orders, sir, but Owsley is right."

Risler bit his lip. These men weren't afraid of him. "All right," he said. "We'll take this matter up when I return. You'll wish to God you hadn't questioned me. I'll have those chevrons ripped from your sleeves!"

Ross walked to the corral to get a horse. Risler was losing his nerve. Something had happened to him. For the first time he had made a play that had backfired.

———

THE ROAD WAS BAKING under the hot sun. Risler rode silently behind Ross. Ross felt his back itch from sweat and a trace of fear. Out on the open road Risler could give him the treatment: let a man run and then shoot him down. God would sort the souls.

Ross eased his left hand beneath his shirt and scratched vigorously, at the same time half-cocking the Colt.

They rested the horses at a dry wash five miles from the station. Ross slanted his cap low over his eyes, watching Risler.

Risler removed his gauntlets and pulled them through his belt. Now and then he looked up and down the deserted road.

"Worried?" asked Ross casually.

"What the hell do you mean?"

"You think you can make those charges stick?"

"You're in a hell of a fix, Fletcher."

"So? Maybe it's the other way around."

Risler's eyes narrowed. "What do you mean?"

Ross leaned against his horse, watching Risler's eyes, waiting for the sudden warning of action. "You know Goddamned well I was ordered out of Tucson to turn back the townspeople. West ordered me. Sergeant Duncan ordered me to scout after the courier detachment. There are twenty witnesses to that. And you know damned well the Chiricahuas cut up that detachment. All you've got me on is insubordination, and you can't hang a man for that."

"You talk big, Fletcher."

"I'll talk bigger. How did Cochise get those guns from the wagons west of Tucson? Where was the escort?"

Risler shifted and lowered his right hand.

Ross smiled thinly. "I told you Cochise planned to close Apache Pass. You didn't see fit to report it to West or Carleton. You rode away from the stage station and left Owsley in a hell of a hole. I saw the look on your face when you returned. What did you expect?"

Risler slowly undid the flap of his holster. Ross did not move.

"Yaqui is dead," said Ross quietly. "I killed that flat-faced son of a bitch. Amadeo Esquivel is dead and so is Luz Campos. That leaves you and Maxwell."

Risler gripped the butt of his Colt. "I always said you talked too much."

"I'm going to do a lot more talking, you renegade bastard!"

Risler freed his Colt. Ross stepped in close. He gripped his Colt with his right hand and cut his left hand down on Risler's gun wrist. The hidden Colt leaped out and was jammed hard into Risler's belly. Ross looked into the cold eyes. "Who's got the deed, Risler?"

"I don't know what you're talking about."

Ross swung the Colt up and slashed the heavy barrel down on Risler's head. The officer went down hard. Ross tossed Risler's Colt into the road and went through Risler's clothing. There was no deed. He went through the saddlebags but there was no deed in them either.

Ross poured water on the unconscious officer. He dragged him to his feet and slapped his face hard. "Talk, you bastard! Talk!"

Blood trickled down from a corner of the thin mouth. "I'll have you shot for this."

"What makes you think you'll live to see Tucson?"

Risler looked past Ross. "Turn around and see."

"An old dodge."

The wind picked up the thud of hoofs and the jabbering of voices. Ross turned. A squad of bluecoats had topped a rise. Dust poured up from beyond the rise. Then he heard the rumbling of wagons and the thudding of many hoofs.

Mike Duncan spurred down toward the two men in the road. Ross picked up Risler's Colt and handed it to him. Risler wiped the blood from his mouth.

Duncan drew rein in a cloud of dust. "Captain Risler, sir, we're on the way to Apache Pass. Captain Roberts is in charge."

The column topped the rise and ground down toward the wash. Troopers on dusty horses and wagons filled with infantrymen. Two howitzers bounced in and out of the ruts.

Roberts came forward and looked down at Risler. "Where's your detachment, Captain Risler?" he asked coldly.

"At Cienega de Los Pinos."

"Why are you away from them?"

"I was taking this prisoner to Tucson to stand trial."

Roberts eyed the officer coldly. "Alone? There's something peculiar about this, sir. Sergeant Duncan reported that you had left the station practically undefended. By a stroke of luck, sir, one man saved those guns and men from Cochise. The man standing there with you."

Risler smoothed his blouse. "This man is a rebel agent."

Captain Cremoney kneed his horse up beside Roberts. "We heard about that too. There's something going on, sir, that stinks to high heaven."

Risler drew himself up. "Watch your tone, sir."

"I'll watch it, damn it! Why didn't you forward the report that Cochise and Mangus Colorado were allying themselves?"

Risler flushed. "This man was spreading rumors. I give him no credence."

Roberts spat. "It wasn't up to you to decide, sir. You will report back to Tucson. You've got some explaining to do, Captain Risler, and I'll be damned if I'd like to be in your boots when General Carleton begins to ask you questions!"

Risler walked to his horse and swung up on it. There was icy hate in his eyes. He spurred the horse from the road and passed the column.

Roberts looked down at Ross. "You did a fine job at Cienega, Sergeant Fletcher."

"Private Fletcher," corrected Ross. "Sir!"

"I need you with this column. You will act as chief of scouts."

Ross looked at Risler, who had reached the top of the rise. "I'd like to report back to Tucson, sir."

"You're going with us to scout."

Ross shrugged. "Yes, sir."

The column moved on. Duncan kneed his horse beside Ross. "Risler is in the fire," he said.

"That son of a bitch will never report."

"Maybe. Good riddance. Isabel is in Tucson, Ross. Captain Cremoney's men found her in the desert. She was dead beat but all right otherwise. She told Carleton of what you had done for her. You're the golden boy of the column, sonny."

Ross shrugged. "I've got to get back to Tucson."

"I know. Orders are orders, Sergeant Fletcher."

"Go to hell!"

Ross rode beside Duncan. Duncan shifted his chew and looked back along the column. "We've got a rough bunch here," he said. "Roberts's Company E, First Infantry. Cremoney's Company B. We'll pick up Owsley's squad on the way and leave a guard detail there. Lieutenant Bill Thompson, of the First Infantry, is in charge of the howitzers. We're bound for Rio de Sauze to establish a camp."

"Is Isabel all right?"

"Yes." Duncan looked at Ross. "You're a lucky man, Ross."

Ross glanced at the big sergeant. "What do you mean?"

Duncan grinned. "That girl talked about nothing but you, according to Cremoney."

There was a mingled feeling of exultation and despair in Ross. He wanted desperately to go back to her.

"You're still in the army," said Duncan.

CHAPTER TWENTY-THREE

It had been a thirsty march from Dragoon Springs. The mules bawled steadily as the teamsters' whips snapped over their sweaty backs. The column slogged up the long, precipitous defile. The foothills to either side gleamed like the bleached skulls of dead men. The Chiricahuas lifted their brooding peaks in phalanx after phalanx. The mountains were almost naked except for sparse timber on the lower slopes.

Ross swallowed dryly. He eyed the somber pass. "I don't like it, Mike," he said.

Duncan nodded. "It's too damned peaceful looking."

Roberts had no flankers out. He had ordered the scouts to stay within two hundred yards of the point. He was too confident of his strength. There was water in Apache Pass, and the command could move no further without it.

They moved through the first narrow canyon. The landscape was wild and picturesque. Two mountain ranges met here and flowed together in a wild jumbled mass of crevices, eroded surfaces, and huge boulders. The great overlapping spurs were sheathed with pines, spruces, manzanita and scrub oak, with the many-colored rock formations showing through the tangled green and gray of the growths.

The tiny watercourse paralleling the narrow stage road was dry. Dust threaded up from the column. If there were Apaches in the pass they had had plenty of warning.

Two-thirds of the way up the pass, Ross drew rein. "I don't like it," he said quietly.

Duncan almost shivered in the quiet. The wind moaned softly through the pass. A lone hawk veered off before the wind.

Ross touched his cracked lips with his tongue. His hands were sweat-greasy on the stock of his Sharps. The column was closing up, tightly packed on the narrow road.

A shot split the quiet and a puff of smoke pushed out from a clump of mesquite high overhead. Then suddenly the growths sprouted red blossoms and cottony puffs of smoke. Ross slid from his horse and led it behind a rock shoulder as slugs whined through the air and screeched eerily from rocks. The head of the column fell back. Ross saw a banded head come up out of a bush. Apache. He fired and reloaded.

Here and there along the cursing column a carbine or rifle flatted off. Then the trumpeter lipped into "Retreat," and the sweating teamsters swung their six-mule teams out on a gravelly shoulder and whipped them down the long grade.

The warriors fired, reloaded and fired again into the weary mass of soldiers. Slowly the Californians fell back, shooting steadily, but there wasn't much to see except smoke puffs.

Ross followed Duncan down the road, hunching his shoulders, momentarily expecting a ball between the shoulder blades. They drew rein far down the pass where Roberts was bluing the air with curses. ' "We've got to get that water!" he roared.

Cremoney wiped the sweat from his face. "We've covered forty miles without it," he agreed.

Roberts eyed the smoky pass. "It's hell's own gate," he said.

Cremoney nodded. "I say we go on."

"Agreed. We'll go in on foot. Tell Thompson to bring up those howitzers. We'll give the Apaches a taste of them."

Ross slid down from his horse. The troopers and beetle-crushers formed under the shelter of a long rock ledge. They started up the pass, darting from one rock to another, firing upward at the smoke purls. The heat was heavy in the pass.

Steadily the troops pushed their way up the pass. Ahead of them was the abandoned stage station. From the two heights that commanded the station and the springs the Apaches poured down a steady fire. Lead splashed brightly on the rocks. Two soldiers went down.

It was an infantry fight in dust and thick smoke. Darting Apaches moved on the heights, faster than they could be led by the cursing troopers. The beetle-crushers fired, drew and bit cartridge, poured the powder down into the hot barrels, plied ramrods with a rattle, capped and fired the big infantry rifles. Troopers fired their Sharps, cursing the limited range of the carbines.

Ross lay behind a rock and reloaded. "Where are those damned howitzers?" he mouthed dryly.

Duncan turned. Something thudded against his head. He slumped down. Blood poured from beneath his dusty forage cap. Ross cursed and dragged the big non-com behind a rock. The slug had creased Duncan's skull. He was still breathing.

Ross looked down the narrow, smoke-filled road. A howitzer bounced from rut to rut and went into battery, followed by the second piece. Coolly the gunners rammed home the charge and cleared the piece. A sergeant sighted the stubby piece and stepped back, holding the long lanyard. He jerked it back. The piece bellowed and pushed out a cloud of stinking smoke. The projectile screeched through the air and burst short of one of the heights. The second piece was manhandled into position and was fired. The projectile was short too.

Thompson yelled. "Elevate, you bastards!"

"We're at extreme elevation now, sir!" yelled a sergeant.

They moved one of the pieces. A wheel bounced from a rock and the piece went over in the road. Dust spurted up as the eager warriors poured fire at it. Big Sergeant Mitchell of the cavalry led six men forward. They heaved at the piece. Ross ran to them. They cursed as they heaved up on the heavy piece until it settled on its wheels.

The Apaches overshot from the heights. Both howitzers roared into action, kicking back on their trails. They were still too short in elevation. The gunners rolled them up on rocks. One gun roared and kicked back, breaking the trail.

The second gun got off five rounds, plastering the heights, and then its trail snapped.

Ross wiped the sweat from his face, peering through the thick smoke. He was a good fifty yards ahead of the guns. A huge Apache was standing on a rock watching the action. His arms were extraordinarily long and were covered with the thick sleeves of a filthy red undershirt. "Mangus," said Ross to himself. "Mangus Colorado. Red Sleeves!"

The famous chief moved about on the rock high overhead, directing the fire of his sharpshooters. Ross capped his Sharps and rested it on a rock. He sighted carefully at the red undershirt and then raised the muzzle until he was aiming just over the huge maned head. The Sharps kicked back against his shoulder.

Mangus shuddered as the big slug smashed into him. He fell backward over the rock like some ungainly bird.

Slowly the firing died away. Apaches flitted through the gathering darkness. The Californians moved on to the springs. Then the silence of the pass was broken only by the sounds of thirsty men and animals as they swilled the clear waters of the spring.

———

MIKE DUNCAN LAY in the stage station, breathing harshly. There was a blank look on his face. Ross bathed the sweat and blood from the big head. Behind him he could hear Roberts and Cremoney talking.

"We've broken them," said Roberts.

"I don't know, Tom. I've had the guns mounted where they can sweep the heights. They'll be back."

"I doubt it."

Ross stood up. He walked to Roberts. "I'd like permission to take those dispatches back to Tucson," he said to the officer.

Roberts wiped his face. "Yes. How's Duncan?"

"He's got a thick skull, sir. Maybe a surgeon ought to look at him."

"There's no surgeon nearer than Tucson."

"I'll take him with me, sir."

"He can't be moved."

Duncan raised his head. "I'll be able to ride, sir. I've got a bitch of a headache, but it ain't any worse than some hangovers I've had."

Cremoney grinned. "Let him go, Tom."

Roberts took the dispatches from his first sergeant. "Ride like hell," he said to Ross. "Travel by night. I doubt if you'll be bothered in the pass tonight."

Ross saluted and went outside to get horses. His plan was working well. Matt Risler was up to no good in Tucson, and Ross wanted Mike Duncan with him for the showdown.

Later, out on the dark road, Duncan groaned hollowly. Ross kneed his horse close to the wounded non-com. "Do you want to go back, Mike?"

Duncan grinned. "Hell no! You think I don't know what you've got in your mind? You can't fool Mike

Duncan, sonny. This time you'll need me to run that son of a bitch Risler into his hole."

Ross eyed the big man. "I always thought that skull of yours would turn a bullet."

They descended the pass. High above them the Chiricahuas and Mimbrenos looked down on the stage station and the dim figures of the dusty soldiers who had used bigger medicine than the Apaches had. Two wagon-guns which had turned the tide against two great chiefs—Cochise and Mangus Colorado. Mangus lay in his blood with a terrible wound. Child of the Water had forgotten his chosen people.

CHAPTER TWENTY-FOUR

Tucson sweltered under a heavy blanket of heat. General James Henry Carleton looked up from the dispatches and eyed the two dusty men standing before him. "You've done well, men," he said in his precise voice. "Orders are being prepared to move re-enforcements to Roberts. With the pass in our hands we'll have the way open to New Mexico, and further glory for my command."

The capable officer was a stickler for discipline, as the men of the California Column well knew. The Down-Easter from Maine had done a masterful job in moving his men the hundreds of miles from California through a parched land.

Carleton pulled at his sideburns. "This business of Captain Risler has taken me by surprise. The man is efficient and capable."

Ross shifted. "He had charge of the wagons which were captured by the Chiricahuas, sir. I've heard it said he was elsewhere with his escort when the wagons were taken."

"Yes. It is a blot on his record."

Duncan coughed. "Captain Risler left Cienega de Los

Pinos station almost undefended, sir. If it hadn't been for Sergeant Ross here, we would have lost those guns too."

Carleton held up a hand. "I've sent for him. Let him face you. I assure you, I'll hear both of you out."

"He'll have to do some damned fast talking," said Ross bitterly.

"What was that, sir?"

Ross flushed. "The man is guilty, General Carleton."

"We'll see."

An orderly tapped on the door and then came in. "I've been to Captain Risler's quarters, sir. A man told me he had left town an hour ago."

Carleton smashed a hand down on his desk. "Where did he go?"

"South, sir. On the Tubac Road."

Carleton stood up. "Get Lieutenant Carter. I want a provost detail to get that man and bring him back here."

"Yes, sir."

Ross stepped forward. "I'd like that detail, sir."

"You're worn out."

Ross shook his head. "Not that worn out, sir."

"Why are you interested in him?"

Ross looked into the general's hard eyes. "I have reason to believe he was involved in the death of my brother, sir. John Fletcher. My brother was murdered and the deed to the Sahuarita silver mine was stolen from him. I tell you, sir, Risler is behind more damned connivery than Jeff Davis."

Carleton nodded. "I knew your brother in Mexico. At Buena Vista. A gentleman and a fine artilleryman. You have my permission to find Captain Risler and bring him in, Sergeant Fletcher."

Ross hurried out of the office. Isabel was staying with the family of Jesus Montoya. Duncan gripped Ross by the shoulder. "I'll get fresh mounts."

Ross nodded. He walked swiftly to the Montoya adobe off the Plaza de Armas and rapped on the door.

Maria Montoya answered his impatient knocking. "Where is Senorita Rand?" asked Ross.

Maria Montoya looked surprised. "Why, she has gone to Sonora, Señor Fletcher."

A cold feeling came over Ross. "Sonora? Why? With whom?"

"She was gone when I came back from the market. See? Here is a note she left." Maria smiled apologetically. "I cannot read."

Ross took the note. He read aloud. "I have gone to Sonora with my friend, Matthew Risler. Do not fear for me, Maria. I am in good hands."

Ross crumpled the note and jumped out of the doorway, pounding up the street in his big boots.

Maria shrugged. "These gringos are mad," she said.

———

DUNCAN WAS WAITING in the plaza with two fresh horses. He stared curiously at Ross. "What the hell is wrong now? Didn't she welcome you, Ross?"

Ross swung up on a horse. "Risler has her," he said. "Heading for Sonora."

"Son of a bitch!" Duncan swung up on the second horse and set the steel to it. "What the hell are we waiting for?"

They hammered out of the dusty plaza, scattering chickens and dogs while the loafing *paisanos* shook their heads at the mad haste of the Yanquis.

———

TUBAC DREAMED of the past under a dim moon. The Diablitos rose to the west and the Santa Ritas to the east. Beyond the abandoned buildings were the decaying peach and pomegranate orchards. Bandit and Apache raids had caused the abandonment of the old settlement founded one hundred years before.

Mike Duncan studied the dim buildings from the rise where they had halted. "Looks deserted," he said.

"We'll take a look."

"Listen!"

The wind carried the noise of thudding hoofs to them. A solitary rider had appeared on the dusty road, riding north.

"Mex," said Duncan.

Ross eyed the lone rider. "Maybe he's seen them."

"I'll cut him off."

Duncan rode down into a hollow and dismounted, taking his Sharps. He faded silently into the brush. Ross waited. There was a startled cry from the road and then Mike showed up, shoving a shivering *paisano* ahead of him. He jammed his cocked Sharps into the small of the Mexican's back.

Ross came close to the little man. "Who are you?"

"Hilario Duran, *servidor de ustedes.*"

"Where do you go, Hilario Duran?"

"To Tucson."

"Where have you come from?"

"San Cayetano del Tumacacori."

"Have you seen anyone on the road?"

"No."

"No white men? An American and a woman?"

Hilario looked away. "No."

The Sharps was shoved hard against the Mexican's back. Hilario cringed. "*Madre de Dios!* I am but a poor man traveling alone. I have done nothing wrong, sir."

The man was lying.

"We are looking for Matthew Risler and a young woman. Isabella Rand. Have you seen them?"

Hilario shook his head.

Duncan let down the hammer of his Sharps and drew out his case knife. "Let me handle this, Ross," he said coldly.

Duncan twisted the Mexican's arm and forced him to his knees. Then he threw him to the ground and opened the knife. He tested the edge with his thumb and gripped Hilario by his baggy white trousers. "Now, Hilario," he said quietly. "You are lying. Perhaps you would like to be a capon?"

Hilario shivered. Duncan ripped away the dirty trousers and sat down on the thin legs of the Mexican. "Before God and all the saints," mouthed Hilario, "I know nothing."

Duncan leaned forward and moved the knife blade suggestively.

Hilario closed his eyes; tears crept from the corners and streaked his dusty face. "What is it you want to know, senores?"

"Have you seen them?"

"Yes. They are at the old mission. There is another man with them. A big man. Nicolas, he is called."

"Nick Maxwell," said Ross.

Hilario opened his eyes. "*Sí!* They sent me out on the road to look for any signs of pursuit."

"You've found them," said Duncan. He stood up and sheathed the blade of his knife.

Ross got the horses. "Get out of here, Hilario," he said. "If we catch you anywhere near the mission you'll go back to Sonora a man in name only. Do you understand?"

Hilario gripped his torn trousers and scuttled back to his horse. He lashed it north on the road and never looked back, riding as though *el diablo* were right behind him. . . .

Ross and Duncan covered the few miles from Tubac to Tumacacori at a steady gallop. They stopped on the same rise where Ross had stood so many months before —before the death of John and the finding of Isabel Rand. The mission looked the same, brooding of past glories in the faint moonlight.

"This is where the Apaches got me," said Ross.

"You think there are some of them around?"

"We'll make sure."

They scouted along the Santa Cruz, through the

willows and shrubbery. There was no sign of the Chiric-ahuas. Ross raised his head. "Woodsmoke," he said softly.

They padded across the littered patio, where Ross had gone down fighting beneath a swarm of Chiricahuas. There was no sign of life in the patio. Then they saw a faint flicker of light through the tumbledown passageway between the cloister and the sacristy.

Ross held Duncan back. He removed his spurs and padded into the passageway. He flattened himself against the wall. A fire flickered in the old sacristy. From some-where in the old church he heard the stamp of a shod hoof and the whinnying of a horse.

"I don't like it here, Nick," said Matt Risler.

"Christ! Hilario is watching the road. Ain't no one goin' to creep up on us. What's the matter? You lost your nerve?"

"Go to hell!"

Maxwell laughed. "You ain't been the same since you got run outa Tucson. Fletcher is miles from here. Cochise is in the mountains. Christ, I hear he was mad as a lobo wolf about that deal at Cienega."

"He'll make those Yankee bastards pay at Apache Pass."

"Maybe. If he does we'll be in the clear with Cochise. If he don't, we'd better jump up plenty of dust down into Sonora."

"You contacted Gomez?"

"Yeah. He says he'll have a hundred good men ready whenever we say the word."

Ross edged closer. Risler was seated on a box. Maxwell leaned against the wall, idly paring his nails with a slim *cuchillo*. There was someone lying on a pile of blan-kets in a corner. Ross felt his breath catch. It was Isabel.

Maxwell looked down at the girl. "We got liquor," he said. "Maybe we could have a little fiesta here. She's a right nice piece, Matt."

"God damn you! Don't you ever think of anything but liquor and women?"

Maxwell grinned. "What else is there to think about?"

Risler spat. "We've got the damned mine deed. She'll make a good hostage with her people down in Sonora. They've got money. Gomez has already contacted them. They'll pay gold to get her back."

Maxwell nodded. "Yeah."

Risler paced back and forth. "I've had a setback. Things were going well. We got Rand out of the way, and John Fletcher too. If it hadn't been for that bastard brother of his we would have made pure hell in Arizona."

"We ain't licked yet. When Carleton goes on to New Mexico, providin' he gets through without gettin' his ass shot off by the 'Paches, we'll have things our own way."

Risler nodded. He smashed a fist into his other palm. "By God, I'll show them. I'll have my own empire here, Nick."

Maxwell's eyes were veiled as he watched Risler. He glanced at the girl and shrugged. Then he took a bottle from a saddlebag and drank deeply.

Ross padded back to the patio. "They're in there," he whispered. "Just the two of them and the girl."

"Keno. Let's go!"

"Go to the front of the church and get into the vestibule. Be quiet. The horses are in the nave. I'll come in through the window that opens onto the cemetery."

Duncan nodded. "Give me time. Count to a hundred before you move in."

They leaned their carbines against the wall and drew the Colts. Duncan faded into the darkness toward the front the church.

Ross went back into the Campus Sancti. An eroded window opened onto it from the sacristy. He edged along the wall.

Minutes ticked past. Then one of the horses nickered. Feet scraped on the dirty floor of the sacristy. The horse nickered again.

"See what's bothering those horses," said Risler.

Ross reached the window. Maxwell grumbled as he

went into the sanctuary. Ross came around the side of the window. Risler stood with his back to Ross. The girl looked up. Her eyes widened as she saw Ross, and her breath caught in her throat. Risler looked at her.

There was a sudden curse from the sanctuary and the scuffling of booted feet. Risler drew a big Remington revolving pistol. "What is it, Nick?"

Maxwell yelled. A pistol shot crashed in the nave, smashing the silence and awakening hollow echoes. Ross jumped into the sacristy as Maxwell screamed from the nave. Then there was a repeated roaring of pistols.

Risler whirled as Ross landed behind him. He fired. The slug slapped into the wall beside Ross; the flash of the pistol blinded him. Risler leaped into the sanctuary, blasting with his pistol. Isabel screamed.

Ross jumped up the steps into the ruined sanctuary. The horses were whinnying in terror. A dim figure moved past them. Ross saw Nick Maxwell on the floor with blood flowing from his slack mouth. Mike Duncan lay beside the well, his smoking pistol in his hand.

Risler darted down the battered nave, heading for the front door and safety. Ross plunged after him. Risler whirled as Ross fell over a pile of plaster. The Remington spat flame.

Ross fired from the floor, rapping slugs into the big door. Risler jumped into the baptistry.

Ross got to his feet and cocked his Colt. He walked toward the baptistry and flattened himself against the thick wall. Feet moved in the small room beyond him. Ross edged into the dark baptistry. Risler fired his last shot and hurled the pistol at Ross. It clanked against the wall. Risler whirled and jumped up the narrow stairway leading up to the unfinished belfry. Ross snapped out his last shot and leaped for the stairs.

Risler waited for him, bracing himself against the sides of the narrow staircase. A boot shot out and smashed Ross back down the stairs. His head thudded against the wall, stunning him.

Risler ran up the stairs. Ross got to his feet, shook his head, and went up the stairs slowly. He came into a small, dark room, with faint lines of moonlight showing through the slit windows. He stopped and listened. There was no sound. He looked up the rickety ladder which led up into the unfinished belfry.

Something scraped on the floor above him. He worked his way up the ladder and thrust his head through the hole. A boot smashed at his hand. He winced in pain, but managed to grip Risler's ankle. He climbed up the ladder and upended Risler. He crashed down to the wooden floor.

Ross stood on the flooring and slashed at Risler's head with the barrel of his Colt. Risler rolled aside. Ross dropped on him, battering at his head with the Colt. There was surprising strength in Risler's spare frame. He threw Ross back, and the Colt fell down the ladder hole.

Ross got up to meet a charging attack. A fist skinned his jaw and another sank into his lean gut. Ross went back through an archway. Risler followed his advantage, clawing for Ross's throat.

Ross bucked him with a shoulder and managed to land a wild punch which staggered the gambler back toward the south archway. Risler cursed as he missed his footing. He swayed precariously. Ross swung with all his strength.

The fist smashed Risler's lips and teeth together in a bloody hash. He screamed wildly and lashed out at Ross.

Ross weaved about, taking the frenzied blows on his forearms. Risler retreated beyond the archway out onto the narrow ledge overlooking the churchyard twenty-five feet below. The moonlight showed his face as a bloody mask of hate and fear.

Ross threw a left to the gut and snapped back Risler's head with a hard uppercut. The man teetered on the edge. Then, with a wild, sobbing cry, he fell backward. He hit the hard *caliche* with a thud, and lay still. Ross caught at the rough brickwork to save himself and clung there, cold sweat pouring from his body.

Risler stared up with eyes that did not see. His head was bent at an awkward angle. The breeze ruffled his coat. Ross felt his gut moil. He staggered a little as he walked to the ladder and went down into the storage room below the belfry. He felt his way down the dark stairs into the baptistry.

The horses were shying and blowing at the odor of blood. Isabel Rand knelt beside Mike Duncan. Ross looked down at her. "How is he?"

She wiped her hands on her shawl. "He'll live," she said quietly. "The bullet went through his left shoulder." She stood up and placed her head against his chest. "Somehow I knew you weren't dead," she said.

He held her close. "I take a lot of killing," he said.

He carried Mike into the sacristy and examined the wound. The slug had gone clear through. He washed the two holes with whisky from Maxwell's bottle and bandaged the wounded man. "Stay here," he said.

He walked to the front of the church and out to where Matt Risler lay, with his wild dreams dead along with him. The deed was in the inner pocket of his coat.

Mike Duncan was sitting up, pulling at the bottle when Ross returned. "We did it, Ross," he said.

Ross nodded. He gave the deed to the girl. "That thing is stained with blood," he said. "I wonder if it's worth it."

Mike pulled himself to his feet. "I don't know about you, sonny, but I've had enough of this haunted place. Let's ride."

"You're too weak," protested Isabel.

Mike grinned. He held up the bottle. "I've got strength in here."

The moon silvered the dome of the church as they looked back from the rise. San Cayetano del Tumacacori had seen violence again, possibly the last of such episodes in a long and violent history.

Isabel placed her hand on Ross'. She smiled at him.

Ross drew her close. An owl hooted from the ghostly ruins behind them. The searching wind rustled a velvet mesquite.

Isabel looked at the place of the dead. She said softly, "Rest eternal give unto these, O Lord, and let perpetual light shine on them."

Then the night wind took over, moaning through the open windows of the ruins, as the three riders rode down the ridge toward Tucson.

TAKE A LOOK AT RIDE A LONE TRAIL AND MASSACRE CREEK:

Two Full Length Western Novels

THERE'S CARNAGE IN THE CONCHAS IN THIS CLASSIC WESTERN DOUBLE.

Ride a Lone Trail

When Ken Macklin left the Double H a few years back, he had sworn never to return. But now that his father had been gunned down in ambush, he had no choice. Someone had to pay.

But as he trailed across the Lazy J spread, he learned he was being followed. It looked as if he were to be drygulch victim Number Two. For things were as bad as when he'd left, only now the valley was about to explode into open range war. All it had needed was the fuse, and Ken was it.

Massacre Creek

Tough cavalryman Sabin Shay faced his Cheyenne captors. He knew the price of defeat—and waited for his own destruction. But then he saw the hatred in the Redmen's eyes. If they just killed him plain and simple, he'd be lucky...

"The joy of reading Shirreffs' work is in his mastery of pacing and his tough, gritty prose." – **James Reasoner, author of Outlaw Ranger**

AVAILABLE NOW

ABOUT THE AUTHOR

Gordon D. Shirreffs published more than 80 western novels, 20 of them juvenile books, and John Wayne bought his book title, Rio Bravo, during the 1950s for a motion picture, which Shirreffs said constituted *"the most money I ever earned for two words."* Four of his novels were adapted to motion pictures, and he wrote a Playhouse 90 and the Boots and Saddles TV series pilot in 1957.

A former pulp magazine writer, he survived the transition to western novels without undue trauma, earning the admiration of his peers along the way. The novelist saw life a bit cynically from the edge of his funny bone and described himself as looking like a slightly parboiled owl. Despite his multifarious quips, he was dead serious about the writing profession.

Gordon D. Shirreffs was the 1995 recipient of the Owen Wister Award, given by the Western Writers of America for "a living individual who has made an outstanding contribution to the American West."

He passed in 1996.